CAUTION: DESTINY IS OFFICIALLY IN YOUR HANDS.

ONE BEGINNING, 150 ENDINGS: THE CHOICE IS YOURS

CHOOSE CAREFULLY. CHANGE EVERYTHING.

© Bruce Christianson / Photologic.com

ABOUT THE AUTHOR

HEATHER MCELHATTON is an independent producer for
Minnesota Public Radio and Public Radio International. Her
commentaries and stories are heard regularly nationwide on
This American Life, *Marketplace*, *Weekend America*, *Sound
Money*, and *The Savvy Traveler*. She also hosts her own live
radio show, called *Stage Sessions*, and will appear with Ira
Glass on the television version of his show, *This American
Life*, premiering this fall on Showtime.

PRETTY LITTLE

HARPER

NEW YORK • LONDON • TORONTO • SYDNEY

LE MISTAKES

MISTAKES

A Do-Over Novel

H EATHER M CE LHATTON

FOR CORRENE

HARPER

PRETTY LITTLE MISTAKES. Copyright © 2007 by Heather McElhatton. All rights reserved. Printed in the United States of America. No part of this book may be used or reproduced in any manner whatsoever without written permission except in the case of brief quotations embodied in critical articles and reviews. For information address HarperCollins Publishers, 195 Broadway, New York, NY 10007.

HarperCollins books may be purchased for educational, business, or sales promotional use. For information, please e-mail the Special Markets Department at SPsales@harpercollins.com.

FIRST EDITION

Designed by Justin Dodd

Library of Congress Cataloging-in-Publication Data is available upon request.

ISBN: 978-0-06-113322-0
ISBN-10: 0-06-113322-1

16 17 ❖/RRD 20 19 18

HOW TO READ THIS BOOK

Don't read this book straight through, as you would a "normal" book. If you did, it would seem like a collage of many different stories, none of them making any sense. Instead, start on page one, and at the end of the first section you'll have a decision to make. Make it, and turn directly to the corresponding section. In this way you will control the story, and the outcome of your chosen life.

As you read through the book you'll sometimes land in completely unique places and sometimes end up right where you were before. Try not to turn back. You never know what life has in store for you. Remember, good behavior is not necessarily rewarded, and sometimes bad decisions can lead to wonderful (and not so wonderful) results. When you've reached the end of your journey, go back to the beginning and start over again, because everybody deserves a second chance—and everybody could always be somebody else. Good luck.

1

Laughter and fistfights. Lasagna thrown on the cafeteria floor, geometry books burning in the garbage cans, Sidra Stanislow finally losing her virginity up against the Dumpsters behind the memorial auditorium. All the janitors are getting high. The teachers' lounge is choked with stifled arguments and the vending machines are empty. It's the last day of high school.

You're graduating. Rushing headlong into the unknown rest of your life. Your friends are drifting off in every direction. Some are going to college, some are going to work, and some are going to their parents' basements to smoke pot and watch reality TV. As you see it, there are two options. Go to college and get ahead or take some time off and go traveling. If you get a degree, you might have a decent income—but if you go traveling, you might have an excellent adventure. Both have merits, both have drawbacks. Neither is permanent, and this makes the decision harder.

Take into account that your boyfriend has already decided to go to college and he wants you to come with him. (You've been together ever since he annihilated your virginity in an abandoned Christmas tree shack by the highway.) He's handsome and he loves you. The two of you have really great sex. He's big. (You know, big.) You see college as the responsible choice and travel as the fun choice, but then again college can be fun and traveling can be disastrous. The choice is yours. Your grandparents have given you a small chunk of money for graduation—just enough to get you going in whichever direction you choose.

If you decide to go to college, go to section #2 (page 4).
If you decide to travel, go to section #3 (page 5).

2

From section 1 . . .

You enroll at the university and get an apartment with your boyfriend a few blocks from campus. The apartment is shitty. It has a refrigerator that lets mold grow in the drawers, a toilet that routinely overflows, and noisy downstairs neighbors who always sound like they're killing cats, having loud sex, or both. You try to fix the place up by painting the walls dark colors and hanging Pier One African art—you were hoping to create an urban Cinco de Mayo look, but instead the place looks like a low-rent voodoo carnival.

Money is tight and you begin to bicker with your boyfriend over little things. *The unpaid electricity bill, the empty pizza boxes, the missing beer, your bras drip-drying in the shower, his socks stinking on the floor.* You thought living together would be *sexy*, that he'd help organize the closets and give you back rubs instead of wanting sex all the time, but he says he thought you'd be wearing a lot more lingerie and maybe even *cook* once in a while, so he thinks you're about even on the disappointment score.

Things are no better at school. It's not what you thought it would be. You're always lost and everything's expensive. There's this general rush around you—like a wild river current you can't quite navigate. Confusion. You also need to decide on your major. How the hell are you supposed to know what you want to be when you grow up? You could get an MFA in art and maybe become the next great artist of this century, or you could go for a PhD in sciences and maybe become a doctor. Who do you want to be?

If you decide to major in art, go to section #4 (page 6).
If you decide to major in sciences, go to section #5 (page 7).

3

From section 1 . . .

While standing in his parents' kitchen, you tell your boyfriend you're leaving. You're *not* going to college. You're not buying into the schedules, the credits, or the points. No standardized success for you. You'll know when you're successful because you'll know when you're happy. He seems upset. He's talking loudly. He's shouting and he starts poking you on the shoulder as he explains to you why your plan is so stupid. When you argue back, he shoves you. You shove him back. Then he calls you *a bitch* and asks you *who the hell you think you are* and he slaps you across the face.

Shit. Didn't see that coming—or did you? Didn't he always sort of have a bad temper? But that was just when finals were looming or his dad was yelling, or his coach was complaining . . . come to think of it, there was always a good reason for him to be ticked off. It all clicks in your head. You've seen enough after-school specials to know what will happen next. *They hit you once, they hit you a hundred times.* They get better at it. So before he can hit you again, you grab the iron skillet sitting on the stove (bacon grease still in it) and you clock him in the temple with it. *Thunk.* He drops over like a sack of wet cement. He's not dead. The bastard is still breathing.

Time to go! But where? You've always wanted to see Europe. The stone buildings, the Renaissance paintings, the dark men. You could also go to California. Who doesn't have fun in California? You even have a place to stay there—some friends who graduated the year before bought a house in LA and told you to come out and crash for as long as you like.

If you decide to go to Europe, go to section #6 (page 8).
If you decide to drive to California, go to section #7 (page 9).

4

From section 2 . . .

You enroll in the Art Department. Strange tribe. There's a guy with wooden spoons thrust through his earlobes, a woman with Maori tattoos and genitalia piercing, and another girl who heats paper clips and sears her arms with raised earthworm-shaped hieroglyphics.

Art students stick together and act superior in an attempt to avoid being mocked by law students and business students. For this reason and perhaps others, communication between you and your boyfriend becomes even more strained. (He's getting a business degree. Both boring *and* embarrassing.) He suddenly seems like an idiot. You stop sleeping with him—his rhythm-free pump and grunts just don't appeal anymore. You have several fights and then several more and then one afternoon he comes home early and catches you splayed over the velour couch with a video artist named Thaddeus. He breaks up with you. Can't say you blame him, can't say you're sorry.

Thaddeus likes to make symphony-sex films, which are movies that have girls wrapped in catgut straddling oiled cellos. Thaddeus also videotapes himself having sex with you. You don't like it that much, but as he says, *What do you know?* Anyway, he films you so often that it becomes normal to have tape running while you're naked in bed, almost pleasing to hear the film run and the shutters click. Halfway through the semester there's a group exhibition at school and you're asked to show a piece of your work. Now, should you enter a technically accomplished piece or a more risky piece?

If you enter the risky piece, go to section #8 (page 11).
If you enter the technically accomplished piece,
go to section #9 (page 12).

5

From section 2 . . .

You major in science and you never knew life could be this *ice-pick-through-the-eye* boring. Your day begins at five a.m. and ends around one in the morning. What do you spend all those hours doing? You spend them memorizing. Memorization is your God. You must ingest thousands of dry and crumbly texts, as though you were being force-fed endless crust without water. *Vacuous vocabulary, tedious tables, tired theorems.* Your own thoughts are not required. You haven't had sex with your boyfriend in weeks. He constantly sits on the couch and complains until he reminds you of a whining rutabaga.

Time blurs. The mountain looms. Every test is a slippery crevice waiting for you to fall and twist your ankle, every final an ice storm trying to kill you off before the spring. The days become weeks, the weeks become months. You have lost all track of your boyfriend and you don't think of him often until you come home early one day to find him with his hand up the shirt of a chubby blond girl named Sharon, an ugly grad student who asked you for an aspirin not a week earlier.

You kick him out and throw all his belongings out the third-floor window. You trash the apartment. *You hate the program, hate your boyfriend, hate your life.* This is not a life. This is not happiness. You want to quit the program and go back and do something that actually matters. Something that you actually care about. It's not too late to do something that makes you happy. On the other hand, there's that dreadfully true saying—*no pain, no gain.* Nobody has an easy time studying science. Do they?

If you stick with the science program, go to section #10 (page 14).
If you quit the science program, go to section #11 (page 15).

6

From section 3 . . .

Screw school—you just got out of school. Why study books when you can study life? Your education will be in the train stations, the museums, the cafés and the clubs of Europe. (Not to mention the beds. You expect there's quite an education there.) Your expectations are justifiably high. You expect intrigue, adventure, romance, and good photos. You expect theater and music and fine wine. You expect culture.

You hate American culture—it's big and it stomps. It's aspirin-packed forced hilarity until you die from laughing. It's megaplex superplexes. It's Wal-Mart, Sam's Club, and McDonald's. It's drywall communities and *Disney on Ice!* It's virgin pop stars and Pepsi. The charities are even vicious. God help you if you tangle with Green Peace or PETA. Europe must be better—they hate Americans.

Your parents are worried. They think Europe is dangerous. They think Europe is expensive and smelly and people don't wash properly. Whatever. You're not about to start letting them run your life now. You sell your car and cash in all your graduation checks. You buy a large nylon backpack and a bedroll. You stock up with maps, a Swiss army knife, travel guides, train schedules, Tums, Imodium, Pepto-Bismol, and aspirin.

You stare at large maps thumbtacked all over the wall and mark the cities you want to visit. You've always wanted to see Italy or England. England for its grand architecture, regal history, and punk rock scene. Italy for its incredible food, Renaissance paintings, and wicked sexy shoes. They both sound fantastic—but you can only choose one.

If you decide to go to Italy, go to section #12 (page 16).
If you decide to go to England, go to section #13 (page 18).

From section 3 . . .

The trip to California is eventful. Your car breaks down just outside Las Vegas, in front of a Kum and Go grocery/gift/bait/tan/tackle shop. It's the alternator that's busted—an expensive ticket. You play slots at a little roadside casino while your car is being fixed—something you've never done before and something you're clearly no good at. The damn machine makes so much noise it sounds like you're winning even when you're not. You're ahead and then you're behind and then when you turn around half your money is gone.

You make the mechanic a proposition. In exchange for parts and service, you tell him you'll have a little fun with him in the back room. (Okay, okay, it's slutty, but nobody here knows you and what else are you supposed to do?) The mechanic jumps at the chance. "Hell yeah," he says and throws his dirty red shop rag down on the counter. "I gotta warn you though," he says, "I got a big wiener."

In his messy office the guy puts on a condom and introduces you to his brown vinyl couch. You now notice his potbelly. His stubbly face. *Ick.* You wear your sweatshirt and socks for minimum contact, but he still gets his oily mitts all over you. You feel like a soft-shell crab split on a stick while his bored yellow Lab watches from the corner.

Afterward you take a trucker bath in the restroom (legs hiked up on the small porcelain sink, lots and lots of grainy white powdered soap). The mechanic is really nice afterward. He gives you some cash for the road and a hot coffee and tells you to "stop back any time."

You race across the desert drinking beer and singing at the top of your lungs so you don't have to think about the very gross thing you just did. (But you had to do it. What else could you have done?) You blare country western music until you realize it isn't country, it's *Christian radio,* and you pound the dashboard until the radio shuts off. Then the silence rushes in and you realize you're out of beer.

As you cross the California state line, you have a decision to make. You have a friend in Berkeley who works at the university. She e-mailed you and told you she thinks she can get you a job, but you also have a friend in LA who knows talent scouts and screenwriters and says you can go on open auditions with her. You need to point the car north toward Berkeley or south toward LA. The sun is setting and you can't stand the silence much longer.

If you go to Berkeley, go to section #14 (page 20).
If you go to LA, go to section #15 (page 23).

8

From section 4 . . .

You enter a risky piece of art into the competition. A series of bronzed vaginas cast from friends' genitalia and welded together to simulate the St. Louis Arch. To make the pieces, models sat on a metal folding chair with their legs open and each foot resting on a bucket. Then the plaster (cold!) was smeared between their legs and they waited for twenty minutes until it hardened.

Your piece doesn't go over that well, mostly because Thaddeus's work is getting all the attention—a large plaster violin with a television monitor embedded inside, which is showing a running loop of the two of you fucking. People gather around the grainy green monitor sipping cheap wine from plastic cups and whispering. You don't remember many of the events in the video; you certainly don't remember the camera being where it must have been in order to capture several unflattering angles. After the show you expect the whispering and stares to die down—but they don't.

The video quickly spreads through school and soon every student seems to have a copy. There are even rumors of a Web site with highlights. This then is your new role. You are the *Art School Scag*. The worst part is when your parents receive a copy of the video in the mail from "a concerned peer" who "felt they should know." All eyes are on you now—you feel ashamed and humiliated. Your parents are mortified and they insist you drop out of school and start over somewhere else before any more damage is done.

If you drop out of the program, go to section #16 (page 24).
If you do not drop out of the program, go to section #17 (page 26).

9

From section 4 . . .

You enter a conservative piece of art. A series of color theory paintings you've been working on all year. Small wedges of color bisecting other wedges of color. People nod politely at them and move on.

During the evening a well-known curator approaches you. He likes your work and asks if you'd like to be in one of his juried shows. Everyone stops and listens; they try to act casual as they eavesdrop. This attention distracts them from Thaddeus's ugly piece in the corner—a large plaster violin with a television monitor embedded inside, which shows a running loop of the two of you having sex. Your friends tell him he's an idiot. They laugh at him as he unplugs the violin and eventually leaves the show early.

"Not many people are given an opportunity like this so early in their careers," the curator says. "I wouldn't ask if I didn't think you had real talent." And there's that word. "Talent." Your teachers don't say it, and certainly your fellow students don't say it. Talent is not a part of the equation in art school. They like to make you think talent is attainable, getable, learnable, but of course everyone knows, the muse *plays favorites*. She's a real bitch. She'll dump talent on some and keep it away from others. How many times have true assholes been brilliant (van Gogh, Mozart, and so on), and then nice, diligent folks are just shit out of luck on the talent score? Anyone who's ever tried at something in vain can tell you—and they don't have to be an artist—just because you want to be good at something doesn't mean you ever will be.

That's the problem with the word "talent." It denotes a universal impropriety, a galactic unfairness that terrifies you into bargaining with God. And what kind of divine being would be so unfair? Who would orchestrate such imbalance? But then, here is the gallery owner, a very handsome man with a stubbly jaw and dark roaming eyes and he is kissing the word "talent" to you. You have it, he says. That red red apple that you want to bite. Shakespeare pinned it to the table: "We know what we are, but know *not* what we may be."

If you say yes to the group show, go to section #18 (page 27).
If you say no to the group show, go to section #19 (page 29).

10

From section 5 . . .

You're staying in school. Your boyfriend can march right through the red-hot gates of hell. You've got to get through molecular physiology and you aren't going to be anybody's coin-operated doll. You cut your hair short, wear boxy clothing, and snarl at anyone who smiles at you. You're not going to be quiet, you're not going to wait patiently, you're not going to be *pretty*.

The classes kill you—but the harder they push, the harder you push back. You go out for extras. Honors. The hours are insane, you read until your eyes are bloodshot and sore, until you can't focus and the words on the page swim. You end up trying what all the med students try—*ephedrine*, otherwise known as trucker speed. It's not a big deal, it only takes two tabs a night to keep you up, but after a couple of weeks it takes five tabs and then ten and then it doesn't work at all, so you have to try what everyone uses.

Crystal meth tastes like Drano but it's made from ingredients far more toxic. Muriatic acid, iodine crystals, and red phosphorus just for starters. The grainy dust rips through your nose and throat like shattered glass. You're careful to only snort one line a night and you never shoot it. *Never*. You feel guilty and nervous—but there's no other way to stay awake.

When you finally graduate you have to decide whether to go for your master's. If you do, you'll be committing yourself to six more years of school. An eternity. Meanwhile, a headhunter for a big pharmaceutical company offers you a lucrative job as a pharmaceutical sales rep. It's a chance to skyrocket into the real world. So what do you do? More school, more debt, or more money?

If you stay in school and get your master's, go to section #20 (page 31).
If you take the pharmaceutical sales rep job, go to section #21 (page 33).

11

From section 5 . . .

You not only quit the science department, you quit school altogether. Why rack up tuition bills when you could go make money? You move back home and decide to permanently and forever stop doing any meth. That was just kid stuff anyway, just experimentation, and you're not going to let it continue. You look for work—there's got to be something else you can do. Your parents are uncertain of your choice—but they don't want to judge you, and of course they want you to be happy. *Are you happy?*

You look for work on the Internet and in the want ads and you call all of your friends to see if they know of anything. You post your résumé online, you send out dozens of letters, you go to open interviews. Nothing. It seems like everyone is looking for work and no one's looking for employees. Being out of school and without a job makes you feel lonely and fat and pathetic. You couldn't even consider going on a date—who would want you?

Then you get a break—a small break. A friend from high school offers you a job at her father's grocery store, which is way up north on Lake Superior, in a tiny town that caters mostly to fishermen and truckers. The hours are right, but the pay is minimal and it's far away. There's also a job fair coming up, where hundreds of employers fill the convention center in the hopes of snagging quality employees. You could wait and see if something comes out of that instead.

If you take the job at the grocery store, go to section #22 (page 35).
If you go to the job fair, go to section #23 (page 38).

12

From section 6 . . .

Eight hours of flying and you're exhausted. You're sticky and cramped and itching in places you'd rather not scratch. You're herded off the plane and into the baffling cacophony of Rome, where you immediately suspect you've made a large mistake. You feel homesick and ugly. At the money exchange a woman screams at you in Italian, in the bathroom there are rape-crisis hotline numbers on the wall, and you can't figure out how to flush the toilet. Safe to say you and Italy aren't clicking just yet.

It's hard to believe the Romans ever produced amazing feats of architecture and marble masterpieces in this chaotic, argumentative mess. Every language is spoken; each street sign is printed in five languages. Crowds of well-fed tourists swarm the streets with maps and digital cameras. They fill gift shops, surround market stalls, and swarm like bargain-hunting locusts. You can tell them apart from the Italians easily. The Italians are slender and well dressed. They wear dark colors. Armani. Prada. They pay no attention to the tourists. They only smile at other Italians, only acknowledge other Italians, and only speak to other Italians.

You end up getting drunk at a small café outside the Colosseum and meeting two Australian girls, red-faced drinkers with matching sunburned grins who teach you drinking games like Never, Wuss, Douchebag, and Twenty-one Aces. Afterward you all stagger to their hotel room in a syrupy ouzo haze and fall asleep in a pile on the bed. You wake up in the middle of the night and find yourself partially involved in a halfhearted orgy, the girls sort of pawing you and each other, some sloppy kisses, and then you fall asleep again.

In the morning you feel awful. You have a boozy hangover headache and you creep out of the hotel at dawn, before the others are awake. You keep your sunglasses on. Sticky shame gums you up, and there's no way to rinse it.

Time to move on to another city. Rome has had you and spit you out. You buy a ticket to Florence, where you hope to stay awhile and set up camp. You're already tired of lugging your pack around and having damp laundry.

Once you're in Florence you find an American college on Via Ginori that needs an English-speaking receptionist to answer phones. Perfect! You take the job. It's here, working at the school, that you meet a young Florentine named Filippo, who has long glossy brown hair and liquid brown eyes. *Bello.* He's an unemployed artist, a bohemian rhapsody with six-pack abs. He brings you to his small apartment across the river, where you make love on his bed, in the kitchen, in the shower, on the floor. He becomes your boyfriend, your *ragazzo.*

You move in with him. At first it's something out of a romantic Italian film, but soon Filippo starts to annoy you. He's cheap. He never pays for anything—always manages to get you to pay for things—and in the end you're even paying his rent and utilities. You buy all the food. He seems to think his job is to look pretty and wait for dinner to be ready. As summer drains into fall and spans out to winter, the relationship gets really boring—and expensive. Filippo is gorgeous and he loves you, but after a while you wish he'd just once take you out to dinner. Then one day a man with an opal pinky ring winks at you. He's well dressed, maybe sixty? He smiles. His name is *Doctor* Sandro Candreva and he asks if he could take you out to dinner. "One of the best, most expensive dinners in Florence," he promises. He doesn't have six-pack abs, but he probably pulls in six figures. Six really sexy figures.

If you go out with Sandro, go to section #24 (page 39).
If you decline Sandro, go to section #25 (page 41).

13

In England the streets are boiling over with accents, East Indian, French, Japanese, Spanish, Somali, British. So many cultures and so many differences, but there's one thing they can all agree on. They all hate Americans. You learn this quickly. You also learn Americans abroad can expect to be called names, to be insulted in restaurants, to be yelled at on the street, to be passed over by taxis, to be ripped off at hotels, to be ignored by waiters, and routinely, very routinely, as if it might be the national way to say *hi there!*, they can expect to be given the middle finger.

So you de-Americanize yourself. Tear off the parts that say Uncle Sam. *No gym shoes, no jeans, no baseball hats, no shorts, no sweatshirts or T-shirts. No gold jewelry.* You buy a navy blue peacoat, a black turtleneck, black sailor pants that button up both sides, tall black boots. You try to blend in. You put your camera away, look complacently at three-hundred-year-old architecture, and drink tea, never coffee.

You stop speaking. No conversations, no questions. Your Yankee accent would give you away. It becomes embarrassing to hear your own voice, so you never ask for directions, even when you're quite lost, which is how you ended up in a strange industrial neighborhood outside London called Wandsworth.

You stop to get your bearings and a cup of tea when a lovely woman accidentally bumps into you in line and drops a glob of chutney on your sleeve. She wipes it off with her napkin and you realize it's the first time anyone has voluntarily touched you in a long time. "Sorry," she says in a deep voice. The voice startles you—it's not a woman, it's a man. A lovely Indian transvestite named Alouette. She has a beautiful almond face, high firm breasts, an enviable waistline, and an ass round as an apple. She asks you to join her at her table. She's warm and friendly and every bit a woman except for her voice, something she hides—which is something the two of you have in common.

She takes you to her apartment, where she removes her wig and shakes out her long black hair. She shows you photographs from her recent trip to Paris, where she frequented a popular sex club called Boxx Man on rue de la Cossonnerie. "Incredible," she says and sighs. "They had absinthe and cocaine highballs and a whole wall of glory holes lubricated with French butter."

She says she'd rather be in Paris but stays in London because she has friends and a decent job at the cosmetics counter at Harrods. Her best clientele are the pale men who come in, nervous, requesting heavy pancake makeup "for their wives." She gives them powders and creams and the names of discreet wig makers and shoe stores that carry women's shoes in large sizes.

Alouette invites you to stay at her apartment, which is cozy and warm—and honestly it's the first time you've felt at home since you got there—but you're not sure you should. Maybe you ought to be out there running around seeing the world? She tells you the Eurostar line has trains running to Paris almost every hour, but she gives you a word of warning. "If you think the Brits are tough on Americans, I don't know if you want to meet the French."

If you go to Paris, go to section #26 (page 42).
If you stay at Alouette's, go to section #27 (page 45).

14

Your friend at Berkeley gets you a job at the UCB library. She tells you "Berkeley Men" are difficult and picky and most of the good ones (prelaw, premed) classify girls in one of two categories: the *marrying* kind and the *nonmarrying* kind. Go out with a guy too fast, sleep with him too soon, and be forever relegated to the *nonmarrying* category. She says if you want a good man, you have to be a *good girl*. Whatever.

The library is calm and boring, except when the head librarians show up. They're dried-up mean little ladies and they do *not* like young women. You have to act busy when they appear (which is always out of the blue) or they'll make you check the disgusting dehumidifiers in the stacks or reorganize the infectious disease catalogues.

When left alone, you daydream. You watch people sleeping in their chairs, staring at their computers, frowning at their textbooks, picking their noses, arranging their balls, digging in their purses, whispering on their cell phones, reading their books. Sometimes you talk to people and sometimes you don't— for the most part people ignore you. Then one day when you're pushing your cart down one of the well-polished hallways, you hear someone whistle. It's a short, sharp, conspiratorial sound that makes the hair stand up on the back of your neck.

An undergrad is standing there, one of those cute little hipster-doofus guys with scuffed brown leather pants and a black T-shirt. You know his type. He's a bad boy. He smiles at you and motions you over. No one else is around. He opens the door to a utility closet, a small dark room with a sink and several drums of ominous-looking floor cleaners. He winks and nods as he steps inside. *He has a cute butt.* You go in after him. Inside the closet, he kisses you hard and you kiss him back. He takes off his shirt and he's got tattoos all across his chest, but it's dark in there and everything happens just a little too fast to make out what they actually are.

He gets you up against the edge of the sink, his hands groping up under your blouse. His breath is heavy and fast (he had something with onion for lunch). You hop up on the edge of the sink and he produces his penis—apparently another of God's private engineering jokes. This slender boy has a penis that might possibly belong to a three-hundred-pound gorilla. It's purple and angry and sticks straight out from a fist of curly black hair. It's ridiculous, it's heaven.

You meet him every day. Same time. Same place. Every day you wear a short skirt and every day he pulls you into this same little utility closet. You never speak. You don't know his name and he doesn't know yours. There are grunts and breathing and bitten lips. No words. So far you've made out tattoos of a Japanese girl, a deck of aces, and the name Marina on his chest.

It's during finals, when the library is packed to capacity, that it all comes to a crashing end. Literally. You're busy enjoying your daily constitutional in the utility closet, ass on the edge of the sink, feet braced against buckets of floor wax, when you hear a groaning shriek, the sound of metal on metal, and the sink you're sitting on gives way and cracks off the wall.

You're on the floor in a pile of wet rubble and metal pipe. Water shoots everywhere and knocks out the light overhead. The closet door flies open and water gushes out into the hall, which is now filled with students and administrators and librarians. You've got your skirt up, your panties down, and your only consolation is that you have a cut on your forehead, which is bleeding, and maybe people will think you are badly hurt, which you aren't.

You manage to get your panties up and your skirt pulled down while people rush around you to get the books away from the geyser. In the midst of the confusion you bump into a tall, startlingly handsome man, a student you've seen around the library several times. *Shit.* Did he see what happened? He might just think you're a victim in all this. An innocent soaking-wet bystander gashed on the forehead by a piece of flying sink.

"You need help," he says (does he mean psychological or physical?) and he leads you to a bathroom around the corner, where a stern head librarian tries to stop you. "Excuse me," she snaps, "this is for faculty, not students."

"Excuse *me*, ma'am," he says, "I'm a third-year med student and this abrasion needs dressing." Then he pushes right past her with your hand firmly gripped in his—and you think you might swoon. The librarian scowls and says nothing.

After he dresses the wound, he takes you outside, into the brilliant sunshine and fragrant air, where all the humiliation you should probably be feeling right now blooms into this shiny bright thing, like a bubble in the center of your chest that's so big it might pop. His name is David, he's six feet two and has black hair, maple-colored skin, and dark slanted eyes. He part Canadian and part Japanese. A tall strong man with delicate features. He's a dedicated scientist and a star student. His thesis is on the genetic networks of microbial cell regulation and DNA extraction. Basically, he likes to make things grow from DNA and stem cells. He likes to play God.

His sweetness, sincerity, and kindness lead you to believe he doesn't understand that ten minutes before he met you, you were partially nude in a utility closet fucking gorilla boy. Thank God for small favors.

After a six-dollar chai latte David brushes a wet stamp of hair off your cheek and asks if you'd like to go out to dinner sometime. You remember what your friend told you about rushing into anything with "one of the good ones." Maybe he did see you in the utility closet. Maybe he's expecting to be in the utility closet with you next? Maybe you should say no and wait for him to ask you out again?

If you say yes to a date with David, go to section #28 (page 48).
If you say no to a date with David, go to section #29 (page 50).

15

From section 7 . . .

You drive to your friends' house in LA, but there's no one there. No lights, no noise, no answer. You sit on the front stoop, popping dandelion heads and watching the bright blue cloudless sky. You're sweating. Heat is funny in California—you could bake to death and never know it—the breeze fools you. Eventually you get back in your car and drive to the beach, where people are roller-skating and jogging on the boulevard under the high, white sun.

You walk slowly while all God's mistakes skate past you. Sausage people and goiter people stuffed into tube tops, thongs, and Speedos. (Someone once told you Speedos were introduced to the world on Bondi Beach in Australia, making that particular beach world renowned not only for shark attacks but for the dangling sweetmeats sharks come far and wide for.)

You sit around for a while and think it's strange your friends haven't called you back. Maybe something happened. Maybe you got the message wrong, maybe they're out of town, or maybe you have their phone number written down wrong. That night, when you still haven't gotten ahold of them, you wonder if you should drive back over to their house one final time or go check into a hotel. Staying at their house would be a heck of a lot cheaper.

If you go back over to your friends' house, go to section #30 (page 52).
If you go to a hotel, go to section #31 (page 53).

16

From section 8 . . .

You drop out of school and no one is sorry to see you go. Nobody calls, nobody comes by. Your parents are barely speaking to you—they sit silently at the dinner table, chewing and staring at their plates. Depression reaches its warm arms around you and you sleep. You become an Olympic sleeper—sleeping fifteen, sixteen hours a day. When you're awake you stay in bed and watch television. You memorize tampon commercials and insurance jingles. Showers seem like too much work and eating is exhausting.

Day after day goes like this. You lose track of time. Weeks drain into months. Your parents' anger has softened into a doughy concern, your mother creeping in with trays of tea and toast, as if you had the flu, begging you to just get up and do something. *Anything.* Concern eventually boils into irritation, and your mother gets active about getting you up. She pours ice-cold water on you while you lie in bed, and then drags you down the hall into the shower. She gets you to the doctor, who prescribes antidepressants.

Then your mother sends you to the Hyatt, the one by the convention center, where a man named Guy Moffat, a motivational speaker, is giving a presentation titled "Turning Blues into Good News." Your mother doesn't know what it is—it just sounded positive and it'll get you out of the house for a while.

"Are you blue?" a man in a blue suit shouts from the Hyatt stage. There are aluminum colored streamers behind him. A few people clap. "I was blue!" he shouts—"and that's when I found the good news!" He holds up a Bible and the audience claps—because you know, it would be rude not to. You learn Guy Moffat is the founder of the VowGuardians, a nondenominational religious group whose goal is twofold. They want to "help you find *you*, while simultaneously fighting for a righteous world." That sounds pretty ambitious to you, but awfully considerate.

He says nobody can have the blues if they're a VowGuardian. It's physically impossible. "You are so filled with excitement and joy," Guy says, "there's no room for those mean old blues!" He says anyone can be a VowGuardian if they run the world with honor, if they run the world according to the Gospel, if they respect women and promise to give them what they need. If they are protectors, promise keepers, hunters and gatherers—but *mostly*, if they have *heart*.

"Do you have heart?" Guy shouts, and the room goes wild.

Guy Moffat is so handsome, almost seven feet tall, with ice-blue eyes that pierce you from under a shock of startling white-blond hair. He smiles at you. (You're pretty sure he smiles at you, but he could be squinting from the glare off the empty metal serving trays at the back of the room where they served lo-cal doughnuts and two percent milk.)

VowGuardians say they are serious about making the world a better place. VowGuardians marry and stay married. VowGuardians do not divorce. VowGuardians do not eat or drink anything to excess. VowGuardians exercise. VowGuardians floss. VowGuardians support their youth; they support the loving care of future VowGuardians and VowGuardians' wives. "It's not for everyone," Guy Moffatt says. "Only the strongest in the herd can run alongside us."

That makes you want to take it on. He says there are several centers around town where people are welcome to come and learn more about this unique way of life, and if anyone is interested, there are volunteers wearing green plastic wristbands in the hallway. After the speech (*energizing! inspirational!*), you speak with some of the VowGuardian volunteers waiting in the hallway wearing green wristbands. They gather around you with questions and compliments, and even though you feel like shit, even though you *look* like shit, they don't seem to care. The women are bright-eyed and have purpose. The men seem warm, but in a *big-brother nonsexual* way. They each and every one tell you that being a VowGuardian is the best thing that's happened to any of them. They invite you to come check out their center.

If you visit the youth center, go to section #32 (page 55).
If you do not visit the youth center, go to section #33 (page 57).

17

From section 8 . . .

Like hell you're dropping out of school. They don't like your bronzed vaginas?
Then you'll make more bronzed vaginas. You don't even try for their approval
anymore. Last week at your critique, you presented a five-foot-tall arrangement of shellacked Twinkies glued together to look like a soft yellow cartoon
vagina. Then you lit it on fire and walked out of the room.

You have your own opening at your own "art gallery" in an abandoned
chemical plant by the river. You assemble your work (vaginas made out of
bronze, foam, plaster, wood, chicken wire, Ho Hos, and so on) and place the
pieces in a large circle. Then you create a giant bonfire inside the circle of art,
and while a punk band from Southside plays hard-core on deafening black
speakers, you invite the audience to burn your art. You videotape the burning
from several angles and call the piece *Decuntstruction*. It's a hit at school, your
teachers like the combination of performance art, video work, and installation
piece. You enter the piece into several national juried shows and film festi-
vals.

By the time you graduate, you have two offers to teach, one at New York
University and the other at the Savannah College of Art and Music. While
New York is an obvious choice for action and adventure, not to mention a
significant career step, it also promises to be expensive and crowded. Savannah offers you a bigger paycheck, housing, and health insurance. It might also
provide heat and hillbillies, but there'll be a never-ending flow of oyster roasts,
gin gimlets, and, of course, Southern gentlemen.

If you go to New York, go to section #34 (page 60).
If you go to Savannah, go to section #35 (page 62).

18

From section 9 . . .

The show is a disaster. The other works on view with your art include loom art, beaded tea cozies, distressed teddy bears covered with duct tape. The show is actually written up in the local paper as a prime example of the decline in local art, of galleries catering to the lowest common denominator in order to make a sale—any sale. Your teachers reprimand you for showing your work before you were ready. Your peers laugh at you and call you "McArtist."

So what? Notoriety is becoming to iconoclasts. *Up their nose with a rubber hose*. You organize a few other disgruntled students and begin a group called HACKY (Hedonistic Art Can Kill You), which supports disenfranchised artists and gives them a chance to go down in a blaze of (relative) glory.

You use a warehouse space down by the river as headquarters. The first organized stunt is to alter billboards across the city. Not with spray paint, like graffiti artists do, but artistically, with carefully matched fonts and photo images altering the ads' original content. You fuck with them so carefully that a person might walk right past and not notice the changes unless they really looked or someone else pointed it out. Like when you changed the large green letters in a KOOL cigarette billboard to read KLAN cigarettes. You use the same antifreeze green letters, the same schlocky font. On the leather jacket of the smiling Aryan cowboy, you put a red-and-black swastika armband.

The newspapers love it. They take pictures of nearly every billboard and call the group the Vigilante Vandals, which just made all of you work harder. Next you break into the zoo, where you tie meat to the cages. (You try to make the meat meaningful; for example, the ostriches get thirty packs of chicken meat tied to their cage. The aquarium floor is scattered with dead haddock.) You forget school altogether and instead run around with your ever-expanding HACKY friends.

Your standard tricks, however, are getting boring and the media's starting to move on to other idiots in the community, so the group decides to get some real exposure and streak across the field at the next local (but nationally televised) college football game. You won't be totally naked, however. The plan is to burst out at halftime while wearing letters made of meat strapped to your torsos. The letters will spell out HACKY, and this will force the eye of the media to focus in on your group and take notice of your work. The plan is a little dicey—you may be revered as a local hero, but you may also get arrested. You're assigned to be the *H*, the first one across the field.

If you strap the meat to your naked body, go to section #36 (page 66).
If you don't strap meat to your naked body, go to section #37 (page 68).

19

From section 9 . . .

You're not ready to show your work. It's unformed, sticky, not fully baked, but what's to be expected? It's *art school*—everyone's work sucks. Everyone but one student—Toru Nishigaki. He's a Japanese exchange student with a tiny withered arm like a broken bird wing and a melty deformed face, as though he stood too close to a fire. His work is fantastic. It's convicted, blunt, moderate, and serene. He creates extra-large canvases, like twenty-by-twenty-foot-tall paintings with blocks of color that look like scratched vanilla and burnt lace mixed with cream. *White on white on white*. Dizzying. Some paintings have sticky twigs glued on them, like an enormous forest sunk inside a blizzard.

His paintings are never ostentatious, never showy, never self-conscious like everything else. (For her thesis Susan Chow glued stuffed animals together and lit them on fire.) He's better than anyone else, and that's why they largely ignore him, exclude him, even make comments about his withered arm and his red face. He'll be free of it all soon though—he's graduating.

When you see his work in the senior show, you have a bad case of pinkeye, which makes the world blurry. But you can tell that amidst all the sculptural monstrosities, the lopsided paintings, and boring photographs—his work is truly stunning. There's something haunted about this particular painting; inside the frame it's completely cement colored, with one single black line running down its middle. There's a simple balance to it. Equanimity.

The senior class graduates, Toru goes away, and his cement white painting haunts you. You try to copy it. Try to re-create it—but with no success. Time passes and now you only have one year left before you graduate. Your painting professor tells you all about a new exchange program in Iceland. It's a relatively new art school based in Reykjavik, and they want to attract a globally diverse student body. They pair students with working artists all around

Iceland who then live and work with the artist for a semester. It's a work-study program, which means you'd be assigned a job either for the artist or at a nearby facility.

Iceland? All you know about Iceland is that it's cold and something about whales and Vikings. Besides, warm clothes make you look bulky. Still, free tuition and housing and a monthly stipend? Of course it might totally suck and you'll be stranded.

If you go to school in Iceland, go to section #38 (page 70).

If you stay in your current school, go to section #39 (page 73).

From section 10 . . .

You go for your master's in biotechnology at Berkeley. You're assigned to a lab, a small white room with fluorescent lighting, six cramped workstations, six irritable grad students, and your surly grim professor who doesn't like you, or anyone else. She makes it clear that being stuck with you idiots is a fate worse than hell. Her name is Professor Shisu, also known as *Shitzu* because of her roly-poly frame and shrill bark.

You meet a med student named David who's six-feet-two and has black hair, maple-colored skin, and dark slanted eyes. He's part Canadian and part Japanese. A tall strong man with delicate features. He's a dedicated scientist and a star student. His thesis is on the genetic networks of microbial cell regulation and DNA extraction. Basically, he likes to make things grow from DNA and stem cells. He likes to play God.

The two of you start dating, as much as you can with your hectic worlds. Sex with David is unusual. He's very domineering—he likes obedience, submission, no suggestions. He likes to cover your eyes. In all positions your eyes are covered by cotton pillows or silk neckties or linen sheets. (Startling at first, but learnable.) He also reveals the fact that he manufactures crystal meth on the side, which pays for his tuition.

He dislikes public displays of affection, sneakers, and any kind of nickname. He's respectful, thoughtful, and punctual. He can also be arrogant, quarrelsome, and picky. You meet (and like) his parents, you meet (and dislike) his ex. You love his aristocratic attached earlobes and his smooth white feet. He likes your shiny hair and white teeth—and his attention makes you boil with pleasure. You like making him happy. He makes you love love.

Through it all—the weekend traveling and late nights studying, the endless lectures and jittery mornings fueled by coffee and meth—the two of you are together. The meth bothers you a little. There comes a time when you think the two of you should cool it, but he says not until graduation. *How else will you get all your work done?* (He's about to graduate but you have two years of school left.)

David surprises you the day after he graduates when he proposes to you. He gets down on one knee right in the quad, all the students and musicians swirling around you, and he produces a small marquis-cut diamond ring. He says he's been offered an internship, and he wants you to quit school and all this awful hard work and come away with him. He promises to take care of you forevermore, to be the one you cherish, the one who cherishes you. People have stopped and formed a circle around you, two bongo players under a tree are rattling off a fake roll call.

If you marry David, go to section #40 (page 75).

If you do not marry David, go to section #41 (page 79).

From section 10 . . .

You go to work for a pharmaceutical company called Pharmacept, which produces cancer treatments. Your job is to travel around your region and convince doctors to prescribe all the expensive treatment systems Pharmacept makes. Essentially you're a door-to-door salesman. *A huckster, a fibster, a Bible salesman.* You're in your car all day, or pounding across the pavement, going from clinic to clinic, hospital to hospital. Thank God there's still meth when you need it, a little vitamin "M" for when you're low.

You work aggressively on sales, and while some inroads are made, by the end of the first year you are not making your quotas. A chief surgeon at the Mercy Hospital burn unit tells you that most of the other reps offer "incentives" to doctors for prescribing trial drugs. When you ask him what he means by *incentives*, he shrugs and pushes the bill across the table. (Later research introduces you to the Kendall Scandal, which started in 1996 when a suspicious relationship was uncovered between doctors and a certain behemoth pharmaceutical company. Inspectors found a list at the company's office with the names of ninety-nine doctors who had agreed to receive "undue incentives." All doctors' licenses were revoked, the company went bankrupt.)

At the office you casually ask a senior sales rep about possible incentive strategies and it comes out that many of the senior sales reps do in fact offer incentives to doctors for trial drugs. It's the only way to make quotas, which is the only way to keep your job. Sometimes this is money; sometimes it's vacations or golf club memberships. (You don't ask if sex is ever used as an incentive—but it does suddenly occur to you that almost all the female sales reps are beautiful. Nonni, the high-cheeked South African woman; Belle, the platinum blond; Portia, who has tits like zeppelins.)

You're told not all doctors accept incentives, so you must be careful who you offer them to, but luckily many of these gods in white coats don't believe laws apply to them anyway. The attitude is: Face it. Unenforced laws make the world go around better and quicker. These incentives aren't illegal unless you get caught. Plus everybody does it, plus they expect you to do it, plus you'll lose your job if you don't, plus you'll make a shitload more money.

So you place a call to the doctor you suspect is most likely to appreciate incentives (Dr. Karlen, an oncologist with a black Porsche 911). When he calls back, he says if you're picking up the tab, he's delighted to have lunch with you. He feels like lobster. Now you just have to figure out—is paying off the good doctor salvation, or a slippery slope?

If you pay the doctor a stipend to try the trial drug, go to section #42 (page 80).

If you do not pay the doctor a stipend, go to section #43 (page 82).

From section 11 . . .

At the grocery store, your job is to stand at the cash register for eight hours a day scanning groceries while shifting your weight from foot to foot. The first week goes by slowly as you learn the ropes. You learn how to ring out your till, how to weigh cabbage, how to clean broken eggs off the conveyor belt, how to clean ice cream off the conveyor belt, how to clean baby vomit off the conveyer belt, how to slide items down the conveyor belt, where the bag boys sulkily dump them into bags, hoping to break or smash everything.

There are lonely groceries. Swanson Hungry-Man frozen dinners and Schlitz. There are harried groceries—with newborn diapers, extra-strength rash ointment, baby formula, and instant coffee. There are young groceries— Mountain Dew, Bugles, and blue raspberry Kool-Aid. There are old groceries—menthol cigarettes, prune juice, and next week's edition of *TV Guide*. There are icicle-through-your-heart groceries—a single can of cat food, a pouch of instant soup, and the want ads.

There are good customers and bad customers. Mean customers. People who assume you know the price of everything by heart, ask you why the lines are so slow, tell you to clean up the aisles, tell you they're going to get you fired because you're rude, because you're stupid, because you put the orange juice on top of the eggs, etc., etc.

It gets on your nerves, but the manager is pretty cool. Auggie is a cigar-chomping union man who plays cards all day long with his old Korean War buddies at a card table in the stock room. They smoke joints and tell the same war stories until you know them as well as they do. There's the time Auggie made "jungle hobo stew" in his helmet over a fire. The time LeRoy took a bullet in his testicle and poured whiskey on it to prevent infection 'cause he was so goddamned worried about losing it. Still—the guys are nice to you and pretty respectful, considering "they'd all had more Asian meat than a Korean barbecue."

Auggie won't let anyone hassle the cashiers. If they do, he threatens to cram lutefisk up their asses or puts them on the much-feared and readily enforced "banned for life" list. The few times people demand to speak to the manager, you point to the smoky back room and say, "Be my guest."

The head cashier, Marta, invites you to poker night, where all the girls make seven-layer hot-dish or taco-waffle platter or Spam-tuna-noodle-surprise (the green peas are apparently the surprise, as all the other ingredients are listed in the name) and bring it over to someone's house and play poker. They use coupons and rebate vouchers instead of money. It's a good time. The women tell stories—they're actually pretty raunchy once they get a few beers in them. They say cashiers make shit for money. The shit of shit. After rent and food there's nothing. Between their ice-fishing husbands and their mall-bound teenagers they don't have money for Kotex. "Wadded up paper towel is good enough for me," Marta grunts.

You tell them about your artwork and how you were never understood and how everybody treated you like a second-class citizen. They all nod and agree and say *people just don't understand—they make snap judgments without knowing you—without knowing the whole story.* Maybe it's the beer or the hot-dish—but by the end of the night you're pretty much in love with all these red-faced heavyset Norwegian women, who all have hard lives, every one, and who never—not one of them—consider themselves or you a second-class citizen.

They laugh and talk about being your age and wanting to do other things with their lives, but then they sort of stop talking and sip their beers and shrug. "Look at your hands," Marta warns you, "soft." She shows you her hands, which are red and chaffed from the endless bagging and register work. They're so pink they look like someone dipped them quickly in boiling water. Your hands are still soft. But for how long?

You wonder if staying at the grocery store is a mistake, but mistake or not, jobs in a remote northern town are limited—well, not *totally* limited. There's always Lili, a beach ball of a woman with penciled eyebrows and a blind tobacco-colored toy poodle she carries under her arm like a purse. She runs a "phone service" for gentlemen called Little Lili's and she's asked you several times if you want to work for her. "Best job in town," she says. "You just talk dirty to men and rake in the cash. The pay is good and you keep your pussy at home where it belongs."

"But who actually calls?" you ask.

Lili thinks for a minute. "I suppose on average we get more truckers than anyone else. That and a handful of perverts in wheelchairs."

If you stay at the grocery store, go to section #44 (page 85).

If you go to work at Lili's phone service, go to section #45 (page 87).

23

From section 11 . . .

You go to the job fair at the Hyatt, which turns out to be a pathetic parade of hack insurance agencies, pyramid schemes, and cheap uniform companies. It turns up absolutely nothing except a subscription to *Employee Times!* and a free plastic whistle. Fabulous.

Lonely, you call up some old friends from high school, but they don't call you back. At night you wander over to the neighborhood indoor skating rink, which has a big bar that overlooks the rink. The skaters are so elegant, you watch them from the bar and sip your beer as you watch how effortlessly they slice and cut around each other, never touching, never landing, always moving forward.

Unless they crash, which they often do. Arms and legs in a sudden tangle like badly cast fishing lines. Red faces and apologies. They remind you of life in general—how you're skating along effortlessly until you accidentally crash into someone and they send you hurtling to the ice, where you sit dazed until you very awkwardly and slowly get up.

That's when you spy a bright yellow index card tacked up behind the bar that says *Part-time help wanted*. You spend all your time here anyway, there's nothing you want to do besides sit here and drink, so why not get paid for it? But that same night an HR recruiter from the *job fair* calls you. She works at a special events organization and they have a spot open in the "party planner and entertainment" field.

If you take the job at the ice rink, go to section #46 (page 89).
If you take the job at the special events organization,
go to section #47 (page 91).

24

From section 12 . . .

Sandro picks you up in his dark blue BMW 7 Series, with butter-colored leather, a chrome stick shift, and burled wood dashboard—not that you noticed. As you get into the car, you feel people looking at you. They must think you're a *principessa* with your silver sandals and swept-up hair. *Pretty glossy shiny sexy.* Of course they don't know what *you* know. That you're actually just a dirt-broke expat with a leech boyfriend and getting into this shiny car is probably a *very* bad idea. Sandro leans over and steals a quick kiss from you, his lips salty and warm.

You go to dinner at Le Volpi e l'Uva, a trendy low-lit wine bar on Piazza dei Rossi, which is owned by an old Catholic virgin spinster who only hires gorgeous male waiters. At dinner (charred shrimp with squid ink fettuccini) Sandro says *you charm him.*

"The air moves around you," he says and picks up your hand, kissing the pads of your fingertips. You feel like a real live princess. "This is a city for beautiful things," he says, "for passionate things. We keep you for a while. You belong here." And here in this beautiful place, you do feel like you belong. The delicate food, the candlelight, it all seems easy and familiar and good. All through dinner, however, your mind reflexively thinks of Filippo. *Will he wander past the restaurant and see you with this other man? Will he somehow know you were here?*

Sandro distracts you from your worries and tells you all about his import-export business and his four grown children, who are an orthopedic surgeon, a college physics professor, an architect specializing in reconstructing historical landmarks, and a drug user. "Massimo." He sighs and checks his gold watch. "Every family needs a black sheep."

"Bah-aaaaaaah," you bleat.

After dinner you drive around the city, the orange-lit storefronts blurring past, the full moon overhead. As you're crossing the Arno, the slow Florentine river that drifts south, Sandro rests his hand lightly on your thigh. You do not move it. It feels good, as if Sandro has put his hand on your thigh many times before, as if you knew this drive by heart.

You ask to be dropped back off at school, hoping he won't ask to go to your apartment (where Filippo is undoubtedly watching soccer in his underpants), and then it dawns on you—*Sandro doesn't care if you have a boyfriend*—Sandro probably has a *wife*. He doesn't wear a wedding band, but in Italy this means nothing. *How stupid*. You should have known. Of course he's married. It's quite accepted in Italy that a man of certain stature will have a mistress, or two. At school he kisses you on the cheek and asks if he can see you again. He's creepy but sweet. Filippo is sexy but poor. Life is always a compromise.

If you agree to see Sandro again, go to section #48 (page 94).

If you decline to see Sandro again, go to section #49 (page 98).

25

From section 12 . . .

Sandro is too polished, too interested, too *something* for you. He drops you off and you hurry down the empty street, happy with your decision to tell him, No, *mi dispiace*, but you're not seeing him again. Now you're laughing, smiling, in love with Florence. You feel just like Audrey Hepburn in *Breakfast at Tiffany's*. *Alive, adorable, in love*. You hurry home and burst through the door to tackle Filippo with a kiss.

But the apartment is dark. Something's wrong. There are sounds coming from the bedroom, and then your eye catches a black high heel on the floor, like a black barracuda resting before an attack. Filippo appears in the doorway, naked, a sheet wrapped around his waist. (It is this small modesty that you will remember later. He used to lounge around the apartment nude, his testicles sagging on the furniture like overripe pink plums, but now he is suddenly shy.) *"Cosa fai?"* he shouts, "you said you'd be gone till later!" as if it is your fault for not sticking to your schedule. Then a woman's long, tan leg appears on the corner of the bed behind him. A tan leg with red toenail polish.

You turn and run. "Wait!" Filippo shouts, but you don't look back. What have you done to deserve this? Your stomach turns queasy—what will this mean? Does this mean you move out? If you break up with him you'll be homeless. You'll be alone in a foreign city across the world from home. *Filippo is all you've got*. Was he even cheating? You didn't see them actually having sex. People say cheating doesn't have to be the end—that it's possible to mend fences—and it's not like you've never cheated before. In fact, if you manage to patch this up, it gives you leverage to make some big changes at home.

If you break up with Filippo, go to section #50 (page 100).
If you forgive Filippo, go section #51 (page 102).

26

From sections 13 and 159 . . .

You travel to Paddington Station in central London, where you buy an expensive ticket that will take you straight through the Chunnel right into downtown Paris. On the train you meet a group of loud young Australian students who offer you cigarettes and shots of whiskey. They tell you they're renting a caravan and driving across Europe, which sounds like a definite party. Aadi has a big laugh and his wife, Kiara, likes to sing Broadway show tunes. Their friend Weevil is a wiry little guy with a broken nose and a scar on his forehead. Dosh has one green eye and one blue and he can balance a beer can on a dent in his head. After some more drinks and a hit or two of weed, they invite you to join them. "Come on!" they say.

Why not go with the Australians? They're wild and fun. Americans and Australians always have a good time together. Plus you won't be an American alone—you won't be such a target. You all spend the rest of the trip singing and drinking, listening to stories about the Outback, the 'roos and the wicked surfing, which is better in Australia than anywhere in the world. Cute Australians.

After a long train ride and then a long cab ride all the way to the outskirts of Paris, you learn that when the Aussies said "caravan," what they really meant was "school bus." You had pictured some happy vehicle with colorful striped canvas and swinging copper pots, but what waits for you is a decrepit old acid-green school bus. The thing is a monster. Rusted grillwork and ancient tires. They say it was once an actual school bus, but you'd rather not picture those unfortunate children.

On board you see it's like a long narrow apartment. The back benches have been ripped out and replaced with bunk beds and a small kitchenette. There's a propane stove and a plastic water barrel for a sink. There's no toilet. You have a funny feeling about all this. Your funny feeling grows into a *definitely bad feeling* when you're about fifty miles out of town, hungover and with a headache, and Aadi, the loudest and one might say "chief" of the group, tells you the school bus is a *chalk truck*. A drug-running bus.

"Mostly Tina," he says. Crystal meth. There are secret compartments hidden beneath the seats where white bricks of meth are already stacked and ready to go. These are not just fun-loving Australians, they're also drug dealers. You try to comfort yourself by drinking some more whiskey and by reassuring yourself that you do actually like them, and friends shouldn't judge each other's hobbies.

You travel on the green bus for months, stopping at the major towns in Europe. Paris, Amsterdam, Luxemburg, Zurich, Bern, Geneva, Berlin, Rome, Florence. Drinking, smoking, sleeping. The drug dealing is all done very discreetly, Baggie by Baggie, mostly to the kids who throw raves in old countryside barns. The green bus stops at every checkpoint and all passports are stamped. Sometimes other travelers come with you, hitchhikers, bicyclists, backpackers, and the occasional drifter. (Once you picked up a whole soccer team that was late for a local match.)

Then one warm night outside Siena, a group of teenagers approach the bus. (How word spreads that the chalk truck is in town you have no idea.) One young girl is with them, her name is either Hélène or Ellène, you never heard exactly right. (You do remember she smelled like cheap shampoo, like bright-red chemical strawberries.) There's nothing really remarkable about her or the other teenagers, they just want to buy some stuff, so Kiara takes a few of them into the bus and they come back out and hang out for a while. Everyone sits around the campfire and parties. Someone drags out a guitar so Kiara can sing "Hello Dolly" in a fake French accent. The fire eventually dies out and the teenagers go home. The rest of you climb onto the bus and into your sleeping bags, except for Dosh, who stays outside to sleep by the glowing embers of the fire.

In the morning you wake to a thundering voice. *"Cunt!"* Aadi shouts. *"Damn you!"* He's throwing stuff all over the bus and kicking things out of his way. Weevil is wiping his eyes.

"What the fuck?" Kiara shouts.

"That!" Aadi points to the sleeping bag on Dosh's bed. There's someone in it—but it isn't Dosh. It's one of the teenagers from last night—and her face is a light lavender blue. It's Hélène/Ellène.

"Jesus," Kiara says. "She never shot up before. Oh Jesus." Bits of foam have hardened at the corners of Hélène/Ellène's mouth and her eyes are still open and glossy. They dry as the morning goes on. They go from glossy to dull construction-paper black.

Aadi slaps the girl hard across the face. You wince. You just want to throw yourself across her and protect her. "Wake up!" he shouts and slaps her again. This is a nightmare. This is not happening. Everybody scrambles the hell off the bus. Aadi says there's only one thing to do. "We dig," he says. "We bury her before anyone else comes around." He walks right up to you and sticks a thick red finger in your face. "You too, Yankee bitch!" he says. "Your passport was stamped with ours in every city from here to Checkpoint Charlie. They catch us, they catch you."

If you help dig, go to section #52 (page 103).
If you take off, go to section #53 (page 107).

From section 13 . . .

You stay with Alouette. You feel comfortable here and you love her strange apartment. It's like a Gypsy medium's house, smothered in silk pillows, Oriental throws, faded tapestries, brocade furniture, tea-stained walls, broken antiques, tarnished candelabras, and the heavy curtains that keep out the light. There's an empty fireplace in which no fire has ever burned. (Sealed by the landlord for safety.) It's now illuminated by tiny white fairy lights buried inside a basket of dried, spider-web-laced yellow roses. The apartment has the look of a ruined opera, of a valiant attempt at something that didn't quite happen.

Later that night as you're walking past the bathroom you catch a glimpse of Alouette standing at the sink. It's a snapshot—Billie Holiday is playing on the radio, the sink covered with waxes, creams, sprays, and powders. She has one long leg up on the lip of the sink as she shaves her thigh. She glides the pink plastic razor all the way up to the knot of black pubic hair that barely hides a small dark shriveled penis dangling like a broken doll's arm.

She bartends at a place down by the river, a transgender bar called Switch, which is just a long narrow room with a slowly turning fan and a small wooden stage at the far end where people sometimes sing. You fall into Alouette's routine. Never up before eleven, never to bed before two. Smoke a pack of menthols a day; eat very little, mostly crumbly toast with marmite and strong black tea. She's from Delhi, but detests Indian food. She hates curry and tandoori and anything with cinnamon. She's left all that behind, she says. Along with her gender and her family, she has become a new person.

Then one day while she's out, you're washing dishes at the sink when the doorbell rings. There stands a short, plump Indian woman with a red bindi on her forehead. She has green eyes and wears a shiny moss-colored agate on a gold chain.

"Is Rashid here?" she asks. Her accent is thick and she shifts her weight uncomfortably from sandal to sandal. You can't take your eyes off her bindi. (She will tell you later her bindi is made from red sandalwood paste *to cool her anger*, the ashes of burnt camphor *to aid in victory over desire*, and sandalwood *to quell her desire to kill Rashid*.)

"There's no Rashid here," you say.

"Rashid," she repeats. "Perhaps Alouette?" She looks down. "He calls himself Alouette sometimes. I am his wife, Amil."

Amil. You let her upstairs, what else can you do? You make her tea. Amil tells you she lives in London along with their children. Apparently Alouette, or rather *Rashid*, had another life before this one, a life where he was a heterosexual, a husband, and a reliable bank teller. A life where he was a man.

You wish *Rashid* would get home. You have some questions of your own. Like, does he see his sons? When did he get married? Amil drinks her tea and keeps her eyes on her sandals. "I would not come here," she says, "but there's a funeral and Rashid must go. He must go." She gives you a long sideways look, and you realize that she suspects you and Alouette are living together romantically.

"No!" you say out loud, and Amil nearly drops her teacup.

The door finally slams. *Alouette-Rashid* is home. He walks into the kitchen and freezes when he sees Amil. He sets down the groceries. Nobody speaks. He looks so masculine to you now. For the first time you cannot see where the woman in him went. Now he is all angles and stubble and sweat.

"How long have you been here?" he asks Amil, and there is no affection in his voice whatsoever. (Alouette will tell you later he had sex with his wife exactly three times. All three times he was drunk. The first time was on their honeymoon and they conceived their first son. The second time "she more or less raped me," he says, and they conceived their second child. The third time he fought her off, detached her retina, and accidentally knocked her front tooth loose.)

Amil speaks rapidly in Hindu; her eyes are bright and wet. Alouette says nothing. You leave the room and try to eavesdrop. An hour later you hear Amil leave and Alouette knocks on your door. Rashid is gone. She's herself now. "I need something," she says. "I know it's a lot to ask, but would you come with me to a funeral in India? I can't face my family alone. They hate me. It's only for a few days and Amil will pay for everything, she is rich, it won't cost you anything to go."

If you go to India for the funeral, go to section #54 (page 108).
If you decline going to the funeral, go to section #55 (page 110).

28

From section 14 . . .

You say *yes* and go out with David the next night to a little Japanese restaurant, where he shows you the proper way to eat eel (while it's still warm) and helps you hold your chopsticks *properly* and makes you try crunchy fish roe, which you don't like, but say you do. You start dating. He introduces you to his world of expensive wine, lacrosse matches, and a case of chlamydia, which he claims is a leftover present from his last girlfriend, who cheated on him. It's no big deal. Once David is introduced into your world—your world changes. Everything becomes, *Would David like this? What would David say about this? What would David do?*

He affects every decision you make, from what you wear to where you go. It's like pouring an aggressive compound into a small, benign environment. It takes up everything. All the breathing room—all the real estate. It changes everything about you—and you love the changes. He's an endless source of advice, information, and class. With David on your arm you feel prettier, shinier, sexier.

He's a dreamboat. A hunk. A man any woman would go knock-kneed and damp to be with. You love introducing him as *your boyfriend*—you strut around the campus, tugging him all over so everyone can see the two of you together. You pull him closer and turn up your nose with a knowing smile at the pinched faces of all the other girls draped around the campus who wear bikini tops and short shorts just hoping to catch a man like your boyfriend. What can you say? Sometimes things just work and life doesn't suck and you get the man you want.

He reveals the fact that he manufactures crystal meth with some friends on the side, which pays for his tuition. He gives you a little to try . . . a thin line of white powder you snort up your nose. It burns at first, but it gives you so much energy and makes sex fantastic. Sex with David is unusual. He's very domineering—he likes obedience, submission, no suggestions. He likes to cover your eyes. In all positions your eyes are covered by cotton pillows or silk neckties or linen sheets. (Startling at first, but learnable.) He dislikes public displays of affection, sneakers, and any kind of nickname. He's respectful, thoughtful, and punctual. He can also be arrogant, quarrelsome, and picky. His temper in particular—sometimes it's scary.

The meth bothers you too. There comes a time when you think the two of you should cool it, but he says not until graduation. *How else will I get all my work done?* You have started to smoke rather than snort, the high is smoother and you avoid the nosebleeds, but you wonder when you'll stop—and if you'll stop. You shrug it off. It's probably just a college thing. You'll quit when you want to.

On the day he graduates he surprises you and gets down on one knee in the quad (still wearing his mortarboard and tassel) and he proposes. He produces an enormous marquis-cut diamond that was his mother's, still in the blue box from Tiffany. *Soooo pretty.* But there are things to consider . . . his meth use (your meth use), his temper, and the fact you want to go to school. If you go become Mrs. David, you'll be a doctor's wife . . . and maybe nothing else.

If you marry David, go to section #40 (page 75).
If you do not marry David, go to section #41 (page 79).

29

From section 14 . . .

You say *no thank you* and enjoy the confused look on his face. You say *you'll see him around sometime* and give him your phone number before you merrily depart. You skip back across the quad. For once you didn't rush it with a guy. For once you play hard to get. Now you can flirt with him and make him work for a date with you. It's good for boys to wait. (Surveys say men like to hunt that which recedes, and tend to back away from anything that advances.)

It's a bright sunny day and you get in your car and head into San Francisco. You want a new dress for your impending date with David. Something appropriately sexy yet irresistibly pure. You're driving across the bridge and all of life is perfect. One of those moments you wouldn't change for anything. The immense girders of the Bay Bridge loom over you, metal arms holding you high above the sea. You sing loudly with the radio and change lanes.

Then there is the sound of screeching. Brakes on asphalt. You see a silver BMW convertible roaring up on you like a silver shark with its jaws open. There's an explosion, an impossible force spinning you, the metal arms overhead all jumbled up, guylines twisted. Your head explodes through the windshield.

Unconscious, you are rushed by ambulance to the nearest hospital, where ER doctors and nurses struggle to reinflate your lungs and keep your heart beating. You hear shards of conversation, like a radio that will not stay tuned. You feel fluttering, bird wings, angel wings, and there's something warm in your head and you can't see. (Your skull has been fractured, one of your eyes punched out.)

Your parents are called and they'll be on the next flight, but for now you're alone. You are a soul-kite drifting along the clean white ceiling of the emergency room. It occurs to you as you bump along the metal ceiling and the ductwork that hospitals are the ugliest places. They are the last place anyone could become well. Sterile and colorless and without light. Hospitals should be made from waterfalls and rocky cliffs and bird sanctuaries. Things that crack you open and let the light in. You feel no pain. You can see everything. You can see the doctors and nurses, the X-ray technicians and the waiting room. Funny, the strange chatter and the bleeping machines.

Behind you, up above the ceiling, is a warm white light. There is a gentle tug, as if you were caught in the mild current of a gentle river, up and away, toward this warm bath of milk-white light. Your heaven is waiting.

If you decide to follow the light, go to section #56 (page 111).
If you decide to return to your body, go to section #57 (page 112).

3o

From section 15 . . .

You start to drive over to your friends' house but decide you should eat first. If they're home they're not going to want to whip up dinner this late, so you stop at an Arby's drive-through. There's a long line of cars already waiting and your mind wanders off to *What's it like being a superstar?* and *How much do they pay for those Botox shots?* when someone taps your passenger window. You roll down the window and this really sweet kid selling candy bars asks if you want to buy some to support the Boys and Girls Club of something-or-other. You're digging around in your purse when you hear another voice—an older voice—and you look up to see a man grabbing the kid and shaking him. It's the manager or something and he's yelling at this kid for selling candy bars again. You shout at him to *stop it*—he's really shaking the kid.

Someone starts honking and you're like *what the hell?* You get out of your car and yell at the manager, *Let go of the kid! I wanted a candy bar! What the hell is wrong with you?* but it's like you don't exist, he's so mad at this kid, and the honking gets louder, people are yelling from their car windows. Someone taps you on the shoulder and you start to explain to whoever it is that *This kid just . . .* when the man, who turns out to be the little boy's emotionally unstable older brother, and who has not assessed this situation exactly correctly, shoots you point-blank in the face with a .38 Special.

You have a very nice funeral, and you get to be a star after all, because the Lifetime channel makes an after-school special about the older brother, who wasn't given proper medical help at the hospital the day before because he didn't have insurance, and so wound up at home and under the supervision of his younger brother, who went out selling candy bars . . . and well, you know the rest. Some lives have bad endings.

31

From section 15 . . .

You find a hotel in Santa Monica called the Vista View. It's a sad-luck pink cinder-block affair that rents rooms by the hour. Your bed squeaks and the carpet is damp. You call your friends. (How long is the space of time between rings? One-one-thousand, two-one-thousand, three-one-thousand.) No one answers. *Are they avoiding you? Are they fighting again? Where are you going to stay?* You put four quarters in the vending machine at the end of the mildewed hall and get a dented can of Diet Coke and go for a walk. Nobody walks in LA unless they're homeless or at the beach, so you head for the boardwalk that ribbons along the Pacific Ocean. The sun is red.

Hungry, you stop at a hot dog stand on the beach and order a Vegas special (kraut, extra onions, relish). There are people sitting at small tables around the wagon eating hot dogs from paper plates. When you get your hot dog, there are no onions. The man in the wagon shrugs and turns off the light. He's closing for the day.

"Excuse me?" you say, "I need onions." He ignores you. You tap on his little Plexiglas window. (Smeared, filthy.) "Come on!" you yell. It's not like you have a lot of money, or this little trip to LA is going that well in the first place, and all you want right now is some fucking onions on your damn hot dog. *Is that too much to ask?*

Apparently it is. The man will not even turn to look at you. He just turns up the radio and cleans his little grill inside the wagon. You tell him you're going to wait outside the door all night until he comes out and then you're going to kick his ass. You want a refund. You're probably overdoing it—yes, you're definitely overdoing it, and people around you are staring. *Up your nose with a rubber hose.* You want onions. You kick at the door and yell at the little man. There's a voice somewhere inside your head telling you to stop, but you don't.

You look insane and maybe the cops will come soon, but you keep on yelling at the man anyway.

So when someone taps you on the shoulder, you're not altogether surprised. Your adrenaline is pumping; you can feel your face is hot, red, and sweaty. But the man holding your arm is not a cop. He's just a guy wearing a yellow silk jacket and a pink scarf. *"You're hysterical!"* he says. "I mean really *funny!* You've got to come see me tomorrow."

He says his name is Arthur, and he's a talent scout at a *big agency* and you should come to his house at noon the next day. You look around the wide, deserted beach. The sun is setting and seagulls dive at the receding tide. Haven't you seen bad movies like this? *Young girl new to big city accepts help from kind, weirdly dressed stranger and ends up shipped to the Philippines for international sex ring.* He hands you his card and asks if you'll come.

If you agree to go to Arthur's house, go to section #58 (page 113).
If you don't agree to go to Arthur's house, go to section #59 (page 115).

32

From section 16 . . .

You decide to visit the VowGuardian center the very next day. Your mother is thrilled and gives you her car, along with fifty bucks for lunch. You follow the directions, which are very good, and you arrive in a cute, quiet neighborhood at a brightly painted, pink Victorian house with a wide wraparound porch.

You're greeted in the cozy living room, which is filled with folding chairs and coffee tables, as though set up for a game of bridge. Everyone is really nice to you, they all remember your name, and someone says they like your hair. What a nice change from the prickly, picky, creepy art students you're used to. These people seem nice and genuine. Like they don't have to prove anything to anyone. One boy in particular, Summer, is very attentive. He has curly blue-black hair and large, sky-blue eyes. He listens carefully to everything you say. Listens to you the way you wish your parents would listen—like what you say is important. Like *you're* important.

Summer says the VowGuardians have changed his life. He was hollow before—he used drugs, cheated on his girlfriend, didn't value anything or anyone. He says living in the house with all these people has given him a new start on life. A new appreciation for *what matters*. He says the best part is nobody in the house has to have jobs or make money—the house takes care of everything they need.

"It's like a commune," he says, "but not really. It's cooler than that. No weird hippie stuff. It's just a house where good people are welcome. Why should life be hard?" And that is a damn fine question. *Why should life be hard?*

You tell him about dropping out of art school, the horrible videotape, and how all your other friends abandoned you when you needed them the most. "That would never happen here," he says. "We would never turn on one of our own."

There's a meeting in the living room and you're introduced to the group, which consists of all different kinds of people—older men and younger women, all colors and sizes. Everyone applauds and thumps you on the back and whistles. Your cheeks burn red with embarrassment. You like these people.

The house is so cheerful—the opposite of the damp ugly basement where you currently reside. The VowGuardians ask you if you'd like to move in. This would be a way out of your parents' basement and into a bright, cheerful house without having to pay rent. Besides, if you don't take them up on their offer, with no job and no prospects, how else could you move out? You might end up becoming one of those tragic forty-five-year-olds who still live with their parents and eat dinner with them every night at five p.m.

"Summer wants to sponsor you," the VowGuardians tell you. "We all want you to become a part of the house. We want to support you and get you feeling better, and stronger."

If you move in with the VowGuardians, go to section #60 (page 117).

If you don't move in with the VowGuardians, go to section #61 (page 121).

33

From section 16 . . .

The word "center," in general, kind of gives you the creeps. (As in processing center, or center for disease control.) You don't think you'd like that. "Could you mail me more information?" you ask—and they frown at you. "No," the lead girl says. "You have to come to the center." This is your exit cue. You've seen enough movies about abductions and cults to know you shouldn't "have to" go *anywhere*.

You tell them you won't be visiting *their creepy center* anytime soon. Immediately their smiles fade, their pamphlets drop. What phonies. They turn like vultures on a fat girl in a green sweatshirt that says "I'm Big But I'm Cuddly." *Stupid cult*. Who would be so retarded?

You don't want the depression to come back. *You've got to get back up on the proverbial horse.* Maybe if someone else believed in you? You know, like if there was a guy in your life who really thought you were special. There's an online dating site called U-Date, one of those big sappy sites that have photographs of happy couples having coffee, happy couples walking down the beach, happy couples getting married. Is that the normal order then? *Coffee—beach—wedding altar?* It makes you so mad, you sign up.

This is just a test to see what men want—you have no intention of representing your *actual self.* Who wants someone overweight, depressed, and living with their parents? So what is it men want? They want *thin*. Okay. You're going to create the perfect woman. On your profile you say you're five feet six, one hundred and twenty-two pounds. Perfect. You cut and paste a model from a Talbots catalog. A pixie blond with a perky nose and little cupcake breasts.

Your interests are: sex, grilling steaks while wearing a thong, watching the game, hanging out with the guys, buying lingerie, and, of course, walks on the beach. No kids, never married, perfect health—and your name? Your name is Delilah. *(Oh, Sampson.)* The e-mails pour in. You get three hundred eighty three e-mails the first week. Men from coast to coast want Delilah. They're in awe of her personality (compliant, submissive) and her talents (nude yoga and grilling T-bones). Everyone says *we'd get along just great!*

You are beginning to hate Delilah. Is it her looks or her personality they like? Only one way to find out. You leave her perky picture up, but give her some problems. Now Delilah has three kids. She has dental problems and she can't spell. Does that distract the men? It does not. The e-mails continue to pour in—nobody cares if a pretty woman can spell or has gingivitis. So you give Delilah some more trouble. You give her an STD and student loans. You change her profile headline to read: YOU BETTER BE READY TO PAY MY BILLS. No change. The men keep e-mailing. So then you change Delilah back to all the original "desirable" information; *I once skied naked in Vail! Sometimes I'm just horny horny horny!* But this time you change the photograph. You put up a picture of you. Granted, your photo was deliberately taken for effect—no makeup, your eyes crossed—but the reaction from your cyber guinea pigs is extreme. Nothing has changed about Delilah except the way she looks. She still likes vacuuming naked and giving marathon back rubs . . . but that doesn't seem to matter. No e-mails. Zero. What have we learned? *If you're pretty, it doesn't matter what you say—men want you. If you're ugly, it doesn't matter what you say, men don't.*

All right. Enough. You make all the profile information accurate. Your actual height, weight, hair, everything. (Why not the horrible truth?) You exchange the goofy photo for one of you a friend took in art school. You looking over your shoulder off at the sky. A week later there are two e-mails in your box. One is from Luis, a sweet sexy boy living in San Diego, and the other is from Harrington, an ocular surgeon living in London. You start e-mailing both of them—and they are different as night and day. Luis is shy and sensitive, an out-of-work graphic designer who writes songs on his guitar and calls you his *hermosa reina,* his beautiful queen. He wants to know your favorite color, your best childhood memory, what food you like, everything about you. He's never been farther east than the Mississippi, and he doesn't want to go any farther. He wants a wife and kids, and a small farm in Northern California. He thinks you might be the one he's been looking for.

Harrington is assertive and strong. He's smart and worldly. He lives in a large modern town house in central London and travels to exotic places like Bora-Bora and Phuket for his frequent vacations. He's a certified deep-sea diver, an adventurer and risk taker. He likes your essay, likes what you had to say about yourself. "You're real," he says, "and I've always had a thing for American women." Both men want you to come visit. Soon.

If you visit Luis in San Diego, go to section #62 (page 123).
If you visit Harrington in London, go to section #63 (page 126).

34

From section 17 . . .

You choose New York, which seems to go sour from the start. You land at JFK late, the heat and noise box your ears, your stomach is still wrestling with the in-flight food, and your luggage is missing. The orientation director was supposed to meet you, but she has apparently never arrived or already left, so you have to take an expensive taxi into Manhattan. The taxi driver either misunderstands you or is just a jackass, and drops you off in a strange part of the city. *Possibly Harlem? Brooklyn?* You don't really know.

While you're trying to hail another cab, some kids start talking to you. One has the face of a pugilist, with a truffled nose and eyes green as a nightjar. "Hey, lady," he asks, "you got the time?" His eyes switch back and forth, green goblins in their cave. His voice is singsongy. *"Hey-Lay-dee. Hey-Lay-dee."* You ignore him and reach wildly in the air for a cab. They all make a sudden orchestrated move—one grabs the purse off your shoulder and the other two grab your carry-on bags and take off. You chase them half a block (what would you do if you caught them?) and stop, heart racing, palms sweaty. The noise of the city surrounds you. Everything is stolen. You haven't been in New York for two hours and everything you have is gone.

The rest of your tenure goes downhill from there. The temporary housing is a closet-bedroom-bathroom with a swayback bed and no dresser. The classes you teach are so far off campus you have to take three trains to get there, and your classroom is in the basement of a cinder-block sauna-hot community center. Your class is required, and so the students who have to be there often sleep through your lectures, or work on other assignments, or play games on their cell phones.

You take refuge in going out with some of the other teachers after work—all recent graduates stuck in a similar leaky boat. It's at one of these sip-and-bitch sessions at an Italian restaurant in Chelsea when you meet the bartender, Rocky. He looks eighteen and he buys you a glass of sweet syrupy grappa. He has shining brown eyes, elegantly sculpted hands, and one tooth turned crooked, which makes him stifle his smiles. The two of you flirt and banter; eventually your friends go home and you're left alone there with him.

After the bar closes you walk through the streets together, talking and laughing. He kisses you. He asks you to come home with him. It's chilly out, the moon is missing from the sky, the wind blows through the leafless nude trees. He is warm where everything else seems cold, but beware stranger danger! You don't know this guy—he could be anybody and he could do anything. If he attacks you in his apartment, which is god-knows-where, who would help you? If he *kills* you in his apartment, what's to stop the papers from running your obituary with the apt headline: LOOSE WOMAN GETS WHAT SHE DESERVES. AGAIN.

If you go home with Rocky, go to section #64 (page 127).
If you go back to your apartment, go to section #65 (page 130).

35

From section 17 . . .

You choose to go to Savannah, to an art school where all the students are prima facie punk rock, but most have trust funds and Southern accents. (Some are exceptionally talented, but others look like the cast of *Hee Haw* made over by Marilyn Manson.) Either way, all of them have found a way to leap the high-tuition hurdle of the extraordinarily successful school. The dean, Dean Dorington, is a shrewd woman with raven hair and fierce eyes. She became dean after she caught her husband (the former dean) with their pool boy, Otto, in the equipment shed. Otto was bent over a beach ball, her husband thrusting him like a steam piston.

First she took his money. The dean divorced her husband, sued him, and in an "undisclosed settlement" received enough money that it bankrupted him. "He cried like a schoolgirl," the court stenographer said. "It was nothing a grown woman should see." Next she took his job. Dean Dorington had her husband ousted from his position at the school through a tireless campaign of slander and legal investigations. She fired anybody who had aided, abetted, or even *knew* of her husband's affair. She called him a duplicitous psychopath in a public statement and had his portrait taken down from the main hall and given to Goodwill.

Finally she took his pride, what was left of it, by turning the school into a fierce financial dynasty. She brokered deals with the city to buy real estate, cut utilities, and give her free restoration crews. She established a board of directors with more money than the Nazis, she started a pricey foreign exchange program (who knew there were that many wealthy Japanese kids who wanted to study art in America?). She hiked tuition up to an astronomical height and then she cut teachers' pay—making the college one of the most financially lucrative colleges in the entire United States.

The schedule they give you is a backbreaker, days crammed with classes, nights dedicated to student reviews and grading work. You haven't had any time to create yourself. You haven't painted or sculpted since you arrived. Some of the only time you even have to yourself is late at night in your tiny apartment, when you manage to cook yourself a meal and stare out at the night sky.

It's on one of these rare nights when you're having an Absolut Vanilla–lemonade at your kitchen table that your eye catches a cluster of flapping gray feathers in the alley. It's a pigeon trapped in the tar. You've heard this happens—tar can turn liquid under the scorching high noon sun and sometimes catches animals. Then when the sun goes down the tar hardens—and they're stuck. You've heard of it—but you've never actually seen it. It's heartbreaking. The pigeon is in perfect health except its little legs are stuck fast in tar. You go outside and use a fork to pry the creature out. After much effort (screaming, squawking, several people stopping to stare), you take the bird to the emergency veterinarian clinic in a shoe box.

While you're waiting, someone leans over and taps you on the shoulder. A bleary red-eyed woman offers you a shot of whiskey from a silver flask. You don't recognize her at first. Her nose is red and she looks like she's been crying. "I brought in my pug," she tells you. "He's vomiting again. Cancer." Then you recognize her. It's Dean Dorington.

She thrusts the flask at you again. "Have a drink!" She's drunk, and she doesn't recognize you are on her staff. (Why would she—you've only met in large groups.) You look around to see if anyone else in the waiting room recognizes her, but they don't seem to. You take a swig, and then she takes a swig. Then another and then another. Time passes. You wait for the pigeon, she waits for the pug. The nurse calls her back. You wait. When the nurse finally calls you, she hands you the shoe box and says, "It's dead." Then hands you a bill. Seventy-five bucks for morphine. You pay it and go. Sometimes life is just stupid.

In the parking lot the dean appears again and she's distraught. You've never seen her with a single hair out of place—let alone weaving through a parking lot drunk. "He's dead!" she says. "Buddha Boy is dead!" Then she bursts into tears. You offer her a ride home. She manages to direct you down the twisting low-country roads to her giant wedding cake of a house on the Wilmington River.

"Have a drink," she says as she stumbles out of the car. "That dog was everything to me. Come on. *Have a fucking drink*."

Inside her palatial home the living room is dripping with French antiques, Chinese mirrors, hand-painted Italian credenzas, demi-marquise settees, and crushed gold pillows. It looks like a museum. There's an entire glass case of Fabergé eggs and Limoges figurines. *Where the hell does this money come from?* I mean being dean of a college isn't exactly minimum wage, but the bathroom has a gold toilet. People have long suspected her business acumen has led her to figure out a way to pad her salary.

You sit together on the couch drinking Pimm's and ginger ale. She tells you about her dog. *On and on and on and on.* You down another beer and then another and then another. Your head is starting to swim. She rests her head on your shoulder. "Buddha Boy came with me to this swamp. He was here during my breast cancer, during all those nights. Buddha Boy was here." The room is light and tipsy. Spinning.

She starts to cry again, tears wetting your collarbone. She's shaking. Her hands are clasped around each other and she looks up with wet eyelashes. She kisses you suddenly on the lips. You're too surprised to stop her.

Your only thought is—*you're going to hell now for sure*. Sure, you were going before, for the cheating, the lying, the complaining, and the general malaise. For caring more about animals than people, for not particularly liking children, for never once adopting a starving African child. Now you're going because you're south of the Mason-Dixon Line and you're a lesbian. That means you're automatically going to hell.

You and the dean start kissing and hugging and rolling around on the floor. She's so drunk she starts telling you secrets as she kisses you. Telling you things she shouldn't. *The board of trustees is made up*, she says. *I cook the books, alter the receipts, take money from the school by paying people who don't exist. My cocaine habit is getting worse.* They come tumbling like rocks down the side of a mountain. You eventually fall asleep with your clothes strewn across the floor. When you wake up, the sun is starting to rise. There isn't much time now.

Pity swells in you, pity for this poor pathetic creature, but anger too. She has bilked tuition money from students, and for what? For diamond-crusted eggs and million-dollar toilets? When she finally drifts off to sleep you shift from beside her, legs creaking, and make your way for the door. Your throat hurts and your head pounds. You should tell someone about the dean's confessions . . . shouldn't you?

If you tell on Dean Dorington, go to section #66 (page 131).
If you don't tell on her, go to section #67 (page 135).

36

From section 18 . . .

Sometimes you find yourself doing stupid things. A series of small choices leads to a highly unusual situation—such as strapping cold steak to your nude body and preparing to run across a football field with thousands of people watching. *How did you get here?* There's no way to know and it doesn't matter.

It's cold out. Frigid. The group enters the stadium secretly, through a service door by the Dumpsters. You all tiptoe down a service hallway that ends at a set of large metal double doors that will open directly onto the field. You can hear the dull roar of the crowd—a buzz saw in your brain—it sounds like *a lot* of people. You try to give yourself a pep talk. Stupid clichés run through your head. *No guts, no glory. No pain, no gain. Damn the torpedoes and full steam ahead. . . .*

You take off your trench coat and shiver. You are starting to have doubts. The crowd outside is screaming, the music is blaring, and everyone in the group suddenly seems tiny and pale. There's no time to think. You're pushed to the front of the line—as your letter is *H*, you're the first to go. You're stone cold. You can see your breath as you pant sharply. This feels really wrong.

Then the halftime siren sounds, your signal to charge across the field, and you burst through the doors. Cold air whips around your body as the meat slaps your chest. *Thump thump thump.* You run across the field, across the sharp Astroturf, past the smeared crowd—away from the roaring in your head. You chug toward the large set of double doors on the far side of the field, where you'll run back inside. If you can make it there, you'll be back on the warm bus before you know it—and all this will be over.

You reach the doors and try to open them—but something is wrong. The doors are locked. You slam against them frantically, jiggling the handle. You can feel the cold metal on your fingertips, the burning warmth over your body.

"It's locked!" you yell to the HACKYs behind you—but when you look they aren't there. There's only a CNN cameraman pointing a camera in your face. Behind him a tide of reporters swells toward you, men carrying cameras with cold blue lenses, wet and shiny like the eyes of spiders.

It turns out no one else ran across the field. *They chickened out, got confused, thought it was the other bell*—you'll never know and it doesn't matter because forevermore you will be known as the girl who ran naked across the field on national television, wearing meat on your chest. You will be known as the Lone Meat Streaker, but this is the least of your problems as stadium security guards swarm you and throw a damp blanket over your shoulders.

At the station you refuse to give your name, your affiliations, your phone number, or your next of kin. It doesn't matter because your parents saw you on TV and they arrive at the station with grim expressions. They want to post your bail and take you home, even though your father can't even look you in the face. You tell them you want to issue a statement. After all, the whole idea was to expose HACKY for what it is—why it exists—and you haven't done that yet. If you go home—you've failed. You want to call a press meeting right there at the police station and deliver your message to the community. Your parents tell you to stop embarrassing yourself and ruining you life as well as their lives and they beg you to use "what little sense you have left."

If you go home, go to section #68 (page 138).
If you stay in jail, go to section #69 (page 142).

37

From section 18 . . .

You have to draw the line somewhere—and you draw it at strapping raw meat
to your tits. Enough already. The others are pretty sore about it—they want
you to come with. You tell them it's better with fewer people and it's important
to keep the group trim, able to make a fast getaway. You remind them they're
all wanted for several misdemeanors if not felonies, varying from property destruction to breaking and entering. It's important they don't get caught. So they
go on without you while you stay to clean the meeting room/meating room.
Cleaning up is the least you can do—you feel a little guilty about bailing.

The room is a mess. Red juice and slush swamp the table, which you try and
scoop up with paper towels. You should get a bucket for this, it's disgusting.
Then there's a knock at the door. (Odd, because HACKY members usually
just barrel in.) A man comes in, a medium-sized guy with dark hair. He's nervous. Something about how he is holding his hands. You remember that. The
radio is on, and he crosses the room quickly. He's suddenly right beside you.

"All this meat!" he says. His face (a blank ovoid) tilts toward you.

"All this meat!" you repeat, your voice higher than it should be. You back
up slowly and he follows you like a rogue wave. He smells salty and raw, like
an open cut. He pushes you up against the table and holds a little silver knife to
your throat. The door is open, you can see the streetlight outside. He fumbles
with his jeans and then with yours. There is red meat all over the table.

He leaves you on the floor and you're not sure what to do next. You get up.
He's gone. It was over so quickly—almost like it didn't happen. It wasn't long
and drawn out like in the movies—he didn't drag you off and keep you in a
cage—it wasn't like any slasher film or after-school special you've ever seen.
It was almost like he didn't want to do it—like he was sorry or nervous or
something. Maybe it doesn't even count.

You bolt the door. *You should have gone to the stadium*. Now, if you go to the police, you're going to have to tell them where the HACKY headquarters are. You're going to have to explain what you were doing and why. You'll expose the identities of everyone in the group—hard workers and single parents, and they all, every one of them, tried to get you to go with them. It's your fault this happened. Now, if you go to the police, you're not just turning yourself in—you're turning the entire group in.

If you go to the police, go to section #70 (page 146).

If you go home, go to section #71 (page 148).

38

From section 19 . . .

You go to Iceland and it's far more beautiful than you'd ever imagined. The country is a thin skin on the earth's crust—a spectacle of mountains, active volcanoes, erupting geysers, pebbly lava fields, black gravel screes, and mossy ridged scarps. The landscape is eerie. Lunar. There are no trees whatsoever, just open plains of black gravel and jutting fjords surrounded by dark water.

There's one main road on the island called Ring Road and it circles the entire edge of the country, following the rocky coastline. As your bus rumbles on, you see few buildings, an occasional gas station, and lots of biscuit-colored sheep grazing in the fields. The bus drops you off abruptly at a gravel crossroads and the bus driver just points. "Now you walk."

You trudge down the wet road, careful to step over the occasional pile of sheep shit, and a half hour later you come to a small stone building with a grim-looking woman standing on the porch. This is your mentor. She's a stone sculptor named Halldóra þórðardóttir (*Hall-dora Thorth-are-daughter*) and lives and works in this house outside the tiny village of Sæberg. Sæberg is tucked into the hillside on a large blue fjord that juts out into the ocean like a crooked green finger. This particular fjord is famous for ancient witchcraft and the polar bears that still occasionally wash up on rogue icebergs that have floated over from Greenland.

Halldóra shows you the town, which has a natural hot spring, a community swimming pool, a run-down apartment complex, a small museum, a youth hostel, and a small elementary school named *Árbæjarskóli*. As part of your exchange program, you're supposed to teach art classes to the eight hundred blond-haired, blue-eyed Icelandic schoolchildren here. (Iceland is a nation of two hundred and seventy thousand of the most genetically similar people on earth.)

Halldóra is a woman of few words. Any indication of her likes or dislikes must be culled from the flickers of expression in her firm mouth and dark eyes.

You can tell she doesn't appreciate anything fancy or formal or [p—] [fis]
her gunmetal gray hair clipped up in a simple bone barrette and [fe]
wool sweaters over paint-smeared jeans, which she rarely washes. [i]

She makes large stone sculptures in the barn and puts you to work
chunks of marble with a diamond pad, a small piece of steel cloth wi
trial diamonds imbedded in it, only they aren't called diamonds when
industrial diamonds, they're called borts.

"Borts are just as strong as regular diamonds," Halldóra says, "but th
imperfect."

"Flawed," you add.

"Not flawed," she snaps, "*imperfect*—which makes them better. Because
they're not little princesses on pinky fingers, they can go on the drill bits that
build steamships and skyscrapers. They're the workhorses of the diamonds.
Those *others*," she scoffs, "the *perfect ones* who end up on engagement rings,
they're the weaklings."

You stop adding comments to anything Halldóra says after this.

She makes you work from five till seven in the morning, and then you go
to the Árbæjarskóli, where you teach second-graders how to finger paint and
glue driftwood into birdcages and make collages with sea kelp and bird feathers collected from the shore. Then after school you go back to the farm, where
you help cook dinner, usually lamb.

After all that, you're finally free to work on *your* sculptures, but you're usually exhausted. Instead you like to go for night walks, like Hemingway and
Thoreau did. The design of a sliver of an iceberg or a tidal wrack is simply
superior to anything you could ever make, and so much more interesting. You
comb the shoreline, feet crunching on wet pebbles, seabirds soaring overhead,
the occasional black seal popping up out of the cold water. It's on one of these
night walks that you find something strange. It's a dried fish head stuck on a
sharp stick, and there's a small piece of driftwood clamped between the fish's
sharp yellow teeth. On the driftwood is strange writing. Almost hieroglyphics. You can't read it, so you dig it up out of the dirt and sea stones and take it
back to Halldóra for translation.

Next morning she's standing by the stove turning bacon when you hold the

head out so she can see. She drops her fork; it skitters across the tiles at her et, and she backs away. "Put it down," she whispers. "Throw it away. Take back in the ocean."

How'd she know you got it at the ocean?

She says it's the old craft, the way farmers used to control the weather. "They put a fish head on a stake and painted a strafe on its forehead with the blood of a baby. A newborn baby." She frowns at you, but you think it's cool that you've uncovered an old piece of ancient witchcraft, an artifact that probably belongs in a museum. But she tells you it isn't old at all. "That was made last week," she says, "a month ago at most. You can still read the writing and the red thread at the base is still there—someone made that thing recently."

"Any babies gone missing around here?" you kid—but she's in no mood to joke.

"I know whose it is," she says. "It's Siggi's, the man who owns the museum. Everybody says he makes them." Then she looks at you carefully. "You must never tell anyone you found this. People are suspicious, they would accuse you. They would turn on you." She tells you people still fear Icelandic witchcraft, they still whisper about the witch burnings and who still practices it—because strafes like these are still found. You agree to throw the thing away and never mention it again, but after she leaves you sneak it out of the compost heap and study it.

It *is* sort of scary looking—but everyone in Iceland is superstitious. They all believe in hidden people and trolls and evil sprits living in the rocks. They think mystical creatures can seek revenge on them or hurt them when they sleep, but that's just because they've been brought up to believe. You know that if you take this fish head to Siggi (you've seen him once or twice down by the waterline—he's a short little man who always carries big books around), you know that if you show him the fish head, he'll tell you more.

If you take the fish head to Siggi, go to section #72 (page 150).
If you throw the fish head away, go to section #73 (page 152).

39

From section 19 . . .

You stay put. You *could* roll the dice—but why? What you have now isn't perfect, but what you could get could be *worse*. You'd rather just leave the fucking dice alone for once. You stay at school and work on your art, but you still can't shake the image of that perfect painting Toru did. The field of white with a single line running through it like a crooked barn fence. You work steadily in your small, cramped studio space, trying to re-create that moment Toru captured on the wall. You work at night, on the one painting that does not come. Over and over you pursue the painting. It comes to nothing.

School is okay. While no one would ever single you out for trouble, no one would ever single you out for anything. You keep your work simple, technical. Never taking too big a chance, never sticking out too far from the crowd. You do your work, you pass your classes, and you graduate. What now? You don't have any definite plan. You take a job as a cashier at a gas station and rent a nearby studio with a few friends. It's a cold-water splinter-floored space with a view of a chemical plant across the street. You set your easel up and keep painting. What else can you do?

You just want to re-create that one painting. Just once and then you can move on. You work and rework your brushstrokes. You paint the canvas, then black it out and paint it again. Maybe the cumulative effect of all this energy on the canvas will amount to something. The Mayans had this technology. They built a pyramid, lopped off the top, built it again, lopped it off again, and on and on, at least seven times, until they believed the energy was so great, so concentrated in that spot, as to induce magic. Your canvas, then, is its own ruin. Gone over and over, lopped off, the fields of white painted over and over again.

You paint all day and then work the graveyard shift at the gas station, from ten at night to six in the morning. Then you sleep until the alarm goes off and then you get up and you paint again. Nothing else matters—not even food. You never really eat, mostly just Slim Jims, orange pop, and popcorn stolen from the gas station.

It always seems to be winter these days. Slush cold. Icy breath, snow crunching underneath your feet—the whole world trapped in a white painting, the trees sprayed with ice, the winter stretching across canvas, the ice field you cannot find, the field of white you cannot paint. You take the canvas out every day and breathe in the paint, which at this point smells like iron, rainwater, and ruin.

Do you know how many colors of white there are? *Ivory, cream, snow, smoke, ghost, bone, bisque, lace, linen.* . . . Which white was that painting? That's the question. The memory presses against your eyelids, leaking into your eyes. In the student records department the woman behind the desk says his name is Toru *Nishigaki* and she even gives you his home address in Japan. Would you dare go find him and see that painting again? It doesn't matter—you haven't got the money to go.

Providence arrives in the form of a cracked tailbone. You slip on the sidewalk in front of an Amoco station one icy afternoon and settle out of court for a sweet twenty thousand dollars. Now you can either start your own business, do something grown-up for once, or you can go hunt down that goddamned white painting before it destroys the whole of your brain.

If you go to Tokyo to find Toru, go to section #74 (page 154).
If you start your own business, go to section #75 (page 156).

40

From sections 20 and 28 . . .

You marry David and the wedding is a baffling ordeal. A six-figure *Town and Country* affair with willowy peach bridesmaids carrying bouquets of Peruvian white lilies and organic kale. They look so happy and single and free you want to bite their faces right off. The gold ring waiting for you seems like a solid gold dog collar.

The basilica is choked with white tea roses; you are choked by a twelve-thousand-dollar lace wedding dress that's so tight you can't breathe. The dress itches, like it's crawling with red ants or skin mites, which to a certain degree distracts you from the oven-hot chapel and the priest who has shockingly bad breath, a cross between imported anchovy and turned tuna.

David yawns during the ceremony and then behaves like a two-year-old during the reception. One of his friends duct tapes a handmade papier-mâché ball and chain to his leg, a symbol of his new warden (you). David finds this so hilarious, such the height of comedic irony, that he refuses to take it off and drags it around the dance floor all night until it's in tatters. You spend your wedding night arguing over who was supposed to bring the check for the caterer and sleeping in separate bedrooms.

The fun doesn't end there. The next week you both check into rehab—something you agreed to do rather than go on a honeymoon. You've both decided to quit meth for good—well, at least for as long as you can. So you admit yourselves into Hazelden and tell the rest of the family you're on your honeymoon in Tahiti.

It's a sixty-day program and you never dreamed it would be so hard. After the initial detox—a harrowing six-day stretch speckled with tremors and vomit—you begin psychotherapy, which is like drilling a pint-sized hole in your head and letting strangers peer in. You learn that you're filled with hidden rage (depression turned inward), an inability to commit, and the knowledge that you have persistent separation anxiety issues. Nevertheless. You both stick with the program and count the days to graduation—but even after you graduate you notice you still get cravings and have dreams about the grainy powder with a sweet acid taste.

You both go home humbled, exhausted, and ready to move on. You end up taking a job as a pharmaceutical sales rep. (*Irony!*) David works at the hospital. Your hours are long, his hours are longer, and it gets to the point where you hardly see each other. No time for dinner together or going out, let alone sex. You never have sex—there's barely even time to sleep. You end up having an affair with a man at work—a quiet, inconsequential guy named Wojahn, who books rooms for your trysts at budget hotels by the highway. (*Wobegone Wojahn* you call him. *Wobegone Wojahn* with a hirsute back and totally bald, bright pink pig testicles.) The affair eventually ends. It's just too boring.

Your life goes on. You move to Boston. That's a good thing—right? David is doing well. You finally get to quit your job, and move into a beautiful brick Tudor house. You get to take some time for yourself; sign up for yoga and get weekly massages at the club. As time goes on David starts his own private practice, and you move into a bigger house, and then an even bigger house, and then the biggest house you've ever seen. It's a twenty-thousand-square-foot drywall McMansion on the edge of a golf club. (You can see out right onto the second green.)

Well, this is the life everybody wants, isn't it? Rest, relaxation, redecoration. You redecorate the house, and then redecorate again. Nice long naps and bubble baths. You're not bothered by traffic or noise and there's a nice group of wives who live on the course as well, and you all meet once a week to drink apple martinis and play bridge. It's the perfect life—only, only it isn't. There's something vaguely wrong, a dulling of the senses, an apathy, a malaise that has settled in like a fog around you. You can't quite put your finger on it, but one day at the club while Kristine is giving you a Swedish-shiatsu combo rubdown, you suddenly feel distinctly as though you're made of duck liver.

There's also the matter of your husband staying out late more and more often. The bridge club says this is normal. "Let them have the leash or they'll give you the collar," the wives tease you. They tell you to take his credit card and buy yourself something nice every time you don't know where he is, and by the end of the month you've already purchased an entire set of Wedgwood china.

You go to Narc-Anon meetings. They keep you sane but they can't help you in the damn giant house. It's deafening in there. You try to take up gardening (black thumb except for orchids, which you love), and then painting (black thumb again), and then you take up bird-watching, which, as corny as it sounds, becomes the one thing that gives you any pleasure. You love watching the darting and whirring wings, the fierce fathers and fiercer mothers. You buy field guides and learn that hummingbirds are not uncommon around your area—they only need to be coaxed to your window with sugar water. So you put up a red hummingbird feeder outside the kitchen window, one of those cheap red plastic ones you buy at the drugstore. You stand at the kitchen sink watching for the hummingbirds. They come. You can hardly believe it. You feel a dizzy mad rush of delight, like maybe you aren't marooned on an iceberg anymore. You watch for hours as the small air-light bodies beat furiously against the wind.

A week later though there's a stern note from the association telling you to remove it. It does not meet with the aesthetic codes of the residence community. The maid takes it down, and the hummingbirds do not come back.

Your husband is definitely fucking around and most probably using meth again. There are signs. Red eyes. Missing money. Late-night phone calls. His absence. Sometimes you sit at the kitchen counter, a large expanse of unbroken white Corian, and stare out at the trees. Somewhere out there is your real life. Here, you are hermetically sealed in a drywall biosphere, a vacuum-packed cloister. So here it is. Wife of a doctor at thirty-eight, rich beyond use, and utterly useless. Powerless. You don't even have the power to feed the hummingbirds.

But you could create power for yourself. You could stay here and use all that money for good—you could donate it to museums and cancer funds and monkey research centers. Children starving somewhere. You could do what all the other rich ladies do. They use their husbands' money to buy the world a better place. You could also just bail. Hit the eject button and start over alone . . . and penniless. You'd lose everything.

If you divorce your husband, go to section #76 (page 158).
If you do not divorce your husband, go to section #77 (page 160).

4 1

From sections 20 and 28 . . .

You tell David you don't want to get married, you think you should finish school. He's acting funny—staring at his shoes a lot—and it's safe to say you aren't ready for what comes next. He gets mad. *Really mad*. Ears red, knuckles white. (Isn't this where he's supposed to get quiet and accept rejection with a dignified resolve?) He tells you that you're being stupid. *What's wrong with you?* he asks. You tell him you've made up your mind and he insists that *no one* is ever going to love you the way he does. You say that's fine by you—his love is feeling a little creepy right now.

That's when David draws back his open palm and slaps you across the face. Just slaps you right there. At first you're not even sure if he hit you. Maybe the ceiling fell down? Have you finally gotten late-onset epilepsy? Is it a rogue earthquake? Then you see the dead black in his eye—like a shark's just before the jaw unhinges and the lid rolls back to white. You know his hand is coming in for another landing. Time to go. You don't even hit him back, you just *run*.

After you graduate, *with your medical degree*, thank you very much, you want to do something important. Something that really helps people. They're looking for doctors at *Médecins Sans Frontières*, Doctors Without Borders, a group of physicians who travel around the world helping the sick and infirm in third world countries. There's also an opening at the House of Human Development—a government agency that places doctors in impoverished at-risk communities in America. The question is, do you want to help at home or abroad?

If you join Médecins Sans Frontières, go to section #78 (page 162).
If you join the House of Human Development,
go to section #79 (page 164).

42

From section 21 . . .

You pay the stipend and the reaction is immediate. Not only does the chief surgeon order a large quantity of your trial drug, he invites you to join his exclusive country club. (Acres of chemically treated green grass and placid man-made lakes with white swans shipped in from Prague.) He introduces you to several other doctors and your quotas improve immediately. You make senior sales rep after shattering quotas and making record sales. You are also snorting six lines a day—and having a hard time keeping it hidden. Someone's always coming in the goddamned bathroom.

Then one day at a Four Seasons Golf Clinic you meet Andrew Sorensen, a particularly young, handsome, and available oncologist. He has green eyes bright like river stones. He asks for your phone number, and without thinking you give it to him. When he calls two days later and asks you out on a date, you realize there's a problem with this. Doctors dating pharmaceutical reps poses a definite conflict of interest. On the other hand, do you know how extremely rare (*like spotting-big-foot-riding-a-unicorn rare*) it is to meet a young, green-eyed oncologist who's available and actually asks for your phone number? You can never tell him you used meth—well, sometimes you still do. *Rarely.*

You go out on the date with the doctor. Who wouldn't? At dinner, his eyes seem particularly green, his lips particularly kissable, his dimples particularly adorable. He's perfect. Dr. Andrew tells you a story about when he was seven or eight and had aggressive eczema. All the neighborhood kids called him Flake Boy and nobody would be his friend. He had a stuffed rabbit for a companion, that was it. "Maybe it's why I went into medicine," he says. "My doctor was the only one in the world outside my family who was nice to me." You find yourself touching his arm, looking into his eyes, and laughing. *So sweet, so vulnerable—which is so sexy!* Everything is perfect—one of those moments you wish you could catch and keep forever under glass. He drives you back to your apartment and earnestly asks if he can come upstairs. He is pale and sincere in the moonlight. A character right out of a Jane Austen novel.

So here is your Darcy. Your Romeo. He's waiting for your answer. But is he a dreamboat or is he a dud? So sweet to look at, a confection this well crafted. He wants to come upstairs and you-know-what with his you-know-what on the God-knows-where, heaven knows how many times. Would a big bite make him taste even sweeter, or would it ruin the perfection altogether? Maybe it's the Cape Cods, or his teddy bear story, or his ever-so-green eyes, but you let him in. He pushes you down on the kitchen table and the two of you go at it right there, knocking a bowl of oranges off the table and sending them rolling around the kitchen floor. In the morning there's a pulpy mash stuck to the sheets, a sex soup of seeds and rind and smell.

When the doctor wakes up you have breakfast ready. Bacon, toast, and eggs. He's groggy. Hungover. He is rumpled and adorable, his hair messed up and a pillow crease across his cheek. You're filled with painful, buoyant love for him. Could you really love him? You do. You *love* him. He smiles at you and takes a bite of toast. Everyone always says not to drop that bomb early, and yet so many of your male friends tell you they want to meet a woman who's passionate about them. Unafraid of adoring them. You *love* him. Do you say so before he leaves?

If you tell Andrew you love him, go to section #80 (page 165).
If you don't tell Andrew you love him, go to section #81 (page 168).

43

From section 21 . . .

You refuse to pay the bribe. It *is* a bribe, isn't it? You feel very satisfied with yourself, even as your sales numbers dwindle and your calls go unanswered. At least you're not doing anything that will land you in superior court. Well, you may have your morals, but soon enough you don't have a job. They fire you. They "regretfully no longer feel you can represent the required standards of the company." Which is bullshit. It also becomes clear that no other pharmaceutical company will have you—it's apparently common knowledge that you're not "a team player."

You eventually have to sell your car and move to a less-than-desirable apartment by the railroad. You try to find solace in the fact that you made the right decision. You can recognize what the right decision is because it's *never* sexy, fun, or naughty and it frequently will piss you off. The right decision will not make you money. The right decision will not make you popular or pretty and it usually requires boring clothes. This particular right decision lands you in a damp apartment on the wrong side of town underneath high voltage lines and working as a receptionist at a dental clinic.

Time passes. You're still unable to get your foot back into pharmaceutical sales, so you stay at the clinic, filing bills and booking appointments for root canals. You have an ongoing affair with the office X-ray technician, Ray. (He warns you that he's tired of the stupid *Ray/X-ray* jokes.) He's a scrawny redhead with a Piper Cub in his pants. You do it doggie style with him on the X-ray machine (complemented with hits of nitrous oxide), you do it missionary style on the receptionist's desk with pencils stuck to your ass, and you create the new and exciting "inverted wheelbarrow" position in the utility closet, a position that requires the stability of a drum of industrial cleaner and the leverage of a broom handle. It's sex and just sex and nothing else. Simple and refreshing in its carnality. What's nice is that Ray never even thinks of asking you out on a date. This little arrangement goes on and off for a year and then Ray falls in love with you. So you decide to fall in love with him. You're not really doing anything else. You had quit the meth for a while, but the cravings sneak back, especially at night, and you give Ray a bump, just to see if he likes it. He does.

Then one day your voice becomes rough and splintered like a sawhorse. It starts with a cough, a spot of blood on your pillow, a headache that won't go away. There are tests and more tests. You're diagnosed with tracheal cancer, which grows rich and healthy like a morning glory through your throat, red vines twisting around your vocal cords. Why did you get cancer? No one knows for sure but they give you a questionnaire. *Do you eat artificial sweetener? Do you drink diet soda? Do you use artificial hair dyes? Do you eat red meat? Do you live under electrical lines?* Oops.

You do the trial drugs, you do the chemotherapy. Ray proves to be a superb nurse, a real sweetheart. You move into his small apartment, chunks of hair falling out here, chunks of hair falling out there. He knows better than to try and cheer you up. You absolutely hate anyone who tries to cheer you up. *Every day is a new chance for life! Think positive! Your hair will grow back in! Until then, here's a creepy wig from the cancer society!*

Chemo makes you feel sicker than the cancer ever did. Just walking up the stairs exhausts you—puts you to sleep for the rest of the day. Nausea, diarrhea, dizziness, irritability. Loss of memory, loss of body hair, loss of all dignity. It seems dying of cancer would be easier than getting treated for it. Two years later, after a fifth round of chemotherapy, the cancer finally goes into remission, *a sleepy-time cancer!* You hair grows back, your white skin gets a rosy hue. Still, your vocal cords need time to heal, you rarely speak, you are careful with your words—they're expensive.

Color takes on a new meaning after your vocal cords have been cut. You spend time at the museum sitting on the metal benches and staring at the paintings, into the Renaissance eyes of princes and the cold crowns of queens and the spicing smiles of children. You watch the white space between the Rothkos. They're quiet—you're quiet. Everybody's quiet. Your treatment is going well . . . the cancer stays in remission and you begin to get your voice back.

The hospital calls and offers you a job working for the hospital counseling people who have been newly diagnosed with cancer. The frightened, the forlorn, the frantic. You could really help. That same week Ray announces he has landed his dream job as an X-ray technician in a hospital in Jamaica. He wants you to come with.

If you stay in America and counsel cancer survivors, go to section #82 (page 171).
If you go to Jamaica with Ray, go to section #83 (page 173).

44

From section 22 . . .

You stay at the grocery store. Becoming a phone sex worker in the great Northwoods is just a little too freaky for you. You're comfortable at the store—you've made good friends and you finally get the right shoes (white orthopedics they sell at the nursing supply store), so your back doesn't ache the way it used to.

Flash forward twenty years later and you're still working at the grocery store, you're now married to Auggie (he proposed in the produce section on *Super Saver Saturday!*), and the two of you are living in his small log cabin on the north ridge. You cook steak dinners together and watch the weather roll across the lake from wide Adirondack chairs on the front porch. You love the big storms that come in low and dark across the water. From far away the rain looks like a corn field collapsing, thistles and wheat stalks falling.

You hardly ever go into the city anymore. It seems far away and noisy. Your days consist of opening the store, checking out the customers (all of whom you know by first name), closing up, going home, putting on some Billie Holiday or Etta James, whipping up a batch of mojitos or martinis and making dinner with your husband. The lake is your source of joy, a large ever-changing canvas of blue and pink, dashed with ducks or barges or white winged sailboats.

You begin a series of paintings based on the lake—abstract watercolors that look like the lake does when you squint your eyes and have a few margaritas. The paintings are smears of color and the absence of color—the broken geometry and sudden chaos of nature. These don't sell very well in the town craft store/coffee shop, but then one day a small man in an Orvis trench coat stops at the store and asks for directions. He buys a long john and a coffee with cream along with several of your paintings. He asks for your phone number—and when he finally gets ahold of you, he asks if he can take your paintings and put them in a show of "outsider art" in some gallery you never heard of in New York City. He also wants you to come out to New York when the show opens and meet the gallery owners.

Auggie says the guy sounds like a scam artist and a creep. "He'll probably take your work and just steal it," Auggie says. "He'll probably clonk you on the head with a ball-peen hammer and rape you right on the streets of New York with everybody walking by and nobody helping. That's the way they are out there—but you know, duchess, it's up to you."

If you say yes to the show, go to section #84 (page 176).
If you say no to the show, go to section #85 (page 177).

45

From section 22 . . .

You take the phone sex job and you name yourself Stormy Sioux. You bill yourself as a wild child *palomino-in-the-storm* type. Men call and want to play games. They like you to play oversexed cheerleader, lost porn star, horny housewife, wealthy widow, bisexual nymphomaniac, space station prostitute, temple priestess . . . and they pay you good money to indulge their every boring fantasy.

Forget Mr. Right, forget someone you are supposed to live with forever, you are capitalizing on "Mr. Right Now" at $3.95 an hour. The phone service gives you a Xeroxed sheet of suggested conversation topics.

IF YOU ARE OUT OF IDEAS, TRY THIS:

- Have sex where you shouldn't. *(Gas station bathroom, pontoon boat, photo booth, the mall . . .)*
- Have sex with his friends. *("So you hunt squirrels with Ed? Would Ed like to see my pussy too?")*
- Let him boss you. *("Are you my daddy? Daddy is bad!")*
- Boss him. *("I'll tell you when you can come, you S.O.B.!")*
- Be a virgin. *("Ow! Ow, ow, ow, ow! It's too big! You're hung like a draft horse!)*
- Sex with authority figure. *(Priest, nun, nursery school teacher)*
- Anal sex fantasy. *(You have to take a poop—but his big dick is in the way.)*
- Oral sex fantasy. *(How will I ever fit this into my mouth. Oh, you're so big.)*

- Pretend to be a lesbian. *(If you actually are one, that's fine.)*
- Pretend to be a celebrity. *(Like Demi Moore or Brad Pitt—but don't insult them if they like a celebrity you can't understand, like one of the Golden Girls or Mercedes Ruehl.)*

*DON'T FORGET TO SAY GOOD-BYE, THANK YOU, AND CALL AGAIN!
**RAPE CRISIS NUMBER ON BACK OF THIS PAGE.

You keep this sheet nearby when you take calls from midnight to three in the morning. While you moan and slurp into the phone you're also doing other things, like clipping your toenails, cleaning the refrigerator, eating garlic bread, or watching *Court TV*. The money is good, the clients not so bad, but it doesn't last long. On a routine call with the guy who likes to be tied up and force-fed red licorice whips, you hear a thump, a crash, an explosion, and then nothing. The line goes dead.

It turns out the guy was driving the family station wagon and had a heart attack just as he was rounding the cliffs on the North Shore. The family traces the guy's last call to Little Lili's—the family is devastated, the wife angry, the children crying, there's a news story and a town meeting and Lili's shuts down overnight.

You are—once again—broke.

Your parents call and they luckily know nothing of the "phone sex scandal." They *do* mention two jobs in the city, one bartending at the ice rink by your house, the other working at a special events company that organizes little kids' birthdays.

If you take the job at the ice rink, go to section #46 (page 89).
If you take the birthday job, go to section #47 (page 91).

46

From sections 23 and 45 . . .

You take the job at the ice rink, which consists of hauling ice to the bar (an irony not lost on you), carding surly teenagers, pouring drafts for the dads and popping open wine coolers for moms. You spend all day with a sweater on, even in the summer. The temperature of the ice skating rink is always sixty degrees. Rain, shine, sleet, or snow—sixty degrees. The fluorescent lights flicker, the blue ice glistens, your skin gets pale from being inside so much. The skaters chop up the ice by day, the Zamboni clears the ice by night. The big machine makes the surface shiny and wet, unblemished as it reflects the red exit lights. You can read it clear as day. *Exit. Exit. Exit.*

Time passes. You move out of your parents' house and into a small apartment a block away from the rink. Easy access. You start to work full-time and pick up shifts on weekends. The rink becomes a reliable timetable of hockey matches, lessons, tournaments, and leagues. You get to know the families. They talk to you between games. Some of them have a lot of money and some of them are poor, but they all have problems.

One family has a kid with cerebral palsy who sits strapped in his chair watching as his brother flies around the rink. Another family has pale autistic twin girls who drift in quiet circles and do not speak. Almost every family is broken somehow. People missing, divorced, or dead. Every family has a flaw, it's the one thing they all have in common. A father who drinks too much, a kid who curses at his mother, a teenage boy with faint bruising around the eye. Even the perfect families have dangling threads, moments when they cannot keep themselves stitched completely together.

Years pass. Your diet of nachos and beer has given you some padding around the middle and your face, which is rarely in the sun, has turned a spooky vellum white. But you've come to feel like part of the families around you. You go to birthday parties and barbecues and are considered by many as family. In addition, you and the handsome, dark-skinned Zamboni driver, Nick, have been doing some heavy flirting lately.

Then one afternoon as you're watching twelve-year-olds hammer each other during hockey practice, the phone rings. Your parents have been in a car crash. You hurry to St. Mark's hospital, where you learn your father is already dead and your mother has lost her eye and her left arm, and is now hovering between life and death. You're not religious, but you pray. You pray at her bedside, you pray in the hallway, you pray in the wood-paneled hospital chapel. You square a deal with God. If your mother lives, you will move back in with her, you will quit the ice rink, you will go back to school. You will make something of yourself. It's up to him. You wait.

God sucks at deals. Your mother dies. Her brain hemorrhages and they can't control the swelling. The funeral is in the dead of winter, on a day when the mercury sinks five below zero. Frigid. At the graveyard you stand with the others in a horseshoe around the coffin, backs to the wind. People hold their hands over their ears and faces, the eulogy lost in the howling wind. When the service is finished, everyone runs for their cars, including the priest, his frock coat swinging like a soundless black bell.

Your parents left you money. Over three hundred thousand dollars. Now you can either go back to work at the rink or you can move on.

If you invest the money and go back to work at the rink,
go to section #86 (page 179).
If you pack up your apartment and move on,
go to section #87 (page 181).

47

From sections 23 and 45 . . .

You take the job at the events place and it turns out you're actually working for a subsidiary operation called Birthday Bonanza! as a clown. Not a proverbial clown, an *actual* clown. You wear a polyester stain-proof, vomit-proof, pee-proof biohazard clown suit. (As a note of interest, the company went through five different fabrics for their clown suits, none of which met EPA standards for protecting the wearer from E. coli bacteria, salmonella, or HIV until they discovered EPI-SHIELD, an airtight material not unlike a plastic tablecloth that hospitals use to protect epidemiologists. This is what your clown suit is made of. You also don a red fright wig, a big red nose, and a pound of white zinc makeup that makes your skin break out in a hive of consistent acne.)

The job doesn't pay much and so you move into your parents' basement. The basement is cozy and familiar, you like it down there. The well-worn couch, the fake fireplace with the plastic rotating flames simulating warmth, the hum of the dryer and the stacks of memorabilia in cardboard boxes. There's even an ancient computer, one your dad doesn't use anymore, which allows you to surf the Web as you perform your nightly ritual of steaming your face and swabbing it down with apple cider vinegar.

You sign up with an online dating service and meet a guy it's safe to say you wouldn't have met otherwise. Mark is an artist. He's charming and debonair, and he rides a black-and-chrome Harley that he polishes with a diaper. The two of you date for six months. You close down your online profile and stop seeing other guys. You actually make a go of it—you actually think this might work—he's a total dream. He's kind, courteous, and charming.

Then one day—for no reason you're aware of—he stops calling. You call him—no answer. You call him—no answer. You know you're not supposed to call guys if they're not calling you, but this isn't some guy you went out with three times, you're in a committed relationship with this bastard. Where is he? Is he dead? In a hospital? You cruise past his house at night and see lights on. Further creeping and peeping reveal he is at home watching television. You call him from your cell phone right there in the box elders and you hear his phone ring not twenty feet from you and you see him look at it—and you see him not pick it up.

He's abandoned you without an explanation. A vanishing act. Anger does not begin to describe how you feel—it's more like a white lacy *rage*. Promises were made. Things were said. Things that ought to hold. You shouldn't be able to say "I'll love you forever" unless you damn well mean it. Suddenly this guy who said you were the most beautiful woman he'd ever laid eyes on and who said he'd love you forever will now not return your phone calls. What the fuck?

Fuck dignity, fuck poise—this is unacceptable. It's fucking *ridiculous*. Someone ought to teach this emotional zombie a lesson. So one night after a particularly humiliating day at work (when a myopic six-year-old actually *urinated* on your lap while his photo was being taken) and after drinking an entire bottle of cheap pinot grigio, you decide it's time for revenge. Big revenge.

You sneak up his driveway and spray-paint his entire bike with a can of hot-pink flocking. The tacky, cotton-candy stuff they use to make Christmas trees look like they have colored snow on the branches. When you're done his bike looks like a big, hot-pink fuzzy stuffed animal. He's going to shit. You can hardly keep from laughing the whole way home.

Someone else must have thought it was funny as hell too—because the next day a photograph of his pink bike is in the paper. *Harley and Easter Bunny have baby?* the caption reads. And then two days later there's a letter to the editor saying, "Was that photo of the pink fuzz bike a bad art experiment or excellent revenge?"

And that gets you thinking.

Revenge. Everybody has at one time wanted it, received it, or dreamed about it. Everyone you know has—if they're being honest. The problem is if you want revenge on someone, they usually know it, and so does everyone else, which makes you a prime suspect. But what if there was someone you could pay to go get revenge for you? A third party, someone totally unconnected? You're not talking about murder or even hurting anyone . . . just some good old-fashioned humiliation served up nice and cold. That could be your next career move. You could become a revenge artist. On the other hand, that could eventually land you in some serious trouble with the law . . . or the target of backlash.

If you become a revenge artist, go to section #88 (page 182).
If you do not become a revenge artist, go to section #89 (page 184).

48

From section 24 . . .

You agree to go out with Sandro again and on your second date he takes you to his house in Fiesole, a small town high up on the cliffs above Florence. He drives a different car this time, a black Mercedes SL, which must stand for *So Lovely*. The wind whips your hair as the sun shines down on your shoulders.

His large pink villa has a white marble fountain in the center court outside the frosted front doors. In the center of the fountain is a Roman god, *maybe Jupiter?* Doing something remotely vile to a swan. There are cypress trees and fig trees surrounding the property, and a sweeping view of the ancient city below—all the terra-cotta rooftops down there so small and distant, as inconsequential as the backdrop of a Renaissance painting.

Sandro shows you the inside of the house, which seems even bigger than the classical facade. It's open and airy, with white marble floors and frescoed ceilings. It's packed with baroque antiques. His wife's taste—surely. Sandro is too masculine for this level of frivolity—with the ceramic floral arrangements and gilded pink satin footstools. Then you hear birds singing. There are two yellow canaries in a black marble cage that chirp at each other as if they'd picked up an old argument that never gets quite settled. Beneath them dozes a large and mournful Weimaraner who snores on a large purple pillow. You can smell cypress in the air and you sigh at the thought of being mistress of this elegant house. Life would be good and luxurious and easy. You can tell by the dead echo of your footsteps—no one else is home.

Sandro takes you upstairs to a garish golden-pink bedroom, which has an enormous bed anchored against one wall like a yellow satin ship tossed up from the sea. This room too is packed with saccharine-sweet antiques. It looks like a bedroom where Versace and Liberace, God rest their souls, would sleep together.

Then you see her. The wife. She's hanging over the fireplace inside a heavy lidded frame. She has blue silver hair and a blue satin dress. Grim smile. There's a smug little dog on her lap. Sandro ignores the painting and so do you. Instead he shows you the balcony, which is unfortunately accessed through his wife's shoe closet. Two entire floor-to-ceiling walls of shoes. Out on the balcony the breeze is warm and the scent of juniper carries up from the garden. Sunlight milks the terra-cotta tiles under your feet. Sandro's arm is around your waist. "I could make your life very easy, *cara,*" he whispers. Easy. *Easy-Peasy-Japon-eezy.* You can't help but smile.

"I have an apartment in the city," he says. "It overlooks the Arno. You could live there." He nuzzles your neck the littlest bit. "Wouldn't you like to be my princess?" You can't help but flash through a litany of images—the one-egg omelet dinners, your thin soles, the beautiful stores you cannot go in, the beautiful clothes you cannot buy. This has not been *la dolce vita,* the sweet life—it's been more like *la stanca vita,* the tired life. The exhausted life—the I-can't-take-one-more-step-on-these-blistered-feet life.

And now he's offering you the answer to everything. He's offering to be your sugar daddy, your sponsor, your overseas benefactor. "What about your wife?" you burst out, stepping back. He laughs a little and takes a black cigarette from his suit pocket. "In Italy we have arrangements," he says. "There are many reasons why my wife and I cannot separate, but we have not shared the same bed in many years." He shrugs and waves the way Italians do when something cannot be completely explained. "It's just understood." *It's just understood* he wants you to be his mistress.

"Take the apartment," he says. "It's beautiful. I take care of everything. Don't worry. Your school too, wouldn't you like to stop work and just be a student? *(Jesus Christ, of course you fucking would.)* I take care of your tuition too," he says. "I take care of everything."

You take the apartment. After all, you deserve it, don't you? A woman who uses sex as a means to an end earns every penny she makes. Besides, sex with older men has its good points. You can always count on lots of foreplay. Older men are tender and they don't waste time asking, *Better like this or better like this?* They know how to read the map, they know the signs. Check for dampness, register moaning. On the negative side, their asses feel like liquid-filled sandwich Baggies and there is a strange softness to the penis, something like rebar wrapped in bread dough.

Filippo is furious when you move out—he tries to grab your arm as you leave, but the burly pug-nosed neighbor, Stephano, steps in and stops him. Filippo wants to know *where you are moving, who is helping you*, but you won't tell him anything. He follows you down the street shouting and shaking his fist—and there's a nasty scene between him and the landlord of your new building. *"Vie via scemo!"* the old man shouts at Filippo, who vows to kill whoever you're moving in with.

After the unpleasantness, you realize your new life suits you. It's *la dolce vita*, complete with an airy penthouse apartment, a house account at the five-star ristorante below, tons of jewelry (black pearl earrings, sapphire rings), and countless pairs of Ferragamo shoes. (Sandro likes you to wear stilettos in bed.) He's nothing but a gentleman. When you see him, which isn't all that often really, he's charming, attentive, and filled with compliments (*your skin is like poured cream, your eyes like distant fire . . .*).

There are trips to Paris and Vienna and Villa Belle Laure, his small French Colonial on the Almalfi Coast. He demands more of your time, and with all the traveling and partying, you eventually drop out of school. He takes you to the opera and the ballet, to elegant benefit dinners and small exclusive after-parties. Sure, a lot of times these places are as lively as a morgue, overrated and under-attended, and yes, rich people tend to be the most boring people on earth, but there's always champagne flowing and sometimes even Vin Mariani, a tasty cocaine-laced Bordeaux.

And then one day you have an argument. It's not even a big one, over nothing in particular, about you being late or him not understanding where to pick you up—something logistical—but after that it's like a light switched off. He cancels dinners and doesn't reschedule. No more invitations to the theater. He stops calling altogether. Your weekly check stops coming. Then, without a word of explanation, the landlord tacks a handwritten note on your door saying Mr. Candreva wants you *out*.

You're also flat broke and you have nowhere to live. You sit on the stoop of your building. What to do next? Then Signora Rossi, the sweet old lady on the first floor, sees you out on the stoop and ushers you inside. *"Sbagliando s'impara,"* she says and sighs. "We learn from our mistakes—and men are always a mistake."

After a long talk and a bottle of the stiff clear liquid, she calls some of her octogenarian friends and fishes out two job offers from them. One is to work at a tiny shoe store in a back alley on Via Ghibellina, and the other is to work in the kitchen of a small bakery by the Pitti Palace. Both sound like a far cry from your glittering previous life as a would-be American geisha, but everyone knows—geishas can't be choosers.

If you go to work at the shoe shop, go to section #196 (page 451).

If you go to work at the bakery, go to section #152 (page 340).

49

From section 24 . . .

You tell Sandro you can't go out with him again. *"Mi dispiace, ma no,"* you tell him. He gives you a parting kiss and bids you a bittersweet *Ciao, bella*.

You go home where you belong. With Filippo. How can you ever make a relationship work if you let yourself be seduced by pretty little things? You're glad you said no to Sandro and you can't wait to kiss Fili right on the lips—but when you get home, the apartment is quiet and dark. Your eyes adjust slowly and you see water spilled across the floor. There's an orange rind on the table. There is music, the smell of garlic. *He's been cooking?* Something is wrong.

There are sounds coming from the bedroom and then your eye catches a black high heel on the floor, like a black barracuda. Filippo appears in the doorway, naked, a sheet wrapped around his waist. (It is this small modesty that you will remember later. He used to lounge around the apartment nude, his testicles sagging on the furniture like overripe pink plums, but now he is suddenly shy.) *"Cosa fai?"* he shouts, "you said you'd be gone till later!" as if it is your fault for not sticking to your schedule. Then a woman's long, tan leg appears on the corner of the bed behind him. A tan leg with red toenail polish.

You turn and run. "Wait!" Filippo shouts, but you don't look back. You run out of the house, into the street, across the Piazza Duomo, muttering, crying, the fat moon overhead. You pass the Medici Palace and see flowers and rosaries woven in the chain-link fence where a pipe bomb had gone off a month before. A museum guard was killed, but several oil paintings were also lost and most of the notes and cards are addressed to them. You take one. Rip it right out of the metal link and shove it deep in your pocket, the hard edges rubbed down to soft rabbit ears. *Madonna mia*, it says. *Ti amo*. You deserve a love letter right now, even if it isn't addressed to you.

You walk back to school, use your key to let yourself into the building, and lie down on a couch in the lobby. You can see a piece of the moon through the window overhead, and you try to make yourself cry but the tears won't come. Only a twisting, creeping anger. Thorny. You sit up. Beside the front desk is a clear Plexiglas box they keep donations in. Not much. How much? You check the box and the lid pops off easily. There's more than you thought there'd be. Enough to go.

Enough to go. Go where? Somewhere warm and far away. Somewhere romantic. Sicily or Santorini. You've always wanted to go—and goddamnit, if life is going to suck, you might as well do what you want to. And there is the moment, the split second when you must make a decision that can forever alter your life. Do you go right or do you go left? Will both roads lead to the same destination? Most certainly not. And how will you choose? No one knows. Who can know the mathematical equation of choice, or the intricate configuration of the one who is choosing. Perhaps only God can know why a willow branch grows one way and not the other, why some fish dive deeper into the fathoms and others toward the light. You scoop up all that cash and run, breathless, for the train station.

If you go to Santorini, go to section #92 (page 193).
If you go to Sicily, go to section #93 (page 196).

50

From section 25 . . .

You tell Filippo *to go fry a fucking egg.* He tries to grab you—but you break away. "You don't belong in Italy!" he yells. "You don't understand the Italian men!" and he chases you halfway to the Arno. You lose him along the stone wall that banks the river, by the makeshift market where South African men sell designer purses. (Five dollars for Prada, six for Chanel, but don't bring them into the rain because the ink will run off and stain everything it touches.) The men don't look twice at you as you race past. They know about running.

Then you see Caribinari coming down the street—Italian police. The South African men throw themselves into a frenzied retreat, shoving purses into garbage bags and scrambling to get away. The police harass them constantly, take their merchandise and fine them for selling without a license. Sometimes they throw these men in jail, where they have to wait for days before a magistrate will see them.

A large man with a white knit skullcap bumps into you. "Take it," he says and thrusts a little metal box toward you. "I cannot go to prison again," he says, and before you know what's happening the police are on him like swarming beetles, dragging him away and down to the waiting squad car. In just a few moments the street is cleared of people. No South Africans, no police, no Filippo. Just you and a little metal box clutched in your hand.

You wait until you've walked across Ponte Vecchio and to a dark square before you open the box. Inside is a small Baggie of hash, three rolled joints, and about a hundred dollars. Not a lot of drugs or money, but certainly enough to put someone from South Africa away for a while. You see why he wanted to get rid of it.

It seems like a sign from above. You *don't* belong in Italy. Now someone from another country has handed you a ticket out of town. Out of the boot.

You know you should be miserable—but you're not. You feel this is a gift—a time to feel good about the next step, and you *do* feel good—especially after you smoke one of the joints and sell the rest of them at a nearby café.

Why the hell should *you* feel bad? You didn't do anything wrong. You intend to meet the universe head-on. Fuck Filippo. These boots were made for walking. You head for the train station. You're getting the hell out of Italy and you're going to try an entirely new country on for size. When you get there, the station is just closing and there are only two trains left. One is going to Berlin and the other to France—but you can't make out exactly where. All you know is you want the fuck out of Italy.

If you take the train to Berlin, go to section #136 (page 302).
If you take the train to France, go to section #135 (page 298).

5¹

From section 25 . . .

You decide to give Filippo a second chance. You believe in second chances—you believe people can change. Besides, where else can you go? When you go back to the apartment Filippo is so happy.

He tells you *he doesn't love her, he loves you* and *he didn't mean it, he was drunk, he was high, he doesn't know what he was thinking, he was stupid, he forgot how much he loves you, he could never live without you, he could never live with himself after this, he will just die if you don't forgive him.*

You're glad you came back too. You would miss him so much, you'd feel like a failure if you left—like you gave up before you should have. In the morning there's the smell of cappuccino and cut roses. Filippo has cooked you breakfast (eggs with rosemary, toast with honey), which you devour despite your wicked hangover and merciless headache. He takes you to bed and makes love to you three times before he lets you fall into a sound sleep.

The tan leg never comes around again and Filippo has stayed true to his word—never staying out late, even getting a job at the market at a vegetable stand. The two of you have fallen in love again but this time with enough money to eat and live, enough time together to make love and watch soccer matches.

Six months later and you're pregnant. (You suspected it. Tomatoes suddenly taste like tinfoil and you can't finish a glass of Chianti without falling asleep.) When the pregnancy test turns blue, you show it to him, and he drops on one knee and proposes.

If you marry Filippo, go to section #94 (page 197).
If you do not marry Filippo, go to section #95 (page 202).

52

From section 26 . . .

You dig. At least you try to, but you can't. You approach the spot where everyone else is scraping at the hard earth with shovels and spoons and your knees get weak and your stomach rolls. *"Please,"* you say to Aadi. *"Let me take her to the police. I won't say anything—I'll just say I found her—"* But your words are cut off as Aadi's fist lands in the soft spot of your stomach. You go down on your knees. You dig. There's only one shovel, so the rest of you use whatever you can. *Dishes, plates, pie tins, your hands.* You dig the hole right behind the bus, so if anyone comes from far down the road, you can roll the bus over the hole and hide it.

The whole time you dig you're thinking of Hélène/Ellène dead in the bus. You can't stop picturing her face. How did this happen? It's surreal. How can a trip to Europe end up with digging a roadside grave? It seems like a ridiculously bad movie, bad plot, bad characters, bad writing.

You keep digging. You alternate with your bare hands and a dirty coffee cup. You lie on your belly for a while until it's too deep and then you drop down in the hole and bend over. It takes most of the day to dig a hole deep enough. The entire time, nobody talks. No one says a thing. There is just you, your damp knees, and the sliding earth in front of you. It's already dusk when the hole is big enough, and Aadi dumps her in—legs and arms tangled. Her toes are painted a pale asphyxia blue.

There's a pause, and then you all simultaneously begin shoving, kicking, dumping dirt on top of her body to cover her. She disappears in pieces, first her face, then her hands and torso and legs, and then finally, because they are raised up against the walls of her grave, her feet. The last pale blue toenail is covered with the red sandy dirt.

Around two in the morning you wake up in the bus, sweating and startled.

You hear Aadi snoring, everyone else sunk inside uncomfortable dreams. The moon is throwing a strange light, a whitewash across the dirty, cluttered bus. Your head aches as if someone had tapped it with a hammer, and you get up and climb down outside. There, in the shadows, you see Dosh, wide awake and tying up his pack. "I'm leaving," he whispers, "he'll kill us next."

You run off with Dosh. It's your only hope. You grab your shit and hitch-hike with him to the station, where he buys a ticket to Germany and you buy a ticket to Rome. On the train you're exhausted. Nervous. Pink peony eyes. Itchy skin.

"Need a cigarette?" a man in blue coveralls asks you.

"Excuse me?"

"Anyone that stirred up needs a fucking cigarette." He smiles. "You've been pacing up and down for fucking an hour and you're giving me a goddamned fucking headache." His name is Eddie and he's American. He's got a big solid gut and a thick white beard—like a slightly pissed-off Santa Claus. He's from Alaska and he's an oil rig worker. "Came out to work on that fucked-up fucker they got outside Sicily."

"An oil rig?"

"A pipeline. One fucked-up pipeline. That motherfucker will never suck cock again." He makes you smile. Everything he says is pretty fucked up. Eddie, or *Big Eddie* as he calls himself, swears more than any person you've ever met in your life. He also knows more about philosophy, religion, and politics than any person you've ever met in your life. While you're on the train he quotes Aristotle, argues for sustainable agriculture subsidies, and claims he makes the best cranberry duck hash in the motherfucking free world.

He's on his way back to Anchorage, where he'll take another plane to Hali-but Cove, a tiny fishing village on an island off the western coast of Alaska. "I live in three big-ass ship containers welded together," he says. "Heats up like a pussy in winter though—even deep winter. I got three fucking wood-burning stoves and I burn cedar. Smells like a motherfucking hippie bus."

You like Eddie. You feel safe around him. His big, avuncular personality makes the insanity of the past few weeks seem distant and improbable. Like a bad dream you can still shake off. When he gets off the train in Rome he invites you to come see some engineering plant where they make combustion engines, and you gladly accept.

After two weeks of following him around, always looking over your shoulder, he pretty much gets the idea you'd like to hang around him, and asks if you want to come home with him to Alaska. *Okay, yes—he clearly wants to get into your pants.* Who cares? You say yes. If you go home, you trail this mess with you to your parents' door. Not good. What better place to hide out from the law than Halibut Cove?—wherever the fuck that is.

Eddie buys you a first-class ticket (Eddie always flies *motherfucking first class*) and the two of you begin the three-day journey home. By the time you reach the remote, tiny fishing village in Katchemak Bay just outside Homer, you are delirious with exhaustion. It's night and you've been awake for forty-eight hours. You can't tell anything about the village or Eddie's shipping crate house except that it smells like fish.

"Actually it's squid ink," he says. Turns out he's a master watercolorist, and he paints with the purple-black ink he removes from squid he catches in the bay.

In the morning you see his easel set up in front of the wide bay window cut right out of the side of the orange shipping crate. (He indeed lives in three shipping crates welded together. One orange, one blue, one yellow—all rusty at the joints.) The boxes are in the shape of a capital *L* and are insulated as well as lined with cedar paneling, making his home smell good and retain warmth. There is indeed a wood-burning stove in each container, keeping the "sleeping container" (his bedroom, a dressing room, and a large bathroom with whirlpool Jacuzzi, double shower head and steam room included), the "kitchen container" (with a large Viking stove, butcher block tables, fierce spice collection, and wide assortment of copper pans hanging overhead), and the "entertainment container" (with wide-screen TV, pool table, leather couch, and vibrating massage chair) all quite warm.

Halibut Cove isn't just a fishing village, it's an artists' community. Painters, sculptors, and metalworkers all live there, inspired by the scenery and the landscape. The nearest bar is across the bay in Homer, so people either migrate from home to home in the cove or they load up on flat-bottomed boats and skip across the bay, where they often become too drunk to come back.

You work in Homer, at a candle store on Main Street. Homer is sort of a tourist town—but there aren't quite enough bed-and-breakfasts and too many bar fights to qualify. One year blends into the next, and then one decade into the next. No authorities ever come looking for you. Life in Halibut Cove is as unique and strange and beautiful as any life you could imagine. Whales breach the water during mating season, school-bus-sized black-and-white fish burst out of nowhere, exciting and delighting everyone on the island. The children run free and wild all over the island, building forts, building rock walls, having campfires and cookouts and catching fish. (You'd like kids, but Eddie is "motherfucking impotent.")

Life goes on and on for you and Eddie. The winters, the summers, the spring and fall, each a fantastic display of God showing off. What's funny is that you don't know one single person who attends church in Homer or Halibut Cove—but everybody believes in God. It's hard not to when you're living in his opera house. You realize every day how lucky you are that you got onto that one train to Rome. What if you would have taken the train before it—or the train after? You never would have met Eddie. This beautiful fate is yours by the narrowest chance. It gives you chills just to think about.

You die in a charter plane . . . a friend had just restored a vintage seaplane with wicker seats and a wooden steering column and invited you and Eddie on its maiden voyage. You're sixty-eight at the time. Eddie is seventy-two. You're holding hands when the engines sputter and the fuel tanks ignite. The plane goes down, nose-first, into the icy waters of the frozen ocean. Your lungs fill with oxygen, everything seems blue and pressed together, blue water, blue sky, blue Hélène/Ellène. You'll all be together now. It'll be beautiful.

53

From section 26 . . .

You tell Aadi to *go fuck a kangaroo*, and you go back on the bus for your shit. Pulse racing, hands trembling, you try not to touch Hélène/Ellène as you collect your things. This is some fucked-up crazy shit. How did this happen? You move carefully, your breath short and jogging.

Your mind hurries to locate the few items of yours strewn around the bus. Your Nalgene in the sink, your toothbrush in the smeared cup, your red-and-black Swiss army watch . . . where is your watch? Screw the watch. Just go. But you can't help sneaking a quick look at her, a sweep of her chestnut hair blown across her face. The foam at the corners of her mouth has dried. Her face is purple, shifting with the shadows, almost animated, as if at any moment she'll spring up and vomit worms on you, take you by the throat and kiss you—maggoty saliva trailing down your throat.

You grab your backpack and heave it up (corpselike) and rush out the door—stumbling down the serrated metal steps and nearly crashing into Aadi, who grabs you by both shoulders. "You shouldn't run, *mate*," he says, smiling.

You feel something warm and spreading and you look down to see a garden spade handle sticking out of your stomach. Aadi is hanging on firmly to the handle and he twists it, turning the world sideways and down. You hit the ground with your eyes open. Now they have two holes to dig.

54

From section 27 . . .

You tell Alouette you'll go with her to India. You don't want to—but you will.
She's so grateful, she gives you a complete makeover using one of her Dusty
Springfield wigs and a pound of pancake makeup. You dance around the apart-
ment and break out a bottle of Pimm's. It's time to celebrate.

But by departure day her happiness has drained. Alouette is outside herself—someone else now altogether. In her stiff dark suit, nails and hair cut
short, makeup off, she is clearly *Rashid*, a conservative and soft-spoken Indian
man. Alouette is completely gone, packed away in medicine cabinets and hidden carefully in combed wigs. Now Rashid takes her place, a square-jawed
man in a tailored suit. He sits on his side of the taxi chain-smoking spiced
cigarettes. He does not speak on the way to the airport.

Eighteen hours later, you land in New Delhi, which is wet and hot and
like sitting inside someone's mouth. Sweat pools at your tailbone, under your
breasts, on your forehead. There is a river of smells—spices, sewers, burnt
honey, tin music, roasted smoke. You're delirious with fatigue, limp and carried along with the swell. Rashid has ordered a car (thank God) and you are
ushered into the cool confines of a backseat and driven far away to his parents'
house, a blurry belle époque building in Old Delhi.

Amil is waiting there at the house, quite efficient as she introduces everyone, prompts you, pushes you, leads the conversation along like a paper boat
caught in a river. Of course you can tell you fool no one. Her sister, Élan,
gives you ferocious looks while standing there in her elaborate hot-pink, gold-
trimmed sari. She has ropes of gold twisted around her neck, from her ears,
her nose. They all turn their noses over you, sniffing for the truth, shooting
looks at Rashid, whispering and shaking their heads. Alouette is not trapped
back in London after all. No. She is right here after all, sitting on this couch

eating a candied fig and playing to her disapproving audience all over again.

The funeral is far away on the banks of the Yamuna River, where a giant pile of expensive wood makes a funeral pyre and the shrouded body of Rashid's grandfather lies on top. He looks so small up there, like a child wrapped in white bedsheets—like lullabies should be sung. *Smoke, haze, cinder.* The fire is blazing, and Rashid's father pours cups of melted butter onto the flames below to make them burn hotter. "The body must be burned," Rashid tells you, "or the soul does not reach heaven. The ashes cool overnight and then they're poured into the river."

"That's beautiful," you say.

"No, it's not," he sneers. "Twenty thousand Hindus die every day. It takes six hundred and fifty pounds of wood to burn a body, which has ruined all the forests. The ashes clog the rivers; it's not only ashes, sometimes it's body parts. This fucking country. It's the twenty-first century and they still dump bodies in the fucking river."

Afterward the family gathers at the house, where there is a buffet table of strange dishes with strange names, *bhapa doi, jhunka, tambli,* and you eat carefully, delicately, because everyone is watching you. After all, if Alouette is a pariah, you are *worse.* You are a pariah's whore. The chattering swells around you and all you want to do is lie down for a nap. Jet lag, strange food, hateful families, it's exhausted you. Drained the marrow from your bones. You are sitting with Rashid on the couch when he turns to you and says, "You can stay and sleep here if you want to. I'm going out for a drive."

If you go with Rashid, go to section #98 (page 209).
If you go lie down, go to section #99 (page 211).

55

From section 27 . . .

You explain to Alouette that you can't go so far away, there are travel visas and shots, and plus, it just seems weird. (You hate to let the thought into your head, but the term "slave trade" keeps popping up like a bright red beach ball. If you go to India you'll probably never come back.) You get into a disagreement with her, then a quarrel erupts and then an all-out fight. Things are said, and Alouette tells you to *get out*. She starts knocking over the kitchen chairs and throwing teacups against the wall.

You hurry to cram all your belongings in your backpack, and you run out of the house. The door slams behind you, and there you are, out on the street. You know she'll never forgive you. Her temper is black and white. If you are out, you are out. It's how she survived all these years—by never looking back.

Once again you are on the road. You have money, you have time—you can go where you want. You're close to Ireland, which seems like a cool country, a symphony of green rock and gray sky and they speak English. Or you could always really change course and go to Greece. You've heard the sunsets on Santorini are the best in the world.

If you go to Ireland, go to section #100 (page 214).
If you go to Santorini, go to section #92 (page 193).

56

From section 29 . . .

You die. You go to heaven, which is a small sunny library filled with answers. Tall walls lined with leather editions wait for you, and a round-the-clock butler routinely brings you coffee and cream in small porcelain teacups. You spend the rest of eternity looking up the reasons why some children are born with cancer, where the Mayans went. It is all before you, in bound edition after bound edition. The answers.

57

From section 29 . . .

You wake up a vegetable. Tubes and wires enter and exit your body from every orifice. You cannot speak, breathe, urinate, defecate, or move your limbs without machines. Even though you cannot move, you are completely conscious. Your family gathers around you and weeps, and there is no way to communicate with them. Your hearing is gone. No more wind through the trees, no more symphonies.

You eat through a tube in your throat and your insides feel like an expanding and deflating cave, a hollow where birds could nest. You live this way for five years, thirty-six days, and twelve hours, until you die from a blood clot that rushes to your heart. You're glad. It was a stupid way to live.

Death turns out to be just like a long sleep, and when you wake you start over. Same exact life, same family, same body—only your memory is completely washed of your previous time through, and of all the decisions you made last time. Now the angels place bets on you, gamble on whether you'll do anything different this time around.

Odds are always that a person will repeat the same mistakes over and over again, life after life after life, because essentially humans are small sentimental creatures who hate change. Sometimes though—sometimes sweeping reforms come on ordinary days. A person takes a chance. Summons courage. They get frustrated and they say, "enough," and they march right down a road they've never been on before. The odds are against you—but it's possible. We'll see.

Go to section #1 (page 3).

58

From section 31 . . .

You decide to give Arthur a try. At noon the next day you drive your rusting car up into the Hollywood Hills to a big modern Greek-Neolithic-Roman house with white marble pillars and a Caribbean blue fountain out front. Trash Posh. *Is he a drug dealer? A porn king? A married millionaire looking for a quickie?* You ring the bell, shifting your feet and twisting your hands. (You left your purse in the car, but your cell phone is clamped tight in your hand. Not that you have anyone to call should this creep attack you. Your damn friends never called you back.) The door flies open and there stands Arthur Shulman with a wide smile and a strawberry smoothie in his hand.

"We're detoxing our assholes!" he says. "*All fruit* for three days."

"No more hot dogs?" you ask, looking around to see if there's anyone with a video camera or a needle of heroin around.

"Ah," he says. "That was reconnaissance. Liability of the job. If you want to find a certain kind of person, you have to go to a certain kind of place."

Three aged dachshunds group around his feet, which he gently shoos away. *"Lousie, Bessie, Zasu, please!"* You step inside. Music is playing and the patio doors are open, letting in a sweep of warm wind from the ocean. You forget your oath not to drink anything offered to you (could be spiked, drugged) and accept a glass of fresh-squeezed orange juice with a lemon slice floating in it. Outside, at the far end of the white marble pool, sits a group of people drinking juice and laughing. You are introduced and you sit down, the warm sun on your back, the cool stone under your feet. After about an hour Arthur gets up and leaves for a while. Then he comes back and tells you *you're fabulous.*

"The screen test is over!" he says. Apparently they have taped the entire conversation with hidden cameras and microphones. (Two lenses in the light sconces on the wall, a slender microphone discreetly placed in the daylilies on the table.) "We believe in stealth testing," Arthur explains. "People get so nervous when they know they're being filmed. We just eliminate the anxiety factor." Everyone at the table smiles and nods. "These are the producers of a new film called *Pink*," Arthur says, "and I'm a casting director . . . professional ingénue hunter." He cocks his head. "You in?"

Four days later your cell phone rings and it's Arthur telling you they've all confirmed the fact they love you, think you're brilliant, natural, fresh, and want to offer you the lead role in *Pink*. The story of a troubled girl who runs away from home and lives on the Santa Monica boardwalk, only to be discovered by a talent scout and made famous.

"Is there nudity?"

"Of course," Arthur shrieks. "*Lots.*"

Now, he didn't kill you—but that doesn't mean he won't. Or sell you into slavery, or make you the star in a snuff film. Hmmmmmmmmmmmmmm.

If you do the movie, go to section #101 (page 216).
If you decline the movie, go to section #102 (page 219).

59

From section 31 . . .

You say, *Sure, buddy, I'll be there, buddy,* and you eat your onionless hot dog. You throw his business card in the garbage can. *Huckster. Fibster. Loser.* You take the long way home, the hot dog sitting in your gut like a fist, your head beginning to ache and your feet hurting. If it weren't so goddamned *lonely*.

Back at the hotel you're bored. There's the sound of a loud vacuum in the hall, and when you open the door you see a young handsome janitor with a square jaw looking at you. Chewing on his gum. Snapping. Looking. You put a hand on your hip. "You're making a lot of noise," you say.

"So?"

"So I'm trying to sleep."

"Sorry, princess."

He unplugs the vacuum and drops the cord on the floor. He stands and walks toward you, slowly. You count his steps. *One. Two. Three. Four.* His face has an aquiline hardness about it—shiny, like after shaving he polished it quickly with gasoline. When he comes up to you, you can smell him. Cologne and sweat and something else. *Pheromones.* Your knees feel weak and you get wet. This makes you angry. (It always makes you angry when you want a man you don't want.)

"Do you always annoy people?" you ask him. "You're good at it."

You step backward into your room—and he follows. His bronze-colored name badge says "Mando." He backs you steadily toward the TV console, a faux wood veneer desk. Without talking you sit up on it and he hikes up your skirt. Works down your panties as you kick off your shoes. The television is on—it's the news. Somewhere in the Valley a little girl has been abducted. The second one this month, but Mando isn't paying attention. He holds your ankles and puts them up on either side of his face. You inspect your pedicure as he grunts. Not bad. Not bad at all.

Afterward there are bruises, a thick red swollen lip, and a painful area on your left side where you caught the hard edge of the table. He pulls his pants up, which somehow stayed around his ankles the whole time. It's dark outside and the weatherman is on now—the blue light filling the room like an aquarium. He's saying it's all sunshine from here on out. He's says it's going to be beautiful.

Six weeks later you're still in LA, working at a pizza place, and you start falling asleep at three p.m. You can't stand the smell of pepperoni. A twenty-eight-dollar test (who has twenty-eight dollars?) and you find out *you're pregnant*. (You thought the slight weight gain, the tender bulge beneath your belly button was from all the free calzones.) You haven't seen Mando again—you go to the hotel to try and find him but he quit weeks ago. You never did find your friends and you're *not* telling your parents. They'd murder you. (You can hear your father booming, "You trade eight minutes of heat for eighteen years of heartache? That sounds about right.")

The problem is you don't have enough money to *take care* of the pregnancy and you don't have health care. You get the number of a Catholic adoption agency from a poster on a city bus and meet with one of the counselors. An overweight woman with a puff of white cotton-candy hair around her red face and an actual wooden cross for a necklace tells you Catholic Charities can help. After reviewing your case she tells you they can help you with adoption, or they can help you financially support the baby.

If you keep the baby, go to section #103 (page 223).
If you give the baby up for adoption, go to section #104 (page 226).

From section 32 . . .

You decide to move into the VowGuardian house, and shortly after you do the house leaders ask to see all your bills and bank statements. The head counselor, Father White, says the VowGuardians will assume *all your debt*. School loans, credit cards—everything. Just like that. Gone. "We want you in a peaceful, prayerful state," he says. "We want to give you a fresh start."

So with some simple paperwork, the VowGuardians assume all your financial responsibilities. "You won't need to work, either," Father White assures you with a gentle pat on the hand. "We'll take care of you." And they do. They take care of your bills, your taxes, and your income. They provide your food, your clothing, your shelter. They schedule the events of the day, they help you with your personal direction and your self-esteem. You feel a new peacefulness and calm growing inside you.

House rules are strictly enforced. No visitors, no family, no television, no newspapers, no radio, no media of any kind. No letters to or from home. "You're tying to cleanse yourself of all your past-life toxins," Father White teaches you. "The mind must stay fresh. Outside influence is the number-one enemy. One cannot stay fresh and light if one is poisoned by the world."

The house is wonderful but mealtimes are unpredictable. Sometimes dinner is at five p.m., sometimes it's at midnight. Some days they wake you up at four a.m. for breakfast and other days you can't eat until noon. You never really know when you're going to eat, and when you do it's usually a very small portion of something vegetarian. Sometimes there's just bread. The good part is you're losing weight and looking as fit and trim as the others—the bad part is you're hungry all the time and get headaches.

Bedtimes are unpredictable too. You're not sure why, but the house schedule changes constantly. They want you up early one day and late the next.

Sometimes they wake you up at three in the morning so you can meditate, sometimes you can't go to bed until dawn. They tell you the goal is to gain control over your habits, to have power over your own circadian rhythms so you decide when to sleep, not your body. They say eventually you'll adjust to it, but for now you are groggy and fuzzy all the time. The world is blurry, like you have a small fever or a head cold, like you can't get anything quite straight.

There's also a lot of prayer and mediation. Like, a *lot* of prayer and meditation. More than you thought there'd be. You don't pray to a God or deity, it's more a prayer to yourself, to your inner nothingness, which must be filled. You pray in group circles, you pray in teams, but you never pray alone. They're afraid you might do it wrong and learn bad habits, so there's always a prayer partner with you.

Your partner for now is Summer, and the two of you pray together at least three times a day in "amulets," which are small porcelain-tiled rooms in the basement. The rooms have tubs in them and you often pray while taking a bath. They say this helps purify you while you pray. You don't totally understand it—but then again you're half asleep all the time. Father White tells you you're doing quite well and that you're almost ready for the next level of understanding.

The next level of understanding comes from Father White himself. He prays with you in an amulet and he tells you to take a bath. Then he tells you to take another. Then another. You can't seem to clean to his satisfaction, and he takes the rough sponge away from you and washes you himself, rubbing hard until your skin is bright red and raw. He instructs you on how to clean your face and feet. How to clean around the vagina, how extra care must be taken with the anus—"like this," he whispers with gritted teeth, "and like this."

Father White gives you a Gideon Bible and tells you to read verses while he checks to see if you are clean. He says this is so you can fortify your mind and build your tolerance to organized religions. You spread your legs and read the psalms. He bends you over while you read the book of Revelation and puts his hands on your thighs during the Gospel of Matthew. You feel his soft-hard helmet rubbing you.

"To become an apostle of the VowGuardians," Father White whispers, "you must receive," and with this he hikes your ass high in the air, pushes hard inside you, and comes. You're shocked at first, but then he's so happy for you. He gives you a VowGuardian ring and tells you you're his favorite student.

Your standing in the house has increased overnight. Your food portions are bigger, you move to a better room, and you're told you'll only pray with Father White from now on. On some level you know what's happening is weird—but you're too sleepy and hungry to really care. Besides, you're happy too. Happy you're doing something well. Happy Father White is happy. Who were you before you came here? Nobody. What would you become if you left? Well, you wouldn't be a top house woman anymore, that's for sure. Would you slide right back into gooey depression? End up fat and friendless like you were? Of course you would.

When your parents finally come looking for you with their accusations and negativity, accusing you of joining a cult and being brainwashed, you tell them they're wrong. They just don't understand. Your mother cries and your father storms out, and it's so unpleasant that you tell them to never come back. Father White is pleased. You return to your days filled with learning, your evenings filled with study and prayer.

Every Friday the house sells homemade candles at the farmers market. You hate Fridays—it's so noisy, and outside people are strange. One day you're off a ways from the group and a girl steps in front of you. "How ya doin'?" she asks.

"Fine, thanks," you say. "Excuse me."

She steps in front of you again. "In a hurry?" she asks. "Someone expecting you?"

"What?"

"I was like you," she says and bites a celery stalk. She looks you up and down—all judgey. She says she was once really into the Looktower, another "youth group," until she realized it was a *cult*. Then you see a man behind her in a blue Windbreaker. You don't like how he's looking at you.

"Your parents sent me," the girl whispers. "You've been conditioned to believe these VowGuardian people love you. They don't. Are they making you have sex yet?"

You step back. "No one makes me do anything."

"Sure they don't."

"I love my life," you blurt out.

"Lots of people think they love their life—when really, it's killing them." Then she tells you the man in the blue Windbreaker is an "exit strategy counselor." That they both work to rescue people from cults. That word again. Cult. Like cut and insult squashed together. It itches at your head.

She says they can help you escape right now if you want to go. Who are they? Did Father White send them as a test. "Just get in that white van," the girl says. "The one by the organic honey stand. We'll get you out of here as fast as we can."

"I'm not a prisoner," you say. "I don't need you to help me *escape*."

"Oh yeah?" She snaps her gum and sticks a hand on her hip. "Then prove it. Get in the van and we'll go visit your parents. Then we'll bring you right back to the VowGuardian house. Word of honor. Promise."

She rolls her eyes and you'd really like to punch her. Then she looks back at the man in the Windbreaker, who taps his watch and hooks his thumb over his shoulder. You look around warily. "How do I know you're not going to kidnap me or kill me?"

"You don't." The girl is losing her patience with you. "Look—if they have no problem with you leaving, then what's wrong with a little trip? Prove me wrong. Prove to me it isn't a cult."

If you get in the van, go to section #105 (page 229).
If you do not get in the van, go to section #106 (page 232).

61

From section 32 . . .

You tell them you're not ready to move in with a group of strangers. The head counselor, Father White, abruptly tells you to *get out*. You think he's joking until he repeats it. You smile at him, confused. He's kidding, right? But he hooks a thumb over his shoulder. "Just go," he says, "and don't come back." Why are they being this way? You thought they were your friends.

The tears don't come until that night, later on, when you're in bed. It all comes out. *The school, the video, Thaddeus, Summer, the VowGuardians, Guy Moffatt*. An ocean of bad choices on which you must sail your pathetic boat. You should have just said you'd move into the house. Now you're alone.

The only job you can find is at the mall as a part-time Easter Bunny. The woman who hires you in the mall HR department (a small windowless room in the basement) chews bright green spearmint gum and snaps it when she hands you once-glossy brochures espousing the merits of clean hygiene while wearing rented costumes. "And I won't double-check your time card," she says. "If you put your time card in wrong, that's your own apple orchard—got it?"

The bunny suit is made of pink plastic gorilla hair and it's hot. The only oxygen source comes from the mesh eyes. You break out into a sweat before you even leave the break room, and you've still got two escalators and a food court to get across. Once seated in your plastic Easter egg you're subjected to a litany of stupid questions, screaming tantrums, and pee. Every child, and even some grandmothers, plop their rear ends right down on your lap for a picture with you. It's nauseating. On your break you've got to cool down, so you take off your bunny head (your face bright red and sweating), and immediately a small child starts screaming. The HR director comes running, tells you that a child seeing a bunny with its head off traumatizes them for life. "For life"—she snaps her gum— "for permanent."

When she doesn't fire you, you figure they must be desperate to find mall Easter Bunnies. But how desperate are they? You show up the next day drunk and flash gang symbols in the kids' photographs. Apparently this is one step too far. Around lunchtime the HR director pulls you off the Easter egg. "Bunny has to hop away now!" she tells the children and then glares at you. "Hop away, bunny!" Around the corner, by the Orange Julius, she fires you.

Time passes. You find a job at a dental clinic, where you have an ongoing affair with the office X-ray technician, Ray. (He warns you that he's tired of the stupid *Ray/X-ray* jokes.) He's a scrawny redhead with a Piper Cub in his pants. You do it doggie style with him on the X-ray machine (complemented with hits of nitrous oxide), you do it missionary style on the receptionist's desk with pencils stuck to your ass, and you create the new and exciting "inverted wheelbarrow" position in the utility closet, a position that requires the stability of a drum of industrial cleaner and the leverage of a broom handle.

It's sex and just sex and nothing else. Simple and refreshing in its carnality. What's nice is that Ray never even thinks of asking you out on a date. He gives you a hit of crystal meth—a spiky shot of energy. You love the stuff, and as long as you're willing to go into the utility closet with him, he's got all the meth you could want. He shows you how he makes it—with stolen chemicals and muriatic acid in his bathroom. "Doesn't that stuff explode?" you ask. "Sometimes," he says and shrugs, "if you don't know what you're doing."

This little arrangement goes on and off for a year and then Ray falls in love with you. So you decide to fall in love with him. You're not really doing anything else. The newfound energy allows you to send your portfolio to your top ten choices for art school, and you're stunned when one accepts you and offers you a partial scholarship. Art school, though—you've had some bad luck with that in the past . . . and what about trying to make a living as an artist? Sketchy at best. That same week Ray announces he has landed his dream job as an X-ray technician in a hospital in Jamaica and he wants you to come with. Do you take the scholarship, or go to Jamaica?

If you take the scholarship, go to section #107 (page 234).
If you go to Jamaica with Ray, go to section #108 (page 236).

62

From section 33 . . .

You choose Luis. You book a ticket to San Diego, and when you arrive you spot him immediately. He's handsome just like his picture. (Which is a relief because you've heard all those stories about the fatties and the goiters and the birthmark people who waltz through the door announcing that *Yes, they are Dreamcatch777*, when clearly they are no dream catch whatsoever.) You're nervous and you feel hot. You wonder what he thinks about you.

He carries your bags. He has big hands, muscular, veined, and the more you look at him, the more beautiful he is. He takes you to a seaside bar, where you order fish tacos and beer. You're both nervous. You can't tell if he likes you. You order a beer and then another and another—it's just past two o'clock in the afternoon and suddenly you're drunk. You decide to go for a walk.

On the pier there are people fishing. One man has caught a baby shark, which lies gasping on the cement deck with its smooth white belly upside down. Your feel bad for it. Your instinct is to pick up the baby shark, hold it tight to your chest, and run.

Luis rents a room in a house thirty minutes away in Oceanside. The house is in a complex of matching rose-colored stucco homes, and his complex is in a hive of other complexes, with names like Oceanaire Estates and Eucalyptus Gables and Honeysuckle Vines.

He brings you upstairs in his house, where you gingerly put down your luggage on his bed. You play with the zippers on your suitcase and he grins at you. He touches your lower lip and the two of you go down on top of the suitcase together. Afterward you still wonder if he likes you.

This will become a question you ask yourself every five minutes or so for the rest of the weekend. Just looking at him makes your heart hurt, but he is distant and quiet. He smiles, but only occasionally. He makes love to you every

PRETTY LITTLE MISTAKES || 123

night, but he still seems distant. The more you pursue, the more he retreats, which makes him more tantalizing by the minute. You want to talk to him, ask him if he really does like you—but his frown, his roving eyes, you feel your heartbeat in your fingertips and you can't ask him anything.

After four nerve-wracking days, he drops you off at the airport. He's weird and fidgety and distant. Doesn't even come in to say good-bye. You cry in a handicapped stall in the women's bathroom. The clothes you brought were wrong, your hair was wrong, you seem ugly, swollen, fish-faced. Everything is wrong. While you are in the stall, wiping your face and trying to wad up your tears in toilet paper, you hear the stern voice of an older woman. "Ma'am?" comes the nasal, official voice. "You're in the handicapped stall, and someone's waiting."

"I'm in here!" you yell.

"I know that, ma'am. It's for handicapped people only."

"I know. Fuck you," you shout. "I'm handicapped too."

Fuck you. I'm handicapped too. It's the phrase that will go on the airport security report. California does not take kindly to those who shout at or about handicapped people—but how could you have known a little girl with legs like twisted pipe cleaners was waiting outside your stall? You pay a fine, miss your plane, and you don't get home until one a.m. that morning, beat up, mascara smeared, and exhausted.

There are three messages waiting for you when you get home. One from your mother, wondering where you are (no way were you going to tell her about your online dating episode), another from a local radio station looking for an intern, and finally there's one from Luis, asking you to call him.

He tells you he's sorry. *Your heart leaps.* He tells you he was nervous. He tells you he wasn't used to spending four days solid with another person—he's been alone too long. He wants another chance. "Come back, baby," he says. "I need you. I screwed up." Your heart is pounding, adrenaline is surging through you—you miss him. What you absolutely hoped was true *is* true—he *does* like you after all! *Giddy, giddy, giddy.* You picture the long tan arms, the deep liquid brown eyes. Still, maybe you've already given him enough of your time. Maybe you should just get to work and make some money. Your friend says she's leaving her job waitressing at a restaurant and you can take her place. "Good tips," she says. "You could just do it until you find something else you want to do."

If you return to Luis, go to section #109 (page 239).
If you take the job at the restaurant, go to section #128 (page 286).

63

From section 33 . . .

You choose Harrington. You arrive in London two days before expected and check into the posh Governor's House Hotel in Kensington, with its grand chandeliers, silver ice buckets, and on-site valet service. (Your credit card may never survive.) You sleep for a day and a half. Then you get up, shower, shave, and call Harrington.

"Surprise!" you say. "I'm here. Come see me."

His voice is a low growl. As if he just woke up. He sounds cranky and irritated. "This is how we're going to do it," he says. "I want you to pull the shades, turn off all the lights, tie a blindfold around your eyes, lay naked in your bed, and wait for me."

"Sorry?"

"You heard me!" he shouts. "I want you to wait for me. I'm going to come ravage you and I want you to wait there. Lay back on the bed. Lights out—complete pitch black and you wait for me. You wait as long as it takes for me to get there and sort you out."

If you do exactly as Harrington says, go to section #110 (page 241).
If you decline this particular mode of introduction,
go to section #111 (page 243).

64

From section 34 . . .

You take a gamble and go home with Rocky. He hails a cab and you both climb into the backseat—where he announces that he lives in *Brighton Beach*, forty minutes outside the city. Brighton Beach? Immediately you think of stalkers, stabbers, rapers, and mutilators. Serial killers. *Jack the Ripper, the Boston Strangler, the Cleveland Torso Killer.* There's a degree of marketing here—killers with catchy names. You wonder why there aren't more female serial killers—and if there were, what would their names be? *The Revenge Artist, the X-Chrome Killer, the Hollywood Castrator, Jane the Clipper, Betty the Bad Wife, Lizzie the Letch.* No, Lizzie's already spoken for.

> Lizzie Borden took an axe,
> gave her mother forty whacks,
> when she saw what she had done,
> she gave her father forty-one. . . .

You take a look at Rocky and realize yours will be a blockbuster death. An after-school special in the making. Your arms hacked to pieces, your shoes missing, and your head in a roasting pan. No, that's crazy. He's just a nice guy who lives outside the city. The cab pulls in front of his apartment building and he leads you upstairs. Okay—now you're thinking he's going to kill you again.

"You want a drink?" Rocky politely asks as he opens the door to his third-floor walk-up. His apartment is large, clean, and warm. It smells like coffee and lemons. The living room has a large white couch and a wood-paneled television in it. There's an enormous tomcat asleep on the windowsill, under ornate lace curtains that look like wedding gowns.

You wait for him to attack you but he doesn't. He takes off his shoes, washes his hands, makes a drink, gets a pack of playing cards, and asks if you want to play gin rummy. You play till four a.m. and fall asleep on the couch.

In the morning, Rocky hands you a cup of black coffee and tells you about himself. He grew up in Russia, in a village whose name you can't pronounce. His parents still live there and he came to America by way of cargo barge. He paid to hide in a container of new Hyundais and he says he discovered a little stray cat who had gotten locked in there with him.

"Stupid cat," he says. "He must have been on his number-nine life."

You wince. *Here's where Rocky tells you he had to eat the cat or kill the cat for survival.* "So what happened to the cat?" you ask, not wanting to hear the horrible answer.

Rocky points across the room to the orange cat snoring on the windowsill. "Oskar," Rocky says. "I fed him on the trip to keep him alive and he still eats like a pig. I gotta get a second job to feed that cat. No joke."

After that you stay at Rocky's house almost every night. It turns out he's a pretty good cook and he can be quite tender and sweet, although he doesn't like talking about his family. You never ask him for his real name—which you assume isn't Rocky. He never tells you. It's a mystery like all the other mysteries.

Life goes on and you continue dating Rocky. Things are pretty good—the sex is phenomenal—but Rocky is dirt broke all the time. You have to pay for everything, and it's really taking a toll on your wallet. Plus, he lives so far away you hardly have time to paint because you're on the damn train all the time. Still, every time you look at him he still makes your toes tingle. If only you could afford new shoes.

Then one day on campus you're introduced to a genteel man named Ben Du Pont (of the Du Pont Du Ponts—the notorious chemical barons who own half of New York). Ben is willowy tall, almost feminine with fine, articulate hands and a very large nose. He's wearing an expensive sport coat with torn blue jeans, which turns out to be his trademark *I'm-filthy-rich-but-I-don't-care-so-you-shouldn't-either* look. "Ben is one of our angel investors," someone says. "He's giving the school ten million dollars for an inner-city youth program."

You've never known anyone with ten million dollars, let alone ten million dollars *to give away*. "Hi," you say, and you know he notices your nipples (which just got hard) under your sweater. You tell him you're a painter, a teacher, new to the city. . . . He's says he's intrigued and wants to know more about your work (or maybe he wants to know more about the saucy lip you deliberately pout or the left hip you deliberately stick out). The two of you talk for a long time. He's funny and witty and sharp, nothing like you thought a millionaire would be.

"I wonder," he says, "if you'd ever go out with an old guy like me? Maybe tonight for dinner?" A millionaire is asking you out to dinner while Rocky is back home making dinner. Who would you rather have dinner with?

If you have dinner with Rocky, go to section #112 (page 246).
If you have dinner with Ben, go to section #113 (page 250).

65

From section 34 . . .

You tell Rocky thanks, but no thanks. *Stranger danger!* Tempting young boys ruin women. Don't you have enough trouble? You lick the salt on your lips as you walk home. You can taste him. You'll probably never see him again—he's too young anyway, his horizon too open. You need men with obstacles. With limits. You walk quickly across Christopher Street, collar up against the cold, and step carefully over a black puddle, streetlight reflected in water. A hand clamps down over your mouth and drags you into the alley.

The hand is heavy and hairy and smells like a urinal cake. It clocks you in the head with something heavy, something hard. (The coroner's report will indicate blunt trauma to the head was caused by a hammer; crime scene investigators will find the ball-peen hammer in a Dumpster.) The silliest thing is to be killed by a complete stranger. No introductions. No arguments. No complaints. This man who kills you is not a sexual predator. He's not escaped from prison. He's just a man with schizophrenia who has no health insurance. He has no medicine, he has no help, so he has a hammer.

The man stuns you like a side of beef. You don't feel pain. The initial sharp-sided sensation, boxy and clear, blends back into something warm and pooling. Comfortable. You are falling back into a warm lake. There you float, watching pictures in a deepening pink sky. Funny pictures. A paper on the Inuit you wrote in college. The dead pigeon you found when you were nine. Your brother making waffles. Your mother's hands smell like White Lilies. Then the pink sky sighs, sinks into red, and you relax back into the warm lake, where there were so many other things to see.

66

From section 35 . . .

You tell the administration everything you've learned about the dean in a long handwritten letter. You spell out why it's so hard to come forward but so necessary. As a front-runner of truth, every educational institution must hold itself to a higher standard, and so you tell them everything—about her drinking, her drugs, her embezzling. You hate to do it—but it must be done.

A week later you're fired. The supervisor of Human Resources calls you into her office. "This is never an easy part of the job," she says, "never." Your office computer is confiscated, your voice mail shut off, your passkey canceled. You get no explanation, no fond farewell, no severance package. There are no cakes, no cards, no teachers that say what a shame this is. You just slink home with your belongings in a cardboard box.

In your tiny apartment you crack open a bottle of wine (and then another and then another). Now you have nothing but time. Time to sit back and think. (When did the countertops in your apartment become so dirty? When did the drapes get so dusty?) The months drain out and the money runs out. You have to find work. Teaching is out of the question; no school near the Mason-Dixon Line will hire you.

Then the strangest phone call comes. A throaty female voice saying, "This is Eileen Ashton." Eileen is the posh ex-wife of a prominent orthopedic surgeon in town known for her extravagant parties and philanthropic gifts. She once threw a fund-raising "wake" for the Children's Cancer Fund (a connection no one really understood, but wasn't questioned), where her high-income guests wore head-to-toe black clothing and nibbled on lobster puffs under their black veils and top hats. She raised eight hundred thousand dollars for the tykes.

"I got your number from Dean Dorington," she says in her saccharine voice. "I was wondering if you could come over tonight—I heard you're good company." *Good company? What the hell? What is that supposed to mean?* (Although by the sound of her voice you get the distinct impression it's something bad.) "Uh—I was going grocery shopping," you say, which is true but sounds really stupid. She laughs a high and bubbling little-girl laugh. A ridiculous but common trait in a full-grown Southern woman. "Well, why on earth spend money when you can make it?" she asks. "Be a good girl and come on over here."

You go over to Eileen Ashton's house, which is a giant antebellum three-story Colonial with green shutters and large white wicker chairs on the porch. Eileen comes from old money. (*Tobacco money. Funded the Civil War money. Landed on Plymouth Rock money.*) Still, when she opens the door, she seems nervous and plays with the gold coin necklace around her throat. She smiles and has the tight, manicured veneer of a well-kept woman who drinks too much when no one else is around.

You tell her you're not sure why you're there and she laughs. *Come on in!* she says. Inside the marina-sized living room is an enormous couch, like a yacht made of white raw silk docked under a crystal chandelier. Eileen hands you a drink—a strong gin and tonic, which is already perspiring when you take a grateful gulp. She makes you another. This is the way in Savannah. *You ought to have a drink in your hand, or you ought to explain why you don't.*

There's a large green parrot perched on a brass ring giving you the evil eye. You almost think it's a clever piece of taxidermy until he lets out an ungodly *MaCAW!* And Eileen says, "Shush, Mr. Biggles!" then laughs. "Don't you mind Mr. Biggles. He's blind and he's stupid, but my husband loved him. Well, I should say soon-to-be-ex-husband, we're getting a divorce and Mr. Biggles here is the only thing he wanted—so he's the only thing I kept. Isn't that right, Mr. Biggles?" She makes kissing noises at the bird. "My husband fed him imported Brazil nuts but I give him cat food . . . more gin?"

You nod, but you know there might not be enough liquor in the world to get you through this. You can't think of anything else to say. "He's blind?"

"Glaucoma. Can't see a thing."

Bitch! the bird shrieks.

"That mouth!" Eileen declares. "*I swan.* My husband taught him some choice phrases." Classical music starts drifting in from somewhere and a silky black cat begins weaving in between your legs. Three drinks and a lot of light banter later and Eileen still hasn't mentioned *what she wants.* All this waiting is making you nervous. You look at the paintings and the antiques in the room. There's more money in this living room than you've made in your lifetime. Eileen is talking and tells you about her mother who lives downtown. *White trash!* the bird screams. *White trash!* And Eileen suddenly throws her entire glass of scotch at the bird, which shatters against the back wall, soaking the wallpaper. The green parrot goes crazy. *What a cunt!* he shrieks, *what a cunt!*

At this point Mr. Biggles is so excited he steps right off his perch and crashes down onto the floor. "Damn feather duster!" she yells. "Why doesn't he just once fly into the fan blade?" You stand up—presumably to help the bird, or maybe to pick up the pieces, but no, really you just want to move away, and Eileen catches you by the shoulder. "Just relax," she says and kisses you on the mouth.

Your head spins. You can hear the classical music, Bach or Mozart or something—her hand is traveling up your thigh and she puts her palm in between your legs. Then the phone rings, like a boxing-match bell, and the two of you break apart. Eileen goes for the phone, which has set the bird off into another round of obscenities as he waddles into the sunporch, where he begins eating from the cat's dish. After Eileen hangs up, she scoops up Mr. Biggles and he flaps his wings crazily. He shrills at her, *I'll smash your face, Eileen! I'll smash your face!* She carries him back to his perch.

"There's a job Dean Dorington wanted me to give you," she says. "I have this house—it was my husband's, but who cares about that. It's on an island called Sapelo. Ever been there? Right off the coast of Meridian. Seven miles out. It's a peach of a place, grand house, indoor swimming pool, but I need someone to stay there permanently. Well—for a while at least. Till the divorce is over. Someone to make sure he doesn't sneak out there and burn it down for the insurance money. It'd just be until I get it in the divorce. If that bastard gets it, I'll pay you to burn it down myself."

Finally you know what the fuck she wants. She wants you to babysit her vacation house. *Sure, fine,* you say. *Why not?* You don't have anything going on here—nowhere to go, no place to be—why not go live on an island. *Where did you say it was?* "Sapelo," she says, "strangest place there ever was."

So take her offer and go to the island, or decline her offer and go it alone? She might really want to help you—but she might want to just get you out there in a remote place where nobody asks questions so she can kill you.

If you go to Sapelo, go to section #114 (page 254).
If you don't go to Sapelo, go to section #115 (page 256).

67

From section 35 . . .

Why rock the boat in which you find yourself standing? *You're not saying anything to anybody*, but there are two fundamental problems with the fact you kissed the dean: (1) You had no idea you could ever kiss a woman. (Is there some lesbian hotline you should call? A sign-up sheet?); and (2) Will she freak out? Will this affect your job? Will she treat you any differently now? Will you treat her differently now? When you do something out of character, is it now in your character for good?

Over the long weekend you wait for the phone to ring, but it doesn't. You start to clean your house. *Wipe, scrub, wipe, wipe, sweep, vacuum, wash, wait.* You do five loads of laundry. You rewash things that are already clean. Then the phone rings. It's the office of Dean Dorington calling. The dean's secretary fires you. Your office computer is confiscated, your voice mail shut off, your passkey canceled. You get no explanation, no fond farewell, no severance package. There are no cakes, no cards, no teachers that say what a shame this is. You just slink home with the contents of your office in a cardboard box.

In your tiny apartment you crack open a bottle of wine and then another and then another until you run out, and you have to get more. The really very good news is that Savannah sells wine everywhere—even at grocery stores. Kroger is the only grocery store in all of downtown Savannah. It's open twenty-four hours a day and it's the only air-conditioned building for miles.

There's a chicken shack out front and a full liquor aisle inside. The cars stall and steam in the heat. As you walk through the front doors, a black man in a stained sports coat shouts over and over, "Whore! You loud-assed whore!" and he does not shut up until the grocery store security guards come. They think they're cops.

The lines at the checkout are endless, the whole of the un-air-conditioned ghetto comes for relief. Men with T-shirts tied to their heads shout at each other in the dairy section. Children tear around in broken shopping carts with frozen steaks pressed to their faces. The mothers, soaked in sweat and dissatisfaction, talk loudly to each other about their neighbors, their money, and their men. They absentmindedly smack the children that swarm at knee level, sending them hollering down fluorescent aisles.

You pick up a green plastic shopping basket and weave through the store. You find an acceptable pinot gris and head for the checkout line. There you notice the room seems quiet. The women have stopped talking, the cashiers are motionless, facing the front of the store. There is a baby crying, but nothing else. Then you see two men with ski hats on. Your first thought is, *Who would wear a ski hat in this weather?*, but then you see their guns. Black, dull, pointing toward the people in line. They are saying something to the cashier, shouting at her, and then a man wearing a blue shirt and a name badge rushes in. An explosion. Like firecrackers. *Pop pop pop!* The man in the blue shirt falls. Then you're turning against your will, like something pushed you hard. Your chest is warm. You seem to be going down on your knees and there is something warm spreading across your chest.

A woman kneels beside you, she's saying something—you never know what, but you think how strange it is for her to be beside you like this, and then you're suddenly not feeling well at all. She must be an angel. The warmth spreading across your chest has edges, as if something sharper lurked behind it. The sound seems to have been shut off in the room. You see the legs of the people standing beside you and the lovely pressure of the woman's hand on your chest.

Then darkness comes. A blank blackness with a dull red center. And the red becomes bigger and bigger until there isn't room for any other color. (Your eyes are filling with blood.) Then there is a tugging, something tugging you toward the center of the red, which seems illuminated now, like the glow from a fire. The warmth feels so good—because you suddenly seem so cold. It becomes clear to you that you have two choices: you can move toward the warm red light or you can stay cold on the floor of the grocery store.

If you follow the red light, go to section #186 (page 426).
If you stay, go to section #187 (page 427).

68

From section 36 . . .

You get in the car with your parents and go home. They're furious—they won't speak to you, and so you lock yourself in the bathroom and take a shower that lasts for three hours. (The meat has left some awful residual smell; you try soap, pumice, perfume—all you can smell is meat, meat, meat.)

The news reporters come around, camp out on the lawn, and break into the garage. Your father has had it. You've never seen him this mad, this red-faced. He yells at you, "You were on national television with your"—he points at your breasts— "with your thingies out!" The photograph taken of you by the CNN reporter (your confused face, your hard nipples barely digitized out, the brown-red meat, which had lost any semblance of the letter *H*, strung around your neck) is now being broadcast from Manhattan to Manhattan Beach. People who before had no access to the insignificant college football game now have total access.

At the front door, in front of the cameramen, you try to make your case. (Thousands of flashbulbs explode, making your eyes go blinding starshine white.) They are on you like vultures. They shout questions. *"Do you know how many kids were at that game? Do you know how many senior citizens and young children account for the football audience? Were you aware there was a Lewd and Lascivious Act in this county, which could put you away for three to five years?"* Then, thankfully, your father yanks you back indoors and slams the front door shut.

You can't go outside, you can't go back to school, you can't go anywhere. Everyone wants to photograph the "meat girl." You get fan mail. Letters and postcards from horny men, college students, upset women, interested solicitors, and violent weirdos. There's a Bible group that says they're loading up in the church vans right now to come and lay hands on you.

Your parents want to get you out of this mess. Out of the public's eye before your reputation is *totally* ruined. (They're overreacting, but you did get another death threat yesterday—maybe leaving for a little while is okay.) You move up north to a small town called Duluth, where you won't be recognized. Up there people don't much care for the media. What with high taxes, low employment, and winter beating the holy living crap out of them half the year, pretty much everything else is irrelevant. There you can blend in. There you can sink into reliable anonymity. It's the perfect place for someone who wants to be gone.

You work at a little diner called Betty's Pies, which has blue-checkered tablecloths and big cheerful women who serve some of the best pie in the world. It's always packed. Betty's faces immense Lake Superior on the North Shore. Lake Superior is the largest body of fresh water in the world. Think about it for a minute . . . the largest body of fresh water in *the world*. When you look out on the horizon of the lake you can't see land, only water, like the ocean. It's that big.

You live in an old trapper's cabin right on the lake—a drafty dusty cobwebby house originally built a good distance from the shoreline. Over time, though, the shoreline has crept closer and closer to the cabin—and now it's just a few feet from the front door. Someday your cabin will be under water. For now, it just has a front-row seat.

From your porch you watch the faraway ships as they make their way to Duluth's harbor. It's eerie. Lake Superior has drowned more ships than any other lake in the world. The water is treacherous, lovely, and black; it's brought down freight ships and luxury liners, tugboats and private yachts. The cargo from these vessels spills into the ink-black water and is never seen again. Model-T Fords, iron ore, yachts and their crew members all hover in the deep, nothing decaying or bloating or rising to the surface, because it's too cold for any bacteria to grow.

Then one day the nineteen-year-old neighbor boy comes over. His name is Peter and he's an Eagle Scout with the stomach muscles of Adonis. He's a very helpful young man, and at first you feel maternal toward him—until he single-handedly carries a two-hundred-pound diesel engine out of the backyard so you can plant a flower bed. He's irresistibly sweet and innocent—and it's obvious he has a pretty heavy crush on you.

At first he makes up excuses to hang around (*I thought I saw a wounded raccoon down here . . . need any help trapping it?*) and then you find yourself inventing reasons for him to stay. (*Could you help me oil the chain saw? Can you start the generator?*) He stays late almost every night for one reason or another and you talk about traveling, art, and philosophy. Peter deVries has unsuspected depth.

There comes the moment when he leans in, brushes the hair from your face—and actually kisses you. It's heaven, heaven, heaven. These things happen. You take his small gesture and run with it—hurry him over to the bed, where you've already imagined the two of you doing every vile thing you can think of.

Under the covers he does not disappoint—he's as big as a draft horse, his penis knocking against his legs like a beef tenderloin. You stay in bed for days on end. Your face permanently flushed, your thighs constantly tingling. He has stamina—but too much stamina is not a good thing. Sometimes you feel like he's trying to saw you in half with his penis. You go around once, and then the little bastard's immediately hard again, pawing your tits like a baby bobcat.

Suddenly living in a northern town doesn't seem so boring. Waitressing at Betty's becomes a happy hobby, an eight-hour respite from your sexy Northwoods boyfriend. He's only supposed to be a chew toy—but you're starting to have these tender feelings toward him. You're starting to picture him living with you, and even building a crib for your chubby Northwoods baby.

You fall utterly in love with him. So when the spring comes and he tells you that he's going to a community college in Minneapolis, it hits you hard. You don't want him to go. You burst into tears. (An all-too-sobering sight for the young Mr. Peter, who shrugs, rubs his nuts uncomfortably, and tells you to "take it easy.") The thought of him going to the city is ridiculous. They'd eat him alive. He belongs here on the iron range, with you. What would get him to stay? What would change his decision to go?

There's only one thing Northerners take more seriously than silence and that's family. If you were to lie, and tell apple-cheeked Peter that you were *pregnant*, he would stay, no question. He'd get a job at his father's lumberyard and move in with you for sure. He'd take responsibility and avoid lots of debt, years of frustration and expectation. (Face it—he'd only land right back here working for his father anyway, and married to some thick-ankled Lutheran girl who would never fuck him the way you could.)

If you tell Peter you're pregnant, go to section #116 (page 259).
If you don't tell Peter you're pregnant, go to section #117 (page 261).

69

From section 36 . . .

You tell your parents to go home without you and your father gets *really* mad. "You can't just run around doing whatever you like!" he shouts, "God sees everything!" Great. It's the perfect time for parental parochialism. You've had it with everyone and their convictions. "Fuck God!" you shout at him, "I'm not concerned with him—he doesn't seem too concerned with me."

Your father storms out, your mother weeping as she follows. What do you care what God thinks? Every mistake, miscalculation, misstep, misfortune, and missed opportunity has received swift punishment. There's no coordination. People say God's an artist—*Look at the Blue Ridge Mountains, lilac trees, monarch butterflies*. Whatever. God might be an artist but he's no fucking choreographer.

So you stay in jail. You're in a cell with a large black woman named Alexis Love who has violent verbal sex night and day with the woman in the cell next door. The state provides a lawyer who arranges a press conference in front of a sea of whirring cameras and bright lights. You tell the frowning reporters that you are a part of a community of activist artists, of students who exercise their First Amendment right to free speech. Your parents post bail, and at home you take a long hot shower.

The next day you're offered a solo show at a boutique gallery in Chelsea. You call the show *RUINED*, and it highlights your work about destruction and reconstruction. About tearing it all down and then building it all back up. You take Polaroids of all the HACKY work and blow it up poster-sized. Billboard-sized. You get chunks of stone and billboard from all the sites you altered and put them down on the gallery floor in inconvenient places, like right in front of the front door and by the exits and by the bathrooms, so that people have to deal with your work the way the public does. Inconveniently.

Smash hit. Rave reviews. You get two more shows, an interview in *ART-news* and a write-up in the *New York Times*. Blame the art world, blame the city's addictive consumption of bullshit, but you're catapulted into the strange jet-set of the HBYA, the Hopelessly Beautiful Young Artists, in New York. You move to Manhattan, go to all the right parties, go to all the right restaurants, and start dating another "talented" artist named Blackjax! who paints things exploding. It's bullshit—but he knows it, so it's funny.

You move in together. You live in a drafty Brooklyn warehouse with chicken wire over the windows and splintery hardwood floors. At first everything is adorably domestic, you grow tomato plants on the fire escape and fry basil omelets for breakfast. He smokes a corncob pipe while he criticizes the *Times* and you make love in the bathtub, which is usually coated with chocolate syrup, maple syrup, or honey. Blackjax! has this thing about things that are sticky.

But then things change. You both become competitive and irritated with each other. You start haggling about money, comparing bank account balances, and splitting absolutely everything fifty-fifty, which you never used to do. Your sex life dwindles away to nothing, especially when he starts snorting cocaine, which he says he *has* to do if he wants to finish his exploding *Eggs! Glorious Eggs!* collection for his upcoming opening in London. What an idiot.

He uses drugs a lot. The grainy white powder is dusted all over the studio—on top of the television, on the kitchen counters, on the lid of the toilet. It gets so you can't pee without getting cocaine on your ass. You wouldn't care—but this shit makes him as spastic as a shrieker monkey. He gets loud, argumentative, and he works on his art twenty-four hours a day without eating or sleeping. (The only way you keep up with him and the amount of bullshit art he's producing is to snort some yourself.)

You both snort or shoot coke every day—it makes everything high and sweet and lovely. Blackjax! gets another show in Tokyo and asks you to come with, which in retrospect was a big mistake. You already fought like Sid and Nancy at home and now you want to mix in international travel? Not good. You're high and combative on the plane, lost and arguing in the streets. He throws a V8 and tonic in your face at a Hentai street carnival. The two of you become notorious for being difficult high-maintenance screaming brats who fight constantly and ruin everything in your path.

The first time he hits you, it isn't even that big of a deal. He's mad, you tell him to *fuck off*, and he pops you in the eye with his fist. You pop him right back. Hard. He laughs and you laugh. It's funny. Maybe that's when you got a taste for it. The sound of your hand hitting someone. You like that sound. It's one of the only satisfying moments in your current life—the sound of beating the hell out of him.

Back in America the two of you fall back into your drugged-out messed-up routines. You're invited to some bullshit upscale party at the docks. (It's so very *now* to have upscale parties in shit-holes.) You put on an apple-green wig for the occasion and cover your face with purple eye shadow bruises. Looking ugly makes you feel prettier.

Between you and Blackjax! you snort almost an eight-ball of meth and get to the docks party pretty late. Everyone there is already smashed and dancing. With your bruises and green wig, nobody even recognizes you, which you like. That means you can dance and dance without anyone knowing or caring. In fact, you don't talk to a soul until you're just about to leave and some idiot starts hassling you by the Porta Pottis. He says you cut in front of him and he calls you *a poser, a loser, a has-been before you ever were.*

Maybe it's because you're high, or used to hitting men, or in need of serious psychological help, but this guy and his *cute little comments* open a reservoir of black anger in your soul. You let him have it. His stupid bald head and his glasses. He's getting things that have nothing to do with him. You start screaming at him and pushing him, and when he fights back you grab a piece of rebar lying by the unfinished concrete wall and you start tapping this guy's temple with it.

The next thing you know it's morning and you're asleep next to your boyfriend. What happened? You can't remember. You get up, chug some ice water, and turn on the television. It's already all over the news. "Man killed at drug rave, killer unknown. . . ." You apparently killed a guy—and he wasn't just a guy, he was an *art critic*. The news anchors joke that legally, killing an art critic might not be a crime, but you're not laughing.

It turns out you killed Jim Dawling Jr., one of the biggest and most feared art critics in New York. You immediately go into hiding, but it turns out to be unnecessary. No one is looking for you. Nobody remembers you even being at the party. (You had on the green wig and bruises.) Are they protecting you because you're some stupid artist? Has it come to that? You can *murder* people now?

Weeks go by, and the reports of the murdered art critic fade away. The problem is the guy had *so many enemies* that the police don't really even know where to start. They question everyone who they know was at the party that night—which is a difficult list to compile, as there is no formal guest list, no formal host. But all the stories conflict, everybody has something to hide, and no one mentions your name. You're getting away with murder.

You get depressed. When you've done something really awful, something you didn't think you were capable of, you start losing respect for yourself. *If I could do that, then I'm sure I could do this, or this, or this.* There's no limit to how much we can disappoint ourselves. You stop painting, stop sculpting. Blackjax! couldn't care less about your decline. He has no time for weakness or insecurity and he starts sleeping with a twenty-two-year-old gallery intern named Erin, who paints cats. You can't live with this guilt—it's eating you inside out. Should you confess to taking another human's life and face the consequences, or not confess and slink off into obscurity—hoping no one notices?

If you confess, go to section #118 (page 263).
If you don't confess, go to section #184 (page 422).

70

From section 37 . . .

You go to the police—that's what you're supposed to do, right? Isn't that what everyone says? Go to the police and they'll help you. You do and they're nice enough. They ask you what you remember—but remembering is what you *don't* want to do. It's all blurry. Fuzzy. You can make out general shapes in your memory, murky outlines in the dark, but your eyes won't adjust and the details won't materialize.

They call it *lacunar amnesia*—the inability to recall a specific, often traumatic event. It's just erased from your memory. Gone. You try to give them a physical description of the guy—but as they ask questions your memory shifts and gives way, like hot water on sugar. It just disappears. You remember useless details instead. The cement floor. The way the little metal chain clinked against the lightbulb in the center of the room. Seeing his shoe.

They don't catch the guy—he remains unidentified while they go ahead and plaster your face all over the evening news. *Poor girl, raped girl, unlucky girl!* Reporters call and bang on the door. Every time the doorbell rings you wince and break into a sweat. Strangers send flowers and your neighbors across the street send over a green bean casserole. *A green bean casserole.*

You find yourself dwelling in the cool porcelain fortress of the bathroom. Nice and simple. Clean. You don't like to leave the house. Your mother gets a trauma counselor to come over, a nice woman whose voice inexplicably turns to mushy static when she speaks. You can't hear her. She can't hear you.

Several months later the counselor convinces you to leave the house for an hour or two and go to a kickboxing class. Real break-an-ankle, bleed-into-your-gloves Tae Kwon Do shit. Not some goofy women's defense training, but some seriously damaging East Asian smack down. You agree to go. At first you're not much good, the sandbag feels like cement, your body feels like marshmallow.

Weeks pass. Months. A year, maybe two. You leave the house quite routinely now and go to the gym, or your kickboxing classes, or your judo tournament, or your kickboxing championship. You also lose weight—a lot of weight—and tighten up your body until you are coiled muscle. You're ready. *Ready for what?* You like to walk alone now. Almost daring someone to mess with you. You walk around the neighborhood where you were raped sometimes. You can say the word "raped" now and when you do, rather than feeling sick, you tighten and your fists harden, and you want to shred someone into pretty pink ribbons. You buy a gun. Why? Why not. You carry it with you everywhere.

It's six months later when you spot him. He's not there—and then he is. *Were you looking for him all this time? Maybe you were. Yes, you definitely were.* You recognize him immediately. Completely. Even though you couldn't remember a damn thing about his face for the cops, now his meat-colored eyes and faint creepy-guy mustache come rushing back with ice pick clarity.

He's carrying groceries (odd to think that he eats), and you realize he must live nearby. He heads east and you follow him, though it's hard to keep up, your legs straining, the air sharp and cold.

He cuts through the Candyman Carwash, the do-it-yourself car wash that has eight cinder-block stalls where people pull in to wash and wax. Eight bays. Eight stations. Eight execution chambers. No one is around. No people around, no cars, nothing. Just wind. You hurry to catch up to him and almost slam right into him as he stops to set down his groceries and light a cigarette inside one of the stalls.

"Sorry!" you nearly shout, panic filling your voice. He smiles—not recognizing you. "In out of the wind." He grins and takes a drag.

You feel the gun in your pocket, heavy and warm. You touch your mouth instinctively, where his mustache once tickled your lips as he jammed his tongue down your throat right before he ripped off your panties.

If you shoot your rapist, go to section #119 (page 267).
If you don't shoot your rapist, go to section #120 (page 268).

71

From section 37 . . .

It's only a big deal if you make it a big deal. Mind over matter. Besides, you can't turn your friends in, you're not a snitch. This will all wash off with soap and hot water. At home you *shower and shower* and then soak in a bath. You stay in there for a long time. Then you drain the suds and refill the tub again. And again. You can't seem to scrub hard enough—you scrub till you're red and raw.

Then comes the big sleep. Ten hours isn't enough, not twelve, not fourteen. You're an Olympian sleeper, you can sleep for up to twenty hours a day, only getting up to use the bathroom. While you sleep you gain weight—at least a pound a week. It's like a sleepy soft barrier between you and everything else. A blanket of protection. No one would choose you to rape now—right? You haven't told a soul. Nobody. Your parents can't understand why you suddenly sleep so much and you convince them you must have mono, *the kissing disease.* HAHAHAHAHAHAHAHAHAHAHAHAHA! When you finally get up, you are pale as a moth, brittle as a root. The sunshine tapping on your window is exhausting.

You eventually go outside, but only to places with lots of other people around. You like going to the Dairy Barn and the Safeway and Super Bob's Pawnshop. The pawnshop has glass counters filled with abandoned engagement rings and wedding bands, stolen power tools, saws, hammers, axes, shiny guns. There's one gun you've asked to hold twice, the pearl-handled Derringer .38 that sits like a jaybird in your hand.

It's six months later when you actually buy the gun (it's for protection, it's for safety), and four months after that when you spot him. Were you looking for him all this time? Maybe you were. Yes, you definitely were. You recognize him immediately. Completely. Even though you couldn't remember a damn thing about his face for the cops, now his meat-colored eyes and faint creepy-guy mustache come rushing back with ice pick clarity.

You see him up on Forty-second Street. He's carrying groceries (odd to think that he eats), and you realize he must live nearby. He heads east and you follow him, though it's hard to keep up, your legs straining, the air sharp and cold.

He cuts through the Candyman Carwash, the do-it-yourself car wash that has eight cinder-block stalls where people pull in to wash and wax. Eight bays. Eight stations. Eight execution chambers. No one is around. No people around, no cars, nothing. Just wind. You hurry to catch up to him and almost slam right into him as he stops and lights a cigarette inside one of the stalls.

"Sorry!" you nearly shout, panic filling your voice. He smiles—not recognizing you. "In out of the wind." He grins and takes a drag.

You feel the gun in your pocket, heavy and warm. You touch your mouth instinctively, where his mustache tickled your lips as he jammed his tongue down your throat right before he ripped off your panties.

If you shoot your rapist, go to section #119 (page 267).
If you don't shoot your rapist, go to section #120 (page 268).

72

From section 38 . . .

You take the fish head to Siggi, he'll know what to do. You find him alone in his museum, back by the arctic taxidermy. There are polar bears, eiderdown ducks, reindeer, and a puffin. All their fake eyes are dusty. When Siggi sees the fish he doesn't say anything at first, he just stares at it. You follow him to his office and he closes the door. He pulls down the greasy window shade, then readjusts his wire-rim glasses before he takes a book down from the shelf. It's a large oxblood leather book with a symbol stamped on the front.

"Read," he says and sets the book on his desk carefully.

He leaves the room and you take his chair. In the book, which takes you the rest of the afternoon to read, you learn about the burnings. Witchcraft was popular in the old days, as were potions and spells and evil charms. But in Iceland, unlike Salem or even Europe, it wasn't the women who were persecuted for practicing magic—it was the men. Mostly men burned alive at the stake, condemned by a very small, related group of people, one family who terrorized the entire continent.

The list of incantations was long and intricate. They all involved chanting and collecting hard-to-get items like the rib bone of a dead child, the scrotum and skin of a dead man, the hair of a virgin, a coin from a widow. There were strafes, or symbols, to be painted in blood, or in the ground, there were incantations to raise the dead, hex your enemies, make more money, control the weather, collect more milk.

One gruesome spell involved breaking off the rib of a dead child, wrapping it in sheep's skin, putting it between the breasts of an evil woman, who would then spit communion wine on it until a phallus-shaped two-headed monster child grew between her tits. It was called a *tilberi*, a little demon child that then hopped end to end all over the land, stealing milk from other people's cows until it was fat as a beach ball, swollen and pink. It would then return to its mother's house, where it would vomit up all the milk into a butter churn. Tilberi butter was a great fear in those times—to eat it was to become cursed.

Your heart nearly stops when a heavy hand drops on your shoulder. It's Siggi—four hours later. Time has collapsed and the windows are inked with night. "You see?" Siggi asks. "This fish is part of the old magic." He makes you a cup of tea and you talk. This will become the first of many long conversations.

You spend a lot of time reading the Icelandic Sagas. You love the warriors and the witches (you think you'd make a pretty good witch). The Sagas were written sometime between the twelfth and thirteenth centuries, and they tell the stories of specific people or of whole towns. *Laxdaela Saga*, *Egil's Saga*, *Eyrbyggja Saga*. Stories of bloody battles, devious knights, women warriors, supernatural events. The writing is fierce. Economical. Strong. The Sagas are considered historical fact—but no one knows who wrote them.

Meanwhile, back at the house, Halldóra starts complaining that your duties are suffering, that you spend too much time at the school and museum. *"Reading, reading, always reading!"* she complains. The accusations fly. "You're sleeping with Siggi, aren't you," she hisses, "you're studying witchcraft, everyone in the village thinks you're a witch!" She tells you that it's for your own good, your own safety that you stop. "People are talking," she says, and she tells you that either you stop going to the museum altogether or she's calling the school and kicking you out of her house.

If you agree to stop going to the museum, go to section #121 (page 269).
If you leave Halldóra's house, go to section #122 (page 272).

73

From section 38 . . .

You agree to throw the fish head away and you never mention it again. Life goes on as usual, and all things, even strange things, can become usual over time. It is no longer unusual to see icebergs the size of school buses drifting by in the jet blue fjord. It is no longer unusual to find the back door flung wide open and a trail of muddy footprints that lead to a neighbor's sheep eating a pie off the table. You find routine in this small village. You find rhythm. Home, school, beach. Repeat.

Then one damp afternoon a geneticist comes to the school, a rugged, square-jawed man from Reykjavik named Jóhann Jóhannsson. He has wheat-blond hair, cornflower-blue eyes, and a warm, firm handshake. He's come as a part of a nationwide survey; he collects DNA from Icelanders (a quick Q-tip swab on the inside of the cheek) for the national Icelandic gene database.

The database is controversial; some feel it will be exploited by pharmaceutical companies, so only ten students have permission from their parents for Jóhann to swab them. He explains to you that because Iceland has had so many catastrophes (black plague, war, earthquake, volcanic eruption) and so little immigration, the gene pool has narrowed and narrowed and narrowed—and now Iceland is essentially one giant family descended from only a handful of forefathers and foremothers.

Because of this it is possible to single out and identify specific genes that may cause anomalies such as cancer. For instance, when the single gene BRCA2 is missing—as it is in many Icelanders—the person is at a great risk for breast cancer. Scientists are slowly mapping out gene codes like these, and the more Icelanders they enter into the bank, the more complete the database becomes.

You follow him around asking questions and helping him locate students. By the end of the day the rain has increased, the wind blustering across the treeless black rock coast. It's over a two-hour drive back to Reykjavik, and you invite Jóhann to stay at Halldóra's farm and he accepts.

The three of you have noodles and soy sauce (one of your latest failed attempts at introducing Halldóra to ethnic food) and talk late into the night. There's no possibility for you and Jóhann to fool around —Halldóra wouldn't have it—so you each sleep in sad little separate beds. You dream about him all night, though . . . about him wearing a Conan the Barbarian cape and shoving you down on a pile of rune stones while simultaneously ruining your virtue.

"Watch out for him," Halldóra warns you in the morning. "He's no good. The geneticists are all evil." But then you see Jóhann at the breakfast table, trying to crack his boiled egg with a chopstick, and your heart melts a little. He smiles and asks if you'd like to go out sometime in the city. He is so, so handsome—but from your experience, the bad ones always are.

If you go out with Jóhann, go to section #123 (page 276).
If you don't go out with Jóhann, go to section #124 (page 278).

74

From section 39 . . .

You go to Tokyo, which is a crush of color, construction, skyscrapers, pink plastic neon, bicycles, vending machines, eye candy, and open-air markets. The turning wheels, deafening noise, swarming citizens, and neon everywhere. The smell of fish, diesel, spice, heat, tar. A bright lime-green cab drops you off in front of Toru's building—a large glass warehouse behind Yoyogi station.

You can see your reflection in the polished cement floors as you walk to number 1931, Toru's studio. You knock and wait for what seems like forever. You're just about to leave when you hear footsteps, a slow clomp and then scraping, like someone dragging something heavy. When Toru finally opens the door, he's out of breath and his sparrow hand is tucked to his waist. He looks at you blankly. He doesn't know who you are.

You remind him you went to school together . . . then a smile flickers across his face. "Sorry," he says, "you're out of context." He invites you into his large studio, which is like a tank or a vault, with narrow rectangular windows high up above, making the room seem like it is underwater—like you were walking on the bottom of a dark lake. He insists you stay with him while you're in Tokyo. "Hotels are too expensive," he says and waves his claw in disgust. "Stay here." You're so relieved. Hotels in Tokyo *are* expensive.

So you stay with him for two weeks—and then two weeks more. You keep waiting for the right moment to ask him about his white painting . . . but the moment is never quite right and then the image of it gets lost in your mind's eye under a slideshow of new frenetic Japanese images. Your flight home comes and goes. The two of you get up late, smoke spice cigarettes, and read the *New York Times*. You eat Japanese junk food. Shrimp-flavored potato chips and betel-nut candy. Since returning to Tokyo he's done quite well selling paintings and he says he needs a studio manager. He hires you to answer his phone and file his slides, but you think it's just a bullshit job he invents to give you some money.

He teaches you Japanese. Tacks up Hello Kitty Post-it notes all over the apartment with words on them. On the front door is *taku* (home), above your bed is *sakkaku* (dream), and on the refrigerator is *hottodoggu* (hot dog). He paints your portrait several times and asks you to pose nude . . . which you do. You feel utterly comfortable with him. Then one day over dinner and cold sake he comes around to your side of the table and kneels. "You know I'm in love with you, right?"

No—actually you didn't. The pieces start to fall into place. The place to stay, the endless conversations, the hot tea waiting for you every morning—he's *in love* with you.

"Kiss me," he says, "and if you can't kiss me you have to leave—I just can't take it anymore. It's torture." You look at his shriveled arm and his half-melted face. His lips blend right into his cheek on the one side—it's impossible to tell where they stop or start. *You're repulsed.* You do love him . . . in a certain way . . . and if you don't kiss him you'll have to go. If you do kiss him, what will he want next?

If you kiss Toru, go to section #137 (page 305).
If you do not kiss Toru, go to section #126 (page 283).

75

From section 39 . . .

You forget the white painting—it'll never be caught and you're not blowing your money on it. Instead, you take the twenty grand, quit your job at the gas station, and buy a business. You buy a hermit crab cart at the Mall of America—the biggest mall in the United States. Besides hundreds of bars, restaurants, and specialty stores (Paperweight Palace, Hooligan Joe's, The Bible Nook, Soap City!), the mall boasts an indoor amusement park complete with roller coaster and Paul Bunyan flume ride. (Big Paul Bunyan tries to cheerfully axe people as they sail between his legs screaming and plummet down three stories in a fake plastic log.) There's also an underwater shark park, a law office, and a wedding chapel. You can meet, get married, have your honeymoon, get divorced, and throw your ex in the shark tank all in one convenient air-conditioned place.

Twenty grand isn't much to start a business, that's why you could only afford the small four-wheeled "Gypsy wagon" loaded with live hermit crabs that have painted Day-Glo shells. You buy it from a guy who's retiring so he can go deal with his cancer or something. Your hermit crab cart is named the Hermit Haven and is stationed in a large vaulted mezzanine alongside dozens of other carts that sell things like organic lotion, kicky wigs, and space-age metal head-rub gizmos.

You become familiar with the workings of the mall, which is really like its own city. It has a water treatment plant, a jail, and a fleet of armed police officers. You'd think police with riot gear and loaded guns would be a bit much for a mall, but the truth is there aren't nearly enough police to keep things quiet. Local gangs love the mall because of its proximity to the airport and several major highways, as well as its warm climate even in the dead of winter. Mall planners, who wanted to create a peaceful environment for weary shoppers, actually created the perfect environment to sell drugs.

The cops carry radios, which crackle and snap with the hiss of the dispatcher's voice. You decode most of the radio lingo. A *9–22 on three-N* means some-one has vomited on the north side of the third floor. A *3–13 on the axe* is a missing child last seen near the Flaming Axe ride, a *5–42 walking* is a shoplifter on the move, and an *8–11* is *a jumper*. A jumper is a suicide—almost always off the top tier of the parking ramp, seven stories of concrete up in the air. Now you'd think a seven-story fall would kill you for sure, but not always. In fact, one man leapt off the top floor of the parking ramp only to paralyze himself from the neck down. "Boy howdy!" one cop said to him as he was getting loaded into the ambulance, "thought you were sorry before!"

Crime in general gets worse during the holidays. It's not unusual to see of-ficers tugging gangly teens toward the detention center after they threatened Santa Claus or peed in the fountain. It's on one mid-December day that a cop is transporting just such a teen when you hear a *Pop! Pop pop pop!*

You look around. People seem to be suddenly running, ducking, dashing into stores and down the long stone corridor. Your stomach hurts. The cop is falling and you look down to a spreading pool of blood blooming on your Hermit Haven apron. You pass out.

Go to section #134 (page 297).

76

From section 40 . . .

You've only lost everything when you've given up on yourself. *Fuck him.* You're getting a divorce—but you don't announce this immediately. *Not yet.* You need to organize. Strategize. Really screw him over. So when he leaves for a weeklong international DNA conference, you gather courage from a bottle of Silver Oak 1987 Cabernet Sauvignon and invite your neighbor, Megan Tewinkel, over for drinks.

She's a wisp of a woman, pale skin, pale eyes, pale hair. Barely there, but with fine blue eyes that flash when she laughs. You tell her everything. About the meth and the women and the lying. You tell her you need a divorce but you also need to not get ruined financially—so you ask her for a favor. You ask her if she'll open a checking account in her name where you can stockpile cash. It'll be totally unconnected to you. Totally untraceable. You're afraid she'll find this utterly ugly, but instead Megan puts her hand on your knee. "My cocker spaniel peed on your lawn once," she says, "and your husband kicked him. I saw him do it." She raises her glass. "Fuck him."

You begin to cancel credit cards, liquidate brokerage accounts, retirement funds, take a loan out against your 401(k), sell off properties, boats, and all the lovely little vintage cars he collects. (He polishes the 1972 Jaguar XKE V12 Coupe with a diaper.) You drain checking accounts, savings accounts, and stockpile all the cash in Megan's account. Limoges figurines, the Oriental carpet in the guest room, the snow blower, his skis, your engagement ring. Everything's got to go. It's a fire sale of divorce proportions. By the time your husband is due home, you have over three million dollars in the bank.

You're wearing your pink diamonds and Chanel suit when your husband pulls up in the driveway. You're not alone. There's you, your lawyer, and an off-duty police officer you rented for the occasion. Neighbors who you have not seen in months (or have never seen at all) suddenly find reasons to be out on their lawns. Your husband looks so confused it's almost pathetic. Your lawyer hands him the papers and the police officer escorts him off the property. He never steps foot in the house again. Megan's sitting on her porch and smiles as she raises her gin and tonic to you.

In court your husband's lawyers scream that there's *money missing, accounts have been drained, property has been sold without consent, and so on,* but there's no money to be found—so what evidence do they have? Your husband is furious. He's belligerent and rude to the judge. His meth habit comes to light, the fact that he's been using again. *A lot.* They get his dealer to testify in exchange for clemency on some other drug bust and your husband is now—*how do they say it in France?* He's fucked for free.

The money is yours to walk away with. Not only that, but you walk away with the house and a vicious alimony settlement. Your husband sits there in his stupid suit, the large desk in front of him, and (for the first time in his God-given life) he's speechless. You're a millionaire a few times over now and you can go anywhere you want. There's an ornithology center in Brazil, which is single-handedly returning several nearly extinct songbirds back to the jungle. Or, you can do what other millionaires do, you can move to a resort town like Palm Beach, take it easy, and soak up the sun.

If you go to Brazil, go to section #129 (page 288).
If you go to Palm Beach, go to section #130 (page 289).

77

From section 40 . . .

You're not divorcing you husband. How could you go? That would be like divorcing your bank account, your safety net, your entire future. He controls all the money anyway. He controls everything. He sets the schedules, the maids, gardeners, handymen—they all arrive and leave at his appointed times, leaving hardly anything for you to even do. So you get pregnant. What else is there?

You give birth to beautiful green-eyed twins, Molly and Michael, and for a while things get better. David spends more time at home—he lays off your imperfections and your shortcomings—but he won't touch you in the bedroom. "It's just so gross," he says. "I mean, I had to watch you give birth. A guy doesn't just get over that."

Then, a few years later, David loses his funding and his job. Money gets tight. He starts drinking again and he might be using meth too—you can't tell. His infidelities become obvious (cell phone bills, a perfume lingering in the house that belongs to no one). His meal requests become more and more elaborate. "I want the roast tenderloin pepper crusted," he'll say, "not pepper *sandblasted* like last time," or "I want *bluepoint* oysters. Not those terrible ones you got last week. Can't you smell when an oyster has turned, and do those kids have to eat in here?"

The salt on the table has to be *kosher rock*, not Morton's. The sugar has to be sugar in the raw, not refined. He likes only one porcelain pattern, and the crest has to be at the top of the plate, like at a French restaurant. Before he eats, he studies the tines of his fork to see if they are the slightest bit dirty or bent. (There was one bent one, a month earlier; the dishwasher had thrown it down into the spinning arm.) He examines every portion of his meal, inspects it, and smiles when he finds something wrong.

Your pulse quickens every day at around three in the afternoon, when meal preparation is in full swing. Everything seems louder, the television, the birds. You drop things, cut your hands on broken glass, shards of terra-cotta fish poachers, and white-wine glasses. The kitchen now seems like a brightly lit Italian-tiled cell.

You could leave, but there's a list as tall as you why you can't. Money, for one. You signed a prenup, and if you go there's no alimony and minimal child care. You have no income, no separate savings, no way to take care of the twins. They'd be devastated if you left. They love their father. You would have no place to live; you have no one who could help you. When you tell him you've been thinking about going, he says, "I know I've been difficult. I hate it when I'm like this. I want to go to counseling. I want us to get better."

If you leave your husband, go to section #131 (page 290).
If you stay with your husband, go to section #132 (page 293).

78

From section 41 . . .

You sign up to work overseas and you're sent to Africa. You're stationed in Chad's capital, a busy industrial town called N'Djamena. The city is plagued with a growing cholera epidemic. The bacterium *Vibrio cholerae* swims through the already polluted water systems and heat helps it grow. It's also the perfect environment for *Candida albicans*, *Neisseria elongata*, *Serratia marcescens*. So many diseases have lovely names.

N'Djamena has a port on the mud-brown Chari River and a marketplace for livestock. It's chaotic and melodious, smoke and music everywhere. You fall in love with the people and the colors and even the heat, which presses itself against you so closely there's never a moment you feel alone. Your hospital is a low stucco building with bars over the windows. Electricity is intermittent. The river of patients you treat have everything from sprained ankles to AIDS.

Sometimes children are dropped off in the night, left inside wicker baskets or plastic buckets on the doorstep of the clinic. They're not sick—just unwanted. You take these children home with you. They have nowhere else to go. A sprawling family grows inside your house, children in every corner, doorway, and drawer. They all take care of each other, and they are so well behaved. The girls cook, the boys collect firewood, it's like you have your own tribe of tough-footed angels.

It's a warm day in October when you are walking in the city past a popular café. You're carrying one of your youngest sons, Eze Anamelechi (who likes to be called by his entire name no matter what), when the café window explodes and there's a tidal wave of sharp glass coming at you full force. You are both killed by an exploding pipe bomb. Your last thought is this: You were noticing the heaviness of Eze, how healthy he's become over the months. You were hugging him close as you padded barefoot on the hot, packed earth. You were noticing how good the street smells. Like roasting coffee and oranges.

In heaven you see the city as it should be. N'Djamena with bright white-washed buildings and sweet, healthy children. No famine, no AIDS, no angry men, no weeping women, no starving animals, no polluted water, no war. Eze is there. It is as if God took a looking glass and inverted the world exactly to its opposite. You are told this is as it must be. The careful balance of the universe requires an exact counterweight for everything. What is bad on earth will be well in heaven. *An eye for an eye, it is said.* Let your kingdom come, and your will be done, in heaven as on earth. Just wait. It will be the perfect reverse.

79

From section 41 . . .

You sign up with the House of Habitat Development, which sends you to Thunderbolt, Georgia, a small town just outside Savannah, which has a lone cinder-block building for a clinic. There you treat the usual ailments. Ear infections, diarrhea, strep throat, flu, broken arms, fractured ankles, STDs. You treat the usual people. Drunks with split lips, homeless men with athlete's foot, bare-knuckle boxers from the nearby gym with their bleeding cauliflower ears.

You see people knocked over, knocked down, knocked sideways by some giant, invisible, deliberate smasher. It's the children of Thunderbolt who make you the unhappiest. They need more than medical care. They need fierce angels to swoop in and save them from the adults. They have mystery burns and bruises. They have parents with short tempers and long days. It's the usual story—social services can't intervene, the police couldn't give a rat's ass, and if you confront the mothers they'll stop bringing their children in altogether.

The days go by like this, the weeks, the months in this little miserable cinder-block clinic. It's cramped and hot and depressing. There's no joy in helping the people, there's no ray at the end of the tunnel, you're just sorting shit sandwiches every day, recording bad stories with hopeless plots and cliché endings. You know you took an oath—but you want to stop. You want to get a love life, a haircut—even going to the dry cleaners would be a serious step in the direction of salvaging what's left of yourself.

If you try to focus more on yourself, go to section #133 (page 296).
If you try to focus more on the clinic, go to section #91 (page 191).

8o

From section 42 . . .

You say *"I love you!"* and you've never seen someone get their shoes on so quickly. You know by his reaction that this will be the end. There will be no more phone calls from Dr. Sorensen—no sweet communiqués. You stare at your cell phone anyway, watch it for signs of life. The days drain out into weeks and eventually months. Nothing. You console yourself with cherry ice cream, salted bagels, and fried chicken, along with the occasional mint cookie milk shake.

You're mostly mad at Jane Austen. The backstabbing bitch never wrote the truth. She only told sweet saccharine lies—her endings always happy and with men who happened to be considerate billionaires. *The lies!* Why was this woman not drawn and quartered? Bucket after bucket of untrue bullshit and every woman you know ready to swallow. Things have got to change.

You quit meth cold turkey. No treatment, no twelve steps, no sponsors. You just lock yourself in your apartment and endure withdrawal, which is like having the pandemic avian flu. You are so mad at yourself for getting this addicted that you quit work. You can't bear to run into Andrew anyway—you're sure he's told your coworkers about your sordid squash-infused one-night stand.

Besides, it's not what you want to do—and if the world is going to suck *this bad*, why not follow your damn dreams right off a cliff? Why not? If people are going to be awful, and think nothing of you or your heart, and if every turn is just as frightening as the last, then why not go down in a blaze of your own self-invented glory?

You find an empty animal clinic for sale—it went out of business when the owner was discovered selling animal tranquilizers to local teens. (Affectionately known as Vitamin K on the trance floor.) Your lawyer and your accountant *and* your broker all think it is a piss-poor idea to buy this defunct, odd-smelling building. They advise you against it—so you buy it. *Over the cliff we go.*

You take out a small business loan and convert the clinic into a no-kill cat adoption agency. But this is no ordinary shelter, this is like the Hilton for cats. *Yes, cats.* Cashmere pillows and classical music in all the suites (*suites*, not kennels). Spring water, chicken liver, and goose gizzards are served in porcelain bowls.

Inner City Kitty opens with an exclusive feature on the nightly news; reporters ask why you have *a feline masseuse* and *an acupuncturist* on staff. Why the screening to adopt is so stringent. Your clinic is a hit. People love the idea of pampered pets, and they come from far and wide to try and adopt your creatures.

Inner City Kitty opens two more clinics and there's talk of launching a national chain. Mark, your operations manager, is a big tall brick warehouse of a man. Square jaw, red hands, sweet soul. He could tear a phone book in half, and he holds the newborn kittens as though they were made of spun sugar.

You rely on him to run all the clinics, manage workers, field problems, and maintain facilities. You meet twice a week at your home, where he gives you the rundown on what needs attention. You can't say exactly when, but somewhere during that time you fall in love with him. Of course you can't say anything because you don't think he feels that way about you, and you're unclear on the sexual harassment laws in your state.

This goes on for months. Late nights talking with Mark, early mornings tending to the animals with him. When you stand close to him, you can feel the electricity coming off him, but you never make a move. Neither does he. Finally the two of you are out of town at an animal rights conference and you both have a little too much to drink in the hotel bar. The kiss comes from nowhere, and goes on forever. Then he is whispering into your ear, fiercely, *I love you, I love you, I love you.*

You marry Mark and the two of you run Inner City Kitty for five decades, taking in the wounded, the hurt, the healing. Treating cats with leukemia, heart disease, wacked thyroids, ruined eyesight, amputated paws, torn ears. You are single-handedly responsible for saving countless cat souls, which you find out, after you die, do live on in heaven. You die of a mysterious virus, one they think you might have picked up from the animals, but doctors are unable to stop it. Mark stays with you till the end. He is the last thing you see in this world.

You continue working in the afterlife, and you're easy to find no matter where you are, as you are the one with all the cats following you, rubbing your legs, purring at your feet. You are the one saying over and over *I love you, I love you, I love you* and you are the one in heaven.

81

From section 42 . . .

You're not saying you love him—you might as well fart at the breakfast table. Besides, men love to be ignored. They respond to neglect. It's proven. They hunt and hunt and hunt, but if they catch their prey, all they can do is club it, scratch their balls, and start hunting something (someone) else. Such poetry.

From that moment forward you employ this tactic and it serves you well. You do not say you love him then—and you do not say it *ever*. It drives him wild—especially on tropical vacations and in ski lodges and during holidays when you get diamond jewelry—moments when you should love him, and should *say* you love him, but still you don't. You adore him, love him mad beyond measure—and as long as you never let him know it, he'll always love you back. This though does feed the white monster inside you—the meth demon. As much as you cannot say you love him is as much as you must snort up. What a hungry, hungry hippo you are.

Nobody knows you use. It's your very best kept secret. You keep the small Baggies of crystals in a Starbucks mint tin in your purse. When the time comes you go into the nearest bathroom and very quietly, diligently grind up the crystals on the back of the toilet. Then you snort them up with the casing of a ballpoint pen. Sexy.

Andrew proposes a year later at his parents' Fourth of July pool party. You're high as a kite at the time. You think about his proposal a minute and then say, "Sure. I guess." There's tentative applause around the pool. Still you do not say you love him. He finds this challenging. Odd. Like a puzzle he has to solve. Still—you will not say *I love you*, even when it burns on your tongue like a white-hot cinder. He will not say it either. It's no big thing really, it's obvious you love each other—your friends all think you do and the wedding costs over fifty thousand dollars, for God's sake.

You move to Connecticut, where you work for another (weary, exhausting) pharmaceutical company. The bribes, the lies, the incentives, it's all routine now. The meth use is high. Too high. You'll get into drug treatment as soon as you have the time. Your therapist says you've got to find more softness in your life, more sources of love, but you don't really have the time after you develop cervical cancer. The doctor says you've already had it *for years*.

You die slowly. You want to end it, end the pain and the sweating and the chemo, the poison that masquerades as medicine. You're like a cartoon character that can't figure out how to die. Jump off a bridge? Drop a toaster in the bathtub? You can't do it. Always something goes wrong. There's always some goddamned person with an aphorism to fly in your face just as you're about to make an exit.

Your husband has never seen you like this—he is frightened by the strength of your hands, the wild look in your eyes. He hides behind the doctors and the machines, hoping you'll pull yourself together. Of course there is no pulling yourself together. There is no treatment for men and women who walk on eggshells, who salt their wounds and then stare out the window. The worst part is that you not only have fucking cancer you are having fucking withdrawals from not having any meth. They tend not to hand that out in hospitals. You can get any other damn drug, but not that.

It was your choice to never say *I love you*, and now you scream it from your hospital bed to anyone who'll listen. The nurses, the janitors, the doctors. Like cash you have to spend in the country you're leaving. Your husband is horrified by your weakness and instability. He drifts back, recedes into the wallpaper and the drapes, where he hangs silently, watching. You're a horror to see. There's one angel. A hospice worker named Lori. A small, high-boned girl who comes every day. She has wispy brown hair clipped in a knot at the nape of her neck and she hums as she knits. Tight knot, purl. Tight knot, purl. She changes your bedpans, checks your morphine. She hums, pats your hand, listens, and knits. She doesn't seem disturbed by your threats of desperate love, doesn't leave when you cry.

Without her you'd be alone. A perfect stranger who loves you. Why not? You never know who's going to be your angel. Then there's black construction paper. Stinging. Stars. Wings brushing your face and you must move on to the next courtroom, where they measure the size of your heart, the capacity of your mercy, and whether you can be recognized by the most sterling angel of them all, a silver-winged horror named Grace. She takes you in her arms and sighs.

82

From section 43 . . .

You decide to counsel cancer survivors. Why not? You tell Ray it's the responsible thing for you to do. He's crushed, but responsibility isn't as bad as people think. Life presents its greatest joys disguised as obligation.

What you have to do, what you're forced to do becomes the lesson. You can take the lesson, or you can leave it. And if you leave it—that's fine, because it's coming back. Sure as sunrise, right as rain, our lessons and our teachers will never give up on us, not even if we walk away from them. *Especially* when we walk away from them. They will pursue us, hunt us, tirelessly, with the full force of the universe behind them.

You're glad you didn't go with Ray; he's a sweet kid but you weren't in love with him and Jamaica seems, well, it seems *big*. A really big life that you're not quite up for yet. You're happy here—you think. You may not always know what makes you happy, but your body will never lie to you. After cancer patients are diagnosed, they usually go back and do an inventory of the time before they were diagnosed. They look for clues. Sensations overlooked, feelings pushed away. "There were no signs!" is the first response. And then a sigh. "Maybe there were a few." *Were there headaches, fatigue, loss of appetite, sharp, unexplainable pains?* Of course there were. *Were you unhappy with any part of your life? Were you stressed or anxious? Were you angry?* Well, don't be stupid.

When you have cancer, there are two wars. The first is not dying, and the second is living. You teach your clients to accept the disease, but to fight the ravages. Fight what it wants to steal—your joy, your sense of humor, your family. Use anything you can to battle it. Zen meditation, church, technology, and pharmacology. You counsel survivors in energy conservation, nutrition, and meditation. Many survive. Many don't. You have one patient, Amaria, a twenty-six-year-old girl who rode horses before she got sick. A champion equestrian. She lived and worked on a horse farm outside the city.

"My horse knew I was sick before I did," she says. "She didn't want me to ride her—she kept herding me back to the barn." Amaria's prognosis is bad. The interferon and chemotherapy don't take; she slips in and out of remission. Her toxicity levels are high; her doctors don't know how many more rounds of chemo she can take. She's depressed, she's anxious, she stops eating. "I used to be afraid I would die on my horse," she says. "Now I'm afraid I won't."

She tries another round of interferon, and loses another ten pounds. She looks like a death camp survivor, a prisoner of her own war. Then she comes in one day, sits in your chair, and smiles. She looks good. Really good. "I'm off the meds," she says. "I stopped treatment. No more chemo, no more interferon, no needles, no bone marrow samples, nothing. I've never felt better. I actually ate scrambled eggs this morning. A whole plate." It's common for a rush of vitality to come when medication is stopped. The problem then becomes the cancer is still in the system, working night and day to gain its foothold—which it will.

When a patient chooses to go off treatment, it is hospital policy not to intervene. Legally, they must describe in detail what will happen, the slow shutdown of bodily functions, the exhaustion that's coming, the cramps and the pain. It will be long, and drawn out. They can offer pain medication, which helps a little, drugs like morphine and Dilaudid, but they also act like hammers, and between missing your life because of pain or missing your life because you're blitzed, it's hard to know which is worse.

"One more ride," she begs. "I need to ride my horse one last time before I can't ride anymore. They say I can't leave the hospital, I'm not strong enough." Her eyes are bright now, her grip on your wrist surprising. "I want you to drive me to Valhalla—where my horse is. Just for one last ride."

In your mind's eye you can see her—hair like a short black flag in the wind, sailing across the fields on her horse. You look at her charts. It's essentially her final wish. If you take her, though, and you get caught, it's grounds for termination.

If you take Amaria to Valhalla, go to section #138 (page 306).
If you don't take Amaria to Valhalla, go to section #139 (page 310).

83

From section 43 . . .

You pack up all your earthly belongings and move to a little cottage over-looking a steep valley in Port Antonio, Jamaica. The house is small but has a wraparound porch and a crow's nest from which you can see beyond the green valley right into the eye of the peacock-blue ocean. You can also see the city, which thrums with life night and day, especially inside Musgrove Market, a maze of vendors selling Maylay apples, avocado pears, pawpaw custard, star apple, sweet sop, sour sop, shrimp curries, callaloo, baby diapers, Bibles, im-ported sneakers, live chickens, French lipstick, pirated movies, used books, fresh bamboo, guava juice, and Appleton Rum.

The city doesn't get many tourists. It's a hard city to get to—a day's drive on nearly decimated roads from Kingston or Montego Bay, and the harbor of Port Antonio is too shallow for the big cruise ships to dock. Port Antonions don't see a lot of people from outside the country, and they don't particularly want to. They're friendly enough with you (the woman who sells jackfruit at the end of your road calls you *Angel Love*), but they're wary.

Outsiders interrupt the rhythm of Jamaica, the flow of even the smallest transaction. Besides not knowing local customs (funeral wakes last for nine days and nine nights and are usually filled with palm wine and playing domi-nos) or local superstitions (never throw a bucket of water out at night or a *duppy*, an evil ghost, will walk over and hurt you), it's hard for you to follow Jamaican patois and you often can't understand anything being said.

Ray loves his new job at the Port Antonio hospital. He's not making that much money—not compared to what he'd make in the States—but as he points out, how many hospitals have a snorkeling club and fresh mango sold in the lobby? Ray is at the beach nearly every day after work; he's devel-oped a cadre of local friends, guys who play dice and give Ray constant crap about his paper-white skin. Ray loves it. You just wish he'd lay off the ganja a little.

About six months later, you find out you're pregnant. You're happy about it—you think. Ray proposes to you and you have a ceremony on the beach at sunset, with all your family and friends in attendance. Life is just heaven for a while. You get the nursery ready for the baby, you read prenatal health care books. (You pledge to never use crystal meth again. It would eat your baby's *brain*.) You assure your mother over and over and over on the phone that yes, you're safe and no, you're not moving home.

You have this glorious vision for the baby, she'll get to grow up in this beautiful house, on the gorgeous mountaintop. She can play in the crystal-clear stream, swim in the ice-blue ocean, eat fresh mango and papaya every day of the year. She'll have the most amazing childhood ever. Then baby Alison is born, a sweet blond baby with chubby cheeks and teeny tiny fingers and toes. She's so precious that even though you're exhausted, endorphins flood your body when you look at her and you're on a permanent rosy high.

Then the bad luck wakes up. Your parents die suddenly in an automobile crash back home and you have to fly home for the funeral. Alison cries all through the services. It's heartbreaking—she'll never know her grandparents.

Then Ray loses his job. He fails a random drug screening test. It's the marijuana he smokes at the beach. *How could you be so stupid?* you scream at him. You think things are as bad as they can be—but then hurricane Betty hits, and high winds thunder across the valley, howling onto your mountaintop, leaving your house in tattered shreds.

The old lady at the jackfruit stand says, *"God neva pramise wi a bed a roses, im nevea tell any baddy dat life ould bi smoode."* It's an old Jamaican proverb. God never promised you a bed of roses, he never said life would be smooth.

Insurance only covers half the costs of rebuilding your house, but still you cling like grim death to your vision. Alison deserves this mountaintop cottage—not a rented apartment in the city. You have to use all your savings, your 401(k) plans, your portfolio, everything you have is used to cover costs. Ray can't get a job anywhere except at an STD clinic, which pays about as much as if he were working at Arby's. Suddenly the dusty people who sleep in cardboard houses on the side of the road don't seem so different from you.

You go back to work as soon as you can, assisting a pharmacist in the city. There you fill prescriptions and count out pills. *Drugs drugs drugs.* They're on your mind a lot lately. You've been getting cravings again. You're always so tired and Alison is learning to walk, shuttling and lurching herself across the house night and day, and you're thinking a bump of meth would let you keep up with her. Times are getting tougher. You and Ray just can't make the bills and Alison has developed an asthmatic condition that requires an expensive medication. You can't even afford to move back to America—and even if you could, you'd be in the same exact position, minus the airfare home, which you can't afford anyway.

That's when you realize you've never seen meth being sold on the island. Jamaica is more of a marijuana and mushroom place, not a cocaine and crystal meth place. *But it could be.* If you produced it on a small scale, for just a little while, you could make enough money to get back home. Maybe even invest a little, get a leg up—for Alison's sake.

If you make the drugs, go to section #160 (page 360).
If you don't make the drugs, go to section #161 (page 362).

84

From section 44 . . .

You say yes to the show and make plans to go to New York. Everybody in town gets a little hysterical about it—they publish an article about you in the *Duluth Gazette* and Diane Lindstrom throws you a going-away party with a bluegrass band. People tell you you're going to be a big city slicker now—and warn you not to come back with any fancy new friends. Nobody in Duluth wants them.

Departure day is clear—not a cloud to be seen. The little single-engine prop plane you take to Minneapolis shakes like a Mixomatic when it hits ten thousand feet. You're glad for your sweater and your shawl because *it's cold*. At fifteen thousand feet the prop starts to sputter in midair, dives sharply and goes nose-down into a barrel roll, a large pillar of black smoke smudging the blue sky. The plane crashes pilot-first into a cornfield. A goose flew into the engine. Typical.

In heaven you meet God, who turns out to be a very irritated and overweight black woman who lives in a big sugar palace up on a hill with about a hundred cats, and she doesn't like to chat. She watches the world on hundreds of flat-screen TVs and sighs a lot, smacks her forehead, talks back to the televisions like the people on them could hear her. "Not again!" She shakes her fist at a pale woman flickering across the screen in a wedding dress. "How could you go back for more? You see that? She's remarrying him. I can't goddamn believe it." She lights a cigar and blows a smoke ring. You ask her questions, like which religion was the right one, and she barely looks up from her soap operas when she tells you one religion isn't much better than the others. "They're all just like airlines," she says. "They all get you to the same place unless it's the Catholics." She sighs. "Then you're screwed." She turns her back on you and blows another smoke ring.

85

From section 44 . . .

You say no to the show. You don't want to parade your little hobbies around like they're something special. Right after that your mother-in-law dies and unexpectedly leaves you a chunk of money. (She was a big woman who could tear a whole chicken in half.)

With the inheritance you and your husband buy a piece of land right on Lake Superior, where the red clay cliffs bleed into the lake, turning the water an iron oxblood red. You build yourselves a bigger log cabin with a sauna and a painting studio and you decide you could generate some income by building another log cabin and turning it into a bed-and-breakfast. Well, honestly, the B&B is mostly your husband's idea—you'd rather open an artists' colony, a place where creative people from the city can come up and share their visions and insights with you. There's not much culture up in the Northwoods. Plenty of beauty, but not a lot of conversations about Germany's resurging Bauhaus movement or how to get linseed oil to dry more quickly on your canvas.

Of course an artists' colony wouldn't generate any money. Your husband shrugs—"Let's build it," he says, "and then we can choose." So you begin construction on a handcrafted log cabin built old-style, without nails or glue, just water-peeled logs cut with tongue-and-groove joints. Your husband gets some buddies to help and they begin in winter when the snow is deep and they can skid the ten-foot-long fir trees over the soft snow without ripping them up. In the spring they pour the foundation and set large round stones pulled from the lake bed. By high summer they start notching and stacking logs.

Up goes a two-story cabin that smells like pine tar inside. It has a high, vaulted ceiling over a large stone fireplace as well as a guesthouse and a fire pit and a sauna. When the house is almost finished, the roof tiled and the shutters hung, the men go in to inspect the electrical box, and a lone hammer (a ball-peen) falls from overhead and quite precisely hits your husband in the cranium, killing him immediately.

What to do? You can continue on with your husband's vision of a bed-and-breakfast—or you could open the artists' colony you wanted. A place where artists could come for two weeks at a stretch and paint. Still, maybe you should honor his wishes. The last thing you need is your dead husband haunting you.

If you build the bed-and-breakfast, go to section #140 (page 313).
If you build the artists' colony, go to section #141 (page 315).

86

From section 46 . . .

With the help of your bank's brokerage service you invest the money in mutual funds and go back to work at the rink. You like it there—why change? Nick shows up with two dozen white roses and tells you he heard about your family. He tried to figure out what hospital you were at, where the funeral was, but nobody knew for sure and so he waited and hoped you'd come back. He invites you over for dinner.

His house is on a little creek at the edge of a cute neighborhood. You tell him you didn't know Zamboni drivers made so much money. He smiles and shows you his secret. In his office are several laptop computers all opened to NASDAQ and NYSE stock pages. "I'm an amateur biotech investor," he says. "It's a little hobby I picked up after I shook my gambling habit. The doc said no more horses, so I found online trading, which is even better."

It turns out that while Nick is by no means rich, he doesn't play ducks and drakes with his money. He plays it safe and steady, which has made him quite comfortable. He works the job as a Zamboni driver because that's what his dad did—and it's sort of an homage, a way to stay connected to his deceased father. "Well," he confesses, "I was gonna quit but then you turned up, and, well, there was nothing that was gonna drag me off the ice then."

"Me?"

He ushers you into the dining room, where he has set out a roast chicken and new potatoes. You spend the evening together and then the next and the next and the next. You still haven't told him about the money you inherited; you haven't even moved out of your ratty little apartment. There was so much change, you just wanted some things to stay the same.

But after three months of dating, some absolutely rigorous, inventive love-making, and many roast chickens, you decide to tell him about the money.

"Three hundred thousand," you say. "I inherited it, and I haven't touched it."
He blinks, holding his fork of new potatoes in the air.

"Marry me," he says.

"What?"

"I mean it. I want kids, I want you in this house, I want it all."

You look at him, his strong hands and beautiful eyes, and you think, *I love this man*. But the fact that he asked you to marry him on the heels of your announcing you had three hundred thousand dollars seems a little . . . odd.

If you marry Nick, go to section #142 (page 318).

If you do not marry Nick, go to section #143 (page 320).

87

From section 46 . . .

You're not going back to work at a fucking *ice skating* rink. Not with three hundred thousand dollars. You can't live on it for the rest of your life, but you could live extravagantly for one year, damn well for two, maybe average for six. Material things don't mean that much to you now anyway.

After they put your mother in the ground, say their prayers, and seal her up, your perspective on the world changes. What seemed important before now seems ridiculous. *Money, rent, clothing, jewelry.* All that crap to haul around, and why? For what? No one's ever seen a U-Haul behind a hearse. You could take the money and start a business, or you could do something wild—like take a trip around the world.

If you go on a trip around the world, go to section #144 (page 322).

If you start your own business, go to section #145 (page 324).

88

From section 47 . . .

You find your first client accidentally while at the hairdresser. The woman sitting next to you starts telling you about her divorce. Her eyes well up with tears and she tells you she hasn't been able to eat *ever since her husband ran off with his proctologist's twenty-year-old assistant*. After another half hour of gut spilling and tears, you ask her if she wants revenge. She looks at you like you're crazy. "Hell *yes*," she says. That's how your career as a *revenge artist for hire* begins.

Scorned women. There are a lot of them and they all feel for each other. After all, who do we go to when our heart is broken? *Our girlfriends*. Who helps us through the rough times, the crying and binge eating and crying? *Our girlfriends*. Since time began and forever on, when the shit hits the fan, when the guy runs out, when he announces he's leaving for a pretty young thing, or when *he just stops calling*, women have been there for each other, and they'll be there now.

You develop a network of scorned women who all pool resources to seek ultimate revenge on the men who've wronged them. Cheating husbands, bad boyfriends, mean bosses, evil stepfathers, no-good sons. The deal is if you want Revenge Artist services, you pay a nominal fee and you agree to participate in someone else's revenge plot. The word of mouth on your new business is phenomenal. You soon have women everywhere from the INS to the IRS in your little black book. You have women who work at the electric company, the phone company, train yards, the stockyards, and the Department of Motor Vehicles. If a guy messes with one of your clients, he can be fucked in a thousand ways, like your motto says: *discreetly, neatly, and completely*.

You take on new clients. You build a roster of disgruntled, wronged women. You right a thousand wrongs. The revenge operations range from funny (dump a hundred cubic yards of cement into a guy's pool) to fairly serious (deliver thirteen severed pigs' heads to an ex-boss's house, one for every year he employed your client). You open an office and hire a staff. The staff orchestrates the revenge plots in ultimate secrecy—and never on the phone or by e-mail. Everything at the Revenge Artist office is done in person and with cash. No paper trail. Ever. What started as a lark spreads its wings into a dangerous bird of prey. These women are fierce.

You don't actually execute any operations anymore—you have people for that—so how you got targeted as the leader you'll never know. You're walking home one night when you hear a *swoosh!* and feel something hit your sternum. You look down to see a plume of blood on your sweater, and the business end of a paintbrush sticking out. *Who the fuck has stabbed you with a paintbrush?*

It was the one who knew you flocked his bike all along. The one who had to suffer so much mocking because of the newspaper article; he threw a temper tantrum at an opening and lost his gallery rep and ended up sweeping an Amoco for a living. It was Mark. He's been following you all along. He waited for enough years to pass that he would fade from memory, sharpened the paintbrush handle down to a sharp point, and used a bow to shoot you. He's not just an artist, he's a fucking poet.

You die slowly in the dark. No one is around to help you. You follow the light ahead of you, which gradually becomes golden orange, crimson red, bruise purple, blue and then black. It feels hollow. The smell of smoke. A crunching beneath your feet, like you were walking on fish bones. There are blue flashes of light, lightning against black water. You wander around, crunching heavily through this subterranean world. You reach a small aluminum bench and you sit down.

Once sitting, you find you can't move. The seat is slick and sticky—your feet are stuck to the pebbled ground beneath you. A movie starts pulsing on the blue wall opposite you. It's a black-and-white documentary of your life, only all the good parts are cut out. Very gritty. Every stupid bad selfish thing you ever did—every revenge, lie, mean act—all caught on video and put on a running loop for you to watch over and over and over again. Every time someone humiliated you, every mean word, every accident over and over and over again. There's no one to talk to—there's no one to ask what's going on—you can't get up, you can't leave. You're forced to watch your personal bloopers for the rest of eternity—and there are a lot of them.

89

From section 47 . . .

One act of revenge is enough. The whole thing is depressing. You didn't want to do it in the first place—your hand was forced. Your hand is *now* forced to a big bottle of wine . . . and then another and another. You drink and drink—until one night, in a semi-blackout, you wander out of the house, down by the highway, into some woods. Before you know what's happening, you're on the highway median and a truck is screeching its brakes as it careens toward you. The truck jackknifes and crashes into the median—the driver thrown right out of the cab window.

When you wake there are tubes and beeping machines and everything hurts. Someone tells you you're lucky to be alive—'cause the other guy isn't. The truck driver is dead. He swerved to miss you and killed himself in the process. *What were you doing on the highway?* They arrest you for public drunkenness right there in the hospital, that and crossing a highway without a motor vehicle, as well as manslaughter. *That word.* "Man-slaughter."

Since it's your first offense and it turns out the truck driver had a blood alcohol content higher than yours, you get off easy. They're not going to send you to prison. You *do* have to go to an inpatient treatment center for alcohol and substance abuse, give one hundred hours of community service, and full financial restitution to the family of the truck driver for funeral costs. You didn't want to be let off easy. You're miserable.

You end up at the House of Mercy, a treatment facility for *serious offenders*. You fit right in. You begin the tedious path to sobriety, which includes group therapy, talk therapy, physical therapy, thought therapy, art therapy, reading from the Big Book, reading from daily meditations, sharing stories, forming personal connections, following the rules. *No drinking, no drugging, no untoward touching with other patients* (in other words, no sex). *No shoelaces* (since that nasty business with the girl who somehow hanged herself by her shoelaces in the craft room). All in all the place is pretty dreary and you don't know how you're going to get through it.

Then you meet Brian. Tall, lean, shaggy hair, square jaw. He comes in one day nearly unconscious and voluntarily checks himself in for treatment after he nearly burned down his house while drunk and trying to make Jim Beam cookies. It's his fifth time through treatment. When he finally comes up for group therapy, he looks like shit—hair standing up on end, face drawn and tired. He smiles at you when he comes into the room and there's a certain lightning bolt of recognition that happens between you—a sense you'd met before and had a good time.

There's this woman who wrote a book about this. (You can't remember the name of the book but you read it in the House of Mercy lending library.) She flat-lined on the operating table for like ten minutes and was totally dead before they resuscitated her. While she was out, she claims she went to heaven, where the angels explained the world to her. Apparently earth is like boot camp for angels—we elect to come here, and only the brightest, strongest angels come. We always come to learn something, like humility or tolerance or hope—things you can learn only through suffering, which life is, in general, a shitstorm for everyone.

She says when strangers recognize each other, it's because they actually *did* know each other in heaven and planned on meeting during the course of their shitstorm. When connected souls meet each other, they recognize it. You gladly welcome Brian into your shitstorm. He's endlessly helpful. When you're forced to make birdcages or to draw pictures of your *emotional landscape*, Brian is there to make you laugh. You sit with him during meals, play poker with him in the lounge, and save a seat for him in every group meeting. You're crazy for the guy.

Things expand from affection to erection and one day he takes you into the craft room closet. Groping you with his wide palms, he tastes like heaven. His lips are salty, soft, and warm. You can't believe he's attracted to you. You try to be sexy, which is hard when you're in a closet packed with industrial-size tubs of paste. Not to mention the fact that with all the phlegm and toxins your body is flushing out, you've become lethargic and chubby, like a listless, insouciant pig. This is illegal, but you want to taste him, you want him to remind you that you were somebody else once.

He undoes your jeans, yanks them to the floor, and he's got his pants around his ankles and your legs spread, and just when . . . just when you're about to . . . the door flies open and there stands a grim nurse with two smirking orderlies in tow. One of the orderlies laughs out loud—and only then do you remember to close your legs.

You are both kicked out of the program. Papers signed, suitcases packed, not a good-bye or *see ya!* to the other patients. Your bed is stripped, your name erased from the community board, your shoes returned to you with the laces *in* them. The message is: *Go ahead and hang yourself with shoelaces if you want to.*

Your parole officer drums her fingers in her office. She's got a *I-knew-you'd-screw-this-up-somehow* look on her face and a half-smoked cigarette in her hand. You've driven her to smoke in a public building. Could anything be worse? She already warned you when you checked in to Mercy House that you were lucky to get in and that breaking parole would mean transferring to Anoka State, a mental hospital with a treatment program that resembles something from *One Flew Over the Cuckoo's Nest.*

You ask to use the bathroom and your parole officer takes you down the hall. The cops wait in her office; they're joking about what a sweet deal being a guard in a women's mental institution would be—and at that moment you realize you're going to have to run. Your parole officer is talking to someone down the hall when you duck out of the bathroom. She's chatting away and you quickly walk alongside a mother and her two young boys as they leave the building. No fuss, no commotion—you're hidden in plain sight. By the time your parole officer goes in the bathroom to look for you, you're at a 7-Eleven buying a Diet Coke.

What else could you do? You're not going to a *mental institution*, you're not letting them shackle you to a wall and pump you full of whatever experimental lobotomizing drugs they use. You feel so stupid. Why do you gamble with your life like this? And for what? You don't ever even see Brian again. After all *he* wasn't under court order to go to treatment, he checked himself in voluntarily—so when he got kicked out he probably just picked up the yellow pages and checked himself in somewhere else, or maybe he ended up in Jamaica cooling himself off with a green palm frond. *Who knows?* The point is—he can do what he fucking wants to and you can't.

You go directly to the liquor store and buy yourself a nice, big bottle of red wine. Maybe your problem is that you've been coloring a little too closely inside the lines lately. Maybe what you need is a nice long drink and a nap.

If you don't drink the wine, go to section #210 (page 490).
If you drink the wine, go to section #90 (page 188).

90

From section 89 . . .

You take the unopened bottle of wine and sit behind a Dumpster. You stare at the ground for a while, feeling lousy. You notice an ant. He's a big ant, one of those big black ones that go fast—and he's got a leaf in his mouth that's four times his size. In fact, if you squint, it just looks like a leaf walking across the ground. He's really struggling with it. He drops it and picks it up. He drops it and picks it up. He climbs over sticks that would be the size of apartment buildings to you.

Right then it occurs to you that life is hard for everybody. Drinking isn't going to change that—it's going to make it worse. A wave of anger rises in you—a surge of disgust with yourself. You hurl the bottle of wine up over your head, it goes sailing out onto the sidewalk . . . and you hear a strange *thunk*, a clip, clatter, and then a piercing shrill *scream*.

A baby's scream—a woman's scream. You jump up from the bushes. Impossible image to decipher. Baby. Stroller. Red wine on sidewalk. Mother bending, her white Keds soaked in blood? Red wine? Splattered everywhere. The baby screaming. Red wine on his head. Blood on his head. You have tossed the bottle of wine out of the bushes and directly onto a passing stroller; a woman had paused at the corner, waiting for the light to change, only to have a liter bottle of cheap merlot sail out of the bushes and crack her two-year-old in the skull. Maybe an ant can't move a rubber tree plant.

Scalps bleed. It's impossible to separate the red wine from the baby's blood. Things you notice: The stroller looks expensive, like an all-terrain stroller with bags and pouches and cup holders. The mother looks nice. Put together and pretty. You're fucked. People rush to help. Police arrive. You are pushed into the center of the crowd, the police are yelling at you—questioning you.

Someone shoves you down. Handcuffs. Squad car. Blood on your shirt. You hear your voice.

Is the baby all right?

Is the baby all right?

Is the baby all right?

Is the baby all right?

The baby is all right—or rather, will *be* all right. He was rushed to Children's Hospital for six stitches in his scalp. (You will learn soon that the baby's name is Brian Bennington, son of Rick and Evelyn Bennington.) Even though baby Brian is *relatively* all right, parents, judges, courtrooms, *people in general* do not look kindly on convicted addicts who break parole and toss wine bottles on babies' heads. They just don't.

To say you had the book thrown at you would be an understatement. It might not have been so bad if a news reporter who covered the story on the "attack" hadn't used the word "attack," and hadn't dug up the number of repeat offenders (an actually alarming number) the state releases into the public (or loses track of, or doesn't have the funding to prosecute), where they can harm, injure, stumble on or malign the rest of society (that is, wander across highways and attack babies).

In court there is a graph and a pie chart showing the increase in drunks and drug addicts released from prison, as well as an in-depth profile on the Bennington family (churchgoing, taxpaying, home owning, God-fearing citizens) and a shocking *before and after* photo of adorable baby Bennington. (*Before* all soft blond curls, *after* all shaved scalp and wiry black stitches.) So due to the extreme circumstances of the case, the fact you are a repeat offender, the media attention, the public outcry, they send you to *prison*. Not a treatment center, not a mental institution, but an honest-to-God orange jumpsuit, steel bars, cable television prison.

You serve three years. Paroled early for good behavior. When you get out, you move to a halfway house for previously incarcerated women reentering society, a narrow Victorian home on the outskirts of town with an antique rose garden in the backyard and a lemon yellow kitchen. Time passes. You have to look for work, but there's not many opportunities for someone recently out of rehab. You go to Denny's and apply for a job as a waitress. Then your friend says she can get you a job on the maintenance crew at the nearby hospital.

If you become a waitress at Denny's, go to section #128 (page 286).
If you go work maintenance at the hospital, go to section #155 (page 351).

91

From section 79 . . .

You want to help the clinic at any price—including denying yourself some comfort. If that makes you codependent or a narcissist or needy or whatever—then so be it. A lot can happen on ordinary days, and it's always on days when you're most bored and most sure that your little life is meaningless that something comes to wake you up. It's just graffiti on the retaining wall of a highway overpass. Some random scrawl that reads YOU GONNA DIE ANYWAY JACK.

It's just some sentence on the wall. But it strikes you. You *are* gonna die anyway—so why not go out fists up, guns blazing, right over a cliff if you have to? Why not? Why not fight for the clinic?

You contact the House of Human Services and get the runaround. You contact the Savannah City Council and never actually get to even talk to a real person. You contact soup kitchens, women's shelters, church organizations, and the White House. Nothing. You keep on. It's hopeless. It's stupid. Nevertheless. You start reaching out to places no one normally would. You just have to keep knocking until someone opens the door. The trick is to keep trying new doors and not stand in front of the same damn one.

Then you contact the Daughters of the American Revolution, a social group of very old, very wealthy ladies in Savannah who eat cucumber sandwiches with their manicured pinkies in the air and can each power down a pitcher of gin gimlets without a twitch. They agree to hear your story. That's when everything changes.

You tell them about the children of Thunderbolt, the state of the clinic, the single mothers, the endless bruises caused by endless need. You compare the small local hamlet to a third world country dropped right in the lace-trimmed lap of Savannah. A travesty, an embarrassment, a disaster but *all fixable, all reversible*—with help.

After your talk you collapse in your chair and watch their snowy white heads drift together as they discuss the situation. Then the miracle comes. The society chairperson, Mrs. Cynda Beyette Talmadge II, stands up and announces that she will *personally* see to it that these poor children of Savannah will never suffer again. The rest of the hens cluck and nod their heads.

These women, who spent their lifetimes organizing fund-raisers and weddings and cotillions, who can negotiate the most delicate of delicate social situations, who have the deepest of deep pockets, who maybe now in their eleventh hour are more reflective and soft than they were a decade ago, they decide to take your clinic and start a family support program. They assign each Daughter of the American Revolution to a single family registered at your clinic. In the end the ladies do more than you ever thought was possible. You'd love to take credit, but the truth is you didn't do anything but tell one story. They did the rest.

It turned into quite a spectacle really—all the women trying to outdo each other with their families—because soft and reflective or not, these ladies are nothing if not viciously competitive. For instance, when Miss Lottie May (who would rather go to hell without her handbag than let Doris Murphy outdo her in any category) heard Doris gave her adopted family a new roof and comprehensive dental care, Lottie bought *her* family a new refrigerator, the exclusive services of a podiatrist, and a powder blue Cadillac. One woman sent her family to her estate in North Carolina to get out of the heat. Another set aside college funds for all twelve of her adoptive children. This went on and on between all the ladies, giving clothing and property and medical care until the adopted families resembled their own.

Your clinic gets a face-lift. When the ladies are done with it, there's a Victorian gabled roof, a wraparound porch, a day-care center, and landscaping that would rival the queen's own Kensington Garden. As the years roll on and your clinic stays a cause célèb in the city, you're able to help other clinics and they in turn help others as well.

You die a very old woman, from a pulmonary embolism, a clot on your lung that stabs you in your sleep and carries you up, up and away into the starry night. You have one thought as you drift swiftly up. YOU GONNA DIE ANYWAY JACK. You smile and wonder what heaven is like—and what will need fixing.

92

From sections 49 and 55 . . .

Santorini is the southernmost island of the Greek chain. The road is not easy.
The trains are unreliable, the ferries are ancient, and the tiny planes are expensive. You begin the journey on an all-night train down the coast of Italy
to the port town of Brindisi, where you must then board a ferry to Athens.
(Tips for navigating the Brindisi port: Avoid eye contact with anyone, keep
backpack strapped to your body at all times, smear off makeup, mess up hair,
make yourself as unappealing as possible.)

Once on the boat you find the sagging freighter is drearily festooned with
crepe streamers and bleeding paper flowers. Your eyes dodge all manifesta-
tions of forced gaiety and instead chronicle decay. The rust that nibbles at
every straining joist, the mystery stains that bloom on the hallway carpet-
ing, and the porthole painted on the bathroom wall, to which some juvenile
passenger has added several shark fins and a desperate stick figure throwing
himself into the sea.

Tips for the boat: Try not to get seasick, try not to drink any water from the
tap, try not to talk to strangers, try to look married, try to get some sleep, do
not use the toilets, try not to get bitten by one of the many spiders, insects, and
unknown flying things that live on the boat. (One guy got bitten on the testicle
by some spider and his balls blew up to the size of pink grapefruits.)

You eventually reach Athens and there's only one rule about Athens: *Get out
of Athens.* Pay a taxi to speed you from the scary seaport to the scary airport,
where you can at least buy an Aegean Airlines ticket to anywhere else. That's
if you survive the plane ride. It's nothing short of a death-defying acrobatic
display challenging all limits of gravity. Are the pilots drinking ouzo? For the
first time in your life you get airsick and end up vomiting in your mouth a little.
Once you land, however, once your churning, angry stomach comes to a stop

and you walk off the tin can of a plane into the fresh salt sea air—everything is well. The blue expanse of the ocean stretches out before you, the blue roofed homes stack behind you, you know the whole horrible trip was worth it.

The cabdriver takes you to a popular youth hostel on the far side of the island that's carved into the side of a black basalt cliff. The hostel can sleep twenty people in the main room, whose walls are washed with a sleepy blue light. The ocean is just five hundred yards away; the sound of the waves crashing is hypnotic. The hostel turns out to be a nexus for professional loafers, budget travelers from every corner of the globe. People come and go every day, every week, every month.

You wander. You explore the busy port of Fira with its winding narrow roads, boisterous restaurants, booming bar scenes, and glittering jewelry shops. You visit the small village of Imerovigli with its expensive homes and well-fed children. You follow the path that leads to the lonely Akrotiri lighthouse and sweeping views of the sea. You bake in the black sand of Perivolos beach, with its thatched straw umbrellas and smiling tan men.

You eat. You eat thick creamy yogurt drizzled with honey, flaky baklava, and rich kalamata olives. You eat whitefish pulled straight from the sea, you eat roasted lamb and garlic. There is a lemon sauce called avgolemono, a rich custard eggplant dish named moussaka. Cloves, ginger, and pepper. Mint, basil, and dill. The food in Greece is the best you've ever had.

It's all white heaven on blue earth until one morning you wake up late, stretch, and wonder what to wear for another day in paradise—only to find your backpack ransacked and your money pouch gone. You spend an hour overturning your mattress, checking and rechecking with increasing hysteria. Your rip off your sheets, your pillows, your shoes. It's gone. All your money, your traveler's checks, your cash, *everything* is gone.

The owner of the youth hostel, a barrel of a man named Macgregor who's bald and has a thick rusty red beard, tries to help you. He calls the local police, who are largely uninterested once they figure out you're not going to sleep with them, and they don't even write your name down. Macgregor makes you a strong mojito—on the house. You sit at the little bar that overlooks the sea. What are you going to do? You've got no money and no way to get home.

You call the American embassy in Athens and wait for three hours on the phone while the perplexing punishment of shrill Greek Muzak blasts in your ear. You're transferred six times and talk to the same person twice before they determine that they can help you—sort of. The American embassy can issue you a temporary passport, get you an airplane ticket home, and give you fifty dollars in spending money, all of which will need to be paid back upon stateside arrival—you have one week to fill out a "citizen in distress" application. After that the office closes for the summer. Only in Greece would an embassy close for the summer.

Macgregor smiles. (Is he smiling or leering? Hard to say. He has brushed up against you twice and you're not sure if the bulge in his linen shorts is a flaccid bulge or a not-flaccid bulge.) "More than one way to skin a cat, love," he says. "I could use some help around here." He sweeps his chubby arms across the room as if it were the easiest thing in the world. "Stay here and work in the hostel. I'll give you room and board and a bit of pay." You can't tell if he's sweet or creepy. He seems to be grinning so hard his face is turning red.

What to do? If you don't go to the embassy now, you'll be stuck here, and you'd have to work for quite a while before you can buy a ticket home. But if you go to the embassy—your trip is over. *Be safe or be sorry?* Everything is wonky and weird. Foreign. You're dizzy. Tired. The ocean seems overwhelmingly loud.

If you take the job at the youth hostel, go to section #151 (page 338).
If you take the embassy's ticket and go home,
go to section #148 (page 330).

93

From sections 49 and 159 . . .

You head for Sicily on a crowded, sweaty train. You transfer to the *Ferrovie dello Stato*, twelve hours straight down the Italian coast to the Strait of Messina. Then you board a rusting ferry to the Sicilian port, and then buy a ticket on a cramped public bus into the city. By the time you reach Palermo, you're exhausted. You walk carefully. With purpose. This city is famous for *Cosa Nostra*, the Italian Mafia, notorious for corruption, extortion, and assassination. Secrecy, blood oaths, and murders. There are legends, stories, myths, and gossip. Like telling stories of the bogeyman or the grim reaper, Italian mothers terrify their children into obedience by telling them Cosa Nostra will get them if they're not good.

You stop in a small bar, La Bella Ragazza, and have a Campari to quiet your nerves. The only person who seems willing to talk to you is a German man who's wearing a very nice TAG Heuer watch and a dark herringbone suit. He seems nice enough. He buys you a few more drinks, and when the bar is closing he says, "You want to stay at my sister's house? No charge and no funny business. I have a daughter your age. I hate to think of her alone in Palermo with no place to stay. Come with me." It's follow him or strike out on your own.

If you go to the German's house, go to section #149 (page 332).
If you do not go to the German's house, go to section #150 (page 335).

94

From section 51 . . .

You agree to marry Filippo. He's ecstatic—punching the air and doing little soccer kicks. He goes to the bar to tell his buddies and you call your parents with the news. They're worried. *"Who is this guy? When did you meet him? You can't know if he's the right one this soon. Is he in the Mafia? Has he brainwashed you?"* It nearly brings you to tears. You can't tell them it's because you're knocked up, so you tell them it's because you're madly in love—which you aren't.

The one good thing is your mother says she's coming immediately to help you with the wedding, which you want to have in a mere three weeks. (The quicker the better, your tummy is going to show soon.) So a month later you have your big fancy Italian wedding. Well—you almost have one. After cinching yourself into your mother-in-law's itchy lace wedding dress and securing the matching scalp-biting veil, you prepare to walk down the aisle. This is it.

Only something is wrong. People are acting weird. Your father is in the hall pacing, and your sister-in-law-to-be, who should be getting ready to walk down the aisle in her peach bridesmaid's dress, is outside whispering on her cell phone.

"What is it?" you ask, but no one can look you in the eye.

Apparently the problem is no one can find Filippo. He's gone. No note, no phone call, nothing. He's just vanished. *Has he been in an auto crash? Is he dead? Sick? Murdered?* All of those things would be better than that he deserted you. Than that he decided you were not enough. Death would be better. At least then you could be a widow and not a single mother—you could tell your baby his father was brave, which he wasn't, and that he was a good man, which he was not.

Eventually your father stands in front of the congregation and makes the oh-so-awkward announcement. *The wedding is off.* The murmuring begins.

The priest comes to do a Hail Mary over you, but you tell him to back off.

Filippo's mother cries into her corsage and says she can't believe he's done this *again*. (It will come out that he called off his last wedding five years ago. He left his bride, a docile girl from Sienna, alone at the altar of St. Mark's.) His brothers tell you they'll kill him, which means they will find him, shout loudly, and then all go get drunk together. His friends roll their eyes, look at their watches, and wonder when the bar down the street closes. The congregation gets up to leave, but they don't go empty-handed. No. They go with a story to tell—the story of the American girl's disaster wedding.

Your parents are numb. Your mother says something about hens and roosters and barn doors being left open. You feel very still. Very quiet. A cold anger is filling you up with ice water. Your parents say they want you to come home. They want you to get away from these awful people and this horrible, hot, noisy city. (They may be the only senior citizens in the world who think Florence is horrible.) You don't know what to do. You've got no reason to go, and no reason to stay.

But why should you go home? What have you done to be run out of town? It's *Filippo* who should go hide—not you. You get your parents to go home by promising them you can only get closure here and that you'll call them soon. (If they'd known you were pregnant, they would have forcibly dragged you on the plane.) Still, your mother is in tears as she gets on the plane, and as you wave good-bye from the terminal window, your stomach seizes and you rush to the women's room, where you're sick in the toilet.

Now to find Filippo. The little oily weasel—he can't be far from his family, they're like cockroaches, they can't keep from swarming all over each other. You ask around town for three days before you get your first clue. Marta, the girl at the bakery, asks if Filippo's oldest brother is back from Venice yet. *Venice*, the city where you were supposed to have your honeymoon. Did he go to the honeymoon hotel without you?

A day and an expensive express train ticket later you find out he didn't go to the honeymoon hotel alone, he went with a woman. *The woman with the tan leg.* You see their names written in the registry and then you see them coming out of Hotel Cipriani together, his arm around her waist, a shiny gold bracelet around her ankle. They're both smiling and nuzzling and you feel your stomach kick. Little bastard. You follow them through crowded narrow streets to a small candlelit restaurant, where a beak-nosed waiter in a tuxedo takes them to their table.

What to do? How do you get back at an Italian man and his whore lover? You're at a loss. Despair is *ovunque*. Everywhere. You wander over to St. Mark's Cathedral, kneel in one of the front pews, and begin to weep uncontrollably. It isn't long until a nun comes up in her long gray-green habit and puts a warm hand on your shoulder. *"Cosa?"* she asks. *"Cosa fai?"*

You throw yourself in her arms and tell her in broken Italian everything that's happened. How Filippo is in your honeymoon bed with another woman, how all you want to do is kill yourself but you have this *baby* growing inside you. She gathers you up and ushers you into the back chambers, to a large kitchen, where more nuns come to listen to your tale. They sit in rapt attention as you explain how Filippo left you at the altar and ran off with this other woman, and now they're having dinner, out in the open, right down the street.

The nuns murmur to each other and someone puts a hot cappuccino in front of you. They pat you on the back and dry your eyes. One of the priests pokes his perplexed head in to see what the gathering is about and the nuns shoo him out.

The nuns seem highly agitated. "Show us," they say, "show us the monster." So you lead them out into the street, through the crowds that always convene in St. Mark's Square. It's amazing how quickly you can cross the square when you have nuns in tow. People make way for them; it's like the Red Sea parting wherever you go. People taking off their hats, bowing, doing Hail Marys over their chests. It's exhilarating, like you're important. Like you're powerful.

By the time you reach the restaurant, a large crowd has begun following you and the nuns as rumor of this beastly man who left his pregnant fiancée at the altar spreads through the street. When you reach the door the maître d' looks up and is too perplexed to speak. The head nun pushes past him without so much as a word and asks you, "Which one?" Everyone in the restaurant is silent and looking at you.

Him, you say and point at Filippo, who is sitting at a large table with the tan leg lady and what turns out to be a large chunk of her family. (She wanted to introduce her new *fiancé* to her family. Papa sprung for a fancy meal at this trattoria so everyone, including his mother, could meet him.) Filippo stands up in protest, but the nun pays him no attention whatsoever and marches right over to him and grabs him by the ear—just twists it hard, and he winces in pain. She begins yelling at him so fast you can't tell what she's saying—but there's no misunderstanding her. She is point-blank telling him off and the entire family is listening. The entire *restaurant* is listening.

It isn't long until the tan leg lady bursts into tears and gets up and runs out, the nuns hissing at her as she goes. Her father is sitting with his head in his hands, the grandmother's face is pressed into an expression of grim recognition. The mother, a handsome woman in a dark dress, holds her butter knife firmly in one hand. (The wedding is called off later that night.)

Filippo has gone utterly limp and has no response whatsoever. (Never underestimate the fear a Catholic has of a nun.) The nuns drag him out to the alley, where he kneels on the ground. He's crying. They're hitting him with sticks, they're kicking him and he lies down. They don't stop. You can't hear what they're saying—you can hardly see him through the black robes. You're feeling wobbly, nauseous. The ground is blurring—you wish they'd stop hitting him—and then you black out.

In the morning you wake in the hospital. You've miscarried—but the doctors don't know why. "These things happen," the kindly doctor tells you, "and when it does, it's always for the best. The body knows what it needs."

You also read in the papers that Filippo is *dead*. He was rushed to the hospital with head injuries and overnight his brain hemorrhaged. It's an unbelievable nightmare—these nuns don't fuck around. In fact, one of the nuns visits you in the hospital, puts her sweet wrinkled hand on your knee, and asks if you won't come visit them when you're released. They'd love to provide you with a place to stay. You're afraid to say no.

Besides, free lodging and a ferocious army of nuns to protect you? *Why not?* You move to the convent and the nuns introduce you to a part of the Catholic Church you never knew existed. It's called *Domini Patri*, a religious sect of women who protect the church through "whatever means necessary." It isn't entirely clear how or when this faction started—there's no information anywhere and members of Domini Patri are kept secret even from each other. You are now a part of the secret society.

The nuns send you to a secret Sicilian retreat up in the hills, where you are taught how to poison, stab, smother, choke, and shoot. The Domini Patri calls killing people "evacuating" them. Your job is to *evacuate* the person or persons you're told to. Three right-wing priests were evacuated last year—each had had serious sexual offense charges leveled at him. A Baptist televangelist and a right-wing radio personality were also evacuated, courtesy of Domini Patri.

You first case is an office clerk in Palermo who "lost" key files in a statutory rape case (priest–altar boy scenario). He's a wormy little man with pasty skin and beady eyes. It's determined that he's a source of constant "accidental" misplacement and so you slit his throat as he enters his apartment on Via Strella. Interesting how easy it is, and how you are whisper quiet, in and out without a sound, a word, or a shred of evidence. You like it, and a private boat picks you up and delivers you back to Rome before the body is even discovered.

Your next case is a statesman who's cut abortion funding and the case after that is the right-wing wife of another nasty televangelist who claims birth control is evil. All evacuated. All paid for by the Catholic Church. You work for Domini Patri for thirty-six years. All told you evacuate over seven hundred men and two women, all enemies of the state. You die one day when you're standing on the yacht of the Duchess of Kent (also a member of Domini Patri) and you drop over dead into the water. She shot you from behind. Apparently your time was up.

In heaven they let you in because, in your own way, you never stopped trying to make the world a better place. It's the couch potatoes who all get french-fried down in hell, because even though they weren't out committing sins, they weren't out committing anything, they just couldn't commit. It turns out that's the biggest sin there is.

95

From section 51 . . .

You refuse to marry Filippo and *Jesus Mother Mary*, let the drama begin. He breaks up with you and tells you he never wants to see you again. He says he won't help with the baby and there's no such thing as child support under Italian law. He threatens to have you beaten up, deported, thrown in jail. He threatens you with just about anything he can think of, including spreading a rumor you're a hairy-legged lesbian—although you're not quite sure why that's threatening.

At this point you don't know if you want to go through with the pregnancy. Filippo tells you to call him when you've come to your senses, but that's the one thing you can't quite seem to come to. You quit school. If you're going to get out of here you've got to make some money and save it. You've got to get a job.

The only job you can find is bartending at a dark little bar called Il Rosso across the river. Away from the tourists, down a small cobblestone street, Il Rosso has a lone creaking mahogany bar perched upon by a tattered flock of Italian men in black trench coats. These men don't come to talk, they don't come to argue, they come to drink. Seriously, steadfastly, drink. One man, Massimo, is a particular case. His wife and little daughter died in a car crash a year ago, and he still carries a lock of his wife's hair in his wallet. He says he was supposed to be with them when it happened, but he had stayed home to watch a soccer game. He should have died too—he thinks he probably did.

It's on a rainy night when you take the trash out that the two of you meet accidentally in the alley. It just sort of happens. You kiss him on the cheek and he smells good. Really good. You kiss him again, sandpaper chin, and again, salty lips. You go home with him. His whole apartment is a shrine to his family, untouched since the day they left. His wife's gardenia perfume and hand lotion are still on the nightstand, his daughter's pale stuffed rabbit still on the floor by her bed where she dropped him that last night. You stay with him, until eventually you're living with him. The two of you lie on his bed with the lights turned off at night and listen to his wife's old Buddy Guy records while he rubs your feet. He tries to convince you to name the baby after a saint. He suggests St. Florian, patron saint of storms. Florian.

You make love to him over and over and over again. Try to stamp out the hurt, stitch up the tear in the fabric, open the locked rooms where he keeps the dark trunks, but there's always a room inside him you can't get into—a space just for them that cannot be touched. You don't hear a peep from Filippo. He doesn't know where you work or live now—he's gone and you're glad for the quiet. Then your parents track you down. They want to know when you're coming home and what's going on with school. Maybe it's because you're exhausted or drained—but you just haven't the energy to keep secrets anymore. You just spill your guts. You tell them everything and your mother listens in silence.

You tell Massimo your parents are coming—and he has a strange reaction. He straightens up and takes a marathon shower. He shaves. When he emerges from a cloud of steam in the bathroom he looks different—not just fresher but more awake. He's trimmed his hair and shaved off his dark stubble. There's life in his eyes you've never seen before. He looks ten years younger.

He wants to fix up his apartment before your parents get there. He cleans out his daughter's room, packs all her toys and clothes carefully in a trunk and puts the trunk in his bedroom closet. He strips the bed and scrubs down the floors. He washes the curtains and rearranges all the furniture—so it hardly resembles the room it once was at all. "So they have a place to sleep," he says and kisses you on the forehead.

Then he cleans the rest of the apartment. He drags all the rugs out of the house and beats them over the back stairwell until the clouds of dust rising off them disappear. He replaces the shower curtain and the kitchen tablecloth and puts fresh flowers on the coffee table. "Does your father smoke cigars?" he asks, and he buys a box of Cubans along with a lamb roast and red potatoes. You hardly recognize this Massimo. Apparently the pressure of meeting your parents has snapped him awake—given him something else to focus on.

He's nervous at the airport, shifts his weight from foot to foot and tugs on his tie. He keeps one arm protectively around your waist and pulls you closer when other men walk by. Your parents look serious and worried. They don't yell, they don't lecture, they just take it all in—in stony silence. At the apartment Massimo makes rosemary-infused lamb with garlic green beans and tomato risotto. He opens a bottle of red wine and pours everyone a glass—you get mineral water. After a toast to your health and the baby, Massimo gets down on one knee and proposes. Now your parents are even more worried. You throw your arms around Massimo and say *yes!*

During their weeklong visit they supply you with every conceivable baby item they can think of (clothing, diapers, changing table, formula, stroller with sun visor, crib, rocker, and so on). They eventually get on a plane and go home. After they leave you're half afraid Massimo might slip into his dark world again, but he seems to have caught baby fever and remodels his daughter's old room into a beautiful nursery.

You go to work at a flower store, La Rosa Rampicante (the Rambling Rose), a cheerful shop owned by the large Donna family of Milan. You arrange flowers and take orders over the phone well into your eighth month, but then take the rest of the time off until baby Flo is born. Massimo won out with his saint.

Filippo never came around to see you once, then he dies in a scooter crash. It's sad—but let's face it, convenient. Massimo asks if he can legally adopt your daughter, and the three of you live in Florence together for years and years. You live a long and rich life—you buy the flower store when the Donnas retire and you inherit their client list as well, which is largely Mafia.

You're now the florist who does all the Mafia weddings and funerals. (Jesus, they love yellow roses!) They take good care of you, pay you well, and protect the store. When your store is broken into once, the captains find the young student who did it and break his legs. Your parents eventually move to Florence so they can be closer to you and baby Flo—who grows up to be an extraordinary girl. She's a fierce cook, has a natural intuition about spices and flavors even when she's young.

When she's older she opens a restaurant in central Florence called Bella Luna, easily one of the best places in town. Massimo builds her a smoke house outside where she roasts the lamb and the ducks. You spend many nights there in the kitchen with the rest of the family, drinking red wine and telling stories as Flo laughs and flies around the kitchen. There you are, the Mafia's high-paid florist and surrounded by your large loving family in the heart of Italy. Who'd have thought your life would be this strangely sweet?

A decade passes and then another. Your parents fall ill, you put them to rest one by one, and then it's your turn to sleep, Massimo and Flo right there by your side. How and when you go hardly seems worth mentioning—the life that led up to it was so luminous and warm, the crossing over was easy and insignificant. When you're in heaven and asked which life you want next, you ask to do the last one over again. Exactly how it was, you say. Not one thing changed. Nothing.

96

From section 151 . . .

You don't give her your journal (it's your *fucking journal*) and you never see the woman again, except in a recurring dream. (She's on a boat sailing across a choppy sea. Her boat comes toward yours, she leans over and hands you a green apple.)

Your parents die in a car accident. There's a telegram, an absurd method of communication, and yet one of the only reliable ones in Greece. By the time you get the notification, they are already in the ground. With the telegram they wire your inheritance, not much by any standard but enough to buy a little blue boat called *The Censio* (Latin for "the decision").

You meet a man named Lazarus who is independent, moody, unpredictable and free. For the next dozen-odd sun-soaked years, you race your boats from port to port, two wooden dolphins speeding after one another, always chasing, never catching. You agree with Zorba, who once wrote, *Bathed in light, fine rain spreading a diaphanous veil over the immortal nakedness of Greece. Happy is the man, I thought, who, before dying, has the good fortune to sail the Aegean Sea.*

Many years later, after your accidental death in Naxos (boating accident, rogue wave), faithful Macgregor cleans out your little shack by the beach, goes through the clutter of beach drift, bleached bird bones and polished sea stones, sticks and kelp, jars of black sand, white sand dollars, through your books and your photographs (three hundred and eight disposable cameras are expensive to develop!) and finds your old journals, all thirty of them. He opens a bottle of twelve-year-old scotch, reads them through, and finds them fascinating.

97

From section 151 . . .

You give her the journal and she snaps it up in her small manicured hands. She takes it with her, and as she disappears your stomach does that cold thing— losing that book would be losing a piece of yourself. *Your history. Your memory.* Like hacking off an ear or a breast. You really start to worry when you realize she left without paying her bill. You get Macgregor to cover for you and dash up the hill on your sputtering moped. *You don't know her name, you don't know where she's staying!* All the people you wrote about drift past you, like passengers drowning at sea. China plates and silver cutlery glimmering away under black water. No lifeboats.

You spend the rest of the night and part of the early morning looking for the journal thief. She wasn't at any of the usual hotels. Not the Atlantis or Tzekos or Villa Soula. You check every lobby, rattle every hotel manager and bellboy. Fifty bucks to anyone who finds the small dark-haired American carrying your journal. You mourn the loss of your own intelligence. You weep for your pea-sized brain and the feeble gerbils running the ruined treadmill. *Idiot. Stupid, careless.*

But in the morning she appears at the youth hostel, fresh as a daisy and grinning from ear to ear. She's holding your book—which you grab back. You're rude to her. (This will change of course in time, after it's all painfully and slowly explained to you. How remorseful you will be of this moment, when you snatch the book back so hard she's almost put off balance! But then again, how could you have known? What identifies a woman as a keen-eyed, highly paid, big-shot editor from New York?)

She turns your stories into a glossy travelogue, a gorgeous collection of short stories and essays, complete with the photographs you took and even the doodles and drawings you put in your journals. The book is called *Passage*, and the reviews sing.

Every shop in all of Greece sells the book. You can get signed copies at Macgregor's youth hostel, which he of course signs himself and says it's your signature. The advance you're given allows you to travel back home and put really lovely headstones on your parents' graves. (They died in a car accident before you made it stateside.) The publishers put out a second book and then a third, each selling more than the last. They encourage you to travel around the world and collect more stories. You've got plenty of money to do it. But then, you've got plenty of money *not* to do it, and so you move back to Santorini, buy a blue-and-white house high on the cliffs of Fira, and buy a little blue boat called *The Censio* (Latin for "the decision").

You spend the rest of your days cruising the Greek isles, until one day you meet a man who is the spitting image of you. Independent, moody, unpredictable and free. Lazarus is his name, with salt-and-pepper hair and twinkling eyes. For the next dozen-odd sun-soaked years, you race your boats from port to port, two wooden dolphins speeding after one another, always chasing, never catching. Zorba once wrote, *Bathed in light, fine rain spreading a diaphanous veil over the immortal nakedness of Greece. Happy is the (wo)man, I thought, who, before dying, has the good fortune to sail the Aegean Sea.* Many years later you die in a boating accident near Naxos. You crash into a thirty-foot Boston Whaler named *The Beginning*. You die on impact.

98

From section 54 . . .

You follow Rashid outside to the street, where he jumps into his father's big silver Mercedes. You barely get inside the car before he peels out, tearing down the wrong side of the road, yelling at the other drivers, honking, swerving and cursing in Hindi. The car rockets forward, and you close your eyes so you won't know when you're about to die. Eventually you come to Connaught Place, an old open-air market. It's a smoky maze of vendor stands selling everything from roasted peanuts and shrieking monkeys to orange marigolds and hand-woven rugs.

Rashid buys a scarf made of green sequined fabric, which he rubs between his fingers, as if he were trying to feel for the other side of him, as if Alouette might materialize like smoke from the sequins. He buys a hot coffee and some small green apples. "You want one?" he asks, handing you the cool fruit. "They're good."

You walk on through the crowds, past the market and up the crooked roads. "They won't give me any money," he says. "My family knows what I am. Amil just wanted to embarrass me, to shame me in front of my grandfather." He turns his eyes toward the stone wall, and fat tears drop from his black eyelashes. "Go home." He wipes the tears with his sequined scarf. "We'll go and get your bags. I'll drive you to the airport, there's no more here. I'll be back home in a week, after the mourning period is over."

You fly home without her, sleep all the way over and arrive with a migraine. Without Alouette the apartment loses its shine. It looks tacky instead of eccentric, crowded instead of cozy. You feel ill. Headache, chills, stomachache. At first you think it's jet lag, then maybe a cold. Your urine is dark. You lie down, can't eat. Only *sleep sleep sleep sleep*. Dark. Dreams. You have a fever you can't seem to sleep off.

Alouette comes home thirteen days later, and when she sees you she catches her breath and rushes you to the hospital.

They show you a mirror and a sickly greenish yellow face looms in front of you. "It's hepatitis A," the doctor says. "Have you had the vaccine?" You don't know. "Have you been to a foreign country?" he wonders, "an undeveloped country?"

"I'll say," Alouette sneers. "She was in fucking India."

"You might have eaten contaminated food," he says. "Vegetables that weren't washed." *The apple.* You hear the doctor whisper to Alouette in the hall, *It usually isn't deadly, but you should have come in sooner, it's advanced.*

The room is blurry and you can't focus, as if your eyes were coated with Vaseline. They put you down in a bed. *The hospital? Your home?* It's cool. You hear your parents' voices, but the lights are so low. A week you stay here, two? Fever out of control, infection leaking into your spinal cord, your brain, your DNA. Eating at you like a colony of black ants, spreading and multiplying until the waves wash over you. There is a breath, a halting comma as you reach, you remember a ballet class when you were little and the teacher told you your pirouette was better than anyone else's. She made you show the class again and again. Then you think of nothing. (It was the apple.)

99

From section 54 . . .

You don't follow Rashid, you stay at the house. Your exhaustion becomes psychedelic. The fake flowers that have been draped around the photograph of Rashid's grandfather seem to be glowing and pulsing. You try to control your breathing. The room is washed in strange colors—red walls, orange flowers, green saris. All the women have such beautiful clothes. You feel like a field mouse caught by peacocks. They wear sweeps of raw silk and embroidered cotton, sheer chiffon. Coral, violet, lime green, peach. The colors swirl in your head, the room is heavy with perfume. You close your eyes.

Amil takes you to a bedroom downstairs. "The funeral will go late," she says. "Sleep." Grateful, you lie down and fall into a deep, dreamless sleep. Later someone's shaking you—a voice is whispering for you to *wake up!* Rashid? Alouette? No. The feminine figure sits down on the edge of your bed and leans over you. It's Élan, Rashid's younger sister. You try to sit up, but she pushes you back and plants her mouth directly over yours. She kisses you softly on the mouth. Her lips taste faintly of burnt cinnamon. Your hand catches her thigh, firm underneath her dress.

Adrenaline is coursing through you. She nuzzles your erect nipples through your shirt. Her hands are kneading your skin, moving pieces of you. A thousand things are charging through your mind. Questions and sermons. Effluvium. You try not to think of the stern picture of Rashid's grandfather or if some Indian cultures mutilate women's clitorises, and you're pretty sure they do. Old Man Rashid was probably an all-time champion clitoris ripper. Lesbians probably got extra-special treatment.

Élan licks your lips like they were sticky with ice cream, her tongue is quick and pink. The two of you roll around, her hands under your skirt, her fingers slippery and wet. Time suspends as you twist the cotton sheets, sweating, laboring against one another. There are hips and thighs and breasts and sighs. You must've fallen asleep—because the next thing you know it's morning and someone is shaking you roughly and yelling. Élan's brothers and father are there shaking their fists and shouting in Hindi. Her father slaps her across the face, which is when you scramble out of bed and run down the hall.

There is more shouting and throwing. Her brother grabs a handful of your hair and shoves you and your belongings out the front door. Where the hell is Alouette? Outside, the brothers keep yelling at you. *"Lesbo! Kothi!"* they say and people are starting to stare. You grab your stuff and hurry quickly down the street before you end up in a bad mob scene with your clitoris ripped out.

You have no idea where Rashid is, so you wander around in a daze—the sky bright, your throat dry, and your head throbbing. You eventually sit down on the curb, under the shade of a fig tree, and try to get your bearings. You're trying to figure out how to get a taxi to the airport when one miraculously appears. A black-and-yellow cab comes screeching around the corner, but it doesn't see you sitting on the curb and runs right over you. It really, really hurts. Then you're dead.

There's commotion. It turns out the driver was the brother of a member of some anti-American watch group called Vastu, and that drags the United States government into the situation. They shut down Vastu, which starts local protests and political debate, and then Rashid's family tells everyone you were *a lesbian* who almost corrupted their daughter. Between the anti-Americans, the anti-lesbians, the armed forces, and the gender activists, your innocent one-week trip to India has ended with your face on the news nearly every night.

They even make two different Bollywood movies about you; in the first one you are the immoral houseguest of an unlucky rich Indian family, and because you are a lesbian, dead old Grandfather Rashid strikes you down in a gruesome curse—in which your fingernails melt, your eyes turn inward, and you become a sort of armadillo-monkey-looking thing. Then the Indian army celebrates and there's a party with dancing . . . it's a little hard to keep track of the plot.

The second movie is a response to the first. Indian lesbians have had enough with the social harassment, patriarchal domination, and people rioting against their very existence. So the first ever all-lesbian East Indian film crew makes a movie called *This Girl*, in which you are recast as a brave woman who refuses to acknowledge traditional gender roles, and you also have a very nice ass. Then there's dancing.

Social conservatives in India try to ban the second film, but in an unprecedented move the Indian censor board says the movie doesn't break any censorship laws, and just because lesbians made the film doesn't make it immoral. It's a small but huge step forward, and they hold a parade in your honor. You even eventually get your face put on an Indian stamp. It's only two rupees, but still.

100

From section 55 . . .

You go to Ireland on a ferry, and during the long trip over there's a storm. The water is black and churning, the boat pitches, catching eight-foot swells and crashing down *ker-pow!* in the white foamy surf. You get seasick. *Vomit, vomit, vomit,* and then no vomit, only retching. You cannot stay belowdecks, where the heaving is worse and your eyes have nothing to focus on. Above deck at least you can stare at the moon through the rain, the only stationary object on the sea.

Then fortune throws you a strange twist. You feel a warm hand press between your shoulder blades. The rain has passed over and you stand soggy against the rail. "Hey." A beautiful woman with a British accent hands you a cup of hot tea. She's tall and slender, awkward with her arms. "You looked like you could use this." She smiles and looks away, her short shaggy black hair falling over her dark eyes. She has a small mole above her lip. She fishes around in her pocket and produces a bottle of Dramamine. "We'll probably be off the boat before these kick in, but it can't hurt." Right then you feel like kissing her. Tasting that mole with your tongue.

You drink the tea and feel a little better. The two of you go inside, sit down in a booth in the cafeteria and talk. Her name is Christian and she's a jewelry designer. She's on her way to visit her grandparents. They're tomato farmers in Galway. They grow heirlooms and cherry and Jersey Devil and early girls. You love listening to her voice.

By the time the ship arrives at port it's late and the dock is deserted except for the disembarking passengers. Christian's grandparents have left her their red VW bug so she can drive herself to the farm. "They wouldn't mind me bringing someone home," she says, "that is, if you need a place to stay?"

Yes, of course you need a place to stay—especially if it's with her. On the way you talk. *You talk and talk and talk and talk.* It's like you've met your twin sister only she's better and different. She says after visiting her grandparents she's going to drive counterclockwise around Ireland all the way to Rosslare, where she'll take the car ferry to Le Havre and stitch her way across Europe.

By the time you get to her grandparents' small stone house you're exhausted. Her grandparents are already asleep. "We sleep in the barn," she says and takes you out back to a cozy little stone building that's been turned into a guest cottage. There's just one bed—it's queen-sized, but you tell her you don't mind sleeping on the floor. Christian laughs and strips down to her bra and underwear.

You sleep together. In bed you continue to talk and laugh and you try to sleep. Finally, around dawn, after being so careful not to touch you, Christian turns on her side and strokes your cheek. She leans in to kiss you. You feel a strange silver liquidity, a lighting bead of white-hot mercury that rockets around your head, your heart, and down to the soles of your feet. She's poised there, ready, waiting for you.

If you kiss Christian, go to section #158 (page 357).
If you push her away, go to section #159 (page 359).

101

From section 58 . . .

You do the movie and it's a runaway smash hit, partially due to the multiple risqué fetish scenes with bowling balls and house paint. On opening night reporters are clawing over you, large crowds of people press up against the police barricades, and at the after-party you're photographed drinking champagne out of Sir Elton John's diamond-studded platform boot.

The very next day glossy gossip starts about you. The tabloids say you're bulimic, you're a lesbian, you're sleeping with the director (which you were, but aren't now, so it shouldn't count), you have a rare blood disease that makes you so skinny. (You're skinny because of three hours of yoga a day, prescription amphetamines, no carbohydrates, and regular colon cleansing. You'd love a rare blood disease. A rare blood disease would be a gift from the Lord.)

Your publicist books you on morning talk shows and late-night comedy programs. You do a Sprite commercial and an AIDS benefit (where you learn Brazil offers free antiretroviral therapy *free* to all its citizens, which has saved the country an estimated $2.2 billion in hospital costs). You do another movie—and then another. You're everywhere. Your face is on billboards, television commercials, bus stops, magazines. People are sick of you. You are sick of you.

Fame hits hard. People recognize you in the grocery store, at Starbucks, on the street, everywhere. They mob you with bizarre comments and requests like *Will you sign my baby's stroller? Can you lend me a thousand dollars? What kind of underpants do you wear? I had a dream about you last night. I couldn't believe you had cellulite on your ass. I have cellulite on my ass too! Are those your real boobs? Is that your real nose? Maybe next time you should lose a little weight. Are you a bitch in real life? Are you a slut in real life? Do you fuck soap in real life? I love you like hell, bitch!*

It goes on until you can't go outside without a bodyguard. They call your kind of fame "celebrity by sudden death," because of its abruptness, its severity, and the deathlike effect it has on your real life. It's like losing who you were. Like throwing away your previous identity and being given a new one. Everything you were *now you aren't*. Everything you had *now is gone*. You don't belong to yourself anymore—you belong to your handlers, your agents, your publicists, your public. Everybody needs a piece.

The agency hires a man to be with you at all times. "The man" will pick you up at seven a.m. "The man" will get your breakfast. Only the man is never the same person twice, the man is an ever-changing man from the agency. The walls get higher and higher. You're slowly shut out from society for your own safety. (Especially since the series of death–rape fantasy letters you've gotten.) The things you thought you wanted—like attention and money and fame—you don't know if you want them at all.

Then fortune throws you a strange twist. On a rainy ferry to Catalina, where you're location scouting for your next film, you get seasick and sneak to the other end of the ferry, where you can throw up over the side in private. You feel a warm hand press between your shoulder blades. The rain has passed over and you stand soggy against the rail. "Hey." A beautiful woman with a British accent hands you a cup of hot tea. She's tall and slender, awkward with her arms. "You looked like you could use this." She smiles and looks away, her short shaggy black hair falling over her dark eyes. She has a small mole above her lip. She fishes around in her pocket and produces a bottle of Dramamine. "We'll probably be off the boat before these kick in, but it can't hurt." Right then you feel like kissing her. Tasting that mole with your tongue.

You drink the tea and feel a little better. The two of you go inside, sit down in a booth in the cafeteria and talk. Her name is Christian and she's a jewelry designer. She's just come back from her grandparents' farm, they're tomato farmers in Galway. They grow heirlooms and cherry and Jersey Devil and early girls. You love listening to Christian's voice. There's something about her that eases you—reminds you that you're a person, not a commodity. "Do you know who I am?" you ask her.

"No," she says. "Should I?" She doesn't know you're a "star" and that makes her all the more appealing. Soon enough she'll find out—and so you enjoy this moment of being normal again. When you get to port, it's late and you offer to let her stay with you in your hotel. She accepts. That night the two of you sleep in the same bed. You lie next to her, breathing, not touching—for hours.

You feel a strange silver liquidity next to her, a lightning bead of white-hot mercury that rockets around your head, your heart, the soles of your feet. Here is something strange. Delicate. She leans over and kisses you—gently, softly. She feels like heaven—she feels like home. You tell her how you feel trapped in your new life—how everything seems plastic. "Quit," she says. "Just walk away. We can travel together, get out of here. It's never too late to disappear." Then your publicist calls and tells you they're remaking a blockbuster version of *Wonder Woman* with Winona Ryder and Meryl Streep. This will take your career all the way to the top, make you a gajillionaire, but Christian says no. Don't take it—or she's leaving.

If you take the blockbuster, go to section #166 (page 372).
If you don't take the blockbuster, go to section #167 (page 374).

102

From section 58 . . .

You say no to the movie. *Pink* is industry speak for *porn*, that much you know. You tell them *you'll call them back later*, which of course you don't. Instead, you drive around LA a few more days, not doing much of anything, and then your racketing, wheezing car finally breaks down and strands you in some postapocalyptic ghetto where you have to give the rest of your money to a mechanic who looks like Pol Pot.

You're out of money and you have no place to go. Bus station? Homeless shelter? You finally drive back to your friends' house and ring the doorbell eighty billion times until you lose all patience and chuck a garden paving stone through the kitchen window. Desperate times call for desperate measures. You carefully crawl inside—where the smell hits you. Something is dreadfully wrong. The house is too quiet. Too hot. Something keeps you from shouting out their names.

Then you notice the garbage all over. An empty ice cream container, chicken bones strewn across the floor. Flies buzz around the sink over the garbage disposal and there's a thick coating of dust on the countertops. You hear a whimpering from down the hall (cold ice stomach, *dread dread dread*), you want to run, but you follow the whimpering sound to the master bedroom.

Lying on the floor, in a decimated state, is Hadley, their yellow Lab. He's panting, bloodshot eyes filmy, foam at the corners of his mouth. His ribs are concave, he looks nearly starved to death. He tries to wag his tail. "Hadley?" You wipe the foam from his mouth, the crust from his eyes. You bring a bowl of water and pour some into his mouth. *Where are they? What happened?*

Now you run through the house, turning on lights, flipping switches (activating the stereo and the television, cacophony filling the rooms). *"Sherri! Misha!"* She's a Midwestern blond from Waukegan, he's a sharp-eyed Russian exchange student from Kiev (always moody and irritated). You search through the house and find no one. Then you see the door to the basement ajar.

Downstairs the smell is worse. A deep rusty aroma like algae and blood clot. *Something is wrong.* Your heartbeat quickens, your hands sweat, your stomach turns over in a knot of nausea. Then you see her. Sherri is bent over the folding table, her legs splayed behind her and arms thrown forward. Motionless. You walk up and touch her shoulder. Cold. Then you see Misha five feet behind her, up against the dryer. You do not look directly at his face, most of which is gone. The shotgun is still clutched in his hand. You're no CSI expert, but it looks like a little murder-suicide action down here.

The entire staff at the Santa Monica emergency pet hospital is in shock at the sight of Hadley. "It's the neighbor's dog," you say. "They moved away and left him tied to the garage." They move into action. People in LA couldn't care less about fellow humans, but hurt an animal? Not tolerated. Hadley receives intravenous vitamins, aromatherapy, antibiotics, and a marine-enriched kelp wrap. He's placed in a hyperbaric chamber with Bach cello suites playing and a small twenty-four-hour television in the corner that airs CNN so he always hears a human voice. He's fed a blend of egg, olive oil, and chopped liver, given smoked jerk house chew toys, and sleeps on an oversized down feather pillow.

Sherri and Misha, however, remain dead in the laundry room. You're too terrified to tell anyone. What if they blame you? No one can prove that you knew they were down there. What if you just hadn't gone in the basement? That's the story you stick with—you found the dog, nothing else, not that anyone's asking you any questions because no one else has found them. You drive by their house every day and the house stays dark. Mail piles up outside the door.

Hadley makes a complete recovery. The nurses just give him back to you and look away. No charge. They'll cover expenses and the rest of their work they donated. You go one last time to Sherri and Misha's house. You dread it—but if you're going to make it back home you've got to store up on some supplies and find some cash to take with you. You figure you can climb in the back window and get all of Hadley's toys and his food. Maybe see if there's any electronics you can sell to get yourself back home. Home. What a beautiful idea.

Hadley waits in the car while you break in and load up two grocery bags full of stuff. You try to work quickly, try not to look at the basement door, still slightly ajar. Just as you are climbing back out the window, the police pull up. A neighbor apparently saw "a suspicious character" lurking around the backside of her neighbor's house.

They take you to the station, where you learn you're the prime suspect in Sherri and Misha's murders. "Your prints are all over the house!" the detective yells. "We found traces of the woman's blood on your sleeve and you had their dog in your car. What are we supposed to think?"

They question you. *Were you having an affair with either of them? Were you addicted to meth, like they were? Did you know anything about the lab in the basement? Did you know there were ten eight-balls of meth in one of Hadley's dog toys? No? We don't believe you. How much did you sell before you were apprehended? Why did you kill them?* Insanity seeps across your life like green poison.

One ridiculous baffling event links to the next. Jail. Lawyers. Testimonies. Questioning. Courtroom. Sentencing. They can't pin the murders on you (not enough physical evidence), but they can give you ten years for drug possession and attempt to distribute an illegal substance. Your parents spend all their money to no avail on lawyers who talk talk talk and full-fare airplane tickets that delay delay delay and congressmen who do *nothing nothing nothing*.

Prison is about killing days. One day murdered after the last. The maximum-security detention center has high, vaulted ceilings with no windows, no ductwork, no wires, no moving air of any kind. Where the oxygen comes from you can't imagine. It's all air-locked, vapor-locked, airtight, vacuum-packed, and sealed off from the rest of the world. The walls are painted a thick muddy beige that remains a constant, unchanging sickish color under the unblinking fluorescent lights. There are no shadows.

You sit in your cell, day after day, and do nothing. Eventually the Women Who Help Underprivileged Prisoners Start Over (WHUPSO) program provides you with a sketch pad and charcoal pencils. You doodle. You draw and sketch and eventually you start a little informal art class for the other women, nothing much at first, just crafts really until you break down and ask your parents to send art supplies.

Your parents send a monthly supply of brushes and canvas and art history books. (No sharp objects. You have to sculpt with soft soap and clay—no wood or metal allowed.) They even send oil paints, but the canvases the women produce aren't very good, they're all twiggy and rough and mostly primary colors. You couldn't get any of them to blend or feather. You don't understand most of the artwork; one painting is just a black canvas with printed white letters that reads: I ALREADY GOT ONE ASSHOLE IN MY PANTS WHY DO I WANT TWO? All the women vote it best painting in the class.

Halfway through your sentence you develop a staph infection. A simple cut on your leg you got on KP duty while cleaning out one of the enormous industrial-sized stainless-steel pots. You think it's just a little cut that won't heal. It's even cut in the shape of a heart—a pretty little mistake. You like it. But it doesn't close, and it gets pussy at the edges. It goes untreated for too long and you develop a fever they can't bring down. Your brain swells and before you can be transferred to the hospital, you die in the infirmary. Your last thought is of trees, and why didn't you get to see more of them.

You go to heaven, which is a big ugly factory, with dirty chicken-wire windows and dusty wide-plank floors. In among the machinery the angels go, pulling levers and oiling springs, constantly tending to the great grinding machine, which takes up almost the entire building.

The machine generates the fates of all human beings. "It's run by the twins," a smudgy-faced angel tells you and points to two small children high atop the lottery machine. The angel is missing a tooth and you're thinking, *What kind of heaven doesn't have dental care?* He says their names are Chance and Catastrophe. Their heads are tilted together. "I guess I don't have to tell you which twin came up with your last life," he says, grinning. "We all had fun watching that one."

103

From section 59 . . .

You decide to keep the baby and seven nauseous, exhausting months later baby Elizabeth is born. Dark brown eyes, long eyelashes. A dream caught. You live in an apartment complex called the Sheltering Arms, with at least twenty other single moms, many of whom are on welfare and struggle to make rent. You're looking down at the courtyard early one morning, exhausted after another night of trying to get Elizabeth to nurse, and all the mothers are trying to get their little ones off to (expensive) day cares, so they can go to work. It occurs to you you're all in the same poorly built boat.

You are all poor, you all spend a lot of money on day care, health care, and food, you all have to work constantly to make ends meet—and none of you has time alone. Ever. If you were to combine forces, pool resources, and share expenses, everything would be a lot cheaper. A *lot* cheaper. Everyone works different hours, there's always at least one mother at the Sheltering Arms, why couldn't you have your own day care here? A system where everyone takes turns watching the kids?

You get all the women together and pitch the idea. After some initial questions and concerns, they begin to realize *they love the idea*. It eliminates them having to pay for day care and keeps their kids home. If you all rotated making industrial-sized dinners, enough for everybody, you'd only cook *one dinner a week*. The more they talk, the more talents they find in the group. One woman is a nurse, another is a part-time mechanic. One is a cashier at Safeway and gets a discount in the grocery *and* the pharmacy.

You implement an elaborate plan. You pick a different apartment every day where all the kids go for day care. Then you all put money in a pot and go to the grocery store, where you buy enough food for fifty people. You divvy it all up and everyone has a different night when they host dinner for fifty (everyone brings their own plates and silverware). Every Sunday you take inventory of supplies left over, supplies needed, and you head out and do it all over again.

Besides cutting your expenses *in half*, the support you get from all these amazing women is overwhelming—and it's more than financial. It's emotional, physical, and spiritual. It works better than any government program—and better than most families. You invent your own family—and you also invent the Ten Commandments for Single Mothers:

1. THOU SHALT allow your children to have impractical pets like gerbils or iguanas. Indulge them—*they only have one parent.*
2. THOU SHALT not bash your evil adulterous husband in front of them, lest they grow up to hate him too—which, when you think about it, would be heartbreaking.
3. THOU SHALT love thy children with all thy heart, even when they are wee monsters capable of amazing atrocities, like jamming peanut butter sandwiches in the VCR.
4. THOU SHALT not be afraid to ask for help, even from the cable guy, when you can't get a jar of pickles open, because no one's going to know how to help you unless you tell them how.
5. THOU SHALT learn to laugh at spilt milk and crayons jammed up noses. Thou must.
6. THOU SHALT believe there is life beyond the Sheltering Arms, and that you will not be poor forever. There's always the lottery.
7. THOU SHALT love this short time with your kids. Even though it seems like an eternity, they'll be gone soon and you'll be lucky to get a phone call.
8. THOU SHALT realize this is a sucky deal, and it's really hard, and thou shalt not beat thine self up.
9. THOU SHALT remember yourself. Always.
10. THOU SHALT remember you are never, ever alone. (And Catholic Charities will still adopt them, even when they're in middle school.)

One day your neighbor invites you to visit her cousin, Luis, in San Diego with her. Well, you and Elizabeth are always up for a road trip, so you pack up an overnight bag, get Elizabeth's favorite toys, and drive south.

It turns out Alana's cousin is a total dreamboat. Luis is tall and tan and handsome. His hands are muscular and lean, his arms veined, and the more you look at him, the more you blush. You all have beer and fish tacos at a crowded restaurant in Ocean Beach. Elizabeth even flirts with Luis, grabs at his hands and smiles big when he tickles her. When it's time to drive home Elizabeth cries and doesn't want to get in the car. Luis says he has this affect on all women and you punch him in the arm.

A week later he calls you and asks you to visit him again. You do. This time you leave Elizabeth with the girls and the two of you go out on an actual real-life date. He takes you to an Italian restaurant in the Gaslamp Quarter and then to the beach, where you watch night surfers drop themselves over and over again into the water, wet suits shining like black sealskin. The seals make you think of how badly you still want to travel—you wish you could become one of them and shoot out across the ocean.

That night, Luis massages the curve of your waist. You've already made love three times, and he's coming in for more. You kiss him and press hip to hip, pelvis to pelvis. You're nearly raw from all the friction but you still can't get enough. It's like you want to get inside him—inside his rib cage, where you can ride around in your own bone cage, safe from the outside world. You visit Luis again and again, until you know the stretch of highway between your houses by heart. The driving and schedule change is disruptive, but the sex is amazing. On the plus side both you and Elizabeth love him. On the down side he's been married once before and his wife left him because "he drinks a little too much." But you know nobody's perfect. After about six months of dating, Luis asks you to move in with him.

If you move in with Luis, go to section #168 (page 375).
If you don't, go to section #169 (page 377).

104

From section 59 . . .

The nurses have set up blue sheets all around your stomach during the delivery so you can't even see the baby as it's pulled out of you. They hurry her out of the room lest some latent and unsuspected maternal instinct rear its ugly head and you spring across the room like a girl warrior and grab your baby back. (It's happened more than once.)

Afterward you hear the nurses talking when you're supposed to be too groggy on anesthesia to hear them. "You can always tell the ones who are giving theirs away," one says. "They never want to see the baby." But you did want to see the baby. You did. When they talk to you they keep their banter light and breezy. No one mentions the baby. *Did you see the sunset last night? I swear, we must be the luckiest people in the world living right here in paradise.*

The baby is taken by Catholic Charities to the adoptive parents, who you declined to meet (*Ed and Laura somebody*). That's all you had to hear, *Ed and Laura*, and you knew they'd be the overly attentive, spoiling, self-sacrificing parents you could never be. You've already signed papers, and when you're released from the hospital—it's over.

After the birth you don't sleep well. Maybe your body is prepared for the late nights with a newborn, even though there's no newborn in the house. You wake in the middle of the night, sweating, nervous, sure you forgot something. Then you get drowsy during the day, it doesn't matter what you're doing, you could be eating a sandwich or talking on the phone or water skiing and your head starts to nod. Your circadian rhythm is upside down—you're alert at three a.m. and dead asleep at three p.m.

When you manage to stay awake, you punish yourself in elaborate and expensive ways. You let yourself gain weight, you drink, you watch reality TV with cultlike dedication, you stop bathing and cutting your hair, you make yourself as ugly on the outside as you are on the inside.

Catholic Charities helps you find a job—they place you in a small brokerage firm as a temporary receptionist. The work is mind numbing, all you do is answer phones, write messages, put a short list of clients through to the brokers and tell everyone else no one is available. The messages you take make no sense. *Sell COII at 32 . . . Margin Call! . . . NIKKEI good idea? . . . Buy 500 APPL at close. . . .* It's all Greek. Hieroglyphics. The only interesting calls come from the head broker's wife (soon to be ex-wife), who leaves messages like *Could you stop by the store after work and pick up milk, and, oh, I don't know . . . maybe a fucking sense of humor?*

Every day you feel like you're stuck in a running loop of one of the most boring days of your life. Eventually there's really nothing left to do but try and decipher what some of these strange phone messages you take down actually mean. You start online at nasdaq.com, where you are introduced to the strange world of investing. All these little letters stand for companies. And the numbers beside them are what a piece of that company costs. You buy *Investing for Idiots*, and as far as you can figure, investing in the stock market is just like gambling. You put some money down and hope you get some back.

You open an online account, take a hundred dollars from your paycheck, and roll up your sleeves. But which companies to buy? You buy penny stocks. Nothing over five bucks a share. You put in a hundred dollars every paycheck. You watch that little blue screen now as intently as the brokers do. You pay attention to the messages that cross your desk and you siphon off information meant for paying clients.

Then a message comes that makes you listen. It's an inside tip from one of their New York analysts who calls and assumes you can't translate his broker mumbo jumbo. "Just tell him Mount Sinai gave the green light," the analyst says. "Dave at the FDA called me. The press release hits Monday and it's called *Thermalink*. You got that? *Thermalink*. One-dollar-thirty a share, and it'll hit three hundred at least on the IPO. Nobody's watching it right now, just us."

What the message means is that if you put all your checking and savings and your entire portfolio on Thermalink and it does in fact go from a *dollar to three hundred dollars* in one week, you'll be rich. A three-hundred-percent return. If it doesn't go to three hundred, if it tanks—you'll lose everything. Either way—you have to act immediately.

If you invest in Thermalink, go to section #170 (page 380).
If you don't invest, go to section #171 (page 384).

105

From section 60 . . .

You agree to go with the man in the Windbreaker, if only to prove him wrong. He says his name is Dave, and he's an "exit counselor." He promises that all he wants is for you to talk with your parents, and after you do you can leave anytime. He drives you home in silence; the radio is on (which you haven't heard in months), and the radio man says there's a storm coming.

Your parents are waiting at the house. Your mom sits in the living room dabbing her eyes with a wadded-up tissue. She looks pale. You want to go to her and tell her everything's all right, but Dave keeps right on talking. He tells you this is *an intervention* and your family has gone to great trouble and *expense* to have everybody here. Message: shut up and listen.

He asks you questions like *Do you enjoy living in the VowGuardian house?* and *Do you ever get to leave the VowGuardian house?*, and at first it's easy to answer him, but he has this annoying habit of starting every single solitary sentence with, *"Yes, but . . . ,"* like, *"Yes, but do you know exactly where your money went?"* and *"Yes, but do you know exactly what Guy Moffat has been charged with in the past?"* For every one of your answers, he has another question. It's tiring. Exhausting.

He asks you to think through the reasons why you became involved in the organization, and whether or not there were sound reasons for doing so without having made a full investigation of the group. "I like it there," you say. "They like me."

"Yes, but *why* do they like you?"

He's irritating. Then vexing. Anxiety-making. You have a headache. Dave shows you a videotape. It's the testimony from several "ex–cult members" who said they thought they had found the perfect community until they realized they were being manipulated to obey the orders of a cult called *the VowGuardians*. Ubermensch misogynist clergy. Sex club for Bible crazies.

You start to listen.

After three days of arguing, you decide that it would be a good idea to stay at home with your parents for a while, just to sort things out. You call Father White while Dave and your parents are in the other room and tell him you'd like to stay at home for a while. "Okay," Father White says. "I totally understand. I'm not happy—but you have to do what you have to do—but you really should come get your stuff," he says. "You know—your special Bible and your things."

"Okay, Father. I'll do that."

You tell Dave and your parents that you'll stay home for a while and they seem really relieved. Dave gives you his "hotline cell" number, which he says he monitors twenty-four hours a day. What a freak. "Thank you," you tell him, giving him a hug as he goes. You sneak out of the house later that night and go over to the VowGuardian house so you can get your stuff and say good-bye. It's the least you can do.

When you first walk back into the VowGuardian house, it looks different than you remember. Smaller. Sparse. No phone, no television, no radio. You never noticed how weird that was before. It sort of went along with what Dave had warned you about—that they cut off contact with the outside world so they can control you. And those small food portions—Dave says they use hunger and sleep deprivation as a mind-control tactic. Maybe he was on to something.

Then Summer appears in the dark living room. You get a sexual jolt just at the sight of him. *So handsome.* But he looks angry. Irritated. What's the matter? What's wrong? He doesn't say hello. He doesn't say anything. He just motions for you to follow him, and you do. *Where is everybody?* you ask.

"Asleep," he says. Odd. You thought Father White wanted you to say good-bye.

The two of you go down in the basement, down the creaking stairs to where the prayer rooms are. You're turning the corner and Summer has disappeared. The prayer rooms seem really creepy. Small. *Crack!* Summer has hit you with something, he's on top of you, shoving you onto the ground, punching. *Is he joking?* Your head is wet and throbbing, you push him to get off you, but you can't. The lights are going down. *What are you doing?* But he's not answering—he's fumbling with his belt buckle and angrily pushing your legs apart.

When you wake up again, you're in the backyard between the box elders and the picnic table. Your hair is matted, dried. There's a pain—where? Your thighs, your legs, between your legs. You stumble up . . . how long have you been there? You stumble home. Should you tell anybody? You can't. You think you deserved it. You got yourself into this mess, and this is the cost for getting out. They'll leave you alone now.

A month passes and you feel *funny.* You take a drugstore pregnancy test and *of course.* You're pregnant. If you tell your parents about this, they'll probably tie you to the bed and make you have the baby—but maybe you *want* to have the baby. The baby didn't ask to be made this way. People say having babies changes their lives. Gives them hope they never expected . . . still, Summer would be the father. You'd always have that hanging over your (and the baby's) head.

If you get an abortion, go to section #172 (page 387).
If you do not get an abortion, go to section #173 (page 391).

106

From section 60 . . .

You are not getting into a *van* with strangers. Nothing good ever happened in a van. Why do they even make vans? So pedophiles and exit counselors can have private workshops? You start shouting at her, *screaming* as loud as you can. People come from all over to see what's the matter, and the girl darts away. The man in the Windbreaker slithers into the white van and leaves. You never see him again.

You return to the VowGuardian house. Time passes. Years. Decades. Your life is as routine as a train schedule, you do not make any decisions for yourself, you do not have any money, you don't even remember your old address. Father White moves away to another house, and is replaced by Father Blue, who likes rough anal sex and is no joy to pray with—try as hard as you do to like it. You are almost forty-five when Guy Moffatt is accused of having group sex with minors and operating ice cream trucks that were delivering kiddie porn to the suburbs in over seven cities. After a year of litigation the VowGuardian organization goes bankrupt. The house loses its subsidy and its support. Father Blue disappears. You try to stay in the house anyway with the others, try to get a job, but things fall apart.

You come home one frigid afternoon, your bare hands chapped, your nose running, and find the front door boarded and displaying a pink *intent to foreclose* notice. The windows have two-by-fours nailed across them and there's a stoic cop sitting in his cruiser right in front of the house. He's bored, drinking coffee. A few members of the house are scattered on the snow-crusted lawn, confused, whispering, wandering around with personal possessions like refugees.

"They came and locked up the house. Kicked us out," someone says. "We couldn't take anything with us. It all goes to the bank."

After a time people start to drift away—someone says they're going to their sister's house, another says they have a friend uptown—and nobody has seen Summer. He's gone. Alone for the first time, you don't know what to do. At a pay phone you call your parents collect. The line is disconnected. You call your overbearing Christian aunt up north and she tells you that your parents are ten years dead in their graves and it was you who put them there. Then she hangs up.

You walk downtown. It's winter, freezing. You walk all day, to the edge of town and back. Where are you going? There's nowhere to go. Head down, you cross the river and look at the swirling dark water. Everything looks wrong, the air tastes strange. Your head aches, you can feel your heartbeat in your temples. Along the riverbank the bare trees scratch the air with their nude black fingers.

You sit at the river's edge, watching the water rush by, trying to catch your thoughts as they tumble together and your heart *beats beats beats* in your throbbing head. If you could only get your head around something, something you've forgotten, like an important errand, a name, a significant date. You'll lie down. Sleep. Then you'll make a fire. Go back to the house and see who else is there. You fall asleep down by the river, sheets of ice blow against your back. The chalk-white river runs. You do not wake up.

107

From section 61 . . .

You take the scholarship and everything gets better. At your new school you begin a series of paintings depicting housewives murdering their husbands. The women in your paintings are in classical poses that mimic religious Renaissance scenes. The backgrounds are ornate with thick damask tapestries and pink-cheeked cherubs. These wives show no anxiety as they kill. They are put-together ladies, well coiffed and serene, not a hair out of place as they hit their husbands over the head with steel skillets, push them down cellar stairs, cut them in half with garage doors, poison their lamb roast, drop plugged-in toasters into their showers, etc., etc.

It seems every woman in Manhattan must secretly want to kill her husband. The large oil paintings sell quickly and people rush to put their names on a growing waiting list. You have several shows, win several awards, and are interviewed by *The New Yorker*, the *Times*, and *People* magazine.

At one of your receptions you meet a dashing Southern gentleman named Thompat Beene, a collector and a talented artist himself. He's got a mess of honey-colored hair and cute little dimples that make him look like an eternally naughty little boy. Somebody who won't be too gentle with you. The two of you start dating, and as you settle into the bliss of regular affection, deep conversations, lingering dinners, and phenomenal oral sex, your paintings begin to change. The women don't come across as happy anymore as they kill. They suddenly seem anxious, as though they're a bit unsure about killing their men. Worried. The murders aren't so creative. Not as violent.

People notice. They ask where the strength went. Where the power went. Your gallery director asks that you at least create some of the original series to feed the long line of people waiting, but you can't. Thompat makes you too happy—you can't find the original anger, the source point. It's gone.

Your solo shows dry up—the people waiting for paintings return them when they arrive. Thompat's work, on the other hand, starts getting serious attention. His work seems to be improving, getting more abstract and bold. A gallery picks him up and offers him his first solo show. Your relationship seems to be having opposite affects on the two of you—your work is weakening while his is strengthening, but the two of you are in love, the companionship and sex are harmonic. Then one day Thompat gets down on one knee, with a wet paintbrush in his mouth, and asks you to marry him. Is your dry spell his fault, your fault, or no one's fault? If you say yes, will you be sorry? If you say no—will you be sorrier?

If you marry Thompat, go to section #174 (page 393).
If you don't marry Thompat, go to section #175 (page 396).

108

From section 61 . . .

You pack up all your earthly belongings and move to a little cottage overlooking a steep green valley in Port Antonio, Jamaica. The house is small but has a wraparound porch and a crow's nest from which you can see beyond the valley right into the eye of the peacock-blue ocean. On the other side you can make out the city itself, which thrums with street life night and day. The open-air markets sell Maylay apples and avocado pears, pawpaw and custard, star apple, sweet sop, sour sop, shrimp curries and callaloo, baby diapers and Bibles, imported sneakers and live chickens, French lipsticks and pirated movies, used books and fresh bamboo, guava juice and Jamaica's own Appleton Rum.

The city is almost devoid of tourists. It's hard to get to—a day's drive on nearly decimated roads from Kingston or Montego Bay, and the harbor of Port Antonio is too shallow for cruise ships to dock. The harbor will always be shallow because of regional geology—to dynamite it deeper would crack bedrock and make fault lines splinter up through the mainland. Port Antonions don't see a lot of people from outside the country, and they don't particularly want to.

They're friendly with you (the woman who sells jackfruit rum at the end of your road calls you *Angel Love*), but they're wary. Outsiders interrupt the rhythm of Jamaica, the flow of even the smallest transaction. It's hard for you to follow the Jamaican accent, and when they speak patois you can't understand them at all. Ray loves his new job at the Port Antonio hospital. He's not making that much money—not compared to what he'd make in the States—but as he points out, how many hospitals have a snorkeling club and fresh mango sold in the lobby? Ray is at the beach nearly every day after work; he's developed a cadre of local friends, guys who play dice and give Ray constant crap about his paper-white skin. Ray loves it. You just wish he'd lay off the ganja a little.

About six months later, you find out you're pregnant. You're happy about it—you think. Ray proposes to you and you have a ceremony on the beach at sunset, with all your family and Jamaican friends in attendance. Life is just heaven for a while. You get the nursery ready for the baby, you read prenatal health care books. (You pledge to never use crystal meth again. It would eat your baby's *brain*.) You assure your mother over and over and over on the phone that yes, you're safe and no, you're not moving home.

You have this glorious vision for the baby, she'll get to grow up in this beautiful house, on the gorgeous mountaintop. You can paint and she can play in the crystal-clear stream, swim in the ice-blue ocean, eat fresh mango and papaya every day of the year. She'll have the most amazing childhood ever. Then baby Alison is born, a sweet blond baby with chubby cheeks and teeny tiny fingers and toes. She's so precious that even though you're exhausted, endorphins flood your body when you look at her and you're on a permanent rosy high.

Then the bad luck wakes up. Your parents die in an automobile crash and you have to fly home with little Alison for the funeral. She'll never really know her grandparents. Then Ray loses his job. He fails a drug screening test—tests positive for marijuana—and you scream at him, *how could he be so stupid?* Then hurricane Betty hits, and high winds thunder across the valley, howling onto your mountaintop, leaving your house, along with all the houses of your neighbors, ripped to tattered shreds. The old lady at the guava stand says, *"God neva pramise wi a bed a roses, im neva tell any baddy dat life ould bi smoode."* It's an old Jamaican proverb. God never promised you a bed of roses, he never said life would be smooth.

Insurance only covers half the rebuilding costs, which you don't realize until the house is half rebuilt. You cling like grim death to your vision. Alison deserves this mountaintop cottage—not a rented apartment in the city. You have to use all your savings, your 401(k) plans, your portfolio—everything you had leaks out to cover costs. Ray can't get a job anywhere except at an STD clinic, which is damned popular but pays about as much as if he were working at Arby's. Checking out in Jamaica is fun, being down and out in Jamaica is not.

You go back to work as soon as you can, assisting a pharmacist in the city. There you fill prescriptions and count out pills. *Drugs drugs drugs.* They're on your mind a lot lately. You've been getting cravings again. You're always so tired and Alison is learning to walk, shuttling and lurching herself across the house night and day, and you're thinking a bump of meth would let you keep up with her.

Times are getting tougher. You and Ray just can't make the bills and Alison has developed an asthmatic condition that requires an expensive medication. You can't even afford to move back to America—and even if you could, you'd be in the same exact position, minus the airfare home, which you can't afford anyway.

That's when you realize you've never seen meth being sold on the island. Jamaica is more of a marijuana and mushroom place, not a cocaine and crystal meth place. *But it could be.* You remember how to make crystal meth, you work at a pharmacy, and if you produced it on a small scale, for just a little while, you could make enough money to get back home. Maybe even invest a little, get a leg up—for Alison's sake.

If you make the drugs, go to section #160 (page 360).
If you don't make the drugs, go to section #161 (page 362).

109

From section 62 . . .

Luis is waiting for you at the San Diego International Airport with a bouquet of white daisies and a shy smile. A thousand thoughts are running through your head. *Are you crazy for coming? Does he look happy or sad? Will it be the same this time? Will it be different?* You stay in a nearby hotel, which he pays for. He takes you out on some lovely dates. He takes you for sushi in the Gaslamp Quarter, for banana splits at Ghirardelli, to the Maritime Museum, to the zoo. Along the boardwalk Luis tells you one of the reasons he has trouble with processing the world is that he's dyslexic, which exhausts him.

"It's like I'm always in a foreign country," he says. "Like decoding and switching back letters and numbers to a language no one else speaks." He says this is why he is tired all the time. Why he needs a solid six hours to himself every day.

When you kiss him, he tastes like sunshine and sleep. At night, as he rolls over in bed, his wide hand comes down on the curve of your waist. You have made love three times, and he's coming in for another. No wondering if he likes you now. You kiss him deeply, roll underneath and press up against him. Hip to hip, pelvis to pelvis. Your vagina is rubbed nearly raw from the friction but you can't get enough. It's like you want to get inside him—inside his rib cage, where you can ride around in your own bone cage, safe from the outside world.

Now that you understand the dyslexia, and know how to watch for the signs, you can read him like a parking meter that expires constantly. He needs to eat four times a day, without fail, without delay. If he doesn't, that clouded look comes back, part confusion, part anger, and he pulls tighter and tighter into himself, the way a turtle does when he's hiding.

He wants you to live with him. To make a life with him. He shows you places where you could get your hair and nails done. He shows you where the supermarket is and the gym and even a yoga studio. He takes you to the beach and gets down on one knee. "Will you move in with me?" he asks. His face is full of love. Still—is this the real him, or was the other him the real him? Will he be this way or that way? Light or dark? How can you know?

If you move in with Luis, go to section #176 (page 398).
If you take the radio internship, go to section #177 (page 401).

110

From section 63 . . .

You agree to his terms because stupidity and crazy-rapist potential aside, it's kind of sexy. Harrington says he'll be there around midnight—he warns you to be *perfectly ready* by then. "No lights," he says. "If I see one light on, I take out the paddle. If you do anything I haven't told you to do, you're going to get seriously sorted out." His voice thrills and frightens you. Whatever is about to happen is going to be big.

At eleven o'clock you get out of your milk-and-ylang-ylang bath and put on a black silk slip. *What are the odds he's insane? A killer?* (He's definitely a killer, how could he not be a killer? This is exactly how killers talk.) What if he slices you up and no one knows? No one *would* know. You call down to the front desk and ask for an early wake-up call. At least if you're dead they'll find you before the noon maids come, before your body is bloated and . . . well, you just tell the front desk to *make sure* you're up. If you don't pick up the phone, they'll send someone knocking. Great security plan.

You get ready. You draw the shades, turn out the lights, and tie a white silk scarf loosely over your eyes. You lie down for twenty minutes before you realize you forgot to unlock the door! You bolt out of bed, unlock the door, and scramble back. Your heart is beating, your hands are sweaty. This is ridiculous. This is the single most stupid thing you've ever done in your life. If you're killed, you deserve it.

Midnight comes—midnight goes. He's making you wait. The last time you checked the clock it was three forty a.m., and the next thing you realize is someone is shaking you roughly. You sit bolt upright and fight him off—only it isn't him! It's the maid, who's afraid you're dead because there's a white scarf around your head.

So the duplicitous asshole didn't even come. You check for semen, blood. Nothing. He doesn't answer his cell phone, and he doesn't call. What the hell? Should you go track this guy down? Is this part of the game? Is he waiting for your move so he can plot his? He probably isn't a killer; a killer would have taken advantage of the situation—he at least would have shown up. Maybe what Harrington wants you to do is act a little naughty, give him a reason to give you a spanking.

If you take a cab to Harrington's house, go to section #178 (page 404).

If you return to the States immediately, go to section #179 (page 409).

111

From section 63 . . .

You tell the deep voice on the phone that while his suggestion is sexy and everything, it's also incredibly unsafe and idiotic. He laughs—and asks if you'll
meet him in the lobby and go out for dinner instead. (You're relieved when he
laughs. It sounds like he knows it would've been stupid.) You agree to meet
him that night.

You take your time getting ready—lots of bergamot-lemon lotion and rose-
water perfume. You're downstairs early, waiting while perched on an uncomfortable sixteenth-century wingback chair. You're trying to look pretty as a
postcard, your legs crossed and your expression sultry yet innocent yet knowing all at once. Nobody pays you any attention. People come and go through
the revolving door. You imagine any of them could be Harrington, you imagine having sex with each one of them . . . the fat bulgy businessman, the bald
grandpa, the stylish gay teenager. . . .

Then you see him. You recognize him instantly. He's a big man, six feet
four, with wide shoulders and a mop of messy tousled hair. You jump up
and grin. "So you're the madman?" you ask. He's absolutely gorgeous—
adorable— and your mouth goes dry.

"The very same," he says and gives you a big warm hug. He takes your arm
and guides you down the crowded street to a small curry house nearby.

It's warm and cheerful in the restaurant with red paper lanterns and low yellow candles. Over coconut soup and peanut-chicken satay you study his face.
His features are stately but somewhat ominous, like a blue mountain range.
His wide forehead, his pronounced nose, everything about him is absolute.
Without question. He's the alpha male for all the other alpha males. You feel
safe and protected with him, as though you somehow know he'll take care of
everything.

He tells you about his travels. About the time he ate fugu, a poisonous Japanese blowfish, about the time he white-water rafted the Bio Bio in Patagonia, about the time he was bitten by a mako shark off Stewart Island. He likes remote places like Bali and Indonesia—he's always wanted a beautiful eloquent travel mate, he says, a woman just like you. After dinner he takes your hand as you walk down the street, and he's so big and strong you feel like a little girl. You walk down twisting cobblestone streets and something is so familiar about it, like you know him already, you know this already, you've been taking this walk together forever.

He takes you to a trendy little bar with printed aluminum ceilings and thick alabaster lamps. "I'm glad you didn't let me ravage you," he says. "That was a test. The unwise abound in this small, dirty world. One must sort them out."

After some more pinot grigio and nuzzling it's time to go home. You don't let him come up—instead you just kiss him good night in the lobby. (Even though you'd like him to come upstairs, you remember his "tramp test" from before, and so you leave it at good night, your lips tingling, your face flush from where his whiskers brushed against you.)

The days that follow are a blur. You spend all your time with Harrington, who plans everything, arranges everything, and at his insistence, pays for everything. You end up canceling your plane ticket home and you move (temporarily!) into his flat on Manor Road. It's a cold two-story condominium with blue glass, brushed aluminum furniture, and every kind of electronic gadget you can think of (flat-screen TVs, stereos, surround-sound systems, intercoms, security alarms . . .).

His bed is a simple cherry platform, and when he puts you in it the first time, he takes off your clothes and slowly strokes your bare stomach. You bite your lip with fear, delight, anticipation. Then he takes out the most massive cock you have ever seen—it's more like two ugly, enormous cocks fused into one. He alternates making love to you gently and then roughly. Whatever he does, he's in full control. He has pet names for you. He calls you his *princess* and his *turtle*. He calls you *peanut* and *tickmouse* and *daisy* and *dove*. At night you cook for him, although to cook for Harrington is to undertake a surgery—he likes everything just so.

Your father calls, telling you it's fine you're over there in England doing *whatever it is you're doing*, but now it's time to come home. There's an internship at the radio station he can get you, if you come home *now*. When you tell Harrington about it, he thinks that's ridiculous. "Why would you go back to mediocrity when you can stay here?" He asks you to move in with him permanently.

If you move in with Harrington, go to section #180 (page 410).
If you go home, go to section #181 (page 414).

112

From section 64 . . .

You go to Rocky's. Poor or rich, some people feel like home. Who knows why. Your heart, your hands, your skin, everything wakes up, hums and vibrates when they're near. Rocky is your somebody. Money can't buy that. His smile makes your edges dissolve, makes things clear and bright. On the down side, he lives all the way out in Brighton Beach. Dissolving edges or not, the cab fare is murder.

Nobody calls it Brighton Beach though—they call it *Little Odessa* because everybody comes from that region in Russia near the Black Sea. Everything in Little Odessa is Russian, even the street signs. You can buy borscht and samovars more easily than a ham sandwich, and speaking English will only get you raised eyebrows and whispers. It's like stepping into another country right in the middle of New York.

You like to walk there, through the spiced air and arguing streets. Nobody bothers you, and even if they did, you couldn't understand them anyway. You don't speak Russian, and there's a certain space provided by people after they figure out you have no idea what they're saying. You drift through the streets almost invisibly, Little Odessa rushes around you.

When your lease is up you move in with Rocky, quit the stupid art school, which is full of pretentious losers anyway, and transfer to a small community college. You start teaching art history to a brigade of Russian immigrants, passionate, argumentative know-it-all World War II historians who often throw chalk. Between classes and making a home with Rocky you hardly go into the city anymore. You can get everything you need right there or elsewhere in Brooklyn or even Coney Island. Downtown Manhattan seems as far away as Egypt now.

Years pass. You continue teaching and Rocky opens a corner bar he refuses to name, because it's bad luck. He just calls it "My Bar" and so does everyone else.

He's known for his infused vodkas, a refined potato alcohol steeped with basil, pepper, or persimmon. He spends all his time there with his Moscow buddies gathered around drinking vodka, eating onions, and arguing the merits of communism (apparently there are plenty). You're happy he's happy—but you hardly ever see Rocky anymore. Sometimes he's home when you wake up, but then he leaves early and he's gone all day picking up supplies and doing paperwork. Then he comes home late at night, or rather early in the morning, and creeps into bed with you quietly so he won't wake you up. You never make love anymore.

You would be rock-bottom soul-lonely except for Sergei, the Russian across the hall. Sergei is a big man who lumbers around with furrowed eyebrows and a deep frown. He was a renowned chess player in Russia once—he keeps his dusty awards and trophies up on cobwebby shelves, along with faded yellow photographs of him with Russian diplomats and celebrities. He smiles in the photographs and he's hardly himself. He's missing.

He invites you into his scrapbook of an apartment almost every night for cherry kirsch and boiled pears. He teaches you how to play chess and he puts his favorite vinyl Russian operas on the old wind-up Victrola that was once his mother's. The two of you philosophize on atypical class structures and the decline of Western civilization. You play solitaire sitting next to each other and watch *Jeopardy!* Rocky hardly even knows you two are friends, he's not around enough to notice.

Like everyone else in Little Odessa, Sergei knows everything about everything, including you. "You want affection so much!" he says, "even with total strangers you act like a little submissive concierge. *Yes sir, no sir.*"

You don't pay any attention to him. He hates it when you don't pay attention to him. He pours another kirsch—"it's no good when you're mewling around people's feet like some kitten. Who cares if you make people happy? I like it when you fight," and he does. He engages you in all manner of debates, arguments, discussions, and all-out wars (mostly on the chessboard). He likes it when you talk back, when you get so frustrated you yell. He goads you into it—you can tell because he'll say something he knows you won't let go, like: "Well, we all know women are happier pregnant," or "Everyone knows French expressionists are fucking queers."

That's when you call him any manner of names, names he inspires, like *idiot*, *chucklehead*, *half-wit*, *lost parakeet*, *Russian aristobilly*, *the caveman of Kiev*, and so on. His eyes always light up when you call him names and color comes to his cheeks. He says when you're around yelling at him he feels like he did back home, with fire in his belly and trouble in his sights. You try to get him to get out more, you call him a shut-in and a scared old man and a paranoid schizophrenic until your badgering finally drives him to dancing with his old buddies at the Veterans' Hall on klezmer night, and they're all so happy to see him they buy him shots of vodka and end up swimming nude in the Atlantic Ocean at four in the morning.

Shortly afterward Sergei comes down with an awful chest cold and fever. He groans and shivers in his sheets and you feel awful because you made him go out. "Idiot," you say to him. "Don't you know better?" You take him chicken soup and aspirin and zinc tablets. You mop off his hot forehead with ice-water-soaked washcloths, and in his delirium he tells you that you're an angel, that your boyfriend doesn't know what he has, that you'd be better off married to a dog. He calls you *his darling*, *his peach*, *his ruined one*, and calls out for you in his sleep.

A week after his health returns, Sergei invites you over for dinner. Your first red flag is the fact that he knows Rocky is out of town. Your second red flag is that Sergei tells you he bought champagne, and your third (and biggest) red flag is that you shave your legs. All these red flags, and still you go to his apartment. What can you do? Sometimes red lights look like green lights.

Sergei pours you a tall flute in his mother's cut-crystal glasses. After you've toasted and emptied them, he presses you up against the counter, knocking the empty soup pot off the stove. He tells you *he's in love with you—he wants to marry you*, and the two of you fall down together on the kitchen floor, him sucking on your suddenly exposed and erect nipples, and you biting at his hair while wrestling with his belt buckle. "Marry me," he whispers hotly in your ear. "Marry me, goddamn you."

When Rocky comes home the next day you're icing up a bruise on your knee and you resolve to tell him. But he's grinning ear to ear. He didn't play paintball—it turns out he finally went to see a dentist and got his poor teeth fixed up. He grins at you and all the old melty feelings swim back. He looks adorable. Sweet. He also bought something for you. It's a ring, a small pear-cut diamond engagement ring. He kneels down and asks you to marry him. You're stunned, shocked and in disbelief. You've been waiting for this moment for so long that you'd stopped waiting for it altogether—but Sergei is just across the hall, and he too is waiting for an answer.

If you marry Rocky, go to section #182 (page 419).

If you run off with Sergei, go to section #183 (page 420).

113

From section 64 . . .

You go out to dinner with Ben—and what a fantastic dinner it is. He takes you to Nobu and you gorge on blue fin, yellow fin, sockeye, caterpillar rolls, and cold sake. He tells you the entire sushi market is run by two brothers in Tokyo, one of whom has coral eye and one who only eats cheeseburgers. He says they dominate the entire global sushi dynasty and have been rumored to kill competitors, which apparently has been many many people. Whatever. You're too drunk on Veuve Clicquot to care. You take another bite of yummy unagi.

You like something about Ben—although you can't say what. *Yes you can.* You like his money. That, and that he looks at you like you're the most expensive piece of blue fin he can buy. He looks like he wants to pack you in his porcelain molars. Swallow you whole and not let anyone else have even a taste. He eyes every man that walks by, and he drags your chair closer to his. "So I can snuggle," he says—but it isn't to snuggle, it's to keep you away from the other fish in the sea.

Ben banters well—he's quick and witty—but he's rude to the waiters. He treats them like faithful dogs or slightly handicapped children. "Do you *understand?*" he says to the beautiful high-cheeked woman who takes his order. "I want the ginger sliced *thin.* Not sort of thin. *Very* thin." (You're sure they spit in his food to the point of refusing a sip of his miso soup.)

Your cell phone rings five times during dinner; you know it's Rocky trying to figure out where you are. You didn't call him like you normally would and he's probably worried. This makes you feel awful, but you didn't want to lie to him—you thought it was better to say nothing at all. You can take a night to yourself, can't you? Jesus, when did you ever sign a marriage contract with the guy. Besides, this is innocent.

Innocent, that is, until Ben takes your face in his hands and kisses you right there in the booth. His lips are soft and wet and dreamy. After that all bets are off. (You're already in trouble—you figure at this point, more trouble isn't going to make any difference.) So the two of you make out in the booth like teenagers. You eat your weight in sushi, drink two bottles of champagne, and laugh your heads off.

After dinner you go to a few more bars, drinking champagne and making out in every one. You're leaning against the bar in a little place called Lucky Strike, the world a happy blur because you're beautiful drunk, when he mentions the fact that he's Married. With. Children.

You're suddenly ugly sober. He has plenty of excuses. *He's unhappy! She's never been the one! They got married too young! They got married too soon! She's fragile! She's naïve! She never found herself! She's too dedicated! Too clingy! Too cloying! Suffocating! Jealous! Leaves the window open at night even though he's asked her a thousand times not to!*

What he wants is . . . what he's never had is . . . what he's looking for is . . . oh, why not just say it . . . a real *bitch*. He wants someone assertive, aggressive, independent, not afraid to ask for things, not afraid to demand things! Someone who can have a good time, kick up her heels a little, let him know when he's out of line, let him know when he's been bad—you know . . . *naughty*. Kick him around a bit. Do you like leather? Leather pants, that kind of thing?

Anyway, he glosses over, he'd love to see you again, he loves young people, to be around the young is to be young, and he's in this ridiculous position to help people, he could make life so much easier . . . he kisses you on the mouth and says he'll call soon.

The very next day a bike messenger delivers a pair of tight leather pants, a diamond tennis bracelet, a copy of *Justine* by the Marquis de Sade, and an envelope with a thousand dollars in it. (The money means you'll not only make rent, but you can get the cable turned back on and buy a new pair of shoes.)

There's a note asking you out to dinner on Thursday night. Yes. You. Do. You tell Ben to pick you up at eight. The nice thing about *an understanding* is that it removes all the awkward chitchat. Takes away the questions. That endless expanse of time before you're sure of someone's intentions. What they want. You know what Ben wants. You know exactly what to wear—the leather pants and the diamond bracelet he sent you. You know exactly what you'll be doing at the end of the evening—something the Marquis de Sade would approve of.

Ben sends a car for you, which delivers you to his large white stone apartment building overlooking Central Park. The evening surpasses your expectations on quantity (dinner at Balthazar, art opening at the Met, drinks at a party in a suite at the W on Union Square, another ride around the city looking for the moon), but it utterly fails on quality. Ben is an ass. He is so rude to the waitstaff at Balthazar you swear the waitress must have gone into the kitchen to cry. He talked loudly, constantly, and always about some aspect of his money. What he has bought, what he will buy, what he could buy, what he should buy, and what he absolutely shouldn't buy—but might anyway.

Then you're disappointed when the sex isn't rougher. He has a very small penis and you want to ask, *What happened? Was there an accident? An angry surgeon at the circumcision?* Size counts to most women, and here he is stumbling around with a nubbin—trying to do his best. You feel sorry for him. Is there still a man alive who doesn't know size counts? (SIZE COUNTS. SIZE COUNTS.)

All he wants you to do is be on top and be loud, tell him *he's a naughty fucker, a bad daddy, his cock is too big for you, you've never seen one that size,* and so on.

Nothing compares to the disappointment you feel the next morning, though. When you're finally back in your apartment and Rocky turns up unexpectedly to tell you he never wants to see you again. Apparently one of his friends is a busboy at Balthazar and saw you and Ben making out like bonobo monkeys. When Rocky leaves, you feel like he dropped your heart in a boiling samovar.

You still have Ben, but you're not sure how much good that is. At least dinners with him are big and extravagant. The wine is always ridiculously rare, and the gifts ridiculously expensive. (A Tiffany gold-plated toothpick, a sixteenth-century ceramic frog, a bracelet with your "family crest" on it—you don't have a family crest—a porcelain jug depicting Egyptian lovers, a dress made of a hideous orange silk.) The way he spends money is so stupid it starts to enrage you. The price of a dinner could put a well in Africa, the price of his cufflinks could pay a family's electricity bill for a year. If you had his money, you're sure you'd do better things with it.

Then one day after dinner he leaves the table momentarily to say hi to a colleague across the restaurant. The check, which he's signed for, lies open on the table. It's one of those old-style receipts that prints out the entire credit card number on the check. You reach over and snatch the receipt. Put it in your pocket. I mean—he'd never know if you put a few more things on his card. He never even looks at his bills, and how could he know if it was you or one of his other girls spending the money?

If you use Ben's credit card, go to section #208 (page 485).
If you don't use Ben's credit card, go to section #209 (page 489).

114

From section 66 . . .

Sapelo is a small island eight miles off the coast of Meridian, Georgia. You're excited to go there—you can only get there by boat and you'll be living all alone in a mansion in your own tropical paradise. But nothing is ever what you think it will be. Never. When you finally make it to Sapelo and wend your way in a rusty old Jeep down haunted, creepy roads to Eileen Ashton's crumbling white antebellum mansion, you learn the house hasn't been lived in for *two years*; it's musty, loaded with palmetto bugs (roaches), and you won't be alone—you'll be living with the parrot, Mr. Biggles, who's every bit as reproachful of you now as he was of Eileen.

Your first night is spent trying to sleep in the hot, pitch-black living room of the old place, on a damp sheet-covered couch with the crickets racketing and Mr. Biggles letting out a *Bitch!* every so often in the darkness. The next day is worse. You're supposed to be checking the generator and all the switchboxes, but you'll be damned if you're leaving the main room of the house. You learn that you're not alone on the island—not even close. There's a community of Gullah who live in a village on the other side of the island called Hog Hammock. They're descendents of the original slaves who were brought here and they're rumored to still practice *African religions* (read Voodoo). They don't like newcomers, or people from the mainland—and boy howdy, they don't like you. A woman with a cloudy eye comes up to the house the first day you're there, and instead of saying, *"Hi there! Welcome to Sapelo!"* she spits on the front steps, does a Hail Mary, shakes a rattle, and leaves. Very neighborly.

The house is totally haunted. You hate wandering through the huge empty rooms. You end up moving your mattress and all your belongings out to the solarium, the glass room with dead plants and an empty swimming pool. You can't wait until the end of the summer, when Eileen's divorce is final and you can get the hell out of here. You hope she does burn it down.

You start to see things. A man standing in the woods with an axe. He's chopping something on the old tree stump out back . . . something bloody. You find red string tied to your suitcase handle and five pennies facedown on the floor outside the solarium door. Five pennies right in a row. They couldn't have fallen that way. You didn't see them before, and that means someone must have put them there. You sleep with Mr. Biggles close by, even though he screams obscenities at you—he's the only friend you have. The phones are out and your cell phone won't recharge. Nothing with batteries is working.

You come down with a light fever. Maybe it's heatstroke, but maybe it's because coming here was a mistake. You sit in the solarium staring out the cloudy windows above the pool, palms spread on knees, eyes held in the white sky, and you watch the birds. The island is in the middle of an Atlantic flyway. A migration superhighway. Hundreds of traveling birds go by. You see herons, egrets, thrashers, thrushes, bluebirds, and shrikes.

As you study the horizon, you notice a thin ribbon of black smoke rising over the bloomless mimosa trees to the east. It must be a fire Hog Hammock has going, and you watch it burn all night. Your fever gets worse. You haven't eaten in days now and you're too tired to even get up to go to the kitchen. Mr. Biggles seems fine. There's a lady who starts to come to feed him. Her name is Majette. She lives in the village and she says Eileen sent her—but you think she's lying. "You rest," she says and holds out a thick finger for Mr. Biggles. To your amazement he climbs on without any fuss. "I take care a the bird now," she says. "You drink this." You're too tired to argue. She leaves you with a pot of foul-smelling tea—which you drink. Which was stupid.

115

From section 66 . . .

You politely tell Eileen and Mr. Biggles that you can't accept their nice offer—and you leave. Fucking weirdos. They'd kill you for sure out there. Instead you look for work and you realize you can't even get a job at McDonald's. Apparently nineteen-year-old store managers don't want to hire bitter, desperate, laid-off postgraduate art students to work their drive-through. You finally find a job out at the Oglethorpe mall, at a store called *Plate Mania!*, which is a Christian store where people paint their own plates.

Your job is to work the kiln, the monstrous metal furnace thing in back, where all the plates people have painted get fired. You load the wet plates in, you take the dry plates out. You wear heavy asbestos oven mitts so you don't burn your fingers, but they don't give you anything to protect you from the noxious fumes that emanate from that thing. *Are they painting with radioactive waste?* You hate this job.

Because it's a Christian store, many of the plates have psalms and pictures of crosses on them. Lots have a recurring image of a little shriveled walnut with hair on it—which you can only take to be baby Jesus in a manger. They all say things, like I LOVE YOU SCRAPPLES! or I LOVE BABY JESUS! or PRETTY PRETTY PRINCESS ME! or MERRY CHRISTMAS DADDY AND HIS NEW WIFE CHARLENE! It doesn't matter what they put on the plates, half of them shatter in the kiln anyway.

You have to move to a shabby little apartment out by the mall. You can't afford anything else. Your old pals—low self-esteem, depression, and anxiety—move right in with you. You all sit together on the couch, eating take-out fried chicken, and you wonder, *What's wrong with me? Why am I working so hard for nothing? Why am I such a loser? Is it the economy? The government? Do I have bad timing? Bad brains? Is there a pill I can take for this? I know heroin addicts who have a better life than this, not to mention more free time.*

You try to cheer yourself up by buying yourself little presents. *Makeup, shoes, bubble bath, jewelry*, anything pretty. A girl needs to be cheered up—right? It's after one such spending spree that you get caught in a sudden rainstorm and dash under an awning with your bags, where you career right into a tall slender man, impeccably dressed in a blue-striped seersucker suit. He's totally bald and carries a gold pocket watch on a chain. He's like a cross between Daddy Warbucks and Colonel Sanders, which gives him an air of charming, avuncular power.

He introduces himself. His name is Colonel Jessup (He is a colonel!), and he owns three Chrysler dealerships and a chain of gas stations all around the South called Big Daddy's. You tell him you don't mean to be rude, but *how did he ever get so much money to buy all that?* and he laughs. The colonel says, "It's easy and there's only one rule. Buy assets, miss, not liabilities." He points at your shopping bag. "That's a liability," he says. Then he points at a run-down building across the street with a FOR SALE sign in the window. "*That* is an asset. Those"—he taps on your shoe box— "will give you sciatica."

When the rain breaks, he invites you to walk over to the building with him. He's meeting his real estate agent and they're putting in an offer. He intends to buy this dilapidated building and turn it into luxury condos. "I have to spend quite a bit of money on it now," he says, "but later it'll make me millions. Get it? You have to be willing to put up with some discomfort *now* for some peace later."

The colonel takes you under his wing. You watch him negotiate—how he never takes *no* for an answer and looks at setbacks as opportunities. It's all a potential deal to him. A game. It's inspirational to you. If you're going to climb up out of this, you're going to have to work hard. You throw yourself into your *Plate Mania!* job and get a second job at the Krispy Kreme factory, working the graveyard shift making doughnuts. Twelve hours of lard batter, hot oil, and listening to the hard-core rap music your coworkers play. (You'll never eat another doughnut again. Never.)

Finally, almost a year later, you have five thousand dollars saved. It was a year of no new shoes, no dinners out, and no lattes—but now it's worth it. You use that as a down payment on a tiny run-down house in Thunderbolt.

Then you work like a draft horse fixing it up—new linoleum, fresh paint, better landscaping—so you can sell it. You make a cool fifteen-thousand-dollar profit. This is only the beginning. The colonel helps you look for real estate. (The things he buys are in the millions and billions; you're still in the thousands.) You turn over ten houses in two years, and you have two hundred thousand dollars in the bank.

This goes on and on. Slowly, slowly, you creep up the ladder buying properties and turning them around. Then you buy some apartment buildings (you're a landlord—weird) and some land for development out by the airport. You get a lawyer, a property manager, and an accountant. You have a team of carpenters, painters, and contractors on call. You have your own empire is what you have. You are becoming a real estate mogul.

You end up marrying the colonel's youngest son, Harry, who makes chokecherry pancakes and thinks even your crooked pinky toes are adorable. You have four children together, as well as two dogs and a parakeet named Mr. Biggles, just for old times' sake. You die an old woman with all your grandchildren gathered around your hospital bed. You slip over to the other side happy as a clam. Once you got your head out of your ass, it was an incredible life.

116

From section 68 . . .

You don't trick Peter right away. You wait a week to concoct your plan. After your "one last time" fuck, when he thinks he's headed out to college, you turn your big blinking doe eyes on him and tell him *you'll be having his baby in nine months.*

He blinks once, twice, and then it's his turn to bursts into tears. (This is not sexy and you'll have to put it out of your mind every time you're in bed with him from here on out.) But true to your expectations, a week later he gets down on one knee and offers you a diamond chip engagement ring and a proposal of marriage. You accept. You go off the pill and try in earnest to get pregnant in order to mask the lie.

It takes awhile—but the pregnancy stick turns blue four months later. Thank God Peter isn't the sharpest tool in the shed and you're able to convince him a thirteen-month pregnancy is possible. He goes to work at his father's lumberyard and moves into the cabin with you—where you cook roast beef and Yorkshire pudding on the wood-burning stove. He chops wood and you plant daylilies. The hummingbirds come around, drink the red fruit water in the feeders, and every day you bring home a pie.

Baby Dilly is born in September. Dilly is an angel baby, and Peter adores her. He builds her a crib and matching rocker, changes diapers, warms bottles, gets up for midnight feedings, does all the things you would not think a North-woods man would do. Silly Dilly.

Dilly grows up wild—she's always outside on the lake or romping deep in the forest, she comes home with scrapes, scratches, bruises, poison ivy, ticks, and a constant stream of adopted forest animals. She doesn't do well in school; her wandering mind can't sit still long enough to latch on. It isn't until Dill is in her senior year of high school that Peter announces he's leaving you. Apparently he met someone in the lumberyard—a woman named Margey, and he's in love with her.

Children of divorce can get angry. Really angry, as Dill displays by breaking the windows of her father's new house and dying her hair neon pink with yellow stripes. They say leaving people is as hard as being left, but that's a load of crap. Being left is much much worse. Dilly takes it hard. Silence, fuming, raging. You know she's sexually active now, you find the condom wrappers in her room. She won't talk to you. By the end of the school year she announces she's pregnant. She's sixteen.

Eight months later little girl Blue is born. That's what Dill names her. *Blue*. You work double shifts at Betty's Pies to pay for all the hospital bills. You dish out Salisbury steaks and smothered pork chops and endless slices of pie. Your ankles fatten up, your arms weigh down, your face drops. You become like the others, smooth and gray as a river stone. Then one day you get a phone call. It's one of the old HACKY team, who's now president of an arts high school down in Minneapolis, and he wants to know if you'd come down and teach art. If you go, Dilly won't come with you. She hates the city—hates you for ruining her life (how you've done this you don't exactly know). But if you go—you'll rarely see her or the baby.

If you go teach art, go to section #188 (page 429).
If you stay, go to section #189 (page 432).

117

From section 68 . . .

You decide not to trick Peter into thinking you're pregnant. Why ruin his life? Why nail his boots to the ground now, when he'll only kick free and stomp off later? You help him pack, buy him a leather jacket for the road, and watch his truck drive away, a cloud of dust filling the space where he was. You stay at Betty's Pies, dishing out Salisbury steaks and smothered pork chops and endless slices of gooey pie. Your ankles fatten up, your arms weigh down, your face drops.

You become like the others, smooth and gray as stone. The winters come, the winters go. The lake freezes over till the barges can't get through and ice houses pop up all over the large sheet of ice. Fishermen drill holes in the ice and reel in sturgeon, and when the ice breaks off in giant plates, drifting away from land, the coast guard has to go rescue them in big red boats. The fishermen never reel in their lines.

Then Peter comes back a decade later with a pretty wife named Margey and a bouncing baby boy. (Their family is so cute, so adorable, you just want to drown them in the lake.) They come in every Sunday for supper and rub their pretty pink happiness in your eye, *pretty and pink* just like conjunctivitis.

In a futile attempt to make Peter jealous, you flirt with the regulars at the restaurant when he's there, especially one of the old iron range workers, Joe Trelstad, who's always had eyes for you, but you've never given him the time of day because, well, because he's just *Joe*, just flannel-shirt-wearing, coffee-drinking, dumb-joke-cracking, IQ-of-a-fence-post *Joe*. But you sit on Joe's lap and don't charge him for pie and make damn sure Peter sees you drive away with him in his big pickup truck. His wife is an insipid little perky-nosed blond, one of the million thoroughbred Swedes that plague the north like albino cockroaches. She waves as you leave.

Joe's place is much nicer than you would have imagined. It's a big log cabin high above Vermilion Creek with a moose head over the stone fireplace and a new generator that kicks in whenever the power goes down. (He's got quite a few beautiful Lakota artifacts he's found while out hunting. Arrowheads and broken pottery and even a piece of an old buffalo hide.) You spend more and more time over there until you eventually move in with him. He doesn't work, but he's got money. You don't know how much, but he's comfortable.

The two of you are married in a ceremony on an old paddleboat in the middle of Lake Superior. Afterward Joe confesses he has a lot more money than he ever let on. *A lot* more. Due to some long-ago insurance settlement with a taconite mine, old Joe is financially set for life. You don't ever have to work again. They throw you a big party at Betty's and Joe buys you a new truck. You become the Grand Dame of Duluth, a wealthy patron of the local arts. You and Joe take up sea kayaking and birding, you buy a house on Madeline Island and spend summers there painting.

You do not die until you are very, very old. Ninety-two. You just go to sleep one night in your bed, next to your husband, and you have a pleasant dream that you never wake up from. It turns out heaven is a junk shop, a vast sweet-smelling place where God keeps all his broken things. There you can find all sorts of things lying next to each other—lost violins and Shakespeare's not-so-great plays. Bad artists and good politicians. Busted dog collars and tangled jump ropes. Confused philosophers and chipped coffee cups. Perfect in its way—broken beauty everywhere.

118

From section 69 . . .

You try to confess to the crime, but in one of those all-to-common twists of fate, no one believes you. They roll their eyes and say, "Uh-huh, sure you did." Unbelievably, nobody recognized you that night—maybe because of the apple-green wig or the dark bruises or because everybody was tweaked out on meth. Plus Blackjax! insists you weren't at the party. *That bitch*, he tells police. *She stayed home that night. She didn't kill anyone. She's just turning this poor guy's death into some "cry for help" performance art—she just wants attention. What else is he going to say? He's an accessory.*

After that, things fall apart. It doesn't seem to matter how awful your work is, or what a jackass you are, you can do nothing wrong. Your career continues to rocket forward. It makes you sick. Every scene you cause, every bucket of tar or barrel of chicken parts you spill on a gallery floor—it's all interpreted as the work of a genius. *A genius.* You're about as far away from a genius as you are from a gay iguana, but as the man said, people believe what they want to.

You start to gain weight. Deliberately. It's your new work—the boundaries of love. How much, I mean *how much* does the public love you? Will they still love you at one hundred eighty pounds? Two hundred pounds? Four hundred pounds? Because one thing you know for sure is New Yorkers make room for the avant-garde and the strange and the bizarre, but they will not make room for the *fat*. They believe being fat should be reserved for Texans and Midwesterners. Sort of like their cultural heritage. Fat fly-over people who live in fat fly-over land.

You pack on about three pounds a week by giving up all physical activity and eating six meals a day, which is not as easy as it might seem. Your gallery owner yells at you. "What are you doing?" she says. "You need new clothes. You're spilling out of everything!" You tell her that's the point. You eat until you become big and bloated, your skin splotchy and coarse. You expand and swell. Everything becomes thicker—your wrists, your ankles, your neck. You sleep twelve hours a day and try to remain immobile for the rest. That's not hard to do—*remain immobile*—since just walking up a flight of stairs wears you out. You'd rather lie on the couch and watch television with everything you need (remote control, a bag of Doritos, a six-pack of Coke, a box of crème-filled Krispy Kreme doughnuts).

As you gain weight, to your satisfaction you fall off a few choice party lists. (See? *Insincere bastards.*) People stop calling you and your next show is inexplicably canceled. You can feel this invisible wall go up around you—only it isn't invisible, it's anything but. The wall is made of skin cells and blood and your very DNA. Your body is the wall. No one calls you, no one comes over, no one even makes eye contact. You can't sell your work anymore, you can't get a show, and so now that you've made your point, it's time to drop the weight. When you are your normal size again you can do a whole piece on perception and self.

Only you can't seem to lose the weight. You can't stop eating now. If you try, your hunger comes back like a sharp-toothed saw cutting into you. You're hungry all the time. You try and throw out all your food, you try and eat only one meal a day, but you break down every time and run for a bucket of fried chicken or a stack of buttered waffles. Broke, friendless, and tipping the scales at three hundred fifty pounds, you move back to the Midwest where you'll blend in.

You move in with your parents, who can't look at you. They just don't understand. They think it's a choice you're making to stay this fat. Every time you lose five pounds, you gain back seven. Your parents get you a dietician and a trainer, but nothing works. You try and be an anorexic, try to vomit up your food after you binge, but every time you put your fingers in your throat, you get grossed out and stop. You need support from people who can empathize with you. So you put an ad in the local paper, calling all local big girls to the first official Fat Grrl club. Admission is free, but everyone is weighed to gain entry, and the starting acceptable size is two hundred pounds.

Twelve women show up to the first Fat Grrl meeting. Together you weigh a collective twenty-nine hundred pounds. One woman comes in a special-size motorized wheelchair and brings an entire bucket of deviled eggs. At first the women are shy, unsure of the situation and generally apologetic about everything—but after a few rounds of margaritas a certain festivity falls over the group. Someone once asked Queen Latifah what the world would be like without men and she shrugged and said, *"I don't know—but there'd be a lot of fat, happy women."*

You talk about the issues. How to lose weight, how to not care about losing weight, how to get a man—if and when you do get a man, what sexual positions will conceivably work. (Pillows are apparently key.) "I stack a bunch of pillows under my ass until she angles up," a woman named Linny says. They all laugh and slap their thighs. It feels good to laugh. It feels good to make fun of everyone else, like you have your own club that nobody else can join instead of the other way around.

The Fat Grrls meet once a month and you grow in numbers exponentially. You start a Web site, which gives personal counsel, advice, diet tips, physicians' notes, and messages of hope. A word-of-mouth wildfire explodes once you're interviewed on *Good Morning America* and the entire nation knows about you. After that you're the number-one weight Web site in the world, known for its thorough diet investigation, balanced recipe reviews, and candid advice.

Despite all your good work and helping thousands of women fight their struggle with weight, your own weight issues come and go the rest of your life. Toward the end it looks like the weight has won when you have a massive heart attack and the fire department has to saw through the living room floor in order to get you out of the basement. They're too late, of course; they've arrived to find you cold dead, legs straight up in the air, skirt over your head with a Mallomar clutched in one hand.

There isn't much pity from the firemen, who are used to their own hard lean bodies doing exactly as they're told. One guy discreetly snaps a digital image of you, *funny fat lady upended on the couch*, and sends it around on the Internet. The Fat Grrls get revenge by suing the city for defamation. The money they win from the suit builds the first Fat Grrl center, the mother ship for many more satellite centers just like it, where women come for free counseling and advice.

In heaven you get to vote for who you want to be in the next life (as we are all just reincarnated over and over again, in God's attempt to make us better and better spirits). After you vote for what you want, your ballot is reviewed by the board (strict angels), who make a recommendation to God, and God makes the final decision on what you're going to be in your next life and why. "Well, you're not going to be fat again," he tells you. "What in the hell were you thinking? Did you think that's what I gave you a body for? To drown it in Velveeta cheese sauce?" He hands you your reincarnation slip, and even though you'd chosen to be a "genuinely talented expressionist artist," the slip says you're going to be a third world rice farmer so you can learn temperance and equanimity . . . and to not be so fat.

119

From sections 70 and 71 . . .

All roads lead here. This moment. You are floating outside yourself, every nuance noticeable, every detail available. (The wet cement floor, his muddy shoes, his dirty jeans, his blue satin Windbreaker, his stubble-beard throat, his sharp bobbing Adam's apple.) *Explosion!* Your hand burns. Time speeds forward, all events at once. His face blows apart, leaving meaty slabs of brain on the wall behind him. Blood overspray. He keels over, the cigarette falls from his hand.

Now sirens are in the distance, long blue howls through the wind. You put the warm gun in your pocket. The parking lot is empty. Nobody's there, not a soul to see. The sirens get louder. They're coming.

If you wait for the police, go to section #192 (page 440).
If you run, go to section #193 (page 443).

120

From sections 70 and 71 . . .

He's grinning at you, one front tooth slightly overlapping the other. Those eyes. Like meat. He doesn't recognize you. "Cold?" he asks, stamping his feet. "Sure is cold. Wanna cigarette?" You take a cigarette.

"What's your name?" he asks.

Your skin is crawling with ice beetles, your feet roasting, your tongue a hive of crawling bees. You run out of the car wash, feet pounding, arms pumping, lungs bursting. You don't look back, you charge like a bull down the center of the road. You hurl yourself onto a city bus and go straight to the police station. "He got off the 21A, he must live near there. He's got black hair, black eyes." You talk as fast as the sketch artist can draw—every facial feature is in perfect detail in your mind's eye.

They find him a week later. Marcus Peterson. Thirty-one years old and a rap sheet lousy with sexual offenses. *Peeping, molestation, rape.* In order to prosecute him fully, they'll need you to go on the witness stand. Full disclosure. Media frenzy. Your name forever linked with *rape.* Even if you testify, there's no guarantee he'll go to jail. The DA has lost every rape case in the past eight months due to incompetent lab testing. Your entire life could be smeared like a bug on the sidewalk, and he could walk away.

If you testify, go to section #194 (page 448).
If you don't testify, go to section #195 (page 449).

121

From section 72 . . .

You tell Siggi you can't stay—you're needed at the farm. He's hurt. He takes back all the books he's lent you, and shortly afterward you learn that he has closed the museum and gone back to Reykjavik. No more old books—no more legends—no more learning. Halldóra keeps a close eye on you ever since she accused you of studying witchcraft. She even removes the oregano from the spice rack, which is nothing short of baffling. Then one damp afternoon a visitor comes to the school. A geneticist from Reykjavik named Jóhann Jóhannsson. He has wheat-blond hair, cornflower eyes, and a warm, firm handshake. He's come as a part of a nationwide survey; he collects DNA from Icelanders (a quick Q-tip swab on the inside of the cheek) for the national Icelandic gene database.

You follow him around, asking questions and helping him locate students. By the end of the day the rain has increased, the wind blustering across the treeless black rock coast. It's over a two-hour drive back to Reykjavik, and you invite Jóhann to stay at the farm with you and he accepts. You take him to the barn, where your sculptures and your sketches for future work are stacked in the corner. After some red wine and heavy flirting he comes up behind you and silently cups your breasts. Does he expect you to turn and kiss him? How long will he stand there? He slowly unzips your jeans. You do not turn, you do not push him away, and you do not say a word. He takes your jeans down, spreads your legs and enters you from behind. You never see his face.

In the morning he's gone. You never hear from him again. Three months later, your time working with Halldóra is finally ending. You pack up and head out for Reykjavik, where you'll catch your plane back to America. Halldóra's on her way to Spain for a two-week vacation. As you leave it's a funny sensation, because you're homesick but you don't really want to leave. You're not entirely sure where home is anymore. You have a late evening flight, so there's time to stop at the Blue Lagoon, Iceland's famous hot springs, for one final soak, where you can ruminate on this beautiful country.

You stash your stuff in one of the big rented lockers, put on your bathing suit and your flip-flops, and go paddle out into the steamy aquamarine water. Heaven. Bliss. You're there for three hours, floating in the pools, standing under the thundering waterfalls, basking in the steam rooms carved into the sides of the volcanic cliffs. When you return to the locker rooms, however, it takes quite a while for your addled, sulfur-soaked brain to comprehend the fact that your locker is wide open and everything is missing. Everything. Your suitcases, purse, wallet, passport, cash . . . everything is gone.

Your mellow buzz snaps into a terror-infused race around the hot springs, trying to get someone to fucking help you. No one helps you. It's late, most of the staff on duty are bored Icelandic teenagers wanting to close early so they can go clubbing, and the few visitors milling around the reception area don't speak English. You have *no money*—not even for a phone call. You manage to hitchhike to the airport with a surly cabbie who probably thought he was going to get lucky (okay, he definitely thought he was going to get lucky—but how else were you going to get there?), but it doesn't matter, because by the time you get to the airport, you've missed your flight.

The airline has zero sympathy. Your nonrefundable ticket is now expired. Care to charge another ticket on your credit card? No? They can't help you— sorry—and you can't sleep in the airport overnight. No exceptions. Your head is a swirl. Halldóra is gone, and your parents don't pick up the phone when you call collect. (That's when you remember this is the month they're off on their golf clinic or whatever it is in Florida. You have no idea what city they're even in.) You hitchhike back to Reykjavik, where you guess you'll look for some stupid quick work, just enough to buy a plane ticket.

Looking for work in Reykjavik is like looking for a deck chair on the *Titanic*. There's no real point. You pound the pavement for two days, eating out of Dumpsters and sleeping in an abandoned car by the side of the highway. You can't stay out here—it's only a matter of time before you get into some real trouble. So you take the only job you can find, dancing at a small strip club called Mr. Beene's, which is built out of two aluminum double-wide trailers and has an unfortunate twenty-four-hour buffet that smells funny. It isn't even an official strip club—Icelandic laws are too strict. You have to wear tit pasties and always something over your vagina, like a G-string or a feather or a strip of black electrical tape. It'll take two weeks collecting sweaty tips in your ass crack to afford another plane ticket. You picture your goddamned parents in Florida drinking their mimosas and practicing their backswings, and you just want to die.

The dancers have names like Essex, Big Candy, Fjorder, and Lunt. The men who watch from their broken chairs are hardly really there. Their jaws are loose, their eyes unfocused. They are always very polite, except with each other. Sometimes they throw a pint glass or a punch at the guy sitting next to them. They are shushed by the heavy Icelandic boys who watch the door, bruisers who can't read but listen to the proprietor, Madame Anika, without question. Madame Anika is a Russian immigrant who got knocked up by an Icelandic fisherman. She says, *What could I do? His prick looked like a beef tenderloin.*

On your third night dancing, you take a wrong step and sail right off the stage, cracking your head on a table and fracturing your skull. The bouncer sighs and dials emergency services—but it's too late, you are dead on the sticky floor. One second you're alive, the next second you're not. Ultimately, all that stood between you and death were your Lucite stiletto high heels. Wait till your parents hear this.

In heaven you meet God, and he's really pissed off, like all the time. "Is it that hard?" he shouts at you. "Really? Because I don't see how I could have made it any easier. How you ended up as a *dead stripper* on the floor of a *double-wide trailer* with ninety-nine-cent chicken wings roasting a foot from your smashed-in head is beyond me." He smacks his green forehead. "Seriously!" he says, and then he storms off to the Parcheesi tournament. He says he'll deal with you later.

122

From section 72 . . .

After a full-on shouting match, you tell Halldóra you're ashamed of her and you'd be *happy* to move the hell out. *Living with a frigid narcissistic stone miner isn't your idea of studying art anyway.* You stomp off down the road to Siggi's house, the wind whipping your hair into a fury, tears approaching. He lets you stay out back in his barn.

Halldóra calls the school and informs them of your truancy—and whatever *pack o' lies* she tells them gets you kicked out of the program. Utterly shut out. Now you're in Iceland and your plane ticket is scheduled for three months from now. So you work at the museum full-time helping Siggi catalogue his artifacts and organizing his impossible files. The manuscripts are brittle and the words minute, giving you frustrated headaches as you try to decipher them. You take notes in a large spiral-bound notebook, writing down what you can understand and slowly piecing things together.

What surprises you is that the books don't speak so much of magic and spirits and the underworld as they speak of chemistry. The science of emotion. It says love *isn't* magic, it's the presence of certain chemicals and neurotransmitters fired in the brain. Fear is just a synaptic episode—a collection of neural transmitters firing on cue. Little train wrecks in your head. The books have recipes that control that very brain activity. Recipes that use herbs, plants, minerals, and animal parts to trigger chemical reactions all over the place, in the neocortex, the amygdala, the media insula, the anterior cingulate, the striatum, and the prefrontal cortex. Recipes that increase or decrease levels of serotonin in the brain. Powders, pastes, teas, salves, poisons, and potions.

Want to make your ex leave his new lover? Brew *Stand Down Tea* and it'll cause neurotoxin levels to accumulate, which causes the sensation of depression, which results in decreased human connection. Want to make someone fall in love with you? Cook up *Salwort*, rolled into little pellets and dropped in wine or water, which when drunk stimulate the prefrontal cortex and cause serotonin levels to rise, which simulate the sensation of affection. You keep everything you're reading a secret, even from Siggi. He doesn't know you've been reading the old books, taking them down to the ocean and poring over them like a loving archaeologist trying to bring them back to life.

You experiment on yourself. Mix certain herbs with seaweed and blue-green algae, pack it in a cheesecloth pouch, and bury it underground for seven days. Then you mash that with sea kelp and spoon it into your mouth slowly, the taste overwhelming and rank—but what happens next can't be explained. You feel a certain euphoria you've never experienced before, a warm buzzing sensation that illuminates you, makes your eyelids flutter, the lips of your vagina hum. The effect lasts for three days, and so you make another potion and then another. You keep detailed notes, adjust your methods for potency, and tell no one.

When Siggi has a heart attack and dies, that's when the villagers start looking at and avoiding you. It turns out Siggi left everything he owned to you—*his only friend*, it says in the will. You inherit his house, his museum—everything. The idea of experimenting with the potions and hexes unfettered and unwatched *is thrilling*. First you try a love potion, an herbal ferment that takes two weeks to make. You pack the gooey green salve inside two chocolates and offer one to pretty Ingar—the wealthy girl who everyone wants to marry—and the other to Hani, the good-hearted but acne-ridden and hopelessly awkward teen from the apartment complex.

You've gotten them together in the hay barn outside town, and for scientific reasons you have to watch them from the hay loft. He has her up on a tractor, bent over the steering wheel as he goes at her from behind. His penis looks massive, like a purple eel darting into a tiny pink seashell. By dawn she's pregnant, and a week later they're engaged. Even after the effects of your medicine have worn off, Ingar has come to rely on and respect her fiancé and Hani is just thanking the gods.

Then you mix a complex carbon solution and pour it into a dark beer. You give this beer to the town drunk (the mean old man who kicks dogs and likes to try and pinch the nipples of young girls), and the next day they find him drowned in the ocean with a suicide note left on his kitchen table at home. The serum you gave him was a despondency trigger, a heavy dose of depression. So *this* is magic. You decide to stay in Iceland permanently.

Meanwhile, Halldóra has been spreading rumors about you, telling everyone in the village you're a witch, that you've already harmed people. You ignore her as much as you can, but then, when word spreads all the way to the next village and you can't even buy groceries without people whispering behind your back, you've had enough. You mix a "muddle tea," meant to slow the cerebral cortex and make people confused, and inject it into her toothpaste. *This is almost too easy.* Within the week no one has seen Halldóra outside her house. She doesn't turn up for her weekly poker game or to the feed auction, and when her neighbors call in on her, she only complains of a headache and a general malaise. She eventually sells the farm and moves to Reykjavik to be with her sister.

You begin to manipulate people all over the village. You silence barking dogs, make rich men fall in love with single mothers, help children learn their times tables. Your name travels across Iceland and you become known as a powerful witch. Someone who can make true loves return and enemies vanish. People come from far and wide to speak with you. They fearfully pay you a lot of money for your potions and do exactly as you say. You try to go back to America after a while, but you just can't work your magic there. Americans have too many antibiotics and antidepressants in their systems for your natural ingredients to work anymore.

You move back to Iceland and live a cloistered, isolated life with your books and your beloved four-leggeds (two cats, a dog, and a mouse named Phyllis). You're all together in a small white cottage on a sharp black cliff overlooking the sea. It isn't lonely, it's just alone. You spend your days mixing potions and reading the ancients. You don't paint or sculpt anymore—now the craft is your craft. The villagers respect you—after all, you're the village freak. It suffices. They only come round for potions and tinctures and the occasional poison arrow.

You die eventually, of incurable old age. The one thing no magic can change. When you pass over you fully expect to meet God or the Goddess or the Buddha or somebody, but it turns out that those were all legends. One time through life is really all there is, no second chances, no do-overs, no penance, no retribution, no rewards. Just dirt and you slowly turning into it. When you die the mischievous craft should have gone with you, but your old books were stolen by one of the village girls, a clever one who took them from your house during the funeral and reads them privately to see what they say. She'll die alone too.

123

From section 73 . . .

You smile and say you'd love to see him again. He trundles off in his little car and Halldóra clucks her tongue in disapproval. *Who cares.* You found yourself a Conan the Barbarian geneticist look-alike.

When you meet him in the city for dinner you're wearing a tight pink dress and pearl earrings. You play with your hair and stare at the ceiling, exposing your neck. Unless he really is a Barbarian, he'll get the damn hint. He asks you out again and again. Reykjavik has a hot club scene, dozens of underground dance halls packed with tall, blue-eyed teenagers, women who stand over six feet tall in their chunky high-heel shoes, and men who are taller than the average NBA player, only these giants are pale and awkward. There are celebrities. You see rap stars from Los Angeles and a whole cluster of Italian movie stars who say the nearby Blue Lagoon is good for their skin.

Jóhann and you spend more and more time together. Days turn to weeks, and when your time with Halldóra is finally over, he asks you to stay in Iceland and move in with him—which you do. He lives in the adorable fishing village of Hellnar, in a tiny red metal house with white shutters that overlooks the sea. The house is cozy, the rooms are lit by oil lamps, and there's a wood-burning stove that makes the whole house smell like smoked pine. His bedroom is small and warm, heavy quilts keep you warm at night.

You love setting up house with him. He's an actually, genuinely happy person. You also love Iceland, even though you can't convince your parents that you're not insane. You stay there for a whole year before Jóhann asks you to marry him. It's a total surprise. You're in a sulfur-crusted geyser park beneath a purple glacier and you stand facing east while he bends on one knee.

You marry Jóhann and only a few months later you discover you're pregnant. You begin to vomit every morning, noon, and night and you have a constant headache. If pregnancy is so natural, why does it make you feel so bad? When you're far enough along, Jóhann insists on amniocentesis, the test that not only determines sex but also searches for the dreaded twenty-first chromosome. The chromosome that means your child will have Down syndrome.

When the tests come back positive, there's really no question. Jóhann tells you a geneticist does not accept genetic flaws. "It's math," he says. "We got unlucky with the egg. You have thousands of others that won't have this chromosome. I'm not embarking on a life of special-ed classes and a child whose life expectancy is thirty years." You tell him you're not sure. He thinks you're being selfish and irresponsible.

If you have the baby, go to section #197 (page 456).
If you decide to terminate the pregnancy, go to section #153 (page 345).

124

From section 73 . . .

You tell Jóhann *thanks, but no thanks.* You're going home soon. You want to concentrate on your work and helping Halldóra until it's time to go.

Three months later, your time working with Halldóra is finally up. You pack up and head out for Reykjavik, where you'll catch your plane back to America. She's on her way to Spain for a two-week vacation. As you leave it's a funny sensation, because you're homesick but you don't really want to leave. You're not entirely sure where home is anymore. You have a late evening flight, so there's time to stop at the Blue Lagoon, Iceland's famous hot springs, for one final soak, where you can ruminate on this beautiful country.

You stash your stuff in one of the big rented lockers, put on your bathing suit and your flip-flops, and go paddle out into the steamy aquamarine water. Heaven. Bliss. You're there for three hours, floating in the pools, standing under the thundering waterfalls, basking in the steam rooms carved into the sides of the volcanic cliffs. When you return to the locker rooms, however, it takes quite a while for your addled, sulfur-soaked brain to comprehend the fact that your locker is wide open and everything is missing. Everything. Your suitcases, purse, wallet, passport, cash . . . everything is gone.

Your mellow buzz snaps into a terror-infused race around the hot springs, trying to get someone to fucking help you. No one helps you. It's late, most the staff on duty are bored Icelandic teenagers wanting to close early so they can go clubbing, and the few visitors milling around the reception area don't speak English. You have *no money*—not even for a phone call. You manage to hitchhike to the airport with a surly cabbie who probably thought he was going to get lucky (okay, he definitely thought he was going to get lucky—but how else were you going to get there?), but it doesn't matter, because by the time you get to the airport, you've missed your flight.

The airline has zero sympathy. Your nonrefundable ticket is now expired. Care to charge another ticket on your credit card? No? They can't help you—sorry—and you can't sleep in the airport overnight. No exceptions. Your head is a swirl. Halldóra is gone, and your parents don't pick up the phone when you call collect. (That's when you remember this is the month they're off on their golf clinic or whatever it is in Florida. You have no idea what city they're even in.) You hitchhike back to Reykjavik, where you guess you'll look for some stupid quick work, just enough to buy a plane ticket.

Looking for work in Reykjavik is like looking for a deck chair on the *Titanic*. There's no real point. You pound the pavement for two days, eating out of Dumpsters and sleeping in an abandoned car by the side of the highway. You can't stay out here—it's only a matter of time before you get into some real trouble. So you take the only job you can find, dancing at a small strip club called Mr. Beene's, which is built out of two aluminum double-wide trailers and has an unfortunate twenty-four-hour buffet that smells funny. It isn't even an official strip club—Icelandic laws are too strict. You have to wear tit pasties and always something over your vagina, like a G-string or a feather or a strip of black electrical tape. It'll take two weeks collecting sweaty tips in your ass crack to afford another plane ticket. You picture your goddamned parents in Florida drinking their mimosas and practicing their backswings, and you just want to die.

The dancers have names like Essex, Big Candy, Fjorder, and Lunt. The men who watch from their broken chairs are hardly really there. Their jaws are loose, their eyes unfocused. They are always very polite, except with each other. Sometimes they throw a pint glass or a punch at the guy sitting next to them. They are shushed by the heavy Icelandic boys who watch the door, bruisers who can't read but listen to the proprietor, Madame Anika, without question. Madame Anika is a Russian immigrant who got knocked up by an Icelandic fisherman. She says, *What could I do? His prick looked like a beef tenderloin.*

On your third night dancing, you take a wrong step and sail right off the stage, cracking your head on a table and fracturing your skull. The bouncer sighs and dials emergency services—but it's too late, you are dead on the sticky floor. One second you're alive, the next second you're not. Ultimately, all that stood between you and death were your Lucite stiletto high heels. Wait till your parents hear this.

In heaven you meet God, who's this all-knowing green praying-mantis thing, and he's really pissed off, like all the time. "Is it that hard?" he shouts at you. "Really? Because I don't see how I could have made it any easier. How you ended up as a *dead stripper* on the floor of a *double-wide trailer* with ninety-nine-cent chicken wings roasting a foot from your smashed-in head is beyond me." He smacks his green forehead. "Seriously!" he says, and then he leaps off to the Parcheesi tournament. He says he'll deal with you later.

125

From section 136 . . .

If you want to run away and join the cirkus, then by God—that's your right. Right? You write your parents a long letter (better than a drama-filled phone call) and you explain that you just can't come home right now. You've found a place where you feel good, and places where you feel good are harder to find than Atlantis.

The cirkus is staged inside a red-and-white-striped tent, which is pitched inside a large empty warehouse. "We used to have it outside," the owner, Maxie, tells you. "But the tent has so many holes now—the rain just pours in." The cirkus is called Sweetlady Cirkus and is populated with freaks, geeks, and outcasts of every kind. The chorus line is comprised of fat German women whose naked, pendulous breasts bang together when they dance. The ticket taker is an albino and there's a fleet of monkeys who have sex with each other on demand.

Maxie is a fiery Gemini with a dent in his forehead and two gold teeth, which he got after falling from the high wire. He says he likes his showgirls *fat*. "Better freak factor," he explains. "People are compelled and repulsed at the same time. It keeps them coming back so they can figure out why they're frowning even though their dicks are hard." The Sweetlady Cirkus also has a snake-eating Spaniard, Siamese twins, and a man who can shove anything up his ass. (He demonstrates with lightbulbs, flashlights, knitting needles, and lingonberry pie.) It turns out they want you to perform in the "ice show," where twelve nude women skate around an ice rink made of white wax. Oliver tells you he think it's great—you're not so sure. You picture your father's face if he ever found out—and you shudder.

The first number you learn is simply called "Barnyard," where several women dressed as farm animals chase a farm girl around the rink until they overtake her and have sex with her in various farm-themed ways. You play the chicken. Your outfit is just a yellow-feather chicken head and nothing else. Germans have a strange sense of what's sexy—because they also ask you to play Anne Frank. *Who wants to see a nude Anne Frank?* Germans do. It's part of the "Heroes on Ice" show, which also features Princess Di, Jackie Kennedy Onassis, and Eleanor Roosevelt.

The act is so popular that Maxie decides to take Sweetlady Cirkus on the road and books performances all across Europe. The crowds love it. You're asked to do several interviews on German, British, and French television while wearing your Anne Frank outfit, which both delights and enrages people. *You're this, you're that—you're evil, you're hilarious.* The controversy heats up, the crowds get bigger and bigger, as does your paycheck. Maxie buys a new fancy tent with laser lights.

Then an overseas phone call comes, it's your aunt crying on the other end of the line. She tells you that your mother has brain cancer and not much longer to live. The doctors have diagnosed her with a cancerous brain tumor, and it's inoperable. You and Oliver rush home, but she dies while you're on the plane somewhere over the Atlantic. When you finally arrive, your father won't speak to you. He won't pick up the phone or answer the door. He doesn't go to the funeral. He gives you a message by way of your aunt. It's scribbled on hard note card in a shaky scrawl. *You killed her. You and your damned selfish ways.*

You break down, fall to the floor weeping on your father's letter until it's soft and rabbity as a baby's blanket. Oliver tries to console you. He puts his arms around you and tells you everything will be all right. "Your father won't stay mad forever," he says. "Let's go back home and give him time." He tells you how much he loves you—how you might only have each other—but it's more than enough. Then he asks you to marry him. You know that if you return to Germany your father will be even more angry with you. Maybe he'll never even speak to you again . . . and you don't know if you can live with that. Should you stay here and patch things up with your family, maybe get a real job that doesn't land you hate mail from Anne Frank supporters?

If you marry Oliver, go to section #185 (page 423).

If you don't marry Oliver, go to section #154 (page 348).

126

From section 74 . . .

Kissing Toru is *not* an option. In fact—this is your exit cue. This is getting creepy. There are many scenes in a disappearing act. Scene one: *comfort*. You smile, reach out, and touch his hair, which is coarser than you thought it would be. It shows you're not afraid to touch him; whatever happens next has nothing to do with his body. Scene two: *the opening*. You step back. Look at him. "You and I are such good friends," you say. "I could never do anything to hurt that. To risk that." His eyes drop. (You could say the fact he's crippled has nothing to do with it, but then you'd be lying on top of being a jerk and leaving. It has everything to do with it. What would you do with that hand? How could you live with that face? You wince every time you look at him.)

You are about to move into scene three, *deflection*, when you realize you never asked him about the white painting. "It was the reason I came to Japan in the first place," you tell him.

He frowns. "There was no picture like that," he says.

"The big one," you explain. "The one in the senior show." *Why had you never seen a picture of it in his slides?*

"I had no painting in the senior show," he says. "I was having a skin graft that day. On my face. I already had a fever, they were afraid of infection, afraid I might die."

"But I saw it!" you insist, "your name was on the wall next to the cement-colored painting. There was a crack in the . . ."

He shakes his head. "My father hung an empty frame on the wall to honor the painting that wasn't there—that might never be there. You must have been looking at the wall. It was cement."

"But the line down the center . . ."

"The line in the cement wall." He stands and walks across the room, shutting off the slide projector, putting you in darkness. "I think you should go."

A cement wall? All this time you were chasing something that wasn't even there? You were going after smoke? You pack your bag in confused, angry silence and head down to Yoyogi station.

Disappearing acts aren't just tough on the audience; they take their toll on the players too. (Things to remember: It's not personal. It was meant to be. Nothing heals if you keep tearing out the sutures.)

If you stay in Japan, go to section #202 (page 470).
If you go back to America, go to section #203 (page 472).

127

From section 136 . . .

It's time to go home. You try to say good-bye to Oliver and tell him you'll write, even though you probably won't. While you're on the plane (Row 32, seat D, window) you decide you've got to make some changes in your life. Really get organized and decide where you're going. Things have been a little thrown together up until now and you want a fresh start. A new beginning. All you need is a positive attitude, a smile, and a cheerful disposition. You even chat nicely with the little old couple sitting next to you, a man and a woman from Kent who're on their first trip to America so they can lay eyes on their grandson.

You go to sleep and stay that way for most of the flight until the distant lights of New York are just visible on the horizon of the black water. The pilot is contacting LaGuardia for flight formation when there's a strange sound that makes him look over his left shoulder, and the plane explodes. Later they will find there was a small eensy-beensy electrical spark inside fuel tank number two, which ignited vapors.

The explosion blasts the big 747 out of the sky. A falling silver whooping crane. The sensation of depth. The ocean is on fire, covered with burning oil. In the seconds on the way down you think of Oliver shouting, *Die Mauer ist gefallt! Die Mauer ist gefallt! The wall is coming down!* He'll never know what happened to you. No one in America will know to call him. No one in America will know he was the one who helped you off the train. The couple beside you have their oxygen masks on. They hold hands. It makes all the sense in the world to you here in this one minute. It's all we have. One Minute. One small minute, and then water. The camera crews are coming, there is debris everywhere.

128

From sections 62 and 90 . . .

You work at Denny's and learn that being a waitress is like being an actress. *You always pretend you're happy, always pretend you want to help, always pretend the customer is right.* Never complain. There is someone right behind you to take your job if you'd like to quit. You are expendable, you are replaceable.

If you work at Denny's, people think you're stupid. That's just the way it is. Your customers are surprised when you can read and write, and they always check your math. They treat you like a vending machine, reading off a list of things from the menu and then expecting it to magically and immediately appear. They seem to think that because they're paying you, they have the right to pinch you on the ass and *ask if they can have you for dessert.*

The cooks are worse. They chase you around the stainless-steel counters, corner you in the stockroom, and accidentally bump into you whenever they can. If you don't let them have the occasional feel, they have ways of getting even. They hold back your orders and screw up the side dishes so your customers don't tip you, and because you get paid shit, they know you rely completely on your tips.

You get a sore back, muscle aches, chapped hands, and varicose veins. You gain weight. You become used to being covered in a film of oil and ketchup. Crying babies are just a routine part of every hour of every day. The manager screams at you like you were a barnyard animal he can't get to move fast enough.

You date a cook named Vinny for a long time, although the two of you never marry. He's fat but he tells you you're the one who needs to lose weight. Your typical day goes like this: up at five a.m., to work by six a.m., work a ten-hour shift without lunch, without sitting, and then get home around five p.m. Cook dinner, a frozen pizza or Lean Cuisine, roll a joint, drink a beer, watch *The*

Simpsons, drink another beer, watch *Everybody Loves Raymond*, drink another beer, watch *Frasier*, drink another beer, watch a rerun of *M.A.S.H.*, argue with Vinny, scream at Vinny, go to sleep. Get up in the morning and do it all over again. Twenty years pass. You are a career waitress.

You die accidentally one day in the kitchen when you peek into a pressure cooker of split pea soup and it explodes all over you. Fifth-degree burns over forty percent of your body. You catch an infection and die. At your funeral people shake their heads and wonder what happened. Then they eat.

129

From section 76 . . .

You're Brazil bound! You cash out several hundred stocks and buy a first-class ticket to the Brazilian rain forest, where you'll stay at a five-star eco-hotel, a hotel that grows its own organic food, recycles all its own waste, takes in wounded jungle animals, and runs a local archaeological dig. You get a brand-new wardrobe befitting of an *upper-class, socially conscious, not-too-pretentious* woman. Crisp cotton shirts and Egyptian linen pants, breezy mauve dresses, and large straw hats. Lots of amber jewelry. You picture finding significant ancient pottery while wearing your new Egyptian linen pants.

But you have to get there first, and while you're still at JFK International, in the chaotic crush of the security line, there's a heavy hand on your shoulder. It's the police. They lead you to a small room and take away your passport. It turns out your husband hired several private detectives to tail you and alert him of any sudden movement of money. (He knew you hid that money *somewhere*, and it was just a matter of time until it surfaced.) They were watching international airports. You call your lawyer, but after hearing about Megan Tewinkel's account, he quits over the phone.

You are sentenced to five years for embezzlement and misappropriation of funds. No more silk slips or truffle pâté or sapphire rings. No more vacations or sunsets or lobster or baths. Your choices will be made for you for the next few years, until halfway through your sentence you develop a sudden staph infection in prison, which goes untreated for too long, and you die with a fever, in the infirmary. Your husband thinks this is hysterical and goes out for lobster.

130

From section 76 . . .

You drive to Palm Beach, where you realize you've got to be a millionaire *ten times over* to even own an outhouse three blocks *off* the waterfront. You rent a nice apartment instead and spend several weeks beachcombing. You quickly learn the city is run like an ancient East Indian caste system—social groups stick to their own kind. To make friends, you've got to have friends. To have parties you've got to go to parties, and you don't go to any parties unless you have friends, which you obviously don't have. Your main friends are the people at the Palm Beach Narc-Anon meeting you attend twice a week.

Then you meet a nice older man on the beach. He's a surfer with silver hair. You can't stop your eyes from roving over his tight wetsuit, which glistens over his fantastic body. He has a tapered waist and muscular thighs—his bare feet look perfectly manicured. He smiles and the world lights up. He says his name is Albert and he's a professional loafer. You have dinner together, and then a spectacular night between three-hundred-and-fifty-thread-count Egyptian cotton sheets.

He doesn't seem to care about your age or your marital status or your money. He teaches you how to surf, holds your waist on the surfboard as the waves push you together. At the end of three weeks together, it's time for him to go to Oahu. He asks you to go with him. Of course you've heard plenty of horror stories from wealthy widows in these parts about nefarious gentlemen who bilk gullible grande dames straight out of their money. Albert could be a silver fox, a crafty scavenger looking for his big meal ticket.

If you go with Albert to Oahu, go to section #206 (page 481).
If you say good-bye to Albert, go to section #207 (page 482).

131

From section 77 . . .

You decide to leave him—but you must do it when David's not there to stop you and when it won't terrorize the children. A window of opportunity comes when your husband leaves for a two-week international DNA conference and the children simultaneously head off for a week at Camp Tamarak.

The plan is that when your husband comes home, you'll be gone. Your bags are packed and waiting in the closet. When the children are done at camp, they'll fly directly to your cousin Beth's house in Massachusetts. You've always liked her but you've never known her that well. Your husband has never met her—might not even totally remember she exists and would definitely never think in a hundred years of looking for you there.

You're nervous. Here it is, a normal day, birds singing, cars driving, but to you nothing is normal now. In this one moment, you are irrevocably changing everything and everyone forever. Those next moments alone are orchestral. Every step significant, every movement placed. You pack the children's suitcases. Make difficult decisions about which stuffed animals are the most important. (*Mr. Pigs was her favorite to sleep with last year. Now it's the blue one-eyed bunny rabbit, but what if she wants to switch back?*) You clean out your medicine cabinet and empty your dresser, your nightstand, your jewelry chest. Gold chain necklaces, perfume bottles, prescriptions all get tossed and jumbled together at the bottom of a paper bag. (This is a getaway. No time for organization.)

At the airport you act like an apologetic fugitive. You're confused, bewildered, shaky. The ticket agent, the security guards, the baggage handlers, you can't look any of them in the eye. Words dart through your head like sharp-toothed vampire bats. *Lawyers, divorce, alimony, irreconcilable differences, custody. Evidence, photographs, battery.*

When you arrive at cousin Beth's rambling old farmhouse there's a fresh tomato pie and a pot of hot coffee waiting. She doesn't make you explain anything or talk when you don't want to—she acts as if you had always been coming, as if this was a reunion planned long ago and certainly overdue. She shows you her herb garden and her chicken coop and where she makes beeswax candles in the barn. She's prepared adorable rooms for the children—collected crayons and paints and even an old vintage bicycle.

Things go well at first. The kids arrive confused but happy to see cousin Beth; they love the old farm and take turns feeding sugar cubes to the horses. They start to ask questions, like *Where is Daddy and when are we going home?* You tell them this is their new home—that Daddy is taking a long vacation and *aren't we lucky to be here, with all these chickens?*

Although you don't know if you're lucky at all. The kids have nightmares and you can't find a Narc-Anon meeting anywhere nearby—which makes you damn nervous. You join an online support group, but it isn't the same. You get the old twitches and dry mouth. At least you have no clue where you could even find meth in these woods. At least there's that.

Two years, a bloody divorce, and a restraining order later, you're still living in your cousin's farmhouse, you haven't used any drugs whatsoever except NyQuil, and best of all—you've got full custody of the children. The judge ruled completely in your favor, gave you everything you asked for right down the line. (Half of all his assets, the house, the cars, and a generous alimony settlement.) As you were leaving the courtroom the judge (an Asian woman known for vitriolic sentencing), gave you the slightest smile, the smallest nod of the head. Her expression said, *We got him, didn't we? We got him good.*

Now you've got your kids, you've got some money, and you've got the rest of your life to never be pushed around again. You want to move on. You don't want to inconvenience your cousin any longer, she's already done so much for you. With this new chunk of money (wicked big alimony and the maximum child support for years and years) you can start a new life. This is your white orchid, the beginning of everything else. You love flowers—and of course you love hummingbirds. Why not do something big—something crazy—something you really want to do?

If you open a hummingbird sanctuary, go to section #199 (page 462).
If you open an orchid farm, go to section #198 (page 459).

132

From section 77 . . .

You stay with your husband for the sake of the children. Don't rock the boat, dig in deeper, spend more time with the kids, go to the gym seven days a week, take yoga, take pills, pray. Three years pass. Three more. You look for strength, or rather, for endurance. You sit still. Energy begets energy. Mass collects mass. Your husband tries to be nice. When you make lobster with fennel he tells you you're clever. He makes love to you. Sort of.

You see your doctor for the many mystery ailments that develop. Asthma, sleeplessness, allergies, a mystery rash—welts and bumps that rise up all over your body. The rash is the worst. The doctor gives you an antibacterial, antifungal cream to reduce the itching of the red flower blooming on your thigh, but it's still terrible, and as your husband sleeps at night, you sit on the bathroom floor raking your fingernails across your skin until it bleeds.

You're losing weight. At first you look amazing—hip bones protruding in your expensive jeans, jaw line cut and aquiline, but then you look gaunt. Emaciated. Like you're disappearing. Food, no matter what it is, makes you nauseous—like your stomach is going to explode. The doctor gives you protein powders and vitamins, suggests you drink a beer every day to beef up. He even suggests you cut back on trips to the gym.

Your husband gets better, then he gets worse. There's trouble at work, a grant he didn't get, a fight with a coworker, and he takes it out on you. He uses the belt, the hairbrush, the lamp. Depends on what's handy. One night as you are lying at the foot of the bed, facedown in the carpet (which he allows—even prefers—because it cuts down on bruising on your face), you look up and see your son's pajama legs at the door. Your son is staring at his father and he isn't crying or afraid—he just seems numb, and you know he's seen this many times before.

Was that when it happened? When you decided? It might have been earlier. *But there it was—like an itch with no scratch. A book you read by—who was it? Edgar Allan Poe?* Doesn't matter. A plan is born. The very next day you buy a big slippery beef tenderloin and stash it in the deep freezer at home. (You have to wait a week to make sure it's frozen solid. It's not so hard to wait, there's a lot to fantasize about.) Then you take a handful of your best jewelry and throw it out. Finally Sunday comes and you send Molly and Michael off to their friend's house. The house is yours. He comes home from his marathon golf game, his mind-numbing, fertilizer-soaked, testosterone-spiked ordeal, and you take the tenderloin out of the freezer. (It's maybe eight pounds? Ten?)

An hour later he's downstairs in his den, watching a game and reading the paper, feet up on his beloved ottoman. You unlock the front door and carry the frozen beef tenderloin downstairs in its roasting pan. (No drips!! No blood!) He's fallen asleep in his chair while the announcer's voice drones on. You set the pan down on the carpet and very quietly pick up the frozen beef in your hands. It's like a meat baseball bat.

The tenderloin high over your head, you get a whiff of his cologne, lemon and musk. You have smelled that scent a million times, on top of you, alongside you, over you. *It's the go flag.* You bring the frozen tenderloin down hard on his head. Crack it like a coconut. You knock him right out of the chair. He falls to the floor, where you smash his face again and again. You break his nose, pulp his face into his eye sockets. Every muscle in your body is straining, you can feel your teeth sharpen, your claws extend.

Afterward you drop the slick beef into the roasting pan and sit on the floor, studying your nails. It's an hour before his breathing and gurgling stops. You check his pulse. Dead as a doornail. You walk upstairs with your roasting pan, set it on the counter, and season the murder weapon with olive oil, salt, pepper, and rosemary. You pop the pan in the oven (preheated to 350 degrees), and you toss in a big stack of dry dish towels, pack them in good at the bottom of the stove, where the red flames lick the hemmed white edges. You go upstairs for a bath, where you scrub carefully, every little fingernail, every inch of skin, and then you go to your bedroom, where you pop four sleeping pills and lie down in your bed.

It's the firemen who wake you; the alarm is blaring in the hallway and there are police in your bedroom. You don't have to pretend to be confused—you actually are. (Those pills are strong!) Did you know your house was on fire? Did you know the front door was unlocked? Did you know your jewelry case was ransacked? Did you know your husband has been brutally mauled down in his den?

Your tears are genuine—only they're tears of relief. (Hard for men to tell the difference.) The children are safe, the murder weapon has been burned to ash in the oven, and the bastard is dead. (It's hard to keep from singing.) The cops are patient and kind; they let you get dressed and refuse to let you downstairs to see your husband. It's too brutal for a woman to see, too horrifying for you. They help you into the squad car, take you to the station, and get you a mocha latte from Starbucks.

Of course over the years there are forensic units and homicide investigations (surely somewhere something of yours has his blood on it). But the thing is—this isn't *CSI: Miami*, and cops are overworked, underpaid, and not all that interested in solving the murders of wife beaters. (A fact quickly revealed during the investigation.)

Besides, it was obviously a robbery gone wrong. The front door was open, the jewelry was missing, the invalid wife was knocked out by prescription sleeping pills. No. The cops say this murder was obviously committed by someone who had cased the house for months. Someone who knew it intimately, who knew when you'd be asleep, when your husband would be downstairs. Someone familiar with the neighborhood, someone who could blend in. Someone *very violent, very strong*. Someone clever.

You and your children live like kings on your dead husband's money. When you die you discover there is no God, no ultimate personal being, just an intricate self-balancing design. You never got caught for murdering your husband because he had committed so many atrocities against you. If you'd just killed him for the fun of it—then you would have ended up in jail. That's the beauty of a self-balancing universe. We all get what's coming to us.

133

From section 79 . . .

Just for once you're going to put yourself first. *That's what they tell you to do—isn't it?* You have to get your dry cleaning so you'll have your green dress for the cocktail party you intend to go to later. The dry cleaners is run by a small albino called the Tomato Man. He's no more than four feet tall and he sits on a small padded stool as he runs the register. He's called Tomato Man because of his chubby red cheeks and the fact that his fingers are always bright red from the pistachio nuts he eats. You ask for your laundry and he frowns at the ticket. "I got your order in the back—one of those dresses had a stain so bad they sent it out for special treatment." Then he sighs and looks down at his legs. "You mind stepping back there to get it?"

You step behind the counter, duck under the wall of dry cleaning hanging on the moving rack. "Way in the back!" Tomato Man hollers, and so you brush past the other side. You hear some scraping and shuffling. "Where is it?" you say, when all of a sudden something heavy and hard strikes you in the back of the head.

They bury you in the Daughters of the Revolution graveyard, which is haunted. You drift outside the wrought iron gates and watch the children at your clinic. Now all you can do to help them is follow them home and knock their parents in the heads with empty beer bottles so they fall asleep sooner. It doesn't always stop the abuse—but it sometimes puts it off for another day, and that's about all that can be done, for now. You're amassing power at the graveyard from visiting tourists, stealing power from their digital cameras and pacemakers. Soon enough you'll be able to push one of the abusive parents right down the stairs. It's coming.

134

From section 75 . . .

You wake up in a flickering fluorescent room with green tiles. One of the nurses takes your chart and checks several things off. You look down, searching for the bullet hole that must be somewhere near your stomach—but there's nothing. Just your hermit crab apron, which is untorn and unstained. Then you notice the nurse's hair is strange, like spun sugar, and the light behind her is very bright. She tells you to exit through a small silver door to the right, and suddenly you're back in the mall. Were you in the mall clinic? Where is the policeman who was shot? The boy with the gun? You look around and your stomach seizes, vertigo spins you, and you are drifting in the air, aimless as a lost balloon, floating up toward the ceiling, unfettered by gravity, weightless, spaceless, drifting through cement walls as though they were made of mist.

Are you dead? *No.* Are you alive? Probably not. The only structures that hold mass against your feather-light frame is the ceiling of the mall (a giant glass-domed window crisscrossed by powder blue iron support beams) and the very outer walls of the building, cement cinder blocks that are cold and icy to your touch.

Was it a movie or a book that said when a person dies in a violent way they haunt that place forever? It turns out the mall has hundreds of spirits drifting in and out of its shops and amusements. All the jumpers are there and a small child who usually hovers near the pay phones at the north end. Spirits that sit in the food court and eat hamburgers with the living, spirits that ride around in women's purses and hang on to old men's hats. They're everywhere, listening in on conversations, staring in the storefronts, riding the roller coaster in the amusement park. This is your community now, a group of silent, floating half-lives. Your neighbors for the rest of eternity.

135

From section 50 . . .

You take a train to Paris. The rhythm of the train tugs you down into a deep warm sleep. There's this quiet, warm delicious French banter all around you—*Ca va? C'est amusant. C'est fou!* You drift in and out on an easy tide of unconsciousness—it's easy to forget the ugliness behind you. When you wake up you're already at Gare Saint-Lazare, the station in Paris. You wipe the sleep from your eyes and stretch your creaking back.

Then something seems wrong. Really wrong. You look around and realize *your backpack is gone.* Everything was in it. Papers, passport, money, underwear . . . *everything.* You search frantically all over the cabin, heart racing, hands groping, but it appears that someone has taken all your worldly belongings.

You stumble off the train in a daze—*what are you going to do now?* When you career right into a porter, a tall gangly boy with a cartload of suitcases. You practically knock him down, but still he smiles at you as he gets up. It's been so long since someone smiled at you—you want to cry. Kindness can be unbearable.

He says his name is Pierre, and you shouldn't worry—you can go to the embassy tomorrow for your passport and he'd be happy to be your escort till then. You walk along together, him pushing the cart and you trying to blink back tears as you tell him *everything you have is gone.* "Ah, madame," he says, "Voltaire said life is filled with thorns, and the only way to get through them—is to go very fast."

You wait around the station, and when his shift is over he emerges from the bathroom in a baggy blue suit. He takes you to a bar in the Latin Quarter called Le Caveau des Oubliettes, which is built deep underground in an old dungeon once used to detain and torture enemies of the state. It's supposed to be the oldest jazz club in Paris. You join a big boisterous group of his friends, friendly people who smoke and laugh and pound each other on the back. After the jazz club they take you to Le Chat Noir. The Black Cat. There the stage show is just beginning, and the curtain sweeps open to reveal a real live waterfall right there on the stage—complete with nude mermaids lounging around its edges and live fish swimming in the clear acrylic tank. In the next act the waterfall becomes an ice rink with topless ice skaters, and then it becomes a western saloon where topless cowgirls ride through on real horses and shoot up the place.

By the end of the evening you're drunk, happy, and exhausted. Pierre offers to let you stay at "his house," which is apparently a boat he has moored on the River Seine called the *Marionette Jolie*, the *Pretty Doll*. You accept his generous invitation—where the hell else are you going to go? He leads you through the busy streets filled with musicians, street performers, and all the other drunks trying to get home.

The *Marionette Jolie* looks more like a barge, and it smells like mildew and diesel. It's lit by antique oil lamps, which flicker up and reveal a small kitchenette and the door to a tiny bathroom (you never do get used to calling it a "head," which is somehow perverse), and farther down a rather spacious bedroom at the bow.

Pierre offers to sleep on the couch, but you tell him it's fine, you can sleep together—you'll just keep your jeans on. So the two of you climb into the triangular space and try to get comfortable without touching each other, which is impossible. It's only about a half hour later when he's inside you—fucking away any memory you ever had of a previous life and an idiot named Filippo.

You end up staying with Pierre on the boat, which doesn't actually run, it hasn't in years. (There are dozens of old boats like this on the river, good for housing their inhabitants, but not transporting them. Dead engines and painted flowerboxes abound.) Pierre inherited the boat from his grandfather—who he says was an avid seaman and would be devastated by the *Marionette Jolie*'s current state. "He would probably just cut it loose and let it sink," Pierre says and sighs, "but if he was going to leave me the boat then he should have left me the money to keep it running!" Still, he vows one day he'll restore the boat, just as soon as he gets the money together—whenever that is.

Life on the *Marionette Jolie* isn't easy; you hit your head a lot on the angular walls, and once you even belly-flop right into the Seine, leaving you smelling like mildew, diesel, plankton, and sludge. (It takes two weeks washing your hair with lemons and tomato paste before the smell is completely out.) Even so—there's something contagious about living on the river. The personality of the water changes, one minute it's calm as glass, the next minute pebbled with irritation and white caps. Your favorite thing to do is sit with Pierre on the stern of the boat and drink Pimms.

Pierre gets you a job at Gare Saint-Lazare as a porter. All day long you take tickets at a small metal window and retrieve luggage from enormous, jam-packed shelves. *Bags, boxes, briefcases, suitcases, valises, violin cases, handbags.* You name it, people leave it. They leave radios and picnic baskets and shopping bags. They also leave things they never come back for. There's a whole section of the vast warehouse where Lost and Found items gather dust. Everything is catalogued and kept under lock and key by the watchful porter master, Le-Grand. He calls himself "porter master," but Pierre assures you there is no such position. He just made it up.

LeGrand is a funny little man with a red face and a nervous disposition. He was powerful once at the station but had some falling out with the wrong person and ended up cast away in the bowels of the station with lost luggage. Instead of complaining or becoming bitter, LeGrand developed a near obsessive interest in luggage. He keeps track of how many items are on the shelves at any given time, makes graphs and memos. He prides himself on the number of valuable items he has in his collection. "Nothing is ever stolen," he tells you, tapping on his clipboard. "A gold urn sat here for eleven years. Until its rightful owner, a man from Marseilles, came and got it."

You wish you could find the job as poetic as LeGrand does, but the truth is it gives you headaches, overly muscular forearms, and a sore back. Your main solace is just living in Paris. Walking through the streets is like drinking wine or breathing color or eating the sweetest slice of the world. Everything, even the smallest detail, is delicious. You even come to love living on the *Marionette Jolie*, she looks so fetching in her slip with her brass rails and teakwood. You love cooking in the small galley, the Friday-night poker games on the stern, which usually go till four a.m. and involve laughing, arguing, heated political debates, and stupid human tricks like the one Pierre can do, taking a sip of beer and then squirting it out of his eyelids.

So when one of Pierre's friends, Marie, tells you about an amazing job opportunity, you're not sure whether to take it or not. It's working on a ship that sails around the word. A ship called the *O.H.* for Ocean Home. Marie says they need one more person in the galley, and they're leaving port in a week. It would be a chance to see the world, but you'd have to leave Paris—and Pierre.

If you go on the ship, go to section #204 (page 476).
If you stay in Paris, go to section #205 (page 480).

136

From section 50 . . .

You take a train to Berlin. The rhythm of the train tugs you down into a deep warm sleep. There's this strange, sharp German banter all around you—*Das glaube ich, Es macht nichts*—and you drift in and out on an easy tide of unconsciousness. It's easy to forget the ugliness behind you. When you wake up you're already in Berlin, and you wipe the sleep from your eyes and stretch your creaking back.

Then something seems wrong. Really wrong. You look around and realize *your backpack is gone*. Everything was in it. Papers, passport, money, underwear . . . *everything*. You search frantically all over the cabin, heart racing, hands groping, but it appears that someone has taken all your worldly belongings.

The steward is a nice guy about your age. *"Es tut mir Leid,"* he says, shaking his head. "I'm sorry." He says his name is Oliver and he'll show you where the police station is. He helps you off the train and into Hauptbahnhof, the busy train station. "Here," Oliver says, "to the police." He guides you through a rabbit warren of hallways to a small police kiosk, where you fill out an extensive report on your missing backpack. (Germans love extensive reports.) They give you the necessary paperwork to apply for a new passport at the American embassy and a map on how to get there. You immediately feel better. Forms and maps quiet chaos. Oliver says that was his last train for the day and he's off work—he'd be happy to show you to the embassy.

On the sunny walk over, Oliver points out all the old ornate Renaissance buildings that have shrapnel marks across their faces from World War II. The old buildings often stand right next to modern buildings, which is how you can tell where the bombs dropped. On the walk you realize Oliver is actually quite handsome and very intelligent. You wish you had some lipstick. After he takes you to the embassy, Oliver takes you on a tour by way of the U-Bahn, the modern trains that stitch themselves across the city. You visit the Brandenburg Gate, which he says was commissioned by Friedrich Wilhelm II to represent peace, and then ironically was the site of many deaths under communist rule. You go to the Charlottenburg Palace, a gift from King Frederik III to his wife, Sophie Charlotte. (When and why did men stop giving palaces as gifts?) Then he takes you to see remnants of the Berlin Wall.

He remembers the night the wall came down. "Someone came running into the bar yelling, *Die Mauer ist gefallt! Die Mauer ist gefallt!* And we ran as fast as we could. People were coming from everywhere with hammers and axes. They were yelling and screaming and it didn't matter what you hit the wall with, just that you hit it hard. When we saw the first hand reach over the top of the wall from the other side—everyone cheered and we kept smashing that wall night and day until it was nothing. Until only pieces were left, like it had its teeth knocked out."

He takes you over to the Kreuzberg district, a gritty but cool side of the city with tattoo parlors and coffeehouses and art galleries. You have sausages with sharp mustard for dinner, and as you walk and talk a general sense of calm comes over you. Sometimes the kindness of strangers is the best kindness there is.

Oliver takes you to buy a toothbrush and then checks you into the Hotel Transit, a youth hostel right in the middle of the district. He says he'll come for you tomorrow, and if you want to, you'll go see East Berlin. He kisses you lightly on the cheek good-bye. How strange to feel so comfortable with someone you've only just met. You feel happy.

You spend the next day with Oliver and the next one after that. You like how he smells, you like how his collars are crisp and his black wingtip shoes are always shiny. Even when your passport comes through a week later you don't feel like leaving. He's got a small apartment on the far end of town where he keeps his extensive jazz collection and a pet mink named One Minute. "One Minute!" he'll yell. "Why do you eat all the breakfast cereal? *Why?*"

Oliver confesses he's in love with you—he has been from the moment he first saw you on the train. He says he didn't know a person could feel this way, like his heart has turned into a carnival, like light is bursting from every pore in his body. You ask him if he says this to all the girls, and he sheepishly tells you he hasn't had sex for a year. Right then and there you push him down hard on his bed and fix that.

You realize that if you're going to stay, you've got to get some money. So you call your parents to ask if they'll send you some cash (you haven't been very good about calling them so far) and they tell you not only are they not sending any more damn money, you'd better come home immediately. Your mother cries. She says she's had migraines and headaches ever since you've been gone. She's not well.

You feel bad—you really have been gone a long time, and the more time you waste goofing around overseas, the more time lost to your career, your life back home. (It *is* still home, isn't it?) But Oliver says he's got a friend who owns a burlesque cirkus and they need help. The money is pretty good and you could stay in Berlin indefinitely. Of course if you stay it would kill your parents. They'll think you've run away from home to join the cirkus—and, well, they'd be right.

If you join the cirkus, go to section #125 (page 281).
If you go home, go to section #127 (page 285).

137

From section 74 . . .

You kiss Toru gingerly, touching the good side of his face with your fingertips. His breath catches. When he pulls away from you, you see something in his eyes you've never seen before. *You see love.* You see another soul shining out, brimming with love for you. It's a startling feeling. You grab him and kiss him again, hard. Over the next months you fall deeply in love with Toru. You never thought you could, but when he holds you it's like falling into a safe memory. When he kisses you it opens every furious moment, every long road, every unfinished piece of music.

You stay with Toru for three years, living in his studio while working on your paintings—but your art really isn't going anywhere. You're locked out of the Japanese art scene and you don't even like the work you're creating anyway. You love Toru, but you do not love your work. That's why when the Walker Art Center in Minneapolis offers you a full-time artist-in-residence position back in America, you're flooded with hope. It would be a chance to debut into the American art scene and focus on a new body of work. If you go—you'll leave Toru and your life in Japan behind.

If you stay with Toru, go to section #200 (page 464).
If you return to America, go to section #201 (page 466).

138

From section 82 . . .

Valhalla is sixty miles outside the city and Amaria sleeps for the entire trip. She looks pale and drawn when she gets out of the car, but manages a smile when the owners of the farm take her to the horse barn, which smells like fresh manure and damp hay. When Amaria walks in, you hear a horse whinny. "He already smells you," the woman whispers.

Opaco is magnificent. Long white legs, strong smooth flanks, large solemn eyes. Amaria steps into the stall and the horse moves toward her. He smells her neck, her face, her hair. His lips brush across the bridge of her nose. They stand there, forehead to forehead, the horse making a low rumbling guttural noise, like purring. "Opaco knew Amaria was sick before she did," the woman says. "He stopped letting her ride him. He wouldn't let her into the pasture and kept herding her toward the house. Look at her now though—she looks so much better!"

There's no point in telling this woman Amaria is still sick, that off medication Amaria is living on stolen, borrowed, and broken time. Can't they see it in her pencil-thin arms? Her sallow, concave face? Sometimes people refuse to see what they're looking at. The farmer tosses a saddle over Opaco's back and adjusts the stirrups. "You sure you're up for a ride?" he asks Amaria.

"It's about all I'm up for," she says and he helps her up. When she's up there she lies down on the horse, her face against his mane, her arms around his neck. She's smelling the horse now, just like he smelled her. "Just take it easy," the farmer says and hands Amaria the reins.

You all walk down to the mouth of the pasture, where dragonflies hum around your feet. You sit on a split rail fence that runs along the top of the wide field as Amaria rides Opaco down the hill. It's beautiful out here. The pasture dips down into a low green bowl and stops at a beautiful river that spills over a waterfall.

You watch Amaria trot Opaco down the slope, his white haunches muscular and strong under her frail frame. She looks like a small child or a tiny old woman on his back and she brings him to the far side of the bowl, where she stops him. She reaches down and strokes his mane again. Then she sits up and snaps the reins. The horse whinnies and charges across the field at a full gallop. "Look at her go!" the farmer says.

"Too fast," his wife says and shakes her head, "way too fast."

The horse thunders across the valley and the farmer takes off his hat. "What the hell's she doing? She's headed right for the river!" That's when Amaria's words loom up in your mind: *I used to be afraid I would die on Opaco, get thrown off his back at full gallop and break my neck, and now I'm afraid I won't. . . .*" You stand up. You want to run—but it isn't as if you could stop them. They are beyond you now. You watch as Amaria drops the reins, her black hair snapping like a pirate flag in the wind. The horse never breaks his stride. You watch Amaria, specific in her task, and she doesn't look sick now. She looks beautiful as the horse gallops along the riverbank, as she lets go and dives headfirst into the river.

The farmer and his wife are already running, the farmer yelling on his cell phone, *"We need an ambulance! We need an ambulance!"* But of course you don't need an ambulance, you need a hearse.

When you reach the riverbed, heart bursting, breathless, Amaria is long gone. Over the falls and onto the next world. Later, they'll fish her body out of the river about two miles downstream. Opaco has circled back now, his empty reins dragging on the grass. He presses his muzzle against Amaria's lone red sneaker, which is lying in the grass. He's making those same noises again, low and guttural—and you're no vet, you couldn't be absolutely sure, but there's every sign to you that the horse is weeping.

Ambulances, sheriffs, search-and-rescue crews, newspaper reporters. It all comes out. It always does. You are held responsible for Amaria's death; her parents threaten to sue the hospital and you, their anger fueled by grief. The farmer and his wife tell their side of the story—*that Amaria gave no indication*

. . . *there was no sign* . . . *she acted of her own free will* . . . but the fact is Amaria wasn't meant to ever be away from the hospital and all the local newspapers use your name along with the ugly term "assisted suicide." You're fired, and there's a probation hearing, which you win—but the damage is done and the whole ugly mess twists itself around your life just the way the cancer did.

So you write it down. *Amaria and Opaco.* The story of a girl, her cancer, and her horse. Why not. You're in the story—albeit the very last chapter, but still. You write it all out and you include pictures of her and the horse, of the valley and the river where she fell. The book is published by a small press, but it's mentioned on a talk show that's discussing assisted suicide, and the book starts to sell. It moves from the self-help section to the front tables. It's in store windows, print ads, hospital gift shops.

With the proceeds from the book and a grant from the state, you start Cancer Companions, a program that pairs cancer patients with animals. The data hasn't been banked, but you don't need a survey to tell you that animals are healing. Petting a dog, feeding a rabbit, watching seahorses swim in the seawater tank, it lowers blood pressure and releases endorphins. It also gives them something to take care of when they've been unable to take care of anything for so long.

Not everyone can have a cat or a dog at home, and not many people have room for horses or potbellied pigs, and so the pets that can't go live with their patients stay at a small farm, complete with woods to walk in, fields to gallop in, and comfortable rooms to play in. There is a doctor on staff for the animals and a doctor present for the patients at all times.

The cancer stays in remission, which allows you to devote yourself full-time to the Cancer Companions program, and the endless details it generates. You never marry, never have children—the animals are your children. At night, when everyone else has gone home, you like to watch the pets sleep. There are over two hundred of them under one large roof, and almost never a fight. Most nights you go out to the stalls and take Opaco out for a ride. (The farmer and his wife donated him to the program, and he's one of the children's favorites.) He likes to walk in the creek, which bisects your land, and along the edges of the property, which looks down over the highway.

When you die many decades later, it will not be from falling off a horse, or from cancer, but from plain old age, the only disease with no possible cure. Your heart stops while you are sleeping in an overstuffed chair by the fire with an orange tomcat purring in your lap. In heaven you are assigned to the green mountains where pets go.

In heaven you see Amaria and Opaco, you see every animal you ever knew. You continue with your work even up in heaven, reuniting the two-legged souls with their four-legged souls. All the pets charge full tilt toward their owners when they come, and often there are many pets coming at one owner all at once, all the pets a human ever had over their lifetime all at once. Every one healthy and whole. There is no disease here, there are no wounds or broken bones. There's also no poop. This *is* heaven, after all.

139

From section 82 . . .

You don't take Amaria to Valhalla—and you never see her again. She dies two weeks later in a sweaty, sour hospital bed, her hands curled tight like dried lilies, her eyes bruised blue. The night nurse said she had terrible pain. "*Terrible*. The sheets were soaked." Amaria refused morphine or painkillers toward the end, even when she convulsed. The vision of it makes you feel sick to your stomach. Depresses you, makes you sleep. Food tastes like tinfoil, you're tired and irritated all the time. You even test to see if the cancer's come back.

But it's not cancer—it's guilt. Guilt that makes the air bitter. (You have a strange rash, your eyelids stay red and raw, like ground autumn leaves.) Your patients at the clinic are suffering, you feel as though you're not helping anyone anymore—and so you quit. You're not sad—you weren't even really planning it—you just calmly walked into the Human Resources office and told them you were leaving. Then you drive out to Valhalla, where Opaco is still boarded. The farmers tell you the family stopped paying for Opaco's feed and they can't afford to keep him much longer.

That's how you start your horse farm. You buy a small, cheap chunk of land way out past the country near the Canadian border. Big woods, cold water. You ask people to bring their unwanted horses to you, the sick horses, the hoof-and-mouth-plagued horses, the malnourished horses, the ill-tempered horses, the wild horses. The horses nobody wants. If nobody wants them— then you want them. You collect these sweet beauties and build a herd of lovely gorgeous broken horses. Magnificent, bruised, but still standing. Just like you. You name your horse farm the Valkyries, after the Nordic heroines of battle, and after Amaria.

Valkyries are exactly who come to help you. First Juliet arrives, a horse doctor from Australia who specializes in herbal cancer treatments. (She treats their tumors with comfrey, goldenseal, maritime pine, and crab apple extracts. She grows nettle, rosehips, and wild oat in the fields where they graze, all natural cancer-fighting plants.) Then comes Afton, a milky white redhead and fierce stable manager who has an insatiable urge to constantly groom, pluck, and preen the horses. Even the sorriest sights, the ones with mange and bad teeth, get thorough baths and their manes braided with sweet grass. Afton coos at them like a Manhattan hairdresser afterward, telling them *marvelous* and *just right* and *feel better?*

After that comes Suzanne and Julie, women from Port Townsend, who build their own yurt out in the pasture. They ride and walk and feed the horses. Then Alison and Jennifer and Moe. All women who drift in on their own steam and join this broken horse farm. There is farm equipment and feed stalls and fire pits. Tough, resilient, and motoring through the local men like they were chew toys, you are modern-day cowgirls. Newspapers begin to cover your efforts to house unwanted horses, and a television crew comes to film these otherwise-doomed creatures now in tranquil repose by the creek.

Then an elderly woman you never met, one Mrs. Suzie Hicks, ups and dies and leaves her entire estate to "Those kind people who help the horses." Seven million dollars after taxes and a piece of land near the coastal village of Svendborg, Denmark. You love her, whoever she is. This donation allows you to start a European branch of the Valkyries . . . horses that would normally be put down in Europe simply because they had outlived their usefulness and had nowhere left to go now had a safe stable and a staff to take care of them.

You die one day while out riding on your horse. You had just trotted past where Opaco was buried, out by the briars, when your horse slips and sends you forward, airborne and headlong into the cold creek bed below, where on impact you hit your head on a submerged rock, and the small zygomatic bone, the one beneath your lower eye ridge, is crushed inward and pierces brain tissue, causing you to hemorrhage and die almost immediately. Almost.

There is enough eternity inside that brief synaptic shorting out of your neurons and electrons to allow a ricochet review of your life. A series of animated postcards that flap through your mind's eye like escaped blue jays, all fighting to get out at once. The science classes, the sales offices, the burn of the meth, the Piper Cub in Ray's pants, the white space between Rothko's bars of color, all those glorious survivors. Amaria and her black hair. The women here who will bury you, and who will go on after you, who will carry it forward.

140

From section 85 . . .

You finish building the log cabin and you open a bed-and-breakfast. Since your husband went and chose to get hit on the head with a hammer, you hire a man named Jens to be your handyman. He'll keep the house running, mow the grass, repair the mosquito screens, chop and stack firewood. You also hire a small Vietnamese woman named Bi'ch. She has itty-bitty hands and feet, but she can kill a chicken in one blow.

It's discovered early on that Bi'ch only cooks Vietnamese food. That's when two guests, Margaret and Maureen (dragged to the woods by their hunting husbands), voluntarily put down their card game and offer to teach her how to cook more American fare. The three of them have a ball in the kitchen making green bean casserole, seven-layer hot-dish, macaroni and cheese, and Jell-O in every color. (Bi'ch tried to make a red square Jell-O with a gold star inside, using raspberry and lemon Jell-O, but it didn't really work.) At the end of their two-week stay Bi'ch presents them with a finale dinner. An entire Thanksgiving dinner. The turkey is made out of Spam.

Your accountant calls and tells you the market has gone into a recession, and you won't be getting any dividend checks for a while, as there will be no profits. Well—you have money saved up from all the bed-and-breakfast traffic, and if you tighten your belt, maybe increase the room rates a bit— you'll be fine. In winter, after hunting season is over, there aren't too many guests, so you shut down the guesthouse and tuck yourselves into the main cabin. Jens can light a fire in under one minute (you've timed him at fifty-two seconds) and Bi'ch has begun to sing to Vietnamese records while she cooks, filling the house with halting, raking hoots and calls. She rescues a white parrot she names Mr. Marshmallow and the bird learns to sing right along with her.

Eventually spring comes, the frozen lake cracks and water rushes in. After they get evicted from their apartment in Duluth, Bi'ch's younger sister, Dung, moves in along with her two young sons, Keanu and Gary Cooper (Dung is a film fan). Her sons play on the beach, especially Gary Cooper, who's five and has quite an imagination. He believes a giant sea dragon lives in the lake and any rocks he picks up by the waterline are potentially dragon poop.

Then you notice Jens. Really notice him. He's lighting a match when it happens. It's as if you'd never seen him before. The man is *handsome*. He's as tall as a three-year-old oak tree, has wide shoulders and a flicker of light in his blue eyes. When he takes you to bed for the first time, you feel as though you've met the reincarnation of Paul Bunyan—a mighty axe indeed. A year later you marry him in a ceremony on a friend's boat in the middle of Lake Superior—which goes mostly well, except for the brief scare with the coast guard, when some friends who came to watch the ceremony from their boat lost anchor and drifted right into you.

The two of you live in the bed-and-breakfast for the rest of your life, watching the lake freeze and thaw, the rain come and go, the Canadian geese fly south and then north again. It is a life filled with sweet scent and regular comedy. You cook at the wood-burning stove, Bi'ch grows a garden filled with medicinal herbs she sells to the locals, Dung gets a rich boyfriend but won't move out of the house, Keanu develops a drug problem, and Gary Cooper goes to college to study dental hygienistry.

Jens eventually dies in his sleep when he is eighty-three years old, during one of the coldest winters you can remember. Ten months after that, you see a sharp white light, sink to your knees, and die. Your husband is waiting for you, and you weren't going to watch the lake freeze without him.

141

From section 85 . . .

You finish building the log cabin and open an artists' colony named Avalon. You contact the university and tell them you'll take six of their top art students for two weeks, free of charge. Well, you'd think you'd asked to *adopt* them. The insurance, the fire codes, the health codes, the site visits, and the headache of an administrator—you eventually just pull your offer and put an ad in the paper seeking artists for your own home-spun competition. *Wanted: artists to send their work for selection in the highly prestigious Avalon Award. Winners receive two weeks paid in full at a lakeside colony!*

Nothing prepares you for the avalanche of bad art that lands in your mailbox. Papier-mâché owls, a stop sign bent in half, photographs of decaying meat, sculptures of blobby amoeba things—it's bad enough to make a painter poke her eyes out. You pick eight semi-decent artists out of the crap heap. A wood sculptor, two painters, a metal artist, a ceramicist, and an uncategorizable artist who urinates on stretched bedsheets. (Can't be afraid of the avant-garde.)

You tell them all to arrive June third, and everything else will be taken care of. Food, lodging, all arranged for; just bring yourselves (and no pets). You can't wait for your colony to begin. You hire a Swedish man named Jens to be your handyman—he'll mow the driveway, repair the mosquito screens, chop and stack firewood, that ilk. You also hire a small Vietnamese woman named Bi'ch to cook. She has tiny hands and tiny feet, but can kill a chicken with one blow.

The artists arrive—and the trouble begins. One is bitten by a spider and another one has hay fever. There's a woman who is apparently a fundamentalist Christian and she begins to try and convert you, and another boy with tarantulas tattooed around his neck shows up drunk and stays that way. The complaints begin. Bi'ch has prepared an impressive tray of chicken egg rolls and rice but no one wants it. One is a vegetarian, another is vegan. You sit at the head of the table, eager to hear the artists strike up some engaging conversation about Rothko's use of absence, or de Kooning's sexual preferences, but the artists start arguing about which highway was the fastest route.

The complaints continue. The house is too hot during the day and too cold at night. They want art supplies. They need canvas and oil paints and clay. They slosh around the house, spilling paint, dropping chisels, hammering sculptures, and making a general wreck of everything. The Christian has been ostracized by the group and two others are missing, which is probably why strange noises are coming from the bedroom.

One artist, Duncan, noisily welds together a giant metal sculpture in the garage. It's made of hubcaps and grillwork, torn sheet metal and car bumpers. You ask him what it is. "Penis," he says. Sure enough, when you stand back you can see it's an eight-foot-tall penis made of hubcaps and grillwork. He takes extra time perfecting the hubcap balls, using heavy wire to simulate hair.

When the two weeks is up, you were originally going to give each of the artists a bottle of champagne and a nice speech about taking creation with you wherever you go, but at this point you have forged a towering hate for each one of them and they all leave without saying good-bye. Many leave their artwork behind. You check the garage, and sure enough the eight-foot penis is still there.

It's later that September when your accountant calls and tells you the market has gone into a recession, and you won't be getting any dividend checks for a while, as there will be no profits. Well, you need to pay the mortgage, so you tell him to sell some of the principal stock. This continues for the entire winter, getting no dividends and dipping into your principal stock, until one day your accountant says, "Fire the handyman, fire the cook, and sell that house. You're not going to survive at this rate." You have no choice but to do exactly that. You sell the land in the spring to a couple who want to start a bed-and-breakfast. You never see Jens again.

You buy a small condo in a senior citizen retirement building. It's a nice, clean, efficient space. They have Parcheesi tournaments and bowling night.

There's a handsome gentleman there named Leinfelder. Leinfelder asks you out for ice cream and to the movies, but later it turns out he already has a girl-friend, a real piece of work down the hall named Hazel.

Your portfolio picks back up and provides you with a small monthly in-come, enough to take the girls out to dinner once a week and take a trip to Key Biscayne once a year. It's not a bad life—but still, you remember your old lakeside home every day, and sweet reliable Jens. You stare at a photograph of him standing in front of the cabin. Your only consolation was that you sold the house to a smug couple with the eight-foot metal penis still in the garage.

You die in a condominium fire that takes the lives of eight other residents. On the way up you look down over the city and see how the glass windows glitter, how the river bends around the city like a protective arm. Next time around you're coming back as a firefighter. This is only the beginning.

1 4 2

From section 86 . . .

You say yes and Nick rushes to his bedroom and returns with a small blue velvet box. "My grandmother's," he says and reveals a gorgeous vintage marquis-cut diamond ring. Dazzling. He'd been planning to propose all along. You toast each other and go to the bedroom, where you have sex like woodland forest animals.

The wedding is in June and you have it right on the ice at the rink. Everyone comes in their ice skates, the bridesmaids and best men as well as you and your groom. The wedding party skates in formal procession around the rink once before coming to a wobbly halt in their general positions. A reporter from the local paper comes and snaps a picture of the wedding. He stays and drinks champagne with the rest of you as you and Nick take a victory ride around the rink on the Zamboni. (There's a close call when your dress catches on the gearshift, but Nick thinks quickly and tears the hem of your dress with his teeth.)

At the reception in the decorated Quonset behind the rink people sit at white picnic tables with paper dove centerpieces. Nick quiets the room and gives a toast. "To my beautiful wife," he says. "Wine comes in at the mouth and love comes in at the eye. That's all we know for truth before we grow old and die. I lift the glass to my mouth, I look at you, and I sigh." The room applauds and the newspaperman snaps another picture.

Nick takes the money you inherited and puts it all on one upstart biotech stock. An obscure pharmaceutical company in New Jersey he's been tracking for some time. You trust him with the money—even if it all goes to hell, there's something comforting in knowing that even if you have to live in a cardboard box, you'll be together. The reporter runs the pictures of your "ice wedding" in the local paper, and a gossip columnist in Los Angeles notices it and prints it up in her national column. A week after that your phone rings, and as you balance the coffeepot in one hand and a plate of bacon in the other, the voice on the other end of the line says it's the producers from *Good Morning America*. They want you and Nick to fly to New York to shoot a story on the most romantic couple in America.

You appear on *Good Morning America* and a cinnamon-blond with crispy bangs interviews you in front of six black-eyed glass cameras. From this moment on, you're famous. Everybody seems to want your strange little life. The interview turns out to be a sort of competition that you've won: viewers voted on the most romantic couple, the couple most deserving of an all-expense-paid vacation to Fiji, and you and Nick are going.

Life is good. The investments Nick made take care of you financially from here on out. You're not rich, but you have enough. As Dickens said, it's a wonderful word—"enough." You live out the rest of your life in happiness, no kids, but lots of travel and good food, until one night when you're out to dinner with Nick and you eat a piece of fish in a restaurant. You have an allergic reaction the likes of which you've never had before. Your eyes swell, your throat closes. The restaurant doesn't have an oxygen tank; there are no doctors in the house, and you die just before the EMTs arrive. It was halibut.

143

From section 86 . . .

You don't like the way Nick asked you to marry him. Telling him about the money was hard enough—and then he turns around and wants to marry you? You look down at your plate. The two of you sit silently for a long time. Eventually, he gets up and starts washing dishes.

You're sure you made the right decision. *He didn't even have a ring when he proposed.* He couldn't have been serious, which makes you doubt everything he ever told you. You cry. It seems silly not to. All the letdowns you ever felt come rolling back—your boyfriend, your parents' disappointment, all the miserable dates and idiot men locked up like embarrassing relatives in the attic of your mind.

The next day at work Nick does not show up. The manager tells you he quit. He just called late last night and said he wouldn't be in. The Zamboni sits stone quiet in the corner with its big green mechanical mouth. You want to call Nick, but what do you say to a man who only loves you for money? The more you think about it, the more it makes you mad. All the talk shows are loaded with women who were taken advantage of—you narrowly averted that. So, when the manager informs you that the owner of the ice rink is selling the business, you cash out your inheritance and you buy it.

No more hauling ice, no more red hands and aching back. You spring for a full liquor license and put in a karaoke machine, which attracts a whole new breed of young adults, kids who ride Vespas and have strange haircuts and a lot of disposable income. They ask for imported cigarettes so you sell Nat Shermans and Dunhills. They ask for cappuccinos so you buy one of those enormous brass coffee machines. They want live music, so you let them start Ice Dice every Saturday night—where they invite rockabilly and swing bands to play while they do the Lindsey in skates.

You do miss Nick sometimes and wonder what became of him. You date other men, but none of them stick around. You spend the rest of your life running the ice rink, and even when you can retire, you don't, because there's nobody really at home, and you love the people who come there.

You die accidentally one day, years later, when the part-time Zamboni driver leaves the machine running on the ice. You're at the edge of the rink, attaching a new league sign to the wall, when the damn machine kicks itself into gear and mows you down, pinning you against the ice rink and spraying cherry-red blood over the ice. All the kids say the rink is haunted after that, that if you stay after hours you can still see a lonely old spinster skating on the ice, looking endlessly for her lost love, wherever he might be.

144

From section 87 . . .

You go on a trip around the world and you have more fun than you ever thought possible. Longtime travelers have this shine to them, this queer road glow. The road smoothes down their rough edges, the strange water and bad weather temper their ambition. You learn one thing is sure: *Everything works out one way or another.* The farther you go, the less anything matters. The more you see, the less you need. In the beginning there are maps and train schedules; by the end your watch has been stolen and the maps thrown away. Now there is only rhythm.

At the end, you're broke and all you have is a worn passport, with extra pages sewn in and a journal filled with notes.

HIGH POINTS
Every time your passport is stamped with a new country
New Year's Eve in Bangkok
The green-bellied birds of Port-au-Prince
The Pyramids of Luxor
The near-death flight from Kathmandu to Lhasa
Glaciers calving off icebergs in Iceland
LOW POINTS
Christmas Day lost in Calcutta
Watching a buffalo get slaughtered at a funeral in Sulawesi
Diarrhea Diarrhea Diarrhea Diarrhea Diarrhea Diarrhea Diarrhea
Loneliness

When you finally stop traveling and return to America (a barren and vast neon expanse of fast-food chains and Wal-Marts), a cloud sets over you. A deep wet depression. You're tired. Bone-marrow tired. Your legs ache, your blood slows in your veins, you put on your shoes every day and stare at the highway. The depression deepens. You sleep and sleep and sleep. The air seems heavy, your head fuzzy, the world blurry.

You try to remember—what was the name of your guide in Lhasa? Which dish was it that gave you diarrhea in Goa? Your journal has some notes—but not near enough. Never near enough. You should have written it all down. You should have saved it. What a waste. You should have Polaroided every single thing. Filmed it. Kept it encrypted, shipped, sealed, signed and carried. Kept it with you, in your pockets, in your molars, in your brain tissue, in your pelvis. You should have videotaped it.

Now you're stuck in the Midwest, flat broke, exhausted, and every friend you ever had has moved away. You can go look for a job or you can hit the road again. Just strike out and rely on traveler's luck.

If you look for a job, go to section #146 (page 326).
If you hit the road, go to section #147 (page 328).

145

From section 87 . . .

You start your own business. You become a sort of jeweler. Your product? Sapphire rings for single things. Haven't you seen thousands of engagement rings on the thin fingers of smug fiancées—diamond rings glittering like eyes at you—you, the one *without* an engagement ring, the one *without* a man, the one *without* an attachment, the one *without* any worth. Why should only girls with guys get diamonds? You'll get your own damn diamond.

True Blue. Isn't that what you call something that goes deeper? Something that is honest and trustworthy and real. Blue—like a sapphire. A piece of solid blue to take with you wherever you go. So the idea of the True Blue Ring is born. Sapphire. The right-hand ring for women who know how to make a fist. For women who don't want a diamond, for women who are engaged to *themselves*. You spend all your money on inventory—about a hundred sapphires. You get a local artist to make the settings—an elegant platinum band for each eye-blue stone.

The rings sell slowly. No one seems to understand the concept at first. The money is running out. You spend everything you have, every last penny. Then one day your luck changes. You're resting your sore feet at an upscale bar when a well-dressed woman smiles at you. "Beautiful," she says, eyeing the sapphire on your right hand.

"It's an engagement ring," you say. "A commitment ring."

"When are you getting married?"

"Never."

It turns out she's the producer for a popular women's talk show. She wants to feature your ring. You do the show, give the host her own ring on air, and from that day forward your life changes forever. Three thousand orders come in that week. The True Blue Ring is featured in *Vogue*, *Cosmo*, and *Vanity*

Fair. Celebrities start to wear them; even women who are married or engaged are wearing them. Apparently to send a "I'm married but I'm still my own woman" message.

You buy a beautiful Truro saltbox house in Cape Cod, which is close enough to New York City for meetings (your flagship store is on Park Avenue) but far away enough that you can smell the sea air and go for walks on your own semiprivate stretch of beach. You buy the estate next door and turn it into a retreat for at-risk teens, inner-city girls who have never seen the ocean, never had an oyster roast, never collected seashells, never seen the horizon so big and wide and blue.

The True Blue Ring spreads to Europe and Asia as more and more women choose to forgo marriage. You date but never marry. You have three satisfying relationships with three men (one for seven years, one for twelve, and one for fifteen) but they end, as all things must, and it's so nice to not have to fill out all the paperwork a divorce would require. Years later, when you're ninety-eight, your funeral is televised. They bury you at sea, ashes scattered from a yacht, just as you asked them to do, so you go down into the true blue beneath it all, sprinkling down deep where the horizons never stop changing.

146

From section 144 . . .

You call around and find an old friend who says she has a job for you. It's assistant producing at a local cable access channel on a travel show called *Let's Move!* It's the kind of show that highlights local apple farms and fudge shops. The geriatric host, Mr. Pedersen, is a octogenarian who doesn't like to move around a lot. (You wonder how a man who won't have a bowel movement outside the privacy of his own home ever became the host of a travel show.) You work for a year with the camera crew and then Mr. Pedersen dies. He has a heart attack on the toilet.

You become the new host shortly after this—now you're the one who has to go to apple farms and fudge shops. Only you think shows about apple farms and fudge shops *suck*, so you take your small camera crew down to the Mississippi River, where there's a small encampment of people who live on houseboats. ("Houseboat" is a loose term. One man has a train car floating on the carcass of an old tugboat.) One resident offers to take you all out for a spin on his homemade wooden boat (it has a cozy little cabin with a coal-burning stove) and you get to see the river from another angle, the bald eagles that somehow live in the city, the turtles, sea otters, trash from the overhead highway.

You interview the man, who's lived on the river for fifteen years, and he tells you about all the murders, suicides, and drownings on the river. He shows you a secret cave right on the water, carved out of limestone, where kids go and smoke pot. It's an urban paradise, and you title the piece "Interview with a River."

It airs that weekend, and the mixture of reviews that floods in range from *It was beautiful, It was refreshing, It was tacky, It was engaging, It was frightening,* to *Where are the fudge shops?*

Your next story is on a tent revival—a Baptist preacher who comes through town and cures people with strep throat and polio by throwing "fire water" on them. You film his sons putting up the tent and his mute wife passing out Bible tracts from a wicker basket at the door. You include highlights from the sermon and an interview in which the good pastor tells you which truck stops have the best smothered pork chops from here to New Orleans. Then you interview the people who attend the revival, before and after, only to reveal none of them has been cured—even a little. This piece, named "Jesus Trip," gets attention. Two papers do a follow-up story and the local news broadcasts a clip of your footage.

You don't look so bad on camera. Something about the lens makes your cheeks look more flush, your hair shinier. A cable travel channel calls. *Would you do a weekly show?*—Um, yes. The weekly segment eventually leads to your own show, and, ultimately, as the years pass, to a show about travel around the world. Now it's not just weird places, but cool places. Having a gourmet picnic on the grassy knoll where Kennedy was shot. Walking the sewers of Paris. You dispatch other travelers. Other reporters who are younger than you now, who still have that wrinkled sheen—those eyes that are always looking over your shoulder to the horizon.

You die one day while you're on a ship. You are on Lake Superior filming a story about the wreck of the *Edmund Fitzgerald* when an aneurysm makes you stop, and you sink down on one knee, a white bolt of pain shooting through you—glorious, dizzying. The last thing you see before the light dies out is the water, all around you . . . the highway around the world, and there you are, at the crossroads of everything.

147

From section 144 . . .

You volunteer with Green Peace, get sent to Malaysia, and then desert the outfit. All you ever wanted from them was the plane ticket. You have a little money—but in this region a little buys a lot. You head out for the Langkawi Islands, only recently developed because it was thought to be cursed by a princess. You take the Malayan Railway from Kuala Lumpur to the smaller city of Alor Setar. From there you take a taxi to the village of Kuala Kedah, and then a ferry to the largest Langkawi island, Pulau.

On the beach of Pulau, you finally relax. You breathe deep and take it all in. (*Hot sand, Maggi Me two-minute noodles, long boats, naked boys, white beach, blue sun, banana leaf.*) You are home at last. Happiness like a ripe strawberry bursting in your mouth. For ten dollars a month you rent a small bamboo house on the beach, which stands on rickety stilts and has a small painted front porch.

You sleep on a straw mat, your belongings on two small shelves by the door. (The cigar box with your cash sits underneath a coffee can filled with rocks.) There's a small cookstove, one burner, and a tiny sputtering refrigerator that keeps things just a tick beneath room temperature. You hire a nut-brown boy named Rut (pronounced Root), who gets your water and cooking oil and sweeps out the sugary sand from your hut every day.

Your neighbor down the beach visits. He comes into your hut and sits down without saying a word. You don't think he speaks English. He's handsome, tall and dark with smoke-gray eyes. When he's there you usually make dinner and hand him a plate of fried fish, chilies, and rice. He eats without speaking, his long fingers scooping up the rice without dropping a grain. He eats every last bite and then sits for a long time on the porch smoking. He is handsome and Rut says his name is Bone Elvis.

Bone Elvis starts coming every night. After he eats, he smokes his pipe while you read on the front porch. The sun falls, the moon rises, the moon falls, the sun rises. The months wear on—and you try not to look too closely inside the cigar box where you keep your cash, because it's getting awfully empty. Even though you fish for your own dinner and buy sacks of rice across the island where it's a few ringitts cheaper, you are running out of money.

Then, sixteen months after you arrive, the cigar box is finally totally empty. You fire Rut, but he still comes anyway. Bone Elvis also still comes for dinner. At first you serve him fresh-caught fish (which you catch yourself) with crushed spices and leftover chilies, until you are out of spices. Then the two of you eat plain fish. He doesn't say a word. Then the rice runs out, and then the oil. Then there is nothing, no way to cook the fish except skewering it on a salted bamboo shard and roasting it over an open flame.

Then there is the night the fish do not bite, and you come home, shoulders low, with nothing. Bone Elvis comes, and when you do not give him dinner, he stands up and leads you down the beach to his house, a small hut up by the rocks. He sits you down on his porch and he goes inside, and cooks you some fish. It's delicious.

You move out of your hut and into his. He makes his money by hunting for cockles on the beach and selling rice from a small paddy a half mile away. The two of you live together for many years, until you are an old woman. Working the rice paddy, walking the beach. Watching the heaviness of the ocean. The sun blares down on you, your skin becomes wrinkled and tough. You die one night when you catch a high fever, and even though the women bring you boneset and cayenne, no one can bring it down.

148

From section 92 . . .

You go home. *What else can you do?* You're miserable. Now the mistakes are stacked like rotten cordwood. *Italy, school, Filippo,* all memories you'd love to erase—but you can't. It's depressing and frightening, you don't know what to do. Your parents urge you to talk to their pastor, and just to get them to climb off your ass—you do.

Pastor Dave isn't anything like you expected (which would have been a pear-shaped, white-haired creep looking for little boys who want candy). Instead, he's a thoughtful young guy who's quite cute and fit. Cute or not, you don't hold back on your questions.

Question #1: What if there is no God? What if there's only quantum mechanics? The ratio of odds. The mathematical likelihood of your life sucking due to certain dumb ass decisions. Question #2: If there's this big fabulous guy up there—why is there so much suffering? Why do children get cancer and bastards get so much money? Question #3: Christians seem to be big on marriage and kids. What if you don't want either?

Pastor Dave doesn't criticize you—he doesn't even argue with you. He just listens. When you're done, he laughs and pours himself a cup of black coffee. "I always get the smart ones," he says. "God picks on me." He tries to answer your questions, and at the same time he admits he doesn't know everything, no one does. "We do the best we can with the information we have," he says. "But we can't know everything. We can't know why some babies get cancer or whether or not we should have children. That's when we need a higher power to lean on. To ask for help. We can let quantum mechanics help us—or we can let God."

"I'll take quantum mechanics," you say.

He laughs and says, "I'll take God."

You and Pastor Dave continue your conversations that day and the next and the next. You like talking to him and trying to fluster him. Then one day he offers you a job as a receptionist in the office. "You're tough enough to handle the bingo ladies," he says, "which is no small task. Plus you're here so often you might as well take a little money for your trouble."

Hmmmmm. A church receptionist? This could be one of those tragic life choices ending thirty years later with you as a mawkish spinster who knits bulky cable-knit sweaters for the blind and has emotional attachments with cats. On the other hand, it might be a simple well-placed stepping-stone in the right direction, a step on a well-lit path that leads you to something even better.

If you take the job as church receptionist,
go to section #162 (page 364).
If you don't take the job as church receptionist,
go to section #163 (page 366).

149

From section 93 . . .

You follow the German through the narrow streets of Palermo. Your legs are made of cement, your head made of clay. You're thick and cold and confused. You try to keep up with him, thanking merciful heaven he offered to carry your pack. There are still people out on the street, mostly men with dark, roving eyes who stand in groups talking, laughing, spitting, smoking. They call out to you when you walk by, *"Bella donna,"* they say. *"Sei una strella!"* *You're a star!* The German gets far ahead of you, and the Campari makes your eyelids heavy.

Where is this house? Why don't we take a bus or a taxi if it's this far away? You cross a bridge and the neighborhoods become darker. Windows are unlit, overflowing garbage cans are lined up on the curb. *Where is he?* You catch a piece of his shadow as he rounds a corner and sprint to catch up with him, painfully twisting your ankle on the uneven cobblestone. *Is this guy an Olympic walker? Can he not see you are a block behind him, and now hopping on one foot?* You call out to him, call again, walk a few steps on your stabbing, pain-shooting foot, and then stop. He's gone.

You sit on the curb, feeling your ankle swell. It's quiet. You can see the stars overhead, punctures in a velvety blue strip of night sky. An orange cat jumps off a garbage can, sending the metal lid clattering to the pavement, and a light goes on behind you, then you hear a thump and three clicks before an irritated woman appears in the doorway wearing an old pink chenille robe. *"Cosa fai?"* she snaps. *What are you doing?*

"Niente," you say. *Nothing.* She looks suspiciously up and down the street and motions for you to come over. You limp toward her, which softens her expression just the smallest degree and she motions for you to come inside.

Her name is Maria Francesca Adonis, and her home is packed with opulent, well-oiled antiques, stern marble busts, and strangely lush furniture. You sit on a green velvet couch and she brings you a towel filled with ice. She asks you how you came to be stranded with a sprained ankle on her doorstep, and to the best of your ability you explain it to her. She's older, maybe in her sixties, but she's well cared for, manicured nails, and her hair, which is pulled into a tight knot at the nape of her neck, is still blue-black and glossy.

Dio mio, she keeps sighing. She brings you gnocchi and a large glass of red wine, which works wonders. You eventually fall asleep on the couch, empty wineglass on the table, wet towel around your tender ankle. In the morning you wake to strange voices and three well-dressed men staring at you. "You see?" Maria says to them as she points at you. "Do something!"

One of the men, handsome in his blue suit, tells her to relax. They'll take care of it. Then Maria helps you to the dining room, where you all sit down for breakfast. She introduces you to the men, her three sons, Baldo, Pippo, and Marco. They nod and grunt, loading their plates with eggs and pepper bacon. "You stay here for a while?" Maria asks you. "Until your leg is better? You can't run around Palermo alone. We'll take care of you." You don't have a penny to your name. Where else would you go? You say *yes*.

Maria is pleased; her sons don't seem to care one way or another. You spend the rest of the week sitting on the green couch, leg propped up on several pillows, the windows thrown open, drinking bottled water with lemon and playing poker with Maria, who cheats. After dinner she usually turns on the television and you watch the news together, and around ten, after your second glass of Chianti, the door slams open and her sons clomp in. *Ciao, Mama!* they call.

One night Marco plops your lost backpack down on the couch. "I got your suitcase back," he says. "It's muddy." Maria is delighted when she sees it. "Brava!" she says, "my good boy." She kisses Marco on the head, who swats her away as he watches the news. *Where did you find it?* you ask him, but he only shrugs. *Did you see the German who took it?* He holds a finger to his lips to shush you and turns up the volume on the television with the remote control. Strange things are quite common in the Adonis family. They say their money comes from blood oranges, shipping the bitter red Sicilian fruit all around the world, but you're suspicious. Since when do oranges produce this much money?

When your ankle is better, Maria takes you out shopping, out to cafés on the square, and she never pays for anything. You never once see money change hands. She must have tabs, house accounts everywhere. The butcher shop, the fruit stand, the restaurants and clothing stores, no one ever asks her, or you, for money. When you venture out alone, which is seldom, and you try to pay for anything, or leave a tip, the proprietor shoves your money back.

The boys come over to the house almost every night for dinner and to drop off their laundry, which Maria handles like couture. She irons each pant leg, starches the pink colors. Folds the cashmere with a straight board. Then one day you see the German. Across the street with his right leg in a purple fiberglass cast. You cross the street to catch him, but when he sees you he sprints wildly (as wildly as one can on crutches) around the corner. He's easy to catch. Much the way you were that first night you arrived. "Hey!" You catch him by the arm. He's acting so strangely—you can feel him shaking under his jacket. Gone is his smile and twinkling eyes. He stares at the ground.

"What the hell happened?" you ask. "You just stole my pack?"

He nods rapidly, closing his eyes. "I didn't know," he says, and then begins repeating it, like a broken marionette, until you clutch his arm harder.

"Didn't know what?"

He shakes his head. "Cosa Nostra," he says. "I didn't know you were with them. I didn't know you were in the family."

You roll your eyes. "Cosa Nostra. Right."

It's his turn to snort at you. "You're living with the mother of one of Sicily's biggest families," he says, "and you don't even think the mob exists?"

If you believe the German, go to section #211 (page 492).
If you don't believe the German, go to section #212 (page 494).

150

From section 93 . . .

Stranger danger. You tell the German *thanks, but no thanks.* You're not in the habit of following strangers to unknown locations. Instead, you ask the bartender where you can sleep that night, and it turns out his cousin Nicky owns a hotel down the street. You lug your bag over there, punch the small doorbell marked PENSIONE, and you're buzzed in. You sleep as hard as you did when you first arrived in Italy, all night and most of the next day.

You wake in the afternoon and stretch, the fresh air reviving you. Downstairs in the crowded café you meet a British couple who tell you they've just come from the nearby town of Canneto di Caronia, which is about seventy kilometers from the volcano Mount Etna. They say it's famous for its spontaneous fires, which break out all the time. Electronics, TVs, microwaves, light switches, blenders, and cell phones—they all burst into flames. The electricity company cut off power to the town and hooked it up to a generator in an attempt to stop the explosions, but then the generator caught fire.

No one can explain the fiery phenomenon—scientists, engineers, priests, police, and paranormal enthusiasts have descended on the town and can't figure out what's going on. It's freaky. The village has all but cleared out. That's enough information for you; you pack your bags and head south to see for yourself.

It takes a long time to get there—bus service in Sicily is unreliable to say the least, but after two misdirected routes and a bus driver who screams at you in his heavy Sicilian accent, you eventually arrive at the all but deserted town of Canneto di Caronia. You check into the only hotel you can find, Hotel Za' Maria, located on the town's main street, sandwiched between a railroad track and the sea. In the other rooms are Swiss seismologists, a volcanologist, a handful of reporters, and an exorcist. (Who knew an exorcist could be a small doughy man with green Harry Potter glasses?)

Been here long? you ask the volcanologist at dinner. (There's only one place to have dinner in Caronia, in the hotel lobby, where dishes are spooned out from metal pots cooked up the hill. No cookstoves allowed, lest the chef go up in flames.) "Too long," he answers. "Only lunatics stay here."

The volcanologist's name is Jed; he's a New Zealander and dead handsome. He tells you there is no fire demon, no devil, no poltergeist. "Only a plumbing problem," he says. "Mount Etna is plugged up. Only a few miles from here magma is spreading out horizontally rather than vertically and it's creating fields of methane underground, which in turn creates electric fields that ignite. That, combined with the decreasing number of eruptions, suggests that there's a big catastrophic eruption in the near future."

He shows you all his seismic data and charts, the precision instruments he uses to register quake activity, fault line movement, and anything to do with the surface of the earth *moving*. You of course always thought of the earth as solid, but around Jed everything seems to change. "I'm just about done with my research here," he says. "I actually leave for Taormina tomorrow. I'm locating hot spots, places where Etna's magma plumbing is near the surface but away from civilization. Mostly underwater sites off the Sicilian coast. I find them with thermal imaging equipment anchored on boats. I know you just got here, but want to come with me and assist?"

You go with Jed. In the morning a hired van picks the two of you up and carts you the short distance to the ferry, which will take you to Taormina, a butterfly-shaped island off the coast of Sicily, with two enormous bays of water and a sweeping view of Mount Etna, which looks quite menacing now that you know about her plumbing problems.

Home to aristocrats of the ages, the Sicels, Greeks, Romans, Byzantines, Saracens, Arabs, Normans, and Spaniards, mysterious and captivating Taormina still has the ruins of its *Gymnasia*, where athletes trained for the Olympics, the Naumachiae (a building named after the ancient naval war game), an Arabian Necropolis, the opulent public gardens, and the old abbey, the Badia Vecchia.

Jed is an intrepid traveler. All his gear collapses and fits in his enormous pack, charts and papers sealed in watertight tubes. He has a GPS and satellite phone strapped to his waist so the university of Hawaii, who employs him, can reach him anywhere and anytime. "How long since you've been home?" you ask.

"I get back to New Zealand in the winters," he says. "But anywhere there's a volcano, that's my home."

Just as Jed promised, you're out on a rented boat that very day, on the Mediterranean sea, setting up thermal imaging equipment that is searching for hot spots on the ocean floor. Veins of magma. Jed explains the only way to avoid a massive eruption is to drill into the magma veins near the surface and vent the volcano from the bottom. The University of Hawaii is working in conjunction with several other teams, who are all out on similar scouts, collecting data and potential drill sites.

At the end of the long day you are sun-soaked, sunburnt, and happy. After collecting data, Jed downloads it into a computer, which uplinks with a computer in Hawaii. You'll go out again the next day, and the day after that. It turns out you have the legs and stomach for even the roughest seas and Jed quickly teaches you how to begin using the thermal imaging equipment.

The days fly by, as does the season and the project. Soon it's time for Jed to move to his "winter volcano," White Island in New Zealand. He asks if you want to come with him. He can hire you as an assistant, so you don't have to lug thermal imaging equipment around for free. But you'd have to sign on for five years, as the university doesn't hand out contracts for less than that. You're not sure what to do. You didn't come over to Europe to become a volcanologist—it sounds dangerous, although this job would give you some money to get home.

If you go to White Island, go to section #213 (page 496).
If you don't go to White Island, go to section #214 (page 498).

151

From section 92 . . .

You take the job, but you have to move out of the cave and live in a drafty, creaking wooden shack behind the cabanas on the beach. Still, you like the sound of the surf and the relative privacy. You work at the youth hostel, checking people in, cleaning the bathrooms, changing the sheets, washing the floors, stocking the small bar in the front lounge (an open-air space, with an enormous wooden trellis overhead made entirely of driftwood trees), and you develop your favorite pastime, collecting the stories of travelers passing through.

There's the guy who survived a camel attack him in Egypt, a girl who shows you her shark bite for a beer, a man who vomited up his own stomach lining after eating chili in Marrakech. You write down these stories in a black book, a moleskin you bought in Fira. Some of the stories are just musings, some are more in-depth. A season passes, and then another. The travelers come and go like the tide. Heavy in the summer, thin in the winter. The stories add up and so do your savings, as there's little for you to spend your money on except journals and pencils and the odd disposable camera, which you use to take pictures of the people you write about.

Macgregor lets you manage the bar. You serve the island's only pomegranate martini and over twenty-eight different kinds of imported beer. "The only place on Santorini you can get a warm Guinness!" Macgregor boasts, although there aren't many takers for warm beer during the roasted Greek afternoons.

But things get lonely. It's ironic that on such a beautiful, romantic island long-term romantic relationships are all but impossible. The native Greek men won't have anything to do with Americans, and the migrant workforce that invades the island during the summer can provide you with exactly three months of company before they have to go home. The small and freakishly unacceptable population of foreigners who live on Santorini year-round hold absolutely no interest.

Still, you have your journal, and your writing is getting better. One day a small woman with piercing blue eyes sits down at your bar. She asks you what you're writing. *Well, you have to think about that. What are you writing?* You tell her about your chronicles. About the people who have come and gone, the bits of color you have managed to pick up and keep in the folds of your book, the names, the places, the calamities and the awe. *The hilarious.* The guy who threw up in his own backpack on a crowded train in Japan so he wouldn't offend anyone. The teenager who had uncontrollable diarrhea during mass at the Vatican.

You tell her the amazing stories. The man who walked fifteen miles through the backlands of Tibet to get a wounded snow partridge proper medical treatment. The girls who took the homeless woman on the beach and bought her a house. People who for no reason stopped their lives, stopped what they were doing, and helped someone else.

This woman at the bar with her blue eyes listens and listens as you go on and on. She switches from martinis to Diet Cokes, and as the sun is setting and the regulars start to come in, she says, "Let me see that journal." She sticks out her hand. "I want to keep it overnight. I'm staying up the hill, at the terrace cabanas. I'll bring it back in the morning."

If you give her the journal, go to section #97 (page 207).
If you don't give her the journal, go to section #96 (page 206).

152

From section 48 . . .

The bakery is by the Pitti Palace and is called Pagnotta. It's a warm, delicious-smelling place where clouds of warm cinnamon and lemon sugar bloom through the sweet air. The Amato family owns the bakery, and they originally came from Sicily, which makes them highly suspect in the neighborhood. People in Florence can be very classist—many people think southern Italy is worthless, that they should chop Italy off mid-boot and let the southerners fend for themselves. There's even a local group called *Lega Nord* who have picketed Pagnotta before and handed out nasty anti-Sicilian literature claiming families like the Amatos should *Vie Via*, go home.

Alfonso, the father, is a chubby man with rolls of doughy skin around his neck and arms. He's very rude to customers and very sweet to his family, which is mainly comprised of his wife, Maria, and his three daughters. (His daughters are chubby too; working around tiramisu and clotted cream puts a healthy hide on each one of them.) The negative sentiments from the neighborhood don't bother any of them. Alfonso says, *"They piss and moan but they always buy my bread."* He shows you how to knead dough, how to twist and beat and bake their famous recipes. You go to work at four in the morning and by six a.m., when the bakery is open, there are trays and trays of cakes and pies ready, warm ciabatta and pane Siciliano, a heavy braided bread with sesame seeds on top.

The bakery works in two shifts. You and the family work the *sole shift*, the sun shift, and Alfonso's cousins, burly men with square chins, work the *luna shift*, the moon shift. The moon shift bakes bread that gets shipped out of the city. You're not sure where it all goes—but they make *a lot* of bread. When they arrive, the cousins are clean and pressed, smoking cigarettes and stepping out of their Armani suits, but by the time they leave (just as you arrive in the morning), they're powdered white with flour and their sweaty faces are flushed rose red from standing in front of the stone ovens. "How much bread do they make?" you ask Alfonso. *He tells you not to worry about it.* You ask him, "Who buys all that bread?" *He tells you to get back to work.* But the more you think about it—the stranger it is. No other bakery in town has a second shift.

Maybe it's because you're bored or lonely or just curious, but you want to know more, so you stay late one night. You hide yourself in a closet and sit on an overturned bucket, where from a crack in the door you can watch the cousins, Guido, Massimo, Andrea, and Baldo. They stumble around arguing. Baldo takes a little brown bag from his pocket and brings it to the center island, where he carefully empties out what look like gold coins onto the table. "How many now?" Massimo asks.

Baldo grunts and uses his thick finger to count the coins.

"How many?" Massimo asks again.

"Am I counting?" Baldo shouts. "Do you see me counting?"

Andrea smacks Massimo on the back of the head and Massimo in turn punches Andrea in the head. They go down to the floor in a strong embrace, yelling at each other and rolling on the floor. Guido breaks them up. By this time Baldo has stopped counting and he says, "One hundred and twenty-three."

"Dio mio." Massimo sighs. "A hundred and twenty-three ciabattas."

At this point you're feeling a little nervous about being in the closet. Whatever these guys are doing, it's more than just baking bread. You have the feeling they wouldn't like knowing you were watching. Three hours later you're ready to fall asleep in the closet. It's hot—every single oven is stoked and firing up bread after bread after bread. Guido is on the phone speaking German with someone, Massimo and Andrea run the ovens while Baldo shapes the dough and puts it on wide metal trays. He takes a chunk of ciabatta dough and molds it roughly into the shape of a woman's breast. Then he takes one of the gold coins from the table and presses it deep into the bread's belly with his thumb. They're baking bread with gold coins inside.

Around one in the morning, Massimo shouts from the back room. One of the ovens has gone out. Baldo and Guido leave the kitchen momentarily to go help their brothers in back. *Now's your chance.* You dart out of the closet and grab a gold coin off the table. It's heavy. Unusual. You just barely have time to get back into the closet when the brothers come back. They'll never miss it.

Except they do. At three in the morning there's one last doughy breast waiting in the center of the flour-strewn table—but no gold coin to put in it. "You said there was a hundred and twenty-three," Massimo complains. "Did one walk out by itself?"

"He just miscounted," Guido says.

"He didn't miscount, he's a thief!"

Guido puts his cigarette out. "He miscounted."

"Thief!" Massimo sneers at his brother.

Eventually the brothers choose to forget the missing coin. They look exhausted and hot and dirty. They clean the kitchen and turn off the lights before they leave. When you stand up your legs cramp and you almost fall over. You've got to be at work in an hour. You study the gold coin—you've never seen anything like it. There's a faint outline of a man in a helmet on one side and you can barely make out some sort of creature on the other. The edge of the coin is thick and greenish colored. It looks very, very old.

At work you keep things calm. Normal. You even act as diplomat when two of the sisters get into a catfight about some man they're both in love with. You tell no one about the coin, and a week later you summon the courage to take the coin to a dealer outside town. He looks at it for half an hour before he comes back and says, "It's Roman and it's old—221 BC. Whoever got this probably found it at sea, judging from the surface." Then he says it's worth twenty thousand dollars.

Alfonso and his brothers have somehow gotten their hands on these ancient Roman gold coins (how they got their hands on them you don't even want to know) and they're smuggling them out of the country in bread. (Bread inside bread.) But what do you do? You've got your gold piece, should you get more? You nearly caused a fistfight last time—how can you get more without them knowing?

You find the cousins' Achilles' heel by following them one night to the place where they drop off the gold bread. You learn after they bake the bread that they take it to the post office, where they leave it inside a red Fiat, which is parked out front. Alfonso makes a call on his cell phone and then they all leave. Five minutes later another group of men in suits appear and get into the Fiat and drive off. You follow them every night for a week, and every night it's the same. Bake the bread, put it in the Fiat, make a phone call, and leave—and every night there's a five-minute window before the other men come.

You decide to be brave. So for five nights you follow the brothers to the Fiat, wait for them to leave, sneak up to the car, open the door while crouching down, reach your hand into the damp, warm box, and fish out one loaf wrapped in wax paper. Every night for five nights. Five loafs and they never catch you.

You have stolen *a hundred thousand dollars* in coins. You quit the bakery and move away before anyone thinks to ask you any questions. The family is sad and they give you an opal ring, a hundred euros in cash, and a bottle of French perfume. You feel bad taking anything more from them—it's obvious that the brothers' coin trafficking is supporting the entire Amato family, but you've taken what you need—and now you're going to start your own life down south.

You move down to Sicily and buy a small green stone house in the hills. Truman Capote lived somewhere near here and created his best work. You can see why. You overlook a green valley and the blue sea, bright as a peacock's eye. Gorgeous so that beauty pushes at your eyelids, makes you see poetry at every turn. Land is cheap here—but the house needs a lot of work. You hire local men to come and fix up the aquifer, the roof, the walls. They mend and paint and scrub, until one day a year later you open your bed-and-breakfast, called *Ovunque*—Italian for "Everywhere." You get your first clients through friends of your family, and then their friends and their friends, until you pretty much book up through the whole summer. You fall in love with a local man named Marco, tall and tan with tight apple checks. (He's Sicilian in every way—easy to anger by day, easy to passion by night.) He's a stone mason and he builds you a large marble fountain in your courtyard with two lovers kissing. You work on the gardens, spend the Amato money very sagely, and by the end of the third year you've created a small paradise.

You're featured on the Travel Channel's "best kept secrets" and *Ovunque* has become a gold mine. Your parents retire and move out there to be near you—you buy a neighboring villa for them and they open a small vineyard. You and Marco have two children named Sasha and Sandro, and you don't die until you are a hundred and two years old. (Some say it's the olive oil and Chianti.) You pass over in your sleep. Heaven for you is staying right there in that stone house, haunting the rooms as the guests come and go. There's a local legend that you, the woman who used to own the house, still walks the grounds and is known for stealing coins out of people's pockets—which is truly still something you love to do.

153

From section 123 . . .

You agree to terminate the pregnancy. You guess it's lucky that you're both on the same page about the whole thing . . . I mean, who wants to face the lifetime of struggle that would invariably come with a handicapped child? Same page or not, from that moment on you and Jóhann fight. Everything he does annoys you. How he talks, how he sleeps, how he chews his food.

After the "procedure" panic attacks regularly rip through your system and you can't eat or sleep. The city seems strange. Hollow. You suddenly hate it here and you want to go home. The pressure builds in your head until you can't stand it anymore. You don't even bother with paperwork or filing for divorce, you just scratch out a good-bye letter on the back of an electricity bill, stick it on the refrigerator with a ladybug magnet, and head for the airport.

On the flight home, you sit next to a nice-looking man named Alex VanderBerg. He has deep-set blue eyes and wire-frame glasses that perch on top of his aquiline nose. He smells like musky cherrywood—a scent created by the pouch of tobacco tucked in his breast pocket. He'd probably look stern if he didn't have wavy long blond hair tucked behind his large ears. You get to talking—and talking and talking and talking, for the whole eight hours home. You like him. His refined manners are calming. You ask him what he does for a living and he smiles. "Misplaced equities," he says.

What the hell is that?

He settles back, orders another gin and tonic, and tells you the story. (You try to listen, but your eyes keep wandering down to his lower lip.) He says it all started back when his great-great-great-grandfather opened one of the first art galleries in Holland, which sold mostly Dutch paintings. Works by Bloemaert, Honthorst, Lastman, Rembrandt, and Vermeer. The all-star smackdown heavy-hitter artists of Amsterdam.

You nod your head and wonder what he looks like naked. Alex doesn't notice your lack of concentration, and the story starts to get interesting. Wealthy aristocrats who collected expensive Dutch art were a limited group and there was a rival art gallery run by the Janssen family. "They were dogs," Alex whispers, "relatives of Napoleon. Started the business with his private collection, which was stolen from all over Europe." *Wow,* you think, *he smells even better close up.*

Then the VanderBerg gallery was broken into and cleaned out. "Absolutely gutted," Alex says. "Canvases cut right off their frames, fragile sketches thrown on the floor." He pauses to consider the lime drifting in his drink, and you notice how long his eyelashes are. "The worst part, though," he says, "was that they took several paintings that were on loan."

That was apparently the beginning of the end for the VanderBerg family. They had to pay restitution for the stolen paintings and they owed money all over Europe. Big money. Then the artists started backing out, choosing the Janssen family to represent them. After all, they had a big clientele list and a gallery that had never been broken into. It was the VanderBergs' opinion that the Janssens were responsible for the theft, which made this even more unbearable.

Shortly after that the family officially went from being art dealers to "rescue artists." They hunted for their stolen art all over Europe, following any lead from Paris to Sicily, becoming more and more desperate to recover what they had lost. Alex says he carries on the tradition to this day, and then pauses, waiting for you to understand . . . which you don't. "I'm an art thief," he says, "an international art thief. I find art that's been stolen, steal it back, and sell it to museums for a reasonable fee. It's a service really. These paintings would be lost forever otherwise. It happens more than you'd think—there's a river of masterpieces that the public never sees, never even *knows about,* because it just changes hands in the same underground circles. I fix that." Right then it occurs to you that you've never had sex on an airplane before.

Several more drinks and you throw caution to the wind. You propose meeting in the aft lavatory. Underwear optional. Alex looks like he was stung by a bee, and you're afraid you might have offended him, but then a sly smile creeps across his face and he looks like he won the lottery. Fifteen minutes and a liquid-soap-covered shoe later, you and Alex VanderBerg, *known international art thief*, are officially members of the mile high club and you can't get the grin off your face.

The plane lands in New York. Alex says he'll call and *actually does*. You go out on exactly three dates, which all end in passionate sex in his bathroom (a running theme), and he asks you, "Want to liberate some misplaced equities with me?" He winks and smiles. *He. Is. So. Cute.* How can you say no?

Alex locates stolen art that's fallen off the radar, small work, like sketches and drawings usually. He locates the work through "the grumblers," a vast network of low-ranking informants who won't make money off the deal unless they snitch—the doormen who let mysterious vans drop off covered canvases, the cargo loaders at the docks who overhear private conversations, the underpaid art restoration assistants who watch their bosses restore stolen work, and so on.

Once he's concluded that the current owner stole the work, or the person they bought it from did, or the person *they* bought it from did, he starts making a retrieval plan. *This job*, he says, is simple. There's a hedge-fund banker-guy who has obtained a questionable Picasso. A stolen painting. Alex needs you to simply and literally "drive the getaway car." Why not? You say you'll do it.

You embark on a long life of profitable international art theft and you eventually marry Mr. VanderBerg. All goes well until you get pregnant. This time you opt *not* to have an amniocentesis, the test that determines whether your baby has Down syndrome, because honestly, you don't care and neither does Alex. Some things matter, and then they don't.

Little boy VanderBerg II is born, and you both give up the heist trade in exchange for your own small gallery and a saltbox cottage in Kennebunkport, Maine. Surrounded by beautiful art, delightful neighbors, lobster roasts, and your own beautiful boy, life really could not be sweeter. Sometimes, though, when you stare out at sea, you think of the other baby you might have had . . . but then something always tears your attention away. You never can know what might have been. You and Alex live there in your small, handcrafted bliss until you're seventy-two. Then you get hit by a newspaper truck, which was speeding.

154

From section 125 . . .

You tell Oliver to go home without you. You can't get married—you have to fix this thing with your father first. Berlin can wait—has to wait because your father can't. Oliver says he understands, but you can tell that he doesn't. His shoulders slump and he won't look you in the eye. He takes back the ring he gave you and the pearl earrings, saying they were his mother's. He flies home without so much as kissing you. Everything seems bent and broken. He won't listen.

Your father meanwhile has turned his house into a fortress. He doesn't answer the phone, he keeps the shades drawn. The car has a film of dust on it. Your aunts say he can't go on living without your mother—he's stopped eating and doesn't want to see you. He somehow blames you for your mother's death. For not being a better daughter, for making her blood pressure elevate with your selfish antics and inability to think of others. After several failed tries at communication, you stop trying. Just give him time, your aunts say. He'll come around.

So you give him time, and in the meanwhile you start your own topless ice cirkus. It's just a small operation at first—you get a dozen strippers who know how to ice skate. (Most of them are originally from the Midwest.) You make costumes for them—American icons like Hillary Clinton, Eleanor Roosevelt, Amelia Earhart, and Harriet Tubman, and then you rent a local theater for the evening. (You don't need ice—you skate on white wax instead, which cuts down on expense and injury.) You call the show *Tits on Ice*. People think it's catchy.

Just like in Germany, the general public catches wind of your characters on ice—and they go apeshit. A local paper runs a story on your show in the Variety section, which is then picked up by Reuters and distributed nationally. *The Frozen Chosen?* is the title of the article. Papers across the country run the story and then talk shows start calling. The religious right swoops in and the Christian Coalition sues you for defamation of something-or-other. It's basically a lot of free advertising. Your ticket sales rocket, you are able to hire full-time strippers and give them health benefits and day care. You move the show to New York, where you have a permanent home just off Broadway in the old Apollina Theater (the stage converted to a permanent ice rink).

You call Oliver and ask him to come back to America and be with you—help run the cirkus, but a woman answers the phone. His new French wife, Daphne. When you hang up you burst into heaving tears. Even with all this commercial success and money, you've never felt so alone. Your father never sees you again. He stays stubborn and mad till the end. Even when he's diagnosed with lung cancer—he moves to California without telling you and dies in a hospital bed alone. His autopsy reveals several brain lesions on the pituitary gland, which the doctor says would account for his irrationality and anger issues toward the end. Still—you feel like it was all your fault.

Tits on Ice continues to do well—so much so you can hire a management company to handle most of the details. You have an executive producer and a stage manager and a costume shop—not to mention twenty-four talented girls and two fabulous gay men to perform in the show. You yourself no longer have to skate.

You die one day in a McDonald's drive-through line. A deranged member of the 700 Club has been following you, a man with bloodshot eyes and a pearl-handled Derringer .38. He walks up to you as you wait for your Quarter Pounder with Cheese and taps on the passenger window. You roll the window down (why wouldn't you? In his V-neck sweater he looks like Mister Rogers in distress) and he reaches in with the gun and blows your face off point-blank.

Great.

In heaven you're in big-ass trouble. God is furious with you for mucking around. "Do you think loveliness is flying around on white wax with your tits hanging out?" he asks. "That that's how I wanted you to spend your time?" You're surprised because you didn't think God would use a word like "tits."

He returns you to earth as punishment, but this time you're the wife of the president of the Christian Coalition, which is the worst thing he can think of.

"You'll see," he says. "You'll see what wasting time actually is. Those people have the personalities of Eurasian milfoil and they wear ugly shoes—like orthopedics even if you don't need them."

You don't know what Eurasian milfoil is and he says *pervasive pond scum*. You're surprised again because you didn't think God would know anything about pond scum or orthopedic shoes, but he shrugs and says at least orthopedics are better than those stupid strappy sandals he had to wear in Jerusalem.

155

From section 90 . . .

Your new job at the hospital is to clean monkey cages. The hospital specializes in neurology and behavioral sciences and is known for their extensive testing involving animals—causing routine protests outside. The program you're assigned to is technically called "Behavioral Sciences of Intra-Monetary Exchange," but everyone in the lab calls them the sex monkeys.

The sex monkeys are just regular monkeys—chimpanzees with all their front teeth removed (because they bite). Originally funded by a private hedge fund whose owner is an alumni, the study was designed to study *primal drive spending habits*. Why do we buy what we buy—what motivates, frightens, or compels a creature to spend money? They used monkeys to find out.

The monkeys live in a huge elaborate room called the tank, and your unsavory job is to clean the tank, shovel out urine-soaked hay, and hose down the cement floors. You're told the monkeys were pretty much happy, had plenty of food, space, socialization, until the scientists introduced the concept of *money* into the tank. They gave the monkeys red and green poker chips, and the monkeys had to "pay" for their food with the poker chips.

The monkeys took to it right away. They understood they had to give poker chips for their food, their toys, anything they wanted. Then the scientists introduced the concept of *inflation*. Now food costs two poker chips instead of one, treats cost more. The monkeys totally understood the concept. They hoarded their chips and fought over them and began paying for things before they were even asked.

So after introducing "money" into the tank, the scientists sat back and watched how the monkeys integrated it into their society. They pretty much just wanted to see if the monkeys would keep it up, or eventually tire of the poker chips and throw them all down the urine drain. Well—the monkeys kept it up all right, and six months later all the male chimpanzees were buying only one thing: sex from the female chimps. The female chimps in turn were taking their chips and buying food for their children. They were buying bananas, shiny toys, animal crackers. You're not sure they needed a million-dollar research project to know that.

They're smart, these monkeys. You spend extra time with them after your shifts. They lift your depression and make you feel needed. There's one monkey in particular, Shenanigans, who's your buddy. He sits in your lap and picks imaginary nits out of your hair. He prefers you to all the scientists, and even though he knows sign language, he won't sign to anybody now but you. The scientists find this interesting and ask if you'd be willing to spend more time with him. Sure you would. They pay you more money—enough so you can get your own place near the hospital.

Shenanigans is your ticket to a higher paycheck. The scientists think he's chosen you for a mate and they want to study interspecies pair bonding. You start spending all day in the tank while they take notes. Besides the noise and the smell, it's pretty interesting. Shenanigans introduces you to the tribe, protects you from the other aggressive chimps, and the two of you like to sit and eat apricots by the waterfall (apricots are Shenanigan's favorite). Your monkey husband even tries to give you a poker chip for sex, which you politely refuse. Shenanigans seems very put out by this, and slaps you in the face. He won't talk to you then. The scientists are distressed. If Shenanigans "breaks up with you," this might be the end of their research.

They ask you a difficult question. They ask if you will have sex with Shenanigans, for the greater good of medicine. How having sex with a monkey would improve medicine, you don't know, but they offer you ten thousand dollars to do it. "It wouldn't be actual penetration," the head scientist tells you. "If he thinks you're rejecting him sexually, he'll stop bonding with you. He'll pick someone else. We just have to make Shenanigans *think* he's having sex with you. Get you partially naked and let him—you know, rub around."

You do it. The day comes and you crawl up to Shenanigans, who rudely tosses a banana peel at you. All the scientists are behind their mirrored glass wall, watching. You hand him a poker chip, which temporarily confuses him until you turn around and try to seductively waggle your butt at him. (You are wearing a matching set of nylon nude-colored bra and underpants, so Shenanigans will think you're buck-naked.) The scientists have urged you to let Shenanigans take the lead, just do whatever he wants, and you're grateful when he drags and pushes you out of view, behind a clump of low-lying palm trees.

He gets to work right away. Monkeys are *strong*. He pushes you down and stands behind you. You feel his muscular black hands clamp like vise grips onto your waist. You try and wiggle a little to loosen his grip but he shrieks and bites you on the ass. This makes you lose balance and fall forward on your chin, at which point you feel something hot and hard banging between your legs. Monkey penises are *bigger* than you expected. Your panties are getting wet from whatever he's doing. You're getting worried. You try and inch out of the palm grove, where the scientists can see you and possibly get this little shit off you, but that's when Shenanigans gives one hard shove with his dick, and breaks through your panties.

You feel the slippery hot thing, like a hot hard tongue, dart in and out of you. Sweaty monkey fur around it. Now you start shouting, and all the other chimps start shrieking, which drowns you out. They've circled around now, sitting in the bushes watching Shenanigans screw you. You manage to get on your hands and knees and that's when Shenanigans screams louder than you have ever heard; his hands grip so tight there'll be black and blue marks later, and you feel him release inside you. The chimps go nuts. They bang their fists on the ground and chatter. You crawl battered and bruised out of the palm grove.

The scientists are really sorry. Having never experienced sex with a monkey firsthand, they really didn't know what it would be like. They give you shots of antibiotics and God knows what else. You wonder if that was their plan all along, for you to be screwed by a monkey, because they measure your bruises and ask you over and over to describe what it was like. *"Now, would you say his penis was rough or smooth? When he ejaculated, was it hotter than human sperm? Was the tip bulbous when erect?"*

You get a lawyer and sue the hospital for twenty million dollars. You settle out of court, the hospital desperate to keep the story out of the papers. *Girl has sex with chimpanzee in hospital lab! Scientists watch as lab assistant is monkey-raped!* No. They hand over the twenty million; you sign the papers to never speak of it again.

You invest all the money and with the help of a greedy and ambitious investment banker double it in no time. You buy your parents a mansion in Bel-Air. You buy one next door. The rest of your life is spent jet-setting around the world, going to Fashion Week in New York, attending the World Cup, the Kentucky Derby, the World Series. You buy art in China and donate money to multiple charitable causes. You marry a Swiss mogul named Hans. You adopt seven children and hire seven nannies and seven tutors.

They grow and marry seven respectable people and the grandchildren start to pour in. You don't like the grandkids until they get a little older. In their terrible twos and threes (and fours and fives) they're like little monkeys all over the furniture, shrieking and pounding their fists. Still, you give them each a trust fund and tuition to colleges of their choice. Shenanigans dies when he's the oldest monkey in the tank, and as per your agreement, the hospital sends him to you stuffed and mounted. You keep him in the attic and the children are frightened of him.

You die at eighty-one, from a mysterious virus, not HIV, but not far from it. Your doctors write papers on your symptoms (sweating, blotchiness, blue eyelids) and on the virus itself, which has a familiar but strange cell structure. You of course do not tell them about the monkey sex, and even though your story makes it far and wide in the medical community, the hospital where it happened does not come forward either.

156

From sections 166 and 167 . . .

You marry Christian in a million-dollar ceremony in Malibu. There's hand-made china, billowing silk tents, and perfect weather. You take her hands in yours and you both pledge the rest of your lives to each other. Hundreds of people are in attendance, celebrities, producers, agents, bodyguards. Helicopters swarm overhead, tabloids trying to get a candid photo—but you don't care, the sky never looked so blue, the sun never felt so warm.

You honeymoon in Galway, in one of the crumbling castles that dot the verdant valleys by the cliffs of Moher. You ride speckled silver horses, eat organic vegetable stew, drink champagne, and stay in bed late. Your own private early girl. You talk Christian into letting you do a few more movies (just to pad the investment portfolio) and then the two of you drift into blissful anonymity. You dye your hair dark black and change your names.

You end up moving to Galway. The two of you never have children; instead you give millions to Unicef and the Children's Cancer Research Fund. You have twenty sheep, sixteen chickens, a dog, three cats, and two passports that need pages sewn into them every year, because the two of you travel so much.

You live on the farm to be old women together. You publish two books and she gets her jewelry in *Vogue* and *Vanity Fair*. In town you're known as eccentrics, literates, strange philanthropic witches. You die as you lived—together. Your Mercedes convertible swerves right off the cliffs of Moher one day, headlong into the water below. You have one distinct thought as the water comes hurtling toward you. *Beautiful.*

157

From sections 158, 166, and 167 . . .

You don't marry Christian and she leaves you. You never speak to her again. Never. It really doesn't matter what you do with the rest of your life—it's inconsequential without her. You start to drink . . . there are a few other details that blur, but it doesn't matter. You give up on yourself and so does everyone else. Christian will haunt you for the rest of your days. Her memory, her face, her smell. You die wondering. There will never be another early girl.

158

From section 100 . . .

You let Christian kiss you. Why not? You're curious. *You want to.* Her lips are soft and light, like butterflies landing on your mouth and then lighting away. She kisses the bridge of your nose and then your eyelids and then the ridge of your jaw. She smells like a good memory. Palms damp, heartbeat irregular, you kiss her back on the collarbone. She tastes slightly salty and damp, her breath is shallow, her clavicle rising and falling rapidly—she's nervous too. You lay there together in the dark, breast to breast, nipple to nipple, and kiss all night, making out like teenagers.

The sun rises in the small window across the room, the sky a brilliant lavender and pink. You hear a barn owl calling. When she wakes, Christian is rumpled and adorable in the light blue sheets, her messy hair, her sly smile. You both have a secret now—and it shows. Her grandparents have breakfast waiting on the wooden kitchen table, black coffee, pease pudding, boiled bacon and saveloy. (It turns out pease pudding isn't just a dish in a nursery rhyme—*Pease pudding hot, pease pudding cold, pease pudding in the pot nine days old*—it's actually a thick stewy sauce made from dried peas.) Her grandparents are sweet and friendly, even if they're almost impossible to understand with their thick brogue accents. They ask if the bed was firm enough, if you two had a good night's sleep. If only they knew.

Later that morning they stand in the yard waving as you and Christian drive away. Now there's just the road and the two of you. Over those first miles you don't talk much; you'll learn over time that with Christian there are no awkward silences, only sweet surrenders when you're just together. No talk required.

You drive down to Rosslare, around the southern tip of Ireland, stopping all the way for every tiny town, every crumbling castle and every scenic overlook. Even though the whole country is a scenic overlook. Ireland is gorgeous. Christian is gorgeous. You're gorgeous. The whole crazy world is gorgeous. You wonder how any place could be so filled with endless moments of orchestrated beauty. You take a ferry to Paris and get matching butterfly tattoos on the smalls of your backs, you get drunk in Munich, lost in Rome, repentant at the Vatican, and sunburned in Greece.

You feel like you've found your soul mate. Your true love. Christian is funny and smart and always making trouble. She steals a fishing boat in Spain and convinces you to go out into the open water naked. You lie there in the boat side by side, drifting in the current and caught by the moonlight. It's a month later in Sienna when she checks her e-mail. Her grandparents have died in an automobile accident. They leave Christian the house, the land, the farm, and a big chunk of money.

You both return to the farm in Ireland. It looks lifeless without her grandparents. Christian wants to move in and set up her jewelry studio. You've already been traveling for two years—no college, no job, and now you have no money. You're actually homesick. When was it you were going to start your life exactly? Maybe you should go back to America and get organized. But then Christian smiles. She gets down on one knee and asks if you'll marry her. You love Christian—but women marrying women in this Catholic neck of the woods—that's a good way to get lynched.

If you marry Christian, go to section #215 (page 501).
If you do not marry Christian, go to section #157 (page 356).

159

From section 100 . . .

You can't kiss her. You stumble up and back away from the bed. It's too weird, it would mean . . . well, you don't know exactly what it would mean but you're not ready for it, whatever it is. *"No, no, no,"* you say, apologizing and hitting your head on a low rafter. *You're sorry, you're not that way, you didn't mean to lead her on. . . .*

You start to collect your things and Christian begs you to stay. She apologizes for making a move, she thought maybe you liked her, and the more she tries to convince you to stay, the more you want to leave. You get everything together and hurry for the door. She says she feels awful—and offers to drive you back to port, where at least you can catch the ferry. You keep a careful eye on her. Your heart is beating, you feel queasy and numb.

The car ride is awful. Deafening silence. The turn of the wheels and a tinny McJibberish Irish voice on the radio. Christian says nothing. You say nothing. Her hands are gripped on the wheel. All the fluency between you is gone. It's not that you have anything against girls who like girls, but you don't like girls—you like them but . . . maybe you would even kiss one, but it's complicated. It's not too late to continue on with your adventure. You really want to go to Sicily. It'll take a long time to get there, but it's supposed to be beautiful. You also want to go to Paris—closer by but certainly more crowded.

If you go to Paris, go to section #26 (page 42).
If you go to Sicily, go to section #93 (page 196).

160

From sections 83 and 108 . . .

You pitch the idea to Ray. "It would be so easy!" After all, you've got access to almost everything you need—you can get the kitchen matches, iodine, hydrogen peroxide, and decongestants at the pharmacy. You can buy the lighter fluid, lye, acetone, antifreeze, and muriatic acid at gas stations and hardware stores without anyone batting an eye. You both decide you'll have to do this covertly and out of the house, away from Alison. There's a little tool shed in back of the house where you keep rakes and paint cans. You clean it all out, hang curtains over the little windows, and set up a laboratory.

Everybody has a job. You tend to the hot plates, Ray diligently scrapes red phosphorus off the kitchen matches, Alison watches Barney videos in the living room. It takes a little time, and you completely mess up your first two batches, but by the end of the week you have six grams of meth to sell. Only you don't sell it—you give it away. People have to experience it in order to want it, and since you intend to sell to upstanding citizens, they won't know what they've been missing.

Ray gets your first clients from his STD clinic. (It seems a likely match.) He clandestinely hands out small Baggies of the powder to the people he suspects would enjoy it—and within the month you already have your first loyal customers. By the end of six months you've built a new Quonset hut on your property, you've employed two local men to help you, and you're producing about six grams of meth a day.

Within no time you have amassed enough money to get back to America—but you want more. You couldn't have this operation in America, but here it's so easy. Labor is cheap and you pay off the local police every month—a little hush-hush money and they look the other way. You've even been able to help a few of your neighbors by single-handedly paying for the new water purifier and you bought the jackfruit lady a brand-new chair.

Years pass. By the time Alison is in grade school, you're supplying the entire eastern half of the island with meth, including Kingston. By the time she's in high school you are one of the wealthiest families in all of Jamaica. You live in a gorgeous plantation-style villa in Goblin Hill, just above the Blue Lagoon. You have donated hundreds of thousands of dollars to Jamaica's educational system, as well as the Holywell Conservation Trust, and Women, Inc., a battered women's shelter in Kingston.

Alison has become quite the athlete and has even been offered a full scholarship at Stanford and a place on their women's swim team. She practices her butterfly at Winnifred Beach (donated by the late Quaker minister F. B. Brown as a place for "missionaries, teachers, and the respectable poor"). You're swimming with her there one day when an undertow comes for you.

As you are rushing headlong out to sea in the invisible cold river, you review your life. You had a wonderful husband, an adorable daughter, and you lived in paradise with more money than you knew what to do with. You were also a drug dealer. Alison is waving frantically at you from the beach, and as you go under for the final time, you wonder what she will grow up to do with her life. Maybe she'll always do the right thing—or maybe she'll be like you and do everything wrong so it all comes out right in the end. The ocean will take anybody.

161

From sections 83 and 108 . . .

You're *not* going to become a drug dealer. You have to set an example for Alison. This means of course you have to move out of your mountaintop home and into a small apartment on the outskirts of Port Antonio, which can be a dangerous neighborhood. Still. You have to teach her right from wrong—and you don't want her to see you dealing drugs—but you soon realize she's seeing drugs being dealt all the time, right in front of the house. You've got to do something. You beg Ray to look for work outside Port Antonio—maybe somewhere more rural.

He finds something amazing. A caretaker's job at a small bed-and-breakfast in the Blue Mountains called Swallowtail, named after the large black-and-blue butterfly of the same name, which used to flourish in the valley, but because of coffee production and logging chewing up their habitat, are now extinct.

The Swallowtail is located at almost forty-four hundred feet and has a spectacular view of Kingston, Port Royal, and Holywell National Park, one of the largest migratory bird habitats in the Caribbean and home to Jamaican bamboo, *Chusquea abietifolia*, which flowers only once every thirty-three years. The next time it flowers won't be until 2017.

You move to these refreshing heights and clean air. (The temperatures change constantly. Even in summer, clouds of mist breeze past your front door, and then evaporate into bright sunshine.) Your job is to clean rooms and do laundry; Ray's is to bring the guests from the Kingston airport and then drive them wherever they want to go on the island. Alison turns into a forest girl, a real monkey climbing trees, roaming far and wide in the forest. It's a good life. A strange life, but a good one.

When the owners retire, you and Ray decide to take out a loan and buy the place. Ray's become quite fascinated with the butterflies in the valley, collecting the small dead bodies of butterflies off the forest floor and pinning their dry wings carefully to cork board. He displays these butterflies, hundreds and hundreds of them in collection boxes, which you hang in all the guest rooms. It's an elderly gentleman, an actual entomologist who's on vacation with his wife, who comes bursting through the office one day with a look of wild excitement on his face.

"I saw one!" he shouts. "It had a wingspan half a foot across!" You can't understand what he's talking about. "I saw Homerus Swallowtail!" he shouts, "*Eurytides marcellinus*! They're not extinct!" He thrusts his digital camera at you and shows you the image of a large black butterfly with iridescent blue patches on its wings perched on a breadfruit tree. It is a truly stunning butterfly.

The reaction is astounding. The Xerces Society (named for the Xerces Blue, the first American butterfly driven to extinction by humans) declares your land a Swallowtail sanctuary, and avid butterfly enthusiasts flood in from all over the world wanting to catch a glimpse of this gorgeous, thought-to-be-extinct creature.

You start your own butterfly farm, as well as a captive breeding program to prevent poaching. You build acres of netted breeding grounds, which protect the butterflies from their predators—birds, lizards, spiders, ants, and wasps. Workers meticulously scour the plants daily to collect the eggs, some of which are as small as grains of rice. You build a larger villa, a hotel that can house up to a hundred guests, and an eco-friendly campground for backpackers. Your swallowtail sanctuary becomes one of the most successful and most-written-about eco hotels in the world. You in turn become rich and live in your own hand-built paradise.

You die when you're a hundred and two years old. Your husband died long ago, and you had the jackfruit lady move in with you—and she became your mother/sister/best friend. Alison runs the hotel now along with her large family. When you die (choked on a mango) the legacy you leave behind in Jamaica will continue for hundreds of years—the schools, clinics, and conservation efforts will thrive.

On your grave they place a marble swallowtail, a symbol to all who see it of your beauty, your rarity, and your wings. You come back in the next life as a swallowtail. Big and blue, heart beating a thousand times a second, on the constant hunt for nectar. It is more fascinating than being a human ever was.

162

From section 148 . . .

You take the job, even though you're well aware that church receptionists are not in general considered sexy. Planning the silver seniors picnic, answering calls about handicap facilities and day-care hours—none of it would interest Hollywood. At first you wear what you think a church receptionist *should* wear—dour dark tights and bulky ill-fitting dresses. That is, until Pastor Dave starts making fun of you. "What is it about church doors that ages women by a hundred years?" he asks. That's a comment that deserves retaliation, and so the very next day you wear a bright yellow sundress with spaghetti straps and white heels. Pastor Dave likes it. He says so.

You like it when Pastor Dave likes what you wear. He likes the sunset palette—yellows, lavenders, sky blue. He also likes Caesar salads without anchovies (he's vegetarian), non-coated Bayer aspirin, putting his heels up on his desk while he's talking on the phone, giving people nicknames (you, for instance, are "the heathen," "little miss sunshine," and "God's greatest challenge"). He likes writing in pencil, strong coffee, and telling you how beautiful you are.

Four years later and you are a regular attendee at church. Not because you subscribe to any doctrine, but because if you don't, things go to hell, so to speak. Pastor Dave can't find his notes, the boiler shuts down, the day-care center temporarily loses a child, and so on. Time passes and you're quite amused with it all.

You eventually marry Pastor Dave. You had to do it—he dared you to. So now you are a pastor's wife. Again, not Hollywood, but there are so many unsuspected things about him, how he loves Greek philosophy, making love in the afternoon, watching old kung fu movies, and eating Chinese food. Things you didn't know a pastor could enjoy.

When you find out you're pregnant, you have no problem anticipating the work. The exhaustion, the cravings, the weight gain, the hemorrhoids, the swollen ankles. The late-night diaper changes and feedings, the colic and fevers. You are well clued in on the downside of children. What you don't anticipate is the love. You find out that when nature hands you a little soft-shell crab, it also hands you amnesia, a complete memory white-out of where the rest of your life used to be.

And so all those memories you wanted to erase are gone, obliterated by this small goggle-eyed creature. (Yes, now there are new nightmares—his health, his well-being, his college tuition, but fear of the future is nowhere near as potent as fear of the past.) Who knows if the old memories will come back, or if quantum mechanics really does give God a run for his money or the other way round, but it doesn't really matter. You're happy, and you've got the rest of your life to figure out.

Your faith grows as time goes on. Prayer, meditation, the support of the church—without it your life would have less meaning. You lead youth groups, attend prayer retreats, you even write a women's prayer book, with examples of ways to "let go and let God." Are you an unlikely Christian? Well, who isn't? Besides, to you Christianity isn't what people tell you it should be—it's what you make it.

You're killed in a rainstorm when you're sixty-two, by a quick flash of lightning. You see black, you smell smoke, you feel your ankles buckle. Your husband tells the reporters that you were a woman of the church, and because of that, God put on a show when he came calling. (He doesn't know yet that God is actually a *She*, and *She* isn't putting on a show for anybody . . . not yet. He'll have to wait for the Rapture for that, and boy howdy is it going to be colorful. She's got the shrieking monkeys and the quantum mechanic antimatter ready.)

163

From section 148 . . .

You don't take the job. Church receptionists are not sexy. A job like that would be the final nail in your already well-built social coffin. Instead you take a job at a nearby art gallery, a modernist place with clean white walls and an owner named Quince, who is stick thin with a mop of black hair and chunky black glasses. You both have cappuccinos and the occasional line of cocaine in the back room.

You go for your degree at a nearby college, argue all your theories in physics class as well as philosophy class. You get a degree in art history, and Quince promotes you from gallery assistant to gallery buyer and starts sending you out on reconnaissance trips scouting for new artists. Your greatest discovery is a gangly girl who makes vaginas out of found objects. Twinkie vaginas, bronzed vaginas, vaginas made out of foam, plaster, wood, chicken wire. She initially has a show at her own "art gallery," an abandoned chemical plant by the river. She created a giant bonfire inside the circle of art, and while a punk band from Southside played hard-core on deafening, humungous speakers, she invited the audience to burn her art. She videotapes the burning, from several angles, and calls the piece *Decuntstruction*. She's fabulous.

Over the years you go to church from time to time—Pastor Dave married the woman who took your receptionist's job, a chunky girl with rosebud cheeks and an easy laugh. Sometimes you even go to sermons, sit in the back, in the shadows of the balcony where Pastor Dave can't see you. He's got a lot to say—some of which you take, some of which you don't. Who knows if the old memories will come back, or if quantum mechanics really does give God a run for his money (or the other way round), but it doesn't really matter. You're happy, and you've got the rest of your life to figure out.

After many decades of running a successful gallery and even showing some of your own work, you're killed in a rainstorm when you're sixty-two. It's a quick flash of lightning. You see black, you smell charred meat and dark smoke, and you feel your ankles buckle. Pastor Dave tells the congregation you were once a woman of the church and you fell from grace, just like God's favorite angel, Lucifer, and because of that God put on a special little show for you when he came calling.

There's no heaven. For you. Not this time.

164

From section 168 . . .

You tell your husband about the money and he breathes a deep sigh of relief. Business hasn't been good lately and he didn't think he would be able to cover the kids' college tuition this semester. You really wanted to go on a trip—but while motherhood falls short on a lot of things, it never falls short on sacrifice.

Elizabeth and Rosie graduate, as does Paulie, and they settle down near you, marry, and have kids. Of course it's wonderful to have your family around you all the time, the children and the grandchildren—the playdates and show-and-tells and hide-and-seeks, but it's exhausting too, as both your daughters are in the habit of dropping off their children at your house every day. Grandma day care. You can't seem to keep enough aspirin in the house. Shouldn't a woman of sixty have a little peace and quiet?

This is pretty much your life until you die unceremoniously on the porch—your heart stops as you're reading a travel magazine, an article about Santorini and the incredible sunsets at Oia. There are pictures of the sky—expert photographs taken with expensive cameras, the greens and golds and blues and heliotrope of a sky you will never see. The pictures are beautiful and tears burn the edges of your eyes. They're beautiful, but they're only pictures. You're touching a photograph of the sky when you feel something heavy in your heart, cold and hard like a five-pound stone, but then the stone blooms open petals of fire—a red heat that licks at your throat, spreads through your arms and legs, heating you and making you arch backward in your chair. The magazine drops.

You die from a massive heart attack. Everyone comes to your funeral, Luis, Elizabeth, Rosie, and Paulie, along with all the grandkids, neighbors, and family. Your life was a noisy circus and now your death is too. Your family goes all out for your coffin—pink satin pillows and locks of your children's hair stuffed inside your clasped hands—oh how they cry, especially Paulie. (Mom should have the best! Mom should rest for eternity on Therm-a-Sleep silk pillows! Mom should wear her best dress and her best jewelry—well, maybe not all her best jewelry—for the sweet hereafter! Now that Mom is dead and gone we should give her what she wants!)

They don't know you can see them. They don't know you're marching around the funeral home mad as a henhouse with no cock. They put things in your coffin—locks of their hair and your granddaughter's favorite stuffed animal. One stranger comes to your funeral. A woman you've never seen before. She has a sapphire ring on her right hand and she looks nervous. Maybe more like determined. She doesn't know you—she's just a woman who read your obituary that morning. A woman who read that you were a loving mother and a devoted wife. That you had always wanted to travel, but never did.

The woman wears a trench coat pulled tight around her waist and she walks directly up to the viewing line without signing the guest book or introducing herself. She walks up to your coffin and puts a creased piece of paper inside. It's sort of a consolation prize. A sympathy card from one soul to another. It's a folded-up map of the world. The closest you ever came to your dream, finally tucked neatly in your coffin.

165

From section 168 . . .

You tell your husband you've inherited this money—and now you finally have enough money for the big trip you've always wanted to go on. He's upset—angry that you're leaving. He says you're selfish but you don't care what he says anymore. If you don't live your life, who's going to live it for you? Your kids? Please. They're busy shoveling up big bites of the world for their hungry selves—why shouldn't you? Ever since that fateful trip to LA ended at the Vista View, you've wanted to get back on the road.

You buy a Eurorail ticket and take yourself all over Europe. You go to London, Belfast, Paris, Luxembourg, Berlin, Rome, Florence, Copenhagen, and Amsterdam all in one trip. You collect photographs and presents for your family all along the way and you can't wait to see them. All this travel has made you appreciate home—but it's made you appreciate yourself even more. You are going to travel more—and that's that. But when you finally go home six months later, your husband isn't there. Your children aren't either. There's a dusty letter on the dining room table with your name on it. The house is strangely quiet. Even the dog is gone.

The letter is from your angry husband, who says he's leaving you—on account of your incredibly self-centered ways. "I'm not telling the kids you took money that could have gone into their college tuition accounts," the letter reads, "it would crush them to know their mother is so selfish, so cruel." He has moved out and gone to his brother's house and he is *filing for divorce*.

Deep depression settles in. You still have travel diarrhea, your legs ache, blood idles in your veins. Time passes and no one comes home. Your husband's lawyer calls. You stare at the highway. The depression deepens. You sleep and sleep and sleep. The air seems heavy, your head fuzzy, the world blurry. You try to remember—what was the name of your guide in Vienna? Which dish was it that gave you diarrhea in Mumbles? Your journal has some notes—but not near enough. Never near enough. You should have written it all down. You should have saved it. What a waste. You should have Polaroided every single thing. You should have videotaped it.

The kids tumble into their own anger and depression. There is fighting, arguing, negotiating, and crying. There are court dates, legal fees, endless negotiations. Your husband gets almost everything, which when your kids find out makes them hate him. Elizabeth rages, Rosie cries, and Paulie crashes his father's car into an off-duty ice cream truck. Your family is in shreds and it's *all your fault*. But you can't help remembering how good you felt on the road. How you felt free and full of energy. How every challenge was met—each goal achieved. The feeling that gave you. *This cow is out of the barn and she won't go back.*

So you leave your little house by the ocean, sign all the divorce papers, and go to work for a tour company in France, a business that takes large groups of people overseas, to Europe and Asia and Pan Africa. You children are terrified. They think you'll be killed, they think you'll be mugged, robbed . . . worse. But in fact you are not mugged or robbed or worse. You live in a cold-water apartment over a Greek restaurant in the Latin Quarter. You don't make much money, you're struggling to learn French, and making friends in Paris is almost impossible—but you are happy. You are finally totally and completely happy.

You don't die for years, and when you do it's on a bright summer day at a café on rue Martinique. You're sipping iced Earl Grey tea from a tall glass and reading a book on Egyptian archaeology when your hearts stops. As you fall forward, the birds are singing and a young couple next to you are kissing. Your temple hits the pavement and everyone around you jumps up. All these details. It's beautiful.

166

From section 101 . . .

You take the movie and it's grueling. You have artistic differences with the director, a "fiscal disagreement" with your agent, a fight with your costar, and an allergic reaction to some funky shrimp salad served on set. You take Christian to the premiere, and all of a sudden it's as if nothing else besides the fact two women are on a date together matters. When you get out of the limo holding Christian's hand there's an explosion of strobe lights as the paparazzi take ECUs (Extra-Close-Ups) of your entwined manicured fingers. They ask you to kiss Christian for the cameras—which you gladly do. Why not? Who cares?

Everybody cares. The studio, the director, your costars, the Screen Actors Guild, the Academy, *People* magazine, Rush Limbaugh, Nancy Grace, Al Sharpton, *Good Morning America*, Fox News, and the Religious Right—just to name a few. Some people think you're *so brave* and some think you're *so disgusting* but nobody thinks you're boring. Your publicist thinks it's fantastic. The attention catapults you into the center of the nation's attention and every magazine and show there is calls to book you.

On the *Late Show* you ask David Letterman why it is that all the unsexy people have the most to say about sex. "I mean, um, *Senator Santorum?*" you say right into the camera, as though addressing the senator personally. "You really don't need to worry about who's having sex with who. Do you actually *own* a mirror? Nobody wants to see you naked—ever." The audience claps and Letterman asks you if you think the Senate will ever grant same-sex marriages. "Look," you say, "Senator Santorum's problem is that this generation of women, be they gay or be they straight, isn't like any other. We're not going to put up with being told what we can do or who we can marry. We don't have to. We are lawyers and judges and governors and we *will* be president of the United States. The Senate doesn't have to grant us anything. We're going to take it."

Cut to explosive applause from audience.

Well, this little speech of yours lands you right in the heart of every public debate, argument, news show, magazine and newspaper in the country. It gets worse after you're voted one of *People* magazine's 50 Most Beautiful People. You and Christian beat back the media as best you can, you dodge the paparazzi who stalk you, camp out in the your yard, lunge out at your car. It's all so surreal.

Who cares who we kiss? you wonder. Loving Christian is as simple as breathing or walking. Something in your parasympathetic nervous system. *Is she a woman? You hadn't even noticed.* To you she's *a person. A soul.* X chromosome or Y chromosome is irrelevant. Irrelevant or not, Christian puts her foot down after about six months of being hounded, pounded, and pursued by the press. She wants a normal, quiet life with you. "Marry me and let's go away. We've got enough money for the rest of our lives. We can quit all this." Marry her? You're all for same-sex unions . . . but you're not sure you want to marry *anybody*. It seems awfully permanent, and if the press got ahold of it—your life would be hell.

If you marry Christian, go to section #156 (page 355).
If you don't marry Christian, go to section #157 (page 356).

167

From section 101 . . .

You don't take the movie. You want to be with Christian—and everyone is making that really difficult. What's all this fuss about who likes to kiss who? Kiss a man, kiss a woman. Kiss an *armadillo*—what does it matter? How does who you kiss help/hurt/inspire/disgust anyone else? Loving Christian is as simple to you as breathing or walking. It's all very confusing to you—all very silly. Fine, she doesn't want you to do the blockbuster? You won't.

It's irrelevant anyway, because the crazy aggressive biotech small cap stock your broker bought for you at forty-seven cents a share (something to do with cancer treatment, lasers or something) shoots, rockets, bitch slaps the NASDAQ and latches on to a funky-fat twenty-eight dollars a share. Your broker—he invested a lot on that little stock. It takes a millionaire to be a millionaire . . . and you're a goddamned millionaire now.

If you marry Christian, go to section #156 (page 355).
If you don't, go to section #157 (page 356).

168

From section 103 . . .

You and Elizabeth say good-bye to the girls and move to San Diego. You're not sure if it's the right choice, but just like Rita Mae Brown said, "A peacefulness follows any decision, even the wrong one." So you settle into your new life. You move in with Luis and two months later you feel a tender knot in your stomach. Free-floating nausea. You can't drink red wine. You're tired all the time. Tomatoes taste like tinfoil, wine like turned egg salad. You're pregnant. Luis is excited but you're uncertain. It's all happening so fast.

Baby Rosie is born, a soft tan girl with dark blue eyes and skin the color of cinnamon mixed with milk. Then a year later baby Paulie arrives, a little thug from the start who never has time for kisses or hugs and runs headlong into the world trailing your heart behind him. Your parents come out to visit—how they adore their grandchildren!

No one ever mentions Elizabeth's biological father. She looks just like her siblings, and you decide early on to tell her that Luis was her father. A lie? Of course it's a lie. Immoral? *So what?* As long as it spares your little girl from feeling abandoned. You don't want her to feel father hunger, that horrible aching emptiness that could never be filled—mostly because you have no idea where her real father *is*.

Luis buys a small printing company that specializes in inking medical information brochures. Business is good and he eventually buys you a house near the beach in Oceanside. It's a tiny white cottage with crooked green shutters and an orange house cat left by the previous tenants. You ask him if you can take a trip somewhere—but money is always tight. Elizabeth takes up ballet (those tutus are pricey!), Rosie wants violin lessons, Paulie plays soccer (forget the tutus, what about the cost of gas for all those out-of-state games?), and they all *three* need braces. When the kids go to college you *really* never have any extra money to travel.

Then a distant uncle dies. You receive a certified check in the mail from his lawyer for ten thousand dollars. You could easily dump this check into the kids' bottomless college accounts and it would be soaked up immediately by their endless needs, or you could keep the money and go on one kick-ass trip by yourself.

If you give the money to your kids, go to section #164 (page 368).
If you keep the money for yourself, go to section #165 (page 370).

169

From section 103 . . .

You can't leave the Sheltering Arms—it's too important to you. What would you do without the support of all the other single mothers? Do you think a single man could take the place of an entire squad of seasoned single mothers. The thought makes you chortle, and you don't chortle easily. In fact, you wonder why this isn't a standard living situation for people who need help. To live in a community-based building where you all take turns, pool your resources; create a family with whoever else needs a family too.

Your parents come out to visit—they want to move you and Elizabeth to a nicer apartment, but you refuse. In fact, all the original mothers have stayed despite life changes, job offers, and the creepy super who you got fired after he tried to corner Li Vang's little girl, Kylie, in the basement. No. You're sticking together.

The women of the Sheltering Arms decide to start a business together. You've seen what—a thousand engagement rings in real life? (Not counting advertisements or billboards. *Actual rings* on *actual fingers*.) These diamonds are wandering around on the thin fingers of smug girls—glittering like mean eyes at hideous you—the one *without* an engagement ring, the one *without* a man, the one *without* an attachment, the one *without* any worth.

You are a group of women who need a man as much as a swan needs a set of radial tires. Women who would rather travel than tan, who would rather eat a date than go on one, who can get their own damn diamond. So the idea of the True Blue Ring was born. The right-hand ring for women who know how to make a fist. For women who don't want a diamond, for women who are engaged to *themselves*. You pool your savings and buy inventory. Not so much—just a hundred sapphires. Alana's sister, who studied jewelry making in college, makes the settings—an elegant platinum claw for each eye-blue stone. Melanie, who has a head for numbers, does the accounting. Juliet helps her. Alana and Ellen organize publicity. Suzanne does all the graphics and marketing. Jackie puts up a Web site with the help of her teenage son. You, Rosa, Riley, and Maria F. are sales reps and you make appointments with retailers big and small to try and get them to sell the rings. Maria M. (who's on disability and actually gets child support) volunteers to watch all the kids full-time.

The first rings sell slowly and things are looking grim . . . but then a producer for a popular daily talk show interviews Li Vang at the Vietnamese community center, someone looking for "minority success stories." When the television show finds out about the right-hand ring and the women of the Sheltering Arms, they get sort of hysterical about it. On air, during the interview, Li Vang gives the host of the show her own True Blue Ring, and from that day forward, everything changes. Three thousand orders come in that week. The True Blue Ring is featured in *Vogue*, *Cosmo*, *Vanity Fair*. Celebrities start to wear them; even women who are married or engaged are wearing them. Apparently it's some "I'm married but I'm still my own woman" message.

Three years later and business is in the black. You all decide to buy a big house in the hills and name it the Sheltering Arms II. The True Blue Ring spreads to Europe and Asia, as more and more women choose to forgo marriage for creative coupling. You date men—but you never marry. You have three satisfying relationships with three men (one for seven years, one for twelve, and one for fifteen), but they end and it is so nice to not have to fill out all the paperwork. You might have been lonely from time to time—but there was never any time or space to get lonely.

Elizabeth grows up, studies sculpture, and becomes a set decorator in Hollywood. She marries a stunt man named Charlie and they have two kids—your absolutely edible grandkids, Colin and Parker. You can never get enough of those two—you love to buy them extravagant gifts, which makes Elizabeth nuts.

At your funeral the girls go *all out* for your coffin—pink satin pillows and locks of Elizabeth's hair stuffed inside your clasped hands. Little do they know you shadow their every step, watch the house in the hills, their children grow and fan out across the country, their marriages (four of them get married) and each respective divorce. Over time, the twelve of you are all joined again, in a big apartment complex in heaven, with a pool at the center and the orange house cat, who still winds around your ankles as the little ones play.

170

From section 104 . . .

You cash out your entire portfolio and buy Thermalink. You're shaking as you do it . . . *just click the BUY button!* Afterward you accidentally snap a pencil right in half. Then you wait.

And you wait. . . .

And you wait. . . .

And you wait. . . .

And you wait. . . .

You wait for anything one way or the other. You watch the NASDAQ ticker like a fetal monitor. *Any sign of life will do.* You become absentminded. For two weeks you forget to answer the phone, misplace files, disconnect people, and just generally blank out. Your bosses are beside themselves. (Generally nice guys, even if their Dockers are a little tight at the waistline and their penny loafers have *dimes* in them.) *What do you mean you left him on hold? I told you to put him through! Where is the Regehr file? Who spilled coffee on the fax machine?*

Then, in your final act of stupidity, you forget to lock the front door one night and over the weekend the office is robbed. They aren't even mad when they fire you, more like confused. They send you home with a pat on the back and a "good luck."

The stock starts to climb. Every day, by two points. You dance around your apartment in your underwear every morning—it doesn't go as high as you'd hoped, but still. You're a *hundred-thousand-aire*. Not filthy fry-daddy rich—but you have enough to pursue your career as a *supa-star!*

You hire a big fancy publicist who starts introducing you as a "relocated Dutch countess who's interested in acting and has more money than the Kennedys. *The old Kennedys.*" You're not even sure if the Dutch have aristocracy—but it doesn't matter. No one in Hollywood really cares about hard facts—their currency is hard fiction.

Your publicist (who has a black Lab) is at a Doggie Day Care Croquet outing and meets up with a casting director (has a pug-beagle mix) who whispers in the ear of a second director (who has a German shepherd with swollen anal glands), who brings your photo in to Steven Spielberg (who has cats). Your photo bounces around like a lottery Ping-Pong ball and for whatever reason they call you in for an audition to star in a movie called *Weevils!* It's an erotic horror flick for kids about those little bugs in their cereal, bugs who mutate and form different tribes, one evil and one good—one hell-bent on devouring the human race and the other hell-bent on saving it. You role is of young sexy MILF (Mother I'd Like to Fu@k) who weds one of the evil weevils and has to be convinced by her brainy science seventh-grader that the weevil she married is evil.

You get the part. You're ecstatic and immediately able to find an agent, a business manager, and an appointment with one of the coveted eyebrow shapers on Melrose. Filming begins right away in Hawaii, where you're in makeup four hours every morning putting on your wig, sunless tan, beauty mark, and lip prosthetics. (They want your lips to be fuller. Not too full, but about 73 percent fuller.)

Your dialogue is a little sparse. You repeat, *"No! Don't! Stop!"* quite a few times to the conquering king weevil until he overtakes you in a steamy shower scene and you squeal, "Oh my! I thought breakfast cereal was just for kids!!" and you both laugh—since you were the one who accidentally mutated these weevils when you knocked over your son's breakfast cereal onto his radioactive science experiment.

After the movie you don't have any more parts to speak of (the producers of the movie made it clear you weren't supposed to come to opening night of the premiere, but you don't know why). Then you get another break, you join the Wobbly Jamboree, a kids' singing group who travel the country in inflatable pink shirts singing songs like "Let's Do the Jumbly Dance!" and "Big Purple Poo" to auditoriums of wild screaming kids.

It sounds like kind of a weird deal at first, but the money is fantastic. All you have to do is wear a pink inflatable dress, lip sync with the prerecorded music that blares out of the plastic palm trees, and *ding!* the triangle you play every once in a while with your big golden wish-wand. Then, on one show, Mrs. Pammel the Flammable Camel comes out and gives you a fake spanking because you "accidentally" drop your triangle on her camel toe. The kids love that.

Wobbly Jamboree starts playing to sold-out arenas, releasing platinum records, and getting huge mailbags filled with fan letters. Who knew a kids' group could be so big? Because you're the only girl member of the group (the guys swear they're guys, but they're so androgynous and Mister Rogers–like that you're not sure what they are), you start to receive love letters from eight-year-old boys and real star treatment from the band's manager, Marvin.

You start to demand more in your entertainment rider, the document that must precede you at every venue, and lists the things you have to have in your dressing room. You must have three bottles of champagne, each chilled in its own silver bucket. Silver—never plastic. You must also have a dozen white roses and a *male* assistant, no older than twenty-five and no heavier than a hundred and fifty pounds. He must be fit. Very fit. You also need a box of Godiva chocolates already opened and all the ones with nuts removed. All that money buys a lot of candy.

These guys in the band, with their fucking pink inflatable shirts and their banjos . . . *what, are they kidding you?* They don't smoke, they don't swear or drink . . . they have nothing to complain about—you don't even hang out with them anymore after shows. You hang out with the lighting guys instead . . . big muscle-bound lads with tattoos and goatees.

You take it too far. It wasn't a good idea to get high with Frankie, the spotlight operator, before the show. Yes, it's probably why he missed his cues and ended up leaving Mr. Pickles in the pitch black during his solo performance of "Choo Choo Baby." And no, having sex with both the dolly grip and the key grip at the same time backstage was not wise—but you were drunk, and how could you resist? You'd been on the road for three months, and between a dolly grip and a key grip, how can a girl go wrong? Well—that's not how Marvin sees it. He puts you on super-double probation.

That's when your daughter shows up and everything really goes to hell. Apparently *your daughter*, who you've never set eyes on before and who is now sixteen and is *pissed off*, has gone to the magazine *Tabloid!* and told them that you are her mother, that she was an unwanted pregnancy, that her father was a janitor (how did she find all this out?), and that *you did not want her* and *threw her away*. Well, she's not wrong about the janitor thing, but why would she call attention to it?

You might have been able to handle the whole thing if *Tabloid!* hadn't sent that stupid covert camera crew who terrorized you at three in the morning when you were leaving the donkey handler's trailer with a half bottle of Absolut Raspberry in your hand. They are shouting at you and your head hurts—you're drunk and hungover at the same time—and someone says *your daughter!* And *the janitor's baby!* And you can't understand, so you say, "What?" peering into the lens like an albino mole with its hair up in rollers. "The janitor baby came back? Where'd she come from?"

And so it becomes headline news, not just in the glossies but in newsprint. WOBBLY JAMBOREE SINGER ASHAMED OF JANITOR BABY! and BABY IN A DRUM RETURNS! You didn't even ask her name (Alisia, you're told, but you never actually meet her) and *Alisia* sues you for some unknown ridiculous reason and actually gets every penny you have. The lawyers suck the marrow out of what's left, and when it's all said and done, you are kicked out of Wobbly Jamboree and now your sacks of mail are from indignant seven-year-olds.

Boy—take away the money and where's the party? All your old pals are suddenly unavailable. Alisia won't return your calls. You're just about to have a press release to announce your big *Losers Can Be Winners* comeback tour, in which you invite Janitor Baby (why not embrace the name, rather than pretend it doesn't exist?) to sing Sinatra's "That's Why the Lady Is a Tramp," with you onstage, to kids and adults alike.

Only you don't make it to your press release; instead you crash into a tree, which is at first listed as a "fatal traffic accident," but then revised at the coroner's office to a "shooting homicide." Someone shot you from behind, right in the spine. No one ever knows who. There were so many people who wanted to shoot you—the police don't know where to start.

171

From section 104 . . .

You can't buy a stock you don't know anything about. What if you lost everything? Every penny you worked so hard for—every small advance you made? No. Better safe than sorry. Better to be a strongbox than a bread box. No crumbling for you. You *do not* place the order and you patiently wait to be shown how your prudent ways are goddamned *good* ways. You wait.

And you wait. . . .

And you wait. . . .

And you wait. . . .

And you wait. . . .

The stock soars. It goes through the roof. It goes beyond its expectations in the first three weeks. You feel like you had a stroke, a heart attack, a lost lottery ticket. How could you be such an idiot? You would have been a millionaire if you'd only taken the chance. So when one of the other girls in the office wants to know if you want to go to Tijuana for a "wild girl weekend," you just think to yourself, *Tijuana. Sure. Cheer myself up.*

That Friday you load up your friend's snappy gold Toyota Prius and shoot down the highway for the Mexican border. You've got a lot of blues to drink away. The adoption, the stocks . . . what else could go wrong?

A lot else goes wrong. (Never, never, never ask what else could go wrong.) After eating a very dicey meal from a taco cart on the street and then drinking three tall Katrina Kamikazes (vodka, rum, tequila, and triple sec with small plastic toys floating around in the ice), you completely lose sight of your girlfriends at Señor Toadstools and then vomit repeatedly on the Prius in the parking lot.

You are sick. Not *too-much-to-drink* sick, more like *Montezuma's-revenge-and-also-drank-too-much* sick. You are exploding from every possible orifice.

You make your way back through the crowded streets, but you can't find your hotel. You just need a fucking bathroom . . . but of course there aren't any, so the ocean will have to do. You stagger over to the wide sparkling marina, which is only a few blocks from where you *thought* your hotel was. *Was it called El Sueno? El Strella?* You don't care anymore. You just want to be sick in peace.

The ocean never looked so beautiful. Like a big salty toilet. You throw up to your heart's content over the edge of the dock and then you crawl into a little dinghy bobbing gently in the water. Your feet are up on the seat, your head cushioned by an old faded life jacket. You feel cozy and safe. That's when you see the humor in all this. You start to laugh as the stars blur and the sweet scent of a bonfire drifts over you. Life is good even when it's bad. You drift into a deep sleep, and dream that you are living in a trailer park where you're allowed to throw up wherever you want to.

In the morning, when the bright sun hits your eyelids, you smile and stretch. It feels so good to be out, to be warm—to be alive. Your friends are going to be in *so* much trouble for ditching you. You're sore and creaky, and sit up to rub your eyes. What appears before you doesn't make sense. You rub your eyes again and squint.

You have no explanation for what's in front of you. You are sitting in the very same dinghy you fell asleep in last night, but you are not in the same place. On all sides of you, as far as you can see in every direction, is open water. Wide, dark blue, open water. You spin around in your seat, trying to not rock the boat . . . it's hardly even a boat! It's a rowboat . . . that's when you realize there is no motor on the boat, and no oars. You are drifting in the middle of the ocean without any idea which way land is.

You try not to panic. Try to recount any survival training you ever knew . . . what the fuck happened!!! Did someone untie you? Was the boat not even tied in the first place? *Were you so drunk you didn't even realize?* . . . and that's when you realize your beaded purse is gone, the one that had your wallet, your driver's license, all your money, and your passport. *Gone.* Everything. Panic, breath, crying. *Close your eyes and count.* Open your eyes and expect the dream to stop. Please! *Jesus God*—we wait for ships, right? Other boats? *There are no other boats*. There's no land—there's *nothing*. The tide is carrying you wherever it wants to. The sun blisters you, beats on your head, and you hide your face under the little wooden bench that propped up your feet last night.

Burning. Everything is burning. Watery lines in the air—like something is there and then it isn't. You hug your knees and rock. You pray. You count to one hundred, you sing "Amazing Grace." Should you swim? Which way? Drag the boat behind you and rest in it when you're tired? That's ridiculous. Meditate. Find your inner space, focus on the light inside your eyes. (*There's light everywhere! It's trying to pry your eyelids open and leak into your brain!*) Rest. Thirst. Like a tickle, a trickle, a scratching claw on your throat. Don't drink seawater! You know that much.

You sleep.

When you wake there's no way to tell if it is the same day or the next day. You paddle your hands in the water and smooth your face. Feels good. The thirst has heat in it now. Pepper. Your mouth, throat, tongue—everything is heated, like it's baking from the inside out.

That's when you see the dolphin. He rolls over, showing his white belly before he dives back under. Dolphins swimming right beside your boat! Curious sweetheart! *I see you! Yes!* You're saved. *Dolphins do things.* Dolphins save people. They have sonar and radar and clicks and whistles and they protect people—every Discovery Channel show you've ever seen comes rushing back to your head.

You feel better. You have to be able to do *something*. The dolphins are schooling with your boat, you're in a current . . . and currents lead places. Just hang in there and you will arrive somewhere. Only this headache. Clarity comes. You should cool your core temperature. You carefully lower yourself over the side of the boat and the coolness of the water revives you. You relax. Breathe. You keep one hand on the boat, and slowly tread water. *Just hang in there*. Someone will come. You let yourself sink deeper into the water—*so cool!* You wish you could swim down where the water is even cooler. Then you feel something hot at your leg, something tugging. A sharp pain. The fish that were schooling with you—they weren't dolphins.

172

From section 105 . . .

You schedule the appointment without telling anybody—you don't want anyone talking you out of it. No baby from the rape. No rape babies. That *word*. You looked it up in the dictionary, fourteen different definitions. Rape was printed between "rape cake" (a cake made from the rapeseed) and "repent." (In this case, to repent might be to buy a semiautomatic weapon and go a-shootin'.)

You still wonder—why had you never gotten pregnant at the VowGuardian house before? You never used condoms. Never once. But no one ever got pregnant—not till Summer rape-caked you. Was there birth control in that gruel they used to feed you? In the water? When you left—were you then off the pill but didn't know it?

Either way, you knew you were pregnant before the words were out of the doctor's mouth. You knew when your belly was just a little too tight, food tasted just a little too strange. But you are clever. *Clever, clever, clever,* and you don't say a word to anyone. You don't cry, you don't ask questions. You drive across town to a clinic you found in the yellow pages and you schedule an abortion on Tuesday. Perfect. Pregnant till Tuesday.

You build up a white-hot fury inside you as you drive. A strength that allows you to tear phone books in half and crush full soda cans in one hand. When you arrive at the clinic there are two old women with picket signs. Their signs say DON'T KILL YOUR BABY! These two are actually *picketing the abortion clinic.* After you collect your things and make your way across the plaza, the little old ladies rush for you, probably thinking they're going to scare you—but what they don't realize is *you're* rushing for *them.*

"What's your name?" you ask the older one before she even gets anything out of her mouth.

"Excuse me?" she croaks.

You repeat, "What's your name?"

She makes a face. "Mary Jane."

"Beautiful," you whisper, "just like the shoes." Then you lean very close to her, so you can smell her stale Gardenia perfume. "I'm pregnant," you say, "and I'm going in for an abortion. I just want you to know—I'm going to name the baby Mary Jane before I put it in a bucket."

The woman looks as if she'd swallowed a bee. She's aghast. You're feeling better already. "I can accept that men don't understand when a woman knows it's time to not have a baby," you growl at the retreating Mary Jane, "but a woman? A woman stopping another woman from doing what she has to? Would you stop me from taking out a tumor or a cancer or anything I can't have living inside me? It's gender treason. It's treachery. It's backstabbing bitchery." Now you feel *much* better. You march inside the clinic, a song in your heart and a bounce in your step. Good old Mary Jane.

At the clinic it's mandatory that you meet with a counselor beforehand just so they know you're not there against your will, which nearly brings you to outright laughter. (Oh no—believe me, *I want* to be here! It's a great fucking honor!) They need charts, forms, papers, signatures. Finally the counselor sits you down in her small office, a lovely Hispanic woman named Marina with full lips and heavy liquid eyes. She asks you a few questions, *just procedure*, but in her checklist of questions, *How much unprotected sex have you had in the past six months? How many sexual partners have you had this year?* she hits some trigger wire, some buried catch switch, and that dam you've been building, heavy brick by heavy brick, breaks. You spill everything.

Before you can stop yourself you're telling her everything, *everything*. This poor woman. You're talking and telling and seething, knees together, fists clenched, *art school, the videotape, Guy Moffatt, the VowGuardians, the House, Summer* . . . but she's not stopping you and she's not asking any questions, she's just nodding with those heavy liquid eyes that give you permission.

You lay it bare. Threadbare.

She doesn't preach or patronize, she just waits for you to finish. When you're done, she takes you to the procedure room. The nurses are friendly, the doctor gentle. Your feet in stirrups. There's the sound of a small vacuum, a pinching sensation, and then you're done. It takes exactly eight minutes. "Do you want to see what I took out of you?" the doctor asks. *Is he crazy? Is he a Pro-Lifer? Is this his trick—to perform abortions and then terrorize the women who came to him? Who the hell does he think he is?*

"Sure," you say. "Show me anything."

He does. He shows you an aluminum tray with a small translucent red disc on it. The disc looks like it's made of jelly—but it's perfectly smooth. No weird medical matter, no material, no baby's arms or feet. "This is where a pregnancy would have grown. These are the cells collecting."

"That's it?" you ask him. "No heartbeats or fingerprints like the billboards say?"

The doctor laughs. "Not hardly."

Afterward you feel relieved. Lighter. As if the badness has been sucked right out of you. It gives you freedom and energy, starbursts of power—so much so that you drive by the house. Not your parents' house, *the VowGuardians' house.* The familiarity of it is foreign. White shutters. Porch. *Summer working on the front lawn.* He's gardening. Amazing. *Rapist in the garden.* Handle rose thorns with care, prune judiciously. You watch him from afar. His scooter is parked in back. Shiny, newly washed. An idea comes to you. Clear, singular, complete. As if a divine angel delivered blueprints.

You sneak around back and measure the height of his scooter, get the exact dimensions. Then you buy razor-sharp wire and nails. You buy everything with cash. You return the next day and wait for him to leave. Then you screw two industrial eyehooks across the alley and string up the razor wire, right at head height. Invisible in the sun. Nearly invisible.

According to the newspapers, when Summer flew down the alley on his Vespa, he must've seen the wire at the last moment and swerved, which caused the wire to catch him across the eyes. It didn't behead him cleanly, like you'd planned. It just tore his eyes out—which on balance isn't too bad. He spends the rest of his brief, medically complicated life in treatment centers and rehab clinics, a few years later tragically dying on the operating table during a controversial procedure to restore partial vision to the left eye. You didn't kill him, the surgeon did.

You go on to live a long time. You get married—go to grad school, start your own real estate company. When the time is right, you have two kids and you love them. When you die, it's in a car accident, and your last thought before you sail through the open passenger window is not of your two children or your loving husband or your fantastically long life.

No. Your last thought is how lucky you were that you got to kill your rapist. It's a joy every woman should know. Maya Angelou wrote: *I been in sorrow's kitchen and I licked out all the pots.* You say: *I been to see my rapist and I kicked out all his nuts.*

You die happy.

173

From section 105 . . .

You can't get an abortion. You don't believe in it. All you can do is replay the moment the doctor told you, "You're pregnant." (Cue lights, fade to darkness. Fall.) When you're jostled awake, everyone talks at once.

Dark rooms connected to dark rooms. Everyone wears slippers. Hush hush, *she's sleeping.* The whole house is underwater. Everyone is quiet. *You sleep and sleep.*

Nine months later, a scrawny, red-smeared, black-haired, screaming *thing* is pulled out of your stomach. Your first thought is: *Kill it.* Awkward smiles all around the surgical suite. A photograph? Jesus. (Somebody name the damn thing. I don't care. Name it *rapist's baby.* Name it *Bob.*) You name it Mark. Get it? *Mark.* A mark on a piece of paper. A mark on your body. A re-mark-able situation. *A marked woman.*

You're alone. You and the black-haired baby. You don't have black hair. Your mother and father don't have black hair—no one you know has black hair, but little bitty baby does! Black-haired baby likes to yell. Black-haired baby doesn't like to sleep.

"What're you doing to the baby?" your mother screams and snatches the thing away. It's crying. It's a monster baby. You've heard of these? They learn to light fires before they can walk. They smear their shit, eat their shit, hit other kids in the face, draw blood, bite hard, kick, scream, curse, hurt small animals. . . .

People on the street look at you. *Bad mother.* People at day care whisper near you. *Bad mother.* In the history of all time it is never the monster baby's fault—it is the *mother's* fault. The two of you are linked. Inextricably connected. He is you and you are it. This idea that a woman's primary function is to give birth. Like you are some breeding machine without any other worth. If only. If only we could hold it over them—Lord it like we were gods, keeper of the race rather than kowtow and whimper.

You purchase a handgun from Shop Mart (who apparently does not cover abortions on their employees' health insurance but does cover Viagra). It's the final choice. At least it's yours. No VowGuardians to ruin it. You are not in bad company. *Cleopatra, Kurt Cobain, Vincent van Gogh, Ernest Hemingway, Hunter S. Thompson, Marilyn Monroe.*

You take the shiny thing into the bathroom, lie down in the bathtub, and aim it at your face. Barrel black-eyed. Monster baby is crying. Always, always crying.

You pull the trigger. Nothing.

You pull harder.

174

From section 107 . . .

You decide to marry Thompat, but the minute a woman chooses her man over her work, she's got trouble. She's got headaches and backaches and migraines and gingivitis. The body starts sounding alarms left and right, giving her rashes and allergies and pinkeye. You take that engagement ring (diamonds can be so distracting!) and promptly fall into a series of long, drawn-out, mystery illnesses. *Fatigue, malaise, low fever.* You stop painting altogether. You sleep long hours, which is fine, because whenever Thompat does manage to come home, he locks himself in his studio and paints.

You and Thompat are engaged for seven years. In that time he becomes an internationally recognized artist, and you begin running a craft cart at the mall. He's very generous, pays all the bills, moves you into a nice house by a creek, and buys you a used Saab. Then you get pregnant with twins. Timothy and Andrew. Aggressive, demanding babies that hit each other in the head with blocks, scream when even momentarily left alone, throw food if served the wrong brand of strained peas, fall into fits of rage if not given the toy they want or not given whatever they want, which could be anything at any given moment.

Motherhood is more demanding than any painting ever was, requires more patience and diligence and understanding. These children are awful. They work in tandem. They take turns making you insane, as if they had shifts. One deliberately takes the safety cover off an oscillating fan and pokes his finger into the blades while the other throws all his stuffed animals into the hot tub and sets it to "boil." At times you want to drown them. Always one of them is wide-awake and shrieking.

They get sick. Despite the fact they are clean and warm at all times, they catch every imaginable disease short of dengue fever. They fight. They're accident-prone. They fall down stairs and lock themselves in the washing machine and once tried to fly out the second-story window like Superman. You're constantly at the emergency room; the nurses are sure you must be an abusive mother, the doctors sigh and patch them up again and again.

When they go to grade school they are unbelievable. They get detention, suspension, they get kicked out. You try home-schooling them and they break into Thompat's studio and have a paint fight. They smear the Egyptian Crimson he has imported from France on the sofa. They have a sword fight with his paintbrushes and whap each other on the backside until they all break.

Thompat can't believe you can't control the children. He can't believe it's *that* hard. He insists you should try harder, he refuses to give them any medication, he stays away more and more, and then he leaves. He says he cannot bear to be around them, he cannot bear to be around you. Life doesn't change much after he's gone. It seems that after the twins came he was never around much anyway. He marries a previous student and the twins light fire to her bouquet right before the ceremony.

You move into Thompat's old studio, and begin a new series of paintings. Your old gallery owner agrees to look at them, and when she does, actual tears rim her eyes. "You're back," she whispers. "They're fantastic." She gives you a show that fall, which is widely praised and completely sold out. The critics try and describe your work in the paper, although they claim they cannot convey its full weight. *Motherhood*, they write, *rewritten à la Lizzie Borden*.

The paintings depict serene, well-coiffed women killing children in creative ways. The children all seem to deserve it—they're ghoulish little brats with greenish skin, runny noses, and screaming tonsils. The women on the other hand seem quite out of place in the pictures. They wear Chanel suits and pearl earrings while pushing children into polar bear exhibits, dropping them out department store second-story windows, escorting them into ovens, and placing them in the spin cycle.

The twins think this is hilarious. They love the paintings. In fact, they grow out of their hideous little personalities into quite lovely people. Timothy opens his own art gallery in New York, featuring your work, his father's work, and the work of his brother, Andrew, who creates video installations. The four of you don't see each other much over the rest of your life—as distance seems to be the necessary ingredient for harmony—but you speak on the phone often, and the boys almost always ask you for another story from their childhood, from the time they were awful.

You remarry a man named Alexander, a poet who dotes on you and caters to your every strange whim. He follows you around the world as you go from show to show, from opening to opening, your work gaining in popularity and price range all the way. He makes sure you always have what you need, good food, plenty of rest, and excellent sex—it took a while to find the right man, a few detours and dead ends, but you finally found someone who lets you be you. Together you spend the next several decades traveling, building your dream house, and buying your impossibly adorable and wicked grandchildren anything they want. Life becomes very, very sweet. In a freak cruise accident, you both get food poisoning at the shrimp bar, and you die together in a small hospital in the Virgin Islands.

175

From section 107 . . .

You realize you can't marry this man, because as wonderful as he is, he's actually your enemy. As someone once said, *You know who your enemies are because they keep you from your work.* You move alone into a large empty warehouse space that was once a bakery. Giant Viking stoves line one wall, and industrial stainless-steel tables line the other. The rest of the warehouse is filled with other artists and sculptors, video installation artists, printmakers, mapmakers, and metalworkers. It is like a cement honeycombed hive of artists.

You try to pick up your series of housewives killing husbands again—but it just isn't there. That anger drained out of you long ago, and you need something else. You start throwing potluck dinner parties for the building, twenty, thirty people at a time. You've got plenty of stoves for it. The deal is, they make the entrées (on any one night you might all be eating lasagna, lobster, pineapple chicken, and tacos) and you make the dessert. Desserts have always been your favorite. You make lemon cakes and coconut cream pie and handmade peanut butter chocolates.

The chocolates are something your grandmother taught you to do—melt down a Hershey's bar in a double boiler, add whatever you want (peanuts, orange rinds), then pour the mixture into molds (ice cube trays), let them cool, pop them out, and voilà. Everybody loves them and you begin to perfect the mixture.

Hershey's bars aren't good enough. You've got to make your own chocolate. You order cocoa beans from a distributor and track down the best bean there is, the Venezuelan criollo bean. You roast small batches on your stoves and buy some molds from a candy-making supplier. But your neighbor, Wednesday (who is a part-time heroin junkie and part-time sculptor), says the molds are boring. They're just flowers and bunnies and hearts. The chocolate would taste better if they were shaped different. She presents you with a gift. A series of chocolate molds she made and named Dead Dude (little skull and crossbones), Devil Babies (babies with horns), Sick Kitties (small cats with X's over their eyes), and Pure Poison (a small bottle with little XXX block letters).

You make your first batch of chocolate to match the names of the molds. Dead Dudes have cinnamon and pepper in them, Devil Babies are milk chocolate, Sick Kitties have white chocolate ears and paws, and Pure Poison has red pepper blended into the chocolate. The woman upstairs who's a papermaker makes you these lovely black, coffin-shaped boxes, and you take a whole batch of them to a chocolatier downtown. He buys them all, and two weeks later orders a hundred more boxes. Your warehouse has become a candy factory. You expand your chocolates beyond Halloween candies, you begin to color the chocolate and make hand-painted Pollackesque chocolates, which win awards and begin to be shipped nationally. A chain of department stores now carries them, as well as several gift catalogues. You are finally painting again, only with chocolate.

You marry once, divorce, and marry again. You adopt two children and an orange cat named Oscar. You live to a ripe old age on a farm where all of your chocolate is made by hand (but not by you anymore, thank God). You die of old age and go to heaven, which is a metropolis of winged things and glass.

176

From section 109 . . .

You move in with Luis and two months later you feel a tender knot in your stomach. Free-floating nausea. You can't drink red wine. You're tired all the time. Tomatoes taste like tinfoil, wine like turned egg salad. You're pregnant. Luis is excited but you're uncertain. It's all happening so fast.

First comes baby girl Rosie, a soft muscle squiggling in her jumper. Then a year after comes her brother, Paulie. He's a little thug from the start, a heartbreaker who never has time for kisses or hugs and runs head-long into the world trailing your heart behind. You love them more than you can bear.

Luis buys a small printing company that specializes in inking medical information brochures. Brochures with titles like *What to do now that you have pinkeye. So you want a breast reduction! Fungus—America's secret. Angioplasties are for Everyone* . . . , and so on. Several hospitals use his shop, as well as some ophthalmology clinics. He works long hours and comes home dirty and covered in toner. He's short-tempered a lot of the time, he doesn't get to eat regularly, and you shoo the children into their rooms when he gets into one of his moods, but business is good and he buys a house near the beach in Oceanside. It's a tiny white cottage with narrow green shutters and an orange house cat that seems to have been left by the previous tenants.

You develop a routine where you become more roommates than lovers. Sex dwindles, you communicate only about dry, everyday things. *Where's the plunger? Did you pay the cable bill? Have you seen the baby's sweater?* That sort of thing. You want to pull him closer, reach out and break through this ever-thickening wall of ice, but it's like every day there's a new layer of chill and all you can do is watch.

Then one morning while you're running on the beach you see a familiar face walking toward you. At first you can't place it—but then you realize it's the waiter from your favorite sushi restaurant. Toru. He's very tall and has articulate, slender hands. He smiles when he sees you. The two of you walk down the shoreline and talk about good restaurants, good dinner companions, how some people are just on the same frequency. The two of you are definitely on the same frequency. An electric one.

You talk about your childhoods and your first loves and your sad stories. It's been a long time since you had a conversation like that, where you're both speed-talking, trying to get everything out. You sit on the breakers and watch the ocean. He brushes a piece of straw off your shirt. You notice his knees—elegant, well-integrated knees. In fact, you've never seen such beautiful knees in your life.

You do not tell your husband about running into Toru—you could have, certainly there was nothing wrong with running into him. Besides, Luis is as usual in no mood to talk. He comes home dirty and angry that night, cursing about so-and-so at work who screwed him again and what's-his-face who can't follow a direction to save his life. You turn over in bed and let him rant—but for some reason you can't stop smiling.

You decide to meet Toru at an out-of-the-way coffee shop. He takes you to his apartment to show you his Japanese print collection, and what happens next can only be described as an Olympics sex-a-thon. Something worthy of Japanese porn. There are silk neckties and kitchen tables and vegetables involved. Anybody would pay to see what the two of you did.

Toru is magnetic. Irresistible. You meet him again and then again. This goes on for days, then weeks, then months, and then over a year. Luis continues to work hard, the children are doing well at school, and you are happy with your two husbands.

Amazing what the mind can block out, how memory and foresight take vacations when you're doing something you shouldn't be. Then comes the sharp-focus day of panic, the moment your folly comes into stark relief. It's the day you realize *you're pregnant* and you have absolutely no idea if the father is Luis or Toru.

You tell the doctor you have to find out if the baby is Asian or not. "There's really no test for that," he says. "Do you want to know if it's a boy or girl? I could tell you that." You start crying. What good is knowing if it's a boy or girl when you don't know whether or not it's Asian?

You aren't the first to stand at this craps table.

If you stay with Luis, go to section #190 (page 434).
If you run off with Toru, go to section #191 (page 438).

177

From section 109 . . .

You take the internship at the radio station. The newsroom of WLUP is like a big-top circus set on fire. Thirty people crammed into a cramped space running to get news from the wires, running to make deadlines, running to edit pieces, running to attend countless meetings. You don't have a desk—there are none to spare. You share a crowded countertop that has six phones on it with six other interns. No one has time to explain anything to you—there's apparently no training seminar or place to ask questions, it's a *sink-or-swim* office policy, and so it's up to you to learn by osmosis or sheer luck or to get the hell out of the way.

The reporters take recorders and microphones out into the world and get sound. Then they bring back the raw tape, feed it into computers and cut the sound into little bits, adding their voices here and there to explain the story. Simple enough—except the recorders are fickle and complicated and the computers used to edit are in Sanskrit. Plus, anytime you step into a production booth to try and learn the system, one of the reporters gives you the hairy eyeball and/or reports you to his superior to get out of the way so they can cut their stories.

So you stay after work to teach yourself. After everyone else goes home, you get into the editing suites and teach yourself ProTools and Digiserves and all the other impossibly complicated systems they use. You get ahold of one of the minidisk recorders (you "borrow" it from an unlocked drawer) and practice recording. Your voice sounds strange when played back. Soft and goofy. Girlish. So you rehearse. Drop your voice an octave and try to sound more professional. You get it down a little bit better, but the real test is how you sound when you interview someone.

You decide to take a recorder out at night, when no one will miss it. But who to interview? You don't dare take the equipment in a bar, where it might get rum sloshed on it or some drunk will grab at it. So you head out for a small coffee shop near the station, sort of a seedy eclectic place with cut oil drums for tables and rows of old airplane seats for chairs. You talk to a guy there named Mouse, a thin, watery-eyed high school student who's nervous but likes the idea of talking into a microphone and then hearing it played back. You sit and chat as people stop by and talk to him. He knows everybody.

It turns out Mouse is a low-level meth dealer at his high school, one of several "sale runts" around the city. After you promise not to use his name, he tells you what it's like to deal, how the chain of command works. He doesn't even know where the stuff comes from; he gets it from behind the bus station, where a kid named Moses trades bread bags full of crystals for cash. He charges a pretty hefty fee, some of which he keeps, some of which he uses to pay his supplier, whoever that is.

You go out night after night with Mouse, talking to the tweaker kids, to their friends, and even to Moses, who likes the attention. Turns out he picks up the shit from a Bible manufacturer in an industrial suburb. The Bibles are hollowed out, packed with meth, and stacked in boxes for him. He splits it up into bread bags for the sale runts at home. So you follow the trail. You take a weekend job at the Bible factory and sneak your recorder in. You talk to the workers who box Bibles, and after a few months you learn where the lab is, at a cabin up north in the tiny town of Montevideo.

By the time you tell the newsroom editor that you have a story for him to hear, you have over sixty hours of tape cut into a progressive series of portraits. The editor takes your tapes, tells you to go away, he's busy, and you wait. It's a week before he drops your CD into a player and listens, but what happens after that surprises even you. They take your tape, clean it up quite a bit, cut it down, get a few more interviews with the mayor and the chief of police, and then they air your series over three weeks, and call it "Blown Away."

You graduate from intern to reporter, and you're assigned the inner-city beat. *Drugs, murders, police corruption.* The fun stuff. You file story after story and eventually take a job at CNN as an investigative reporter. You join the league of elite investigative reporters who travel all over the world working on in-depth pieces. Stories on the drug trade in Africa, the sex tours of Thailand, corruption in the Mexican government, deregulation of European pharmaceutical cartels.

You never marry or have children, but in your memoir (a best seller titled *Away and Beyond, One Woman's Journey Through Thirty Years of Investigative Reporting*) you confess your stories are like your children. Some successful, others struggling, all of them out in the world, doing their work, archived on the Web, affecting or effecting people's thoughts and opinions long after you stopped working on them.

A month before you die, *Time* magazine does a cover story on you, and they ask you what you remember most about your life. "I never stopped following the shadows," you say. "Always trying to illuminate what was dark."

"And now that you've retired?" the reporter asks.

"There is no retirement. Even as I go out—I have all my lights on."

178

From section 110 . . .

You take a cab to Harrington's apartment, which is in a neat row of narrow red-brick buildings with steep roofs and white shutters. *What are you going to do?* You watch the people walking down the street. Old woman in a green peacoat, deliveryman in a yellow jumpsuit. Starlings overhead. It's eight in the morning. It's cold.

Then you see Harrington. He looks like his picture—but bigger, a refrigerator wheeling around in a trench coat. He checks his watch and starts to walk down the street, so you follow him all the way to the tube, which he takes to the city. You trail him to a shiny office building near Trafalgar Square. Here you're not brave enough to go in, so you write the name of the building down, the Baltimore, and sit down at a café across the street. Four hours later he comes out and takes the tube back home. There is no sign of distress in his face. Nothing that would indicate he had left a woman alone, *blindfolded*, in a hotel room.

You follow him every day for a week—and then one day you let him go to work without you in order to look around his world. Why? You don't know. Because it's a mystery. *He's* a mystery. You want to know more about him, and you figure the easiest way to do this is to root through his garbage. In the Dumpster out back you find an oily paper bag with his crumpled-up phone bill inside. Amazing what information people literally leave out on the street. You find his alternate mailing address, his unlisted phone number, even his Visa card number.

You take notes on the garbage. *He like bananas, white fish, chutney. Seems to go through a lot of paper towels. Subscribes to numerous car trader magazines. . . .* All this sleuthing is turning your humiliation into a prickly sweet feeling of power. Now he is the one who has no idea what's going on.

It's his apartment you're dying to get into. Think of the information within. *His sock drawers, his refrigerator, his computer.* The thought makes you dizzy. You can't resist. In back of his building there are large metal Dumpsters underneath a vertical gutter and a small brick ledge. If you stood on the Dumpster, held on to the gutter, stepped up onto the ledge, you might be able to hoist yourself up to his kitchen window.

You break in. It's almost overwhelming—where to start? His bedroom. The cherry platform bed, the perfectly made duvet, a nightstand with sleeping pills, condoms, and lo! A stack of porn. *Sperms of Endearment*, *Heather in Leather*, and *Rimmerama*, just to name a few. His computer is still on, and it wakes up when you touch the mouse. You find his e-mail messages—all the ones he sent you—and then you see he's sent duplicates of these same e-mails to *hundreds* of other girls all across the globe. Girls in London, Los Angeles, Connecticut, Frankfurt, Paris, and Cairo.

Hundreds of e-mails saying "I love you" and "you're the one." He's engaged in different levels of cybersex with all of them. Some still chatting, others hard-core. There are lots of pictures of these women, some pretty, sitting in gardens, some nude, bent over bathtubs and car hoods. The worst e-mails are the ones where the girl appears to be in love with him—the ones who ask when he's coming to visit, if he got the present they sent. . . .

So. You have a cyber predator on your hands. What to do? Well, first you must tell the girls what's happening. But if you say he's been cheating on all of them, they might think you're just a jealous competitor out to ruin Harrington's good name. No. You must send them something they'll take seriously.

From: London Health services

To: Partners of Harrington H******
It has come to this clinic's attention you may have had sexual contact with one Mr. Harrington H*******. Your name was provided by the client, and while we are not allowed to tell you what the diagnosis is, it is this clinic's responsibility to inform you that Mr. Harrington H******* has been recently

diagnosed with multiple contagious sexually transmitted diseases (STDs) and you should see your doctor immediately.

Thank you for your prompt action.

London Health Services on behalf of Mr. Harrington H*******

You send this to every woman in his e-mail inbox, including his mother. You get on the next plane to America and hurry back to your hometown, where you feel ashamed and humiliated. *You actually flew to another country and waited for a complete stranger on a hotel bed.* You can't tell your family or friends, because then they'd be disgusted. No, it's just the two of you. You and the dirty little secret.

And you wonder about secrets. Why do they want so badly to be told? It's like holding a bright red beach ball under water—you can do it for a while, but you get tired and the secret *never* gets tired. It's always right there, ready to pop up. Are you the only one in the world with a secret? There must be others. There must be millions of people who would feel better if only they could tell someone—anyone—their secret.

So you start a Web site where anyone can anonymously post their secret. People can choose to put their secrets in a variety of different pages, Sad Secrets, Dirty Secrets, Funny Secrets, Love Secrets, Evil Secrets, and Miscellaneous Secrets. Then their secrets can be read by anyone in the world but no one knows who the secret belongs to.

It's like a cyber confessional and you're the priest. Indeed, you read all the secrets religiously. Some of them are heartbreaking (*I'm twelve years old and I just found out today that I am pregnant . . .*), while others are hilarious (*I work at a pet shop and today I sold a dead guinea pig to a customer by convincing him that it was just "sleeping"*). People pay to see the Adult Secrets section (*I'm sexually attracted to animals, not any animal, just squirrels. I don't know why—they're just perfect, the way they look. I wish I could be with them all the time. Is there a name for this?*). It's all fine and good—the Web site grows and you're making a nifty living—but then one day a secret comes across the screen that makes you uneasy. *I'm going to kill three people next week. A man paid me to do it—I'm scared but I need the money.*

What's your responsibility here? What are you supposed to do? The whole premise of your secret site is that it's *secret*. The truth is that the system automatically stamps the unique IP address of the author, or at least the computer it was sent from, onto the secret. No one can see these identifying numbers but the system administrator, and that's you—and you never look at them. You wouldn't know what to do with them anyway, they're just binary code gobbledygook. But some people would know what to do with that address—some computer cowboy could take the binary number 1011000.00011011.00111101.10001001 and connect it to a computer in a public library in Texarkana. Not you—but somebody.

Then another chilling secret comes through with the same IP address. *I bought the gun to shoot them up with. It's a sin to kill but God don't seem to be around here much anymore. I hope the little kids is sleeping when I do it.* Little kids? Even if they're joking, even if they're really talking about lambs on a veal farm—enough is enough. You call the cops, who are surprisingly responsive. They come out to your house immediately, grill you for three hours, and confiscate your computer. They contact the hosting company that owns the IP address and obtain the name, address, and phone number of one Mr. Andy Peterson, a mildly mentally handicapped, out-of-work ex–coal miner in West Virginia. He's just the killer-for-hire. They still have to find the guy who hired him.

West Virginia authorities pick up Mr. Peterson outside a hardware store, where he'd just purchased duct tape and a blue waterproof tarp. Mr. Peterson seems almost relived to confess (all secrets want to be told). He leads them to the fat, square-jawed Mr. Gabler, the mine owner who has paid Mr. Peterson five thousand dollars to kill his wife and their two-year-old twins, Jamie and Joey. The murders were planned for that very evening. Mr. Gabler would have collected over a million dollars in insurance. "Times in West Virginia are hard, gentlemen," Mr. Gabler says as he's led to the squad car. "Very hard."

"Well, sir," one of the officers tells him, "I expect being a wife-murdering kid-killer in Joliet is gonna be a whole lot harder."

The whole mess winds up on the front page of every newspaper and gossip rag. This all makes your Web site some sort of a national treasure to people, some vigilante justice machine. You carry on with the Web site, but you don't read the secrets anymore. Some secrets want to be told—but they ought not be. Some secrets should stay secret.

You die one day when you slip on some liquid laundry soap in the basement. It was Tide. They speed you to the hospital, where a rogue blood clot, a little nasty that's been waiting, has finally been loosened and speeds to your heart and stops it. Kerpow. It's the little things that kill us.

You go to heaven, which is a dry white desert illuminated by a trinity of suns. You learn that everybody goes to heaven, even evil people. Even Mr. Peterson and Mr. Gabler, who died in prison eight days after he was sentenced. (Knifed in the butthole while he was taking a shower. Figures.) The angels tell you everyone is essentially good but they get all screwed up on earth. They say the mercury content in the oceans alone guarantees nasty tempers, and what with the politics of world hunger, the ozone thing, and the general loss of social morals, it's a wonder not everybody is murdered.

The angels like to watch the antics on earth. They gather around a big movie screen every night and watch daily bloopers, grisly murders, and sad suicides. The angels aren't bothered. They shrug and say the whole thing is preposterous anyway—to put a soul in a body made of flesh is like putting it in a roast beef sandwich. It's designed to fail, so what do you expect? They offer you popcorn and a Pepsi. You spot Harrington in the corner and he waves, but there's no time to talk to him now—the blooper reel is starting and a hush falls across the wings of the celestial beings in the audience. Time to see the outtakes. All the mistakes are waiting.

179

From section 110 . . .

You try to leave immediately, but your flight can't be changed without an enormous fee, so you stick it out for the week. It could be worse. Just be glad you weren't raped, beaten, clubbed, held down in the river. You're angry at yourself, ashamed you played with your life like you would with poker chips. Now you have an entire week to kill before you go home, so you try to make the best of it and become the consummate tourist. You go to the drafty museums, the claustrophobic tourist-packed churches, and the mind-numbing walking tours. You even take one of those stupid double-decker buses, but a pigeon shits on you in Trafalgar Square.

On your last day in London you go to a spa and get a sea salt scrub, aromatherapy, hydrotherapy, and a mango-chutney hair treatment. Even if you had a crappy time in England, at least you'll *look* great when you get back. They finish you off with a French pedicure, your feet soaked in slippery rose oil. After the spa you go to Covent Gardens for one last walk before it's time to go to the airport. At the garden there's a reflecting pool where the notoriously aggressive ducks swim. Children hurl cookie chunks at the ducks in an attempt to feed them—but nobody gets too close.

As you walk by the pool, you slip and squish around in your shoes (rose oil!), lose your balance, fall, and crack your head against the cement edge of the pool. Everything goes blurry and black. The ducks come over and peck you. *Are you made of bread?* they're quacking, *Pound cake?* Passersby shoo the ducks away (although the red welts on your face will have to be explained to the coroner) and you die in the ambulance, which is very colorful and noisy.

180

From section 111 . . .

You move into Harrington's world, made comfortable by three-hundred-thread-count Egyptian cotton sheets, five-hundred-dollar coffeemakers, and priceless hand-blown King Louis IX glass chandeliers. His apartment is gorgeous but demanding. Everything is so elegant, you feel as though you have to be too. There's no place for sweatpants or runny noses. God forbid you need deodorant or Tampax. They're hidden under the sink. Harrington is paying the rent, so you don't mind helping out around the house, but you feel like he has a free live-in maid. Your list of chores seems a little long. Daily straightening, vacuuming, and dusting are just starters. You also have to wash the sheets, clean the lint traps, polish the piano (which no one uses), and cook dinner, *including* an appetizer—and Harrington has very specific tastes.

He likes sockeye salmon but *not* smoked salmon. He likes the lightly salted butter of Échiré, which is rare and shipped in from France. When he does want salt, he only wants sea salt from *the Dead Sea*. (Jars are shipped monthly.) You find yourself poring over gourmet cookbooks and wondering if you should buy avocado mashers from Williams-Sonoma or lemon zesters from Harrods. Harrington is also demanding in the bedroom—he brings in satin ropes and fur-lined handcuffs and he binds your hands together. Ties you up, ties you down—every position imaginable. It's tedious. At first you like it, but then he never wants to do anything else but restrain you.

He gets some big promotion at work and begins to buy truly expensive things. It starts with a fifty-foot Boston Whaler, which he keeps at the yacht club. Then there are watches and jewelry and stereo equipment. Not just equipment—an entire surround-sound system, connected to the Internet, so streaming stereo from everywhere in the world blasts through the house, even the bathrooms.

He's generous. You'll give him that. He spends money on you—clothing and trips and things. But he becomes obsessed with what is *the very best* of everything. "I don't want *excellent*," he tells all the shopkeepers, "I want the *best*." And this becomes his obsession—is what he's buying *the best*? Is there a better boat? A better watch? He becomes easily bored with things. He gets rid of stuff just about as fast as he acquires it. You wonder how long it will be until he turns the perfection laser at you.

Time passes. A year, and then another. Everyone at home has given in to the fact that you're an expatriot and not likely to come home. Then Harrington has a scare. A lump in his testicles, which turns out to be malignant testicular cancer. He's hysterical and weeps in bed. Fast action is required. They're going to take out the lump, give him site-specific chemotherapy, and see what happens. He's miserable. Can't eat anything, can't pee without pain. You help him on the toilet, in the bath, help him get dressed, tie his shoes, eat.

So it comes as a great relief when Harrington is released from the hospital with a clean bill of health. He can come home and recover—they'll retest him in a month. Until then, it's just rest and relaxation. He plans a trip to the south of Spain. Three weeks in the sun, no stress, no workload. You will be happy to get out of the oppressive apartment, with all its shiny gadgets and technologically advanced software.

The night he comes back from the hospital, you have white orchids, chilled champagne, and a poached sockeye salmon over a bed of fennel field greens waiting, so you're pretty confused when he says he's not hungry, takes you by the hands, and says, "I'm sorry, sweetheart, I met someone else. A radiologist at the hospital, she's amazing—well, never mind that, but you know I believe in clean cuts and fresh starts, so I'm going to Spain with *Anna*, well, her name doesn't matter, but—by the time I get back, you should be gone."

And then *he's* gone. Poof. Harrington has gone to the south of Spain with *Anna*. You sit on the bed and weep the first day, and then lie in the bed and sleep for the second and third. By the fourth day you're ready to drive to Spain and see if Harrington was maybe *joking*, but then by the end of the first week, the anger starts to set in. Everything around you attempts to remind you about your inferiority. The stereo, the jewelry (are you supposed to leave the jewelry behind?), the clothes, and the vast computer system. All better, faster, quicker, and lovelier than you will ever be.

You finally get out of bed and have an idea that makes you feel better. The sign isn't hard to make, a brown paper bag and a black marker does the trick. You put it up outside the front door with electrical tape and then prop open the door.

Everything must go. Everything Free.
Third foor.

It takes some time for the first stragglers to come up—they're bewildered and wary. "Everything's free," you tell them. "Just take what you want. There are some paper bags under the sink for smaller stuff." People get a little braver and more aggressive. They take the televisions, the computers, empty out the jewelry cases, both his and hers. Someone holds up Harrington's Rolex. "Are you serious?" they ask.

At one point there are well over a hundred people in the flat, ripping and tearing, hauling and moving as quickly as they can. They take the refrigerator, the door hinges, the curtains. People take things you wouldn't think were valuable. Harrington's family photo albums, his toothbrush, his phonebook. They take his file cabinets, all his medical books, the chocolates from the coffee table, the coffee table itself, the modern lamps and green plants and the rare rosebush Harrington prunes carefully on the porch. They take the titanium deck chairs, the couches, the rugs—and then piano movers show up for the piano. As the apartment empties, your spirits lighten. Everything removed is a brick off your heart, and the air—the fresh air—is wonderful. You're only sorry you won't be here to see the look on Harrington's face when he sees his empty apartment. *"Pity,"* as he would say.

You move back to America and work at a used clothing store in New York. Vintage fashion, recycled retro. While working there you come up with some of your own designs that the owner likes, and she shows you where to get your designs made cheap in Chinatown. They sell very well at the little store, but after you go to some aesthetician's birthday party, where the Gotham Chamber

Opera performs, you end up making out with a guy named Switch, a bisexual clothing buyer for Saks, and your line is unexpectedly picked up by the mega department store the very next week. You start to design full-time. Your line is called Artemis (goddess of the hunt), and you create your designs from your cozy Cape Cod house, a renovated saltbox house where the light is perfect and you have the ocean to inspire your designs.

Switch, your fabulous *sometimes-into-girls/sometimes-into-guys* friend moves in with you on the Cape. Sometimes he's your lover, and sometimes he brings in party boys from the city. (There are bowls of condoms all over the house.) Some of your more stoic neighbors find this arrangement upsetting, but you couldn't care less. You haven't lived well until you've lived with an ongoing stream of gorgeous talented gay men who decorate your house for you, who cook *moules au safran* (mussels steamed with shallots, cream, saffron, onion, garlic, and chopped tomatoes), and bring you free sample sale Chanel, because they think you're a *lunatique fantastique*.

Your clothing line is bought out by a big wholesale outfit, a company that makes clothes and sells them to department stores all over the world under different names. You're only selling them your name, they'll design the rest of the clothes from here on out, which gives you and Switch a chance to catch up on reading romance novels on the beach, throwing oyster roasts, and wondering who to have sex with next.

You drown when you're sixty-four. You're taking your daily swim in the ocean when you're swept out to sea by a freak riptide. You learn that all the people that die at sea stay at sea and become fish. You become a tuna, a big gorgeous one that reaches over four hundred pounds before you're caught by Japanese fishing boats and diced up for sushi restaurants all over the world.

181

From section 111 . . .

You tell Harrington you're going to go check out the internship, and if it doesn't work out, you'll come back. "Go," he sneers, "but don't bother coming back. It won't be hard to replace you." He starts storming around the apartment and throwing your stuff into a garbage bag. Sweaters, shampoos, bras, lotion all chucked together. (Peach bath oil breaks open and oozes all over.) He throws the overstuffed bag out the window. *Right out the window!* It nearly hits a woman pushing a stroller. Then he shoves you out the door, no good-bye, no discussion, no kiss, just slams the door shut. You never see him again. You pick up your shit and head for Camden Market, where you can buy a proper suitcase. *Good riddance, Harrington!*

You fly home and take the internship at the radio station. Harrington's humiliation makes you set your jaw—*you have to make this work*. That will be hard. The newsroom of WLUP is like a circus set on fire. Thirty people crammed into a cramped space running to get news from the wires, running to make deadlines, running to edit pieces, running to attend countless meetings. You don't have a desk—there are none to spare. You share a crowded countertop that has six phones on it with six other interns. No one has time to explain anything to you—there's apparently no training seminar or place to ask questions, it's a sink-or-swim office policy, and so it's up to you to learn by osmosis or sheer luck.

The reporters take recorders and microphones out into the world and get sound. Then they bring back the raw tape, feed it into computers, and cut the sound into little bits, adding their voices here and there to explain the story. Simple enough—except the recorders are fickle and complicated and the computers used to edit are in Sanskrit. Plus, anytime you step into a production booth to try and learn the system, one of the reporters gives you the hairy eyeball and/or reports you to their superior so they can cut their stories.

So you stay after work to teach yourself. After everyone else goes home, you get into the editing suites and teach yourself ProTools and Digiserves and all the other impossibly complicated systems they use. You get ahold of one of the minidisk recorders (you "borrow" it from an unlocked drawer) and practice recording. Your voice sounds strange when played back. Soft and goofy. Girlish. So you rehearse. Drop your voice an octave and try to sound more professional. You get it down a little bit better, but the real test is how you sound when you interview someone.

Honestly, you still miss Harrington, as unbelievable as it seems. He did treat you well in certain ways—and his reaction to you leaving must have been so big because he didn't want you to go . . . you decide to call him. So one night, when you're out at the mall to see who you can find to interview, you stop at a pay phone by the arcade to place an international call. The phone rings and rings. The operator asks if you want to keep trying. No, I guess not.

"Hey," a squeaky voice says, "I need the phone." There stands a pipe-cleaner-thin girl, with a black mop of hair and the initials D.P. crudely tattooed on her arm. She looks thirteen, and she seems nervous. She's biting her lip and looking around.

"Is something wrong?" you ask.

"*No,*" she says too quickly. You step out of her way, sit on the palm-tree planter next to the phone booth, and set your recording kit down.

She keeps looking around. "Aren't you going to make a phone call?" you ask her.

"No. I don't need it for that." You keep sitting there, and after a while the girl looks curiously at you. "Are you waiting for Dante too?" she asks.

"Sure."

"Really? 'Cause he said he'd be here an hour ago."

"I'm kidding. I don't know who Dante is." She looks crestfallen. You tell her you're a reporter. This piques her interest, but when you tell her it's for *radio* she's clearly disappointed. "You should try to be a reporter for TV," she says. "That would be *so cool.*" She's so sweet—the way she jumps up next to you on the planter and swings her feet back and forth, like there's still a little girl under all that eyeliner.

"I'm just learning how to be a reporter," you tell her, "I need people to practice on." She thinks that's cool. You ask her if you could interview her—just for practice. She chews on a fingernail.

"Sure," she says, "just till Dante comes."

So you take out your minidisk and start the interview. The girl is excited now—she becomes very professional. "My name is Julia," she says clearly into the microphone, "and I'm twelve, but I'll be thirteen next month. I'm in the sixth grade at Brockton Junior High School. My favorite things are music, rhinestones, and my mom, who's dead, but it still counts." You ask about the rest of her family and she charges on without pausing. Her dad is in prison, her brother ran away, and her other brother beat her up, so there's a restraining order against him. She ran away from her third foster home, but everything's okay since she met Dante.

Dante is in high school, a building right across the road from her middle school, and she met him in the parking lot. Dante is the most popular kid in the whole school and so she "almost died" when he told her he wanted her to work for him . . . then she catches herself and looks around. "This is practice, right?" You tell her absolutely. She can tell you anything in the world and it'll be your secret. The truth is, you're starting to get nervous yourself, and whoever Dante is, you hope he doesn't show up.

Julia goes on. Dante has all the very cutest girls in school, who he calls "*his little dimes,*" working for him. Mostly junior high girls, but some high school girls too. He brings them to the mall or the shopping plaza down the highway and they go wait for the high school boys who have already paid Dante ten bucks to come and "do things" to them. It's hard to keep the microphone still. You ask *where* they go do things, and she says, "Usually in their cars, if they have them. Sometimes downstairs in the movie theater bathrooms." At this point your battery dies. (It's an important lesson, a mistake you never make again. *Always bring an extra battery.*)

You tell Julia she's really good at this—and can you maybe talk to her again sometime? *Sure. That'd be cool.* Then she sees someone she recognizes across the mall. "There's Elle!" she says, pointing to a young girl in a pink miniskirt coming down the escalator. "I gotta go," Julia says. "You can call me about the interview."

You scribble down her cell phone number on the back of your hand. "Can I drive you home?" you ask her, not knowing what exactly you're supposed to do. (*Are you supposed to drag her bodily to the cops? Maybe she's not telling the whole truth? Maybe she's making all this up?*)

"No, Elle and I take the bus. We live with Dante, and if anybody drops us off he gets super mad. Bye!" Then she's gone.

She *lives* with the bastard. You call the police and social services right away, but you're immediately introduced to the inefficiency, inequality, and *inanity* of "the system." You get mired in a nest of case numbers, social workers, and paperwork until you shout at some woman on the phone, "There are little girls selling sex at *the mall*." Enough. You call Julia and ask for another interview. You ask her to bring some of the other girls that work for Dante and meet you at Starbucks. You want to practice interviewing on them too.

When they arrive you buy them all coffees, into which they dump large quantities of milk and sugar. Julia is happy to see you—she talks about Dante and the high school boys and how giving blow jobs *is gross*. The other "dimes" talk too. Sweet young girls who roll their eyes when they talk about how Dante is sending them older guys now—college guys—and they wonder if he's serious about renting a *hotel room* for the girls and doing two at a time.

It's all on tape, and you ask them, you *beg* them to let you make the story public. *No way! You said it was just for practice!* They clam up. Julia is furious. You try to reason with her—you tell her *she's better than all this, she doesn't have to put up with this, you want to help her*, but she grabs her backpack. "If you tell anybody," she seethes through little white teeth, "I'll tell Dante where you work and they'll come *rape you*."

It's this last sentence that gives you the courage to go to Allen, the senior editor of the newsroom, with your tape. (A scary man who shouts more than he talks and has never so much as said two words to you.) It's the word "rape." It's as if Julia knows she's being raped—as if she's shouting, "Go tell them they rape me!" She wouldn't have the idea in her head, so at the ready, if she didn't know deep down what was really happening.

Allen takes your tape into a meeting with all the other editors and closes the door. *Are you in trouble? Will they be able to air the tape without consent?* When they come out of the meeting, grim faces and eyes down, Allen takes you into his office. He tells you that because these are minors, the station doesn't need their consent, but they do need to protect their identities. Allen frowns. "The tape is . . ." You're waiting for him to say *awful, naive,* or *poorly recorded.* But what he says is ". . . amazing. None of my guys could have gotten girls to talk like that. You really did it."

Bam. The editors cut together a six-part series on high school prostitution rings called "Innocence Lost." Dante gets put away for thirteen years and Julia goes to a privately run group home in the country along with several of her friends. When you speak to her on the phone, she sounds like a completely different person. "They have horses!" she bubbles. "My favorite one is Harvey, and I ride him almost every day."

You graduate from intern to reporter, and you're assigned the inner-city beat. *Drugs, murders, police corruption.* The fun stuff. You file story after story and eventually take a job at CNN as an investigative research reporter. You join the league of elite investigative reporters who travel all over the world working on in-depth pieces. Stories on the drug trade in Africa, the sex tours of Thailand, corruption in the Mexican government, deregulation of European pharmaceutical cartels.

You never marry or have children, but in your memoir (a best seller titled *Away and Beyond, One's Journey Through Thirty Years of Investigative Reporting*) you confess your stories are like your children. Some successful, others struggling, all of them out in the world, doing their work, archived on the Web, affecting or effecting people's thoughts and opinions long after you stopped working on them.

A month before you die, *Time* magazine does a cover story on you, and they ask you what you remember most about your life. "I never stopped following the shadows," you say. "Always illuminating what was dark."

"And now that you've retired?" the reporter asks.

"There is no retirement. I'm still illuminated. Even as I go out—I have all my lights on." You die at age eighty while choking on elk jerky. It's embarrassing.

182

From section 112 . . .

You and Rocky get married at the beaux arts Palm House in the Brooklyn Botanic Garden. There's borscht and vodka, nettle soup and lemon pashka. Little Russia in big Brooklyn. Afterward you take a quick honeymoon right in the apartment—stock up on croissants and champagne and don't leave the house for three days (fuck and fuck and fuck and fuck). Sergei eventually moves away. All his classical Russian records—Shostakovich and Verstovsky and Tchaikovsky and Chesnokov—waltz right out the door behind him. Wistful is the only thing you feel for him now.

Rocky is a good husband at first—the other wives say so anyway. Most of their husbands come home drunk and throw their dinners against the walls, and when they don't, that's even worse. "Something is wrong," your neighbor complains. "My husband hasn't hit me for three days! Nothing!" But as time passes, Rocky hardens. Draws away from you. He hardly ever has a kind word—and he only wants the most impersonal and perfunctory sex. This goes on for months and months and then a year and then more. You miss Sergei. His company, his hands—everything about him haunts you. You stop eating. Russian food is starting to disgust you. Russian tea, Russia vodka, Russian people—they all seem rote and overbearing.

Rocky comes home early one night and catches you in bed with Vassily, the building super. A fat bear of a man. What's stupid is you don't even like the super, you're just bored and tired of doing nothing. Rocky pulls out a hammer from the tool drawer in the kitchen and runs around until he catches Vassily and clonks him on the head with it. You're next. Killing someone with a hammer doesn't take as long as you might think. Your death makes "News of the Weird," and that's about it. Some lives just don't add up to much.

183

From section 112 . . .

You run off with Sergei. *How could you not?* His cock is shaped like a baby's arm holding a peach. Plus you love the way he talks. "That guy is *green*," he says about the kid who joined the Russian chess team, "and he's not gonna brown." You also love the way he cooks; each meal could win a blue ribbon at the Russian State Fair, if they had one. The two of you move to the south side of Brighton Beach, away from Rocky and into an even tinier, shabbier apartment.

Besides his aggressive and frequent lovemaking, Sergei turns out to be quite a slob. Socks on the kitchen counter, toast crumbs in bed. He's a pig, but *he's your pig*. Even when you shout at him about his underwear on the bathroom floor or his pipe tobacco all over the kitchen table, you secretly find it adorable, but you'd never tell him. Your attraction is built on mutual indifference and irritation.

Rocky tracks you down in your new apartment, kicks his way through the door while pretending to be the building electrician. He socks you across the jaw and you come at him with a full bottle of Chianti, which you smash over his head. You can't tell the blood from the wine. Sergei is making a sandwich in the kitchen this whole time. He's nonplussed and doesn't intervene. He takes a big bite of corned beef on rye as you have Rocky in a headlock under the kitchen table.

"What the fuck?" you shout at him after you finally shove the bleeding and wet Rocky out the door. "Why didn't you help me?"

He shrugs and says, "You had it under control." That's Sergei. Never one to get too upset about anything. Not even when you get pregnant one, two, *three* times. You wanted to annoy Sergei with all these loud and baffling children, but they don't annoy him. He loves them fiercely.

The five of you live in that tiny apartment and Sergei refuses to get a bigger place. He thinks half the trouble with families today is that houses are too big. Parents don't know anything about their children's lives because they can't *see* what their children are doing. Matteo, Marcus, and Misha are always in the same room as you; you know every disgusting boy detail of what they're doing, whether you want to or not.

They grow up. Matteo gets a good job with the city as a sanitation inspector; Marcus follows in the footsteps of his father and becomes a poet, with several books published by small presses; and wee Misha moves all the way to Russia, where he owns a popular coffee shop called Barabu. You and Sergei visit him several times and end up moving to cold, gorgeous St. Petersburg.

There you start painting again, this time on your work. You don't care about classes, teachers, or critiques. Paintings that are just for you. A small gallery in the city center likes them and shows them. They actually sell quite well, well enough to take the family on vacation once a year to Santorini. Marcus and Matteo move to St. Petersburg as well, where they marry healthy Russian girls and produce eight grandchildren in four years. You have a wonderful life.

The whole family is on a train headed for Peterhof, the royal estate on the Baltic Sea, where Marcus is going to have a poetry reading. You're wearing a blue dress and Sergei a blue suit. Your sons look so handsome, your grandchildren bright as poppies. The train hits a bad section of track and goes headlong into a field of wheat. Everyone is killed. The last thing you remember is your husband looking at you and smiling. "Orchids," he said, "we should have bought orchids."

184

From section 69 . . .

You don't confess. Instead you go and kill yourself by jumping off the Brooklyn Bridge. There's not much to it—no real planning on your part. It's easy to jump . . . just climb up the guylines a way, hop over the safety fence, and voilà! All the shining sea before you. (Well, it's the East River, but who has time for details.)

It's a clear blue sky and nobody on the bridge tries to stop you, despite the fact there are dozens of young, pie-eyed Jehovah's Witnesses standing around. On your way over the railing, it occurs to you that you're committing suicide in front of two dozen "missionaries" and underneath a building that's labeled THE WATCHTOWER. Just what the fuck are they watching? People jump off the bridge? You start to laugh as you claw the air. You hit the water and it's as hard as a Moses tablet.

185

From section 125 . . .

You tell Oliver you'll marry him and you both return to Berlin without laying eyes on your father. This makes your heart heavy—you don't even know if you'll ever speak to him again. Planning the wedding helps your spirits—a little. It's hard not to cheer up when the cirkus folks are all around you throwing you parties and giving you champagne toasts. Plus, there are caterers to hire and the dress to buy—all these details to distract you, at least momentarily, from that dark prickly question that won't go away. *What if your father was right? What if you killed your mother?*

You make your wedding a grand spectacle, a one-night-only show. Every single person in your wedding party is nude, except for paper flowers and elaborate hats made by the cirkus wig maker, Ad Frank. Your dress is fiery bloodred and covered with pink pearls. Oliver wears a crushed-blue velour tuxedo and the two of you step inside an ornate oversized birdcage to exchange vows. You wish your father was there—you've written him several letters, but they all come back unopened.

The cirkus starts touring and Oliver comes with. He's quit his job and now he follows you, helping book gigs and paying off city officials. You tour all summer and spend two weeks in each city. Paris, Amsterdam, Prague, Milan, you never thought you'd see Europe like this—while flying naked across a white wax ice rink. Still, you're becoming something of a cult legend. The cirkus sells posters and T-shirts and key chains with your face on them. Time passes. It's a lovely sticky collage of strange cities and all-night parties and ankle bandages. You're making six figures a year now, which you've been diligently socking away in an online international e-trade account.

Then out of the blue a television network offers to buy out the cirkus. They toss out an astronomical amount of money to buy the rights to the concept, to the acts, and the characters. They want you to *cease and desist* the show so they can create some big network television show called *Circus Freaks*. Maxie sells. The money is too good to turn down. He says he could always come up with another concept—but for now he's bought a thirty-foot sailboat, which he's going to sail with his nineteen-year-old girlfriend to Spain.

Oliver suggests you take some time off and sit still for a while, which sounds pretty good to you. The two of you buy a small stone farmhouse outside Prague and do just that—*sit still*. You grow a lovely vegetable garden and cook delicious, simple, farm fresh meals. You drink local wine and sit for hours in the garden just reading or staring at the sky. Reporters still come around from time to time, asking for an interview with the legendary Mother Theresa Chicken Lady—the cult hero who has disappeared—but you always decline the interviews. It's silence you're after now.

Your father keeps his word and never forgives you. You have a hundred letters he's returned, which sit in a box under the bed. You've thought about returning home to the States to face him—but who can stand up under the heat of such anger? Then one hot day in June you get a letter from your aunt. She tells you he's died in his sleep during an afternoon nap; he had an untreated heart disease no one knew about. The funeral is set for three days from now but your aunt tells you not to come.

> . . . He made it terribly clear. His dying wish was that you didn't come to the funeral. It's in his will. He was always so stubborn and he loved your mother so much. If there had been more time I know he would have set down his blame and his anger. Only there never seems to be enough time in this world, does there. I'm so sorry. I love you.

She includes a photograph of your parents and your father's funeral notice from the paper. You're not even listed in the people who survive him. You're not mentioned at all. Oliver lets you cry day and night without telling you to *hush*.

You and Oliver live together in this lovely stone cottage for the rest of your lives. You have one girl, Hannah, who illuminates even the darkest parts of your soul. At sixteen she runs off in the night to join *a performance academy* in France, where she meets and marries a Gypsy boy you can't stand. You tell her to come home. She does sometimes—the rest of the time she lives in Giverny with the Gypsy and paints.

You live to a very old age on your little farm. You and Oliver become old people. Hannah moves back with your granddaughter, Celeste, who is like a firefly, darting around the garden. When you die, it's from a stroke, and you start to drift up to heaven. Follow the white light . . . but you quickly step outside the light and sink down to earth, where you will roam the earth as a disembodied spirit. You're not going up—no way. There's not enough celestial music or angels in the world to make you face Anne Frank in heaven.

186

From section 67 . . .

You follow the red light. You drift in a bone canoe down a sticky red river. Black tree branches scrape along the bottom of your boat. You have the sensation of floating, of being able to dip in and out of any place or thought you choose. The red river goes through a deep green steam, a mist thick as curtains, and when you clear, the river has ended and you are standing beside a small wooden pulpit.

Behind the pulpit there is a wrinkled old root of a man with waxy skin and floss-yellow hair. He opens a ledger. "In the fair schoolroom of the sky," he says, "what *never matters, never minds*." He flips through pages until he finds the right spot. "Some go up," he says, "and some go down."

He leans over and sears your forehead with a white-hot pencil. Cracks of lightning reverberate through your brain. "Marked!" he shouts and smiles, revealing pale blue teeth sharpened to needle points. He flips the ledger shut. "Now be a good creature and head on down to the skinning grotto," he whispers, "they're waiting."

187

From section 67 . . .

You resist the red light. The pressure of the woman's hand holds you steady and you try to see who it is helping you, but the tangled branches crack and give under your weight and you fall into some dark unconscious place. When you wake up, there are bright blue lights and the smell of stainless steel. There is beeping, speaking, the sensation of motion. You are being hurried down the corridors of a white hallway.

Darkness again, and then breaking awakening. Your eyelids are like dried flowers. It hurts to breathe. The pain feels elaborate and intricate, glowing and warm, as thought it were made of gold leaf and filigree and built by masters. Lasting. Your lung had been punctured, your ribs broken. Stainless steel and catgut hold you together. Part woman, part machine. Old ironsides.

The reporters come wanting details. You say a few things, nothing much. Then you stop talking to them—and then you just stop talking. You never go back to work at the college. The dean must be nervous about your little episode together, because she suddenly reverses herself and offers you an extremely large severance package as well as the school's fleet of lawyers to go after the grocery store. There's a lawsuit. Your prosecution team is strong, the defense is weak, the jury angry. It all ends in an enormous financial settlement that guarantees you'll never have to work for a living again.

Just about a year after the shooting you buy a lovely brick Colonial house along the Wilmington River with an open view of the sea. There you drink ginger ale and Pimm's and watch the big ships as they go out to sea. You paint. The woman who held your hand in the grocery store, Marietta, lives with you now.

She makes coffee thick as tar and cuts it with condensed milk—she brings a hot steaming mug to the sunporch every morning. That's where your easels are set up. The canvases seem to be getting bigger and bigger, wide as the ocean, which stands just to the left of your sunlit room. Every painting you finish seems to be another scale from your skin peeled off and put away. One blue, one aquamarine, small lines and boxes of color, dashes and breaks, as if you could decode a foreign language only your birds know. You have two large parrots, Socrates and Plato, and they argue just like old Greek philosophers.

That is your family. *You, Marietta, Socrates, and Plato.* Four hearts beating in the house. It is a heaven of sorts. This pile of seaside brick, a surly Creole, and your wicked winged philosophers. You will spend many years here, with the canvases running through you like freight trains, stopping to pick up their color before they move on toward the galleries and collectors who buy them. They are like mischievous children who wander out in the bright of day and are never heard from again.

You die one day when you are a hundred and two. Just a short breath, a sharp pain, and a bright light. As natural as swimming. You didn't mean to live so long—you just never got around to dying. You're in an easy chair overlooking the sea and you were trying to remember the names of all your paintings. Heaven knows where your darlings are now; you'd kill them all if you could find them.

188

From section 116 . . .

You take the job and move down to Minneapolis. City of salt, city of time. But there's a certain poetry in this city of blue lakes and white steam, you just have to find it. The notion of found poetry inspires the class you develop, Found Objects, where students create art out of everyday life. Out of things they find in their houses, on the ground, at junk shops, salvage yards, city dumps, lying around wherever. They bring in car hoods, pie tins, rogue Barbie doll heads, broken robin eggs, martini glasses, dried rose petals, cracked vinyl records. . . . Then they assemble those things in some sculptural way that redefines their meaning.

You can't believe you almost didn't move here—almost missed out on teaching—almost passed it all up for dishing out *pie*. (Albeit good pie.) You find your students to be the most engaging, intelligent, curious creatures on earth and you love their eager, facile minds. Nothing against the truck drivers and taconite miners up north, but they're not always ready for a rousing argument on the impact Gilles Deleuze had on postmodern art or the homoerotic subtext of the Bauhaus movement. (Truth be told, you're not always ready for that either.)

You teach Joseph Cornell, master of creating poetry from missing parts. Piecing together found objects. You show them photos of his cramped studio in his mother's house on Utopia Parkway in Queens, you show them his legendary boxes, small cigar boxes, shoe boxes, all with found objects glued inside them—scraps of papers, ripped maps, broken champagne glasses, birds' eggs, feathers, pencils; they're all meaningless on their own, but when put together in a new context they highlight the beauty of the broken world.

Your one grief, and it's a deep, abiding grief, is not seeing your daughter Dilly or your adorable granddaughter, Blue. They never come down to the city, and with classes and student meetings and papers to grade, you can hardly ever make the four-hour drive up north to see them. Dilly seems to have repaired her relationship with her father, which is good, but it feels like they've started a club for just them, a club you can never join. You call Dilly all the time, send up letters and clothes for Blue, but her wild side prevails (where do these children get such spirit?) and she rarely calls you back.

Years pass. Your students do well, a few even go east, where they take on the fickle affections of the New York art world. You marry Gus Gustafson, the jolly black-and-white photo teacher. He's a big horse of a man and he holds you tight at night, his arms a vise grip around your waist, the heat coming off his body like an endless sauna, cleansing and detoxifying. He makes futuristic metal sculptures that look like Brancusi-inspired spaceships have dropped from the sky.

Eventually, with the salt and sugar of time, Dilly even softens toward you and one summer sends her coltish, bright-eyed, fifteen-year-old Blue down to stay with you. "She needs culture," Dilly says, "or something. I caught her at the VFW on polka night last week because she wants to learn more about *ballet*. I don't know what she wants with ballet but I'm pretty sure there isn't much of it on the Iron Range."

Blue ends up attending the arts school later that year and immediately excels in dance and rhythm classes. Dilly starts her own restaurant up north and doesn't have even the slightest desire to step foot outside the county. (You visit her once a month and help out in the kitchen.) Gus has a show in San Diego and darned if some Hollywood producer doesn't see his work and decide to buy every single piece Gus has on hand—and then orders a bunch more, finally setting you both up with a nice retirement plan and some money to spare (read vacation to Hawaii).

On days you're not teaching you spend a lot of time in your studio working, and it feels so much better than the HACKY days. Who would have thought you would end up living in Minneapolis with your granddaughter, teaching art and married to a man who wears size forty-two pants? Your life is a found object, put together from torn scraps of paper and bird eggs.

You do not die until you are very, very old. Ninety-two. You just go to sleep one night in your bed, next to your husband, and you have a pleasant dream that you never wake up from. It turns out heaven is a junk shop, a vast sweet-smelling place where God keeps all his broken things. Lost violins and Shakespeare's not-so-great plays. Bad artists and good politicians. Busted dog collars and tangled jump ropes. Confused philosophers and chipped coffee cups. Perfect in its way—broken beauty everywhere.

189

From section 116 . . .

You stay. You can't leave your daughter—not even if she doesn't want anything to do with you. Whether or not she knows it, she needs you. Even though she's pretty much repaired her relationship with her father (he takes her duck hunting in the fall and deer hunting in the summer), she's still prone to mood swings and not picking up the phone. You continue to work at Betty's Pies. You know the menu, the people, the specials by heart. Monday is fried chicken, Tuesday is meat loaf. Wednesday is baked chicken with gravy, Thursday is hot dish, Friday is fish dinner, and Saturday and Sunday are up for grabs.

The town is small, the culture minimal, but the seasons are orchestral—the way the weather changes across the lake and moves in so you can see rain slake across the surface of the water, turning it black and rippling, like a flock of blackfish speeding toward you. In summer the trees are verdant green, in winter they're stick black and stark white.

You take up with one of the old ironworkers who comes to the diner a lot. Joe Trelstad has always had eyes for you, but you've never given him the time of day because, well, because he's just *Joe*, just flannel-shirt-wearing, coffee-drinking, dumb-joke-cracking *Joe*. But one day he asks you over for dinner, so just once he can serve *you* pie, and you say, "Well, sure!"

Joe's place is much nicer than you would have imagined. It's a big log cabin high above Vermilion Creek with a moose head over the stone fireplace and a new generator that kicks in whenever the power goes down. (He's got quite a few beautiful Lakota artifacts he's found while out hunting. Arrowheads and broken pottery and even a piece of an old hide.) You spend more and more time over there until you eventually move in with him. He doesn't work, but he's got money. You don't know how much, but he's comfortable.

The two of you are married in a ceremony on an old paddleboat in the middle of Lake Superior. Afterward Joe confesses he has a lot more money than he ever let on. *A lot* more. Due to some long-ago insurance settlement with a taconite mine, old Joe is financially set for life. You don't ever have to work again. They throw you a big party at Betty's and Joe buys you a new truck. You become the Grand Dame of Duluth, a wealthy patron of the local arts. You and Joe take up sea kayaking and birding, you buy a house on Madeline Island and spend summers there painting.

You do not die until you are very, very old. Ninety-two. You just go to sleep one night in your bed, next to your husband, and you have a pleasant dream that you never wake up from. It turns out heaven is a junk shop, a vast sweet-smelling place where God keeps all his broken things. There you can find all sorts of things lying next to each other—lost violins and Shakespeare's not-so-great plays. Bad artists and good politicians. Busted dog collars and tangled jump ropes. Confused philosophers and chipped coffee cups. Perfect in its way—broken beauty everywhere.

190

From section 176 . . .

You're not going to break up your family—destroy the kids' home all because of a little carnal pleasure. (Even if it wasn't little.) You tell Toru you can't see him anymore and he drifts away from you—no tears, no shouting, just a complete vanishing. After that his number is disconnected and the restaurant says he quit.

Eight months later you give birth to an eight-pound seven-ounce Asian baby boy. *Damn the luck.* Black hair, creamy vellum-colored skin. Like an opal in a blue blanket. You have to tell Luis what you did with Toru—why your baby is Asian—and Luis breaks a fire extinguisher off the wall in the hospital corridor and smashes it on the floor.

Luis doesn't kick you out, but he won't touch the baby. You beg him not to tell the kids . . . and for their sake and *their sake only* Luis agrees to go on pretending you're a family, but he makes it clear to you that this gives him *full license* to sleep with whoever he wants to—whenever he wants to. "I'm through with you," he sneers and moves his bed into the den.

Baby Billy has it tough from the start. Luis won't touch him and his siblings know something is wrong. People seem to instinctively stay away from him. When he's old enough, you tell Billy his father is *in heaven*, and that he's watching over Billy, but the kid is too damn smart. He knows something is wrong. He knows you're lying. What's worse is that he doesn't say anything. He just stares at you with those black eyes, that tight expression, waiting.

Billy grows up tentative, apologetic, frightened. In grade school he's musically inclined, shy and introverted, and persecuted by classmates for being a bastard as well as being a *"fey, gay, faggot, sissy queer."* You keep thinking that hanging on to the family unit is the thing that will save you all. If you can avoid a divorce, avoid making him any more "different" than he already is, maybe things will come around and he'll get along better with everybody.

He reverts into himself, cries easily, develops an eating disorder, and starts to cut himself. (Tiny slashes, no bigger than paper cuts, lined up vertically on his thigh. Ten this way and then ten that way. Like a herringbone pattern in blood.) When he's a sophomore in high school you finally discover the secret "medical kit" under his bed, an old makeup case filled with scissors and razor blades and pins. You try once more in vain to get ahold of Toru, to track him down anywhere . . . but he's utterly gone.

You eventually get Billy into a treatment program, a place for teen alcoholics and bulimics and all the other mucked-up kids who have taken action with their grief. You can't say you blame any of them. They all have awful stories, alcoholic fathers, absentee mothers, and of course there's your son, who had a perfectly intact family, which is perfectly broken as well. Billy is there for a week when the counselors urge him to tell you his secret . . . that he's gay. This is one too many abominations for Luis, who screams at Billy, *"You're a bastard and now you're a fag too?"*

You ask Luis for a divorce that night. You see now staying with him was the worst mistake you could have made. You loved Toru. Madly. You forced your son to live with a man who never loved him, all in the name of decorum and decency, when really it was the most indecent thing you could have done.

Then Billy disappears from the hospital. He's run away. You hunt high and low for him, contact the police, hire private eyes, light prayer candles, comb the streets, but you know it's no use. No detective, no police officer, no one is going to find him. He's too smart and too hurt. Time passes. Five years. Every day you jump up for the phone, run for the doorbell, hope against all hope he'll come home.

Rosie gets into Columbia and Paulie gets married. They both have kids and Luis does well with his work—but nothing can console your bruised heart as you continue to search for Billy. You hire another private investigator, a very expensive one, and you tell him the whole story. He calls you back almost immediately.

"Found 'em both," he says. *So soon?* He tells you what he knows. Far from being the drugged-out street prostitute you were afraid Billy had become, he's living in Paris and enrolled at the Sorbonne on a full scholarship. *"Paris, France?"*

"He got the full scholarship, on merit—and probably also because he wrote on his application that all his family was dead." He goes by *William* now, and he's the prize student of a distinguished violin professor named Otto Van Parys. Then the investigator tells you that while locating your son, he also located Toru, who is living in a suburb of Paris with his wife and son. You don't understand. "Did Billy . . . did William go there to be with his father?" Your heart is racing . . . fingertips pulsing. "Does he know his father is alive?"

"No, ma'am," the detective says. "It's just a coincidence. Not that I believe in coincidences—but right now neither one of them knows the other exists and they're both living in Paris not five miles from each other."

You hop on the very next plane to Paris and head straight to the dormitories where Billy lives. When you see him, you hardly recognize him. Gone is the frail, apologetic boy you knew, and in front of you stands a tall, resolute young man. He looks completely different. He's definitely William now . . . Billy is gone.

The expression on his face is both of gratitude and fear. He's happy you came—but he won't go back home. "I'll never go to America again," he says, lighting a cigarette defiantly, "and I'll never see that man you married again. Never." He means Luis, of course, and you tell him he doesn't have to do anything he doesn't want to. You tell him everything. Who is father is, how you never meant to give him anything but the best life you could. He goes through seasons of moods. Shocked, unbelieving, and then mad and then confused. You arrange a meeting. Toru is also in shock (as is his French wife, a woman with two previous children) but wants to meet William immediately.

When they do meet, it's like they're carbon copies of each other. The same mannerisms, the same expressions, the same graceful hands. They both love French cuisine and Bach cello suites. They both play chess and rugby, even though Toru gave it up because of his bad knee. They just get along. Instantly, completely. Like Billy and Luis never did. Even when William announces he's *marrying* his violin teacher, Toru doesn't judge him. They spend all their time together, catching up on a lifetime missed.

You go to William and Otto's opulent French estate wedding without complaint. Your time making decisions for William are long over and you see that he can choose for himself better than you ever could. He's gay. *So what?* Who cares who loves who?—as long as they really and truly love them. Your other children even fly over for the wedding, Rosie and Paulie showing an enormous regret that they treated their youngest brother differently than they should have. William makes Paulie his best man.

To see Toru married to another woman is difficult at first, especially since she has despised you ever since your arrival, but *c'est la vie*. You can't really blame her. It's obvious Toru prefers William to his adopted children. (It's so nice to finally see your child preferred over others.)

You end up moving to Paris, and with Toru's help you open a small art gallery–café outside Paris called Chaton. It's nothing particularly fancy, just a little place where you can pour red wine, meet fascinating people, hang lovely pictures on the walls, and play as much Billie Holiday as you like. Billy comes every Thursday to play his violin for the patrons, the old men play chess at their tables, and unlike in America, the little dogs can come and sit right on your lap if they want to. You buy a pug named Otis, who sleeps at your feet all day. Heaven.

You don't die for many many years, and when you do it's on a bright summer day, at your café, as you are sipping an iced Earl Grey tea behind the counter and reading a book on Egyptian archaeology. Fascinating, this big world. Then your hearts stops, right there, as the birds are singing and a young couple in the corner are kissing. It was a beautiful life, and heaven, as it turns out, is the right to come back and do it all over again, starting on page one.

191

From section 176 . . .

You run off with Toru. Your children will hate you, but someday maybe they'll understand. Or maybe they won't and instead will write a tell-all *Mommie Dearest*-type memoir. Small comfort it will be that you did what you had to for your own happiness. Still, you love Toru. What can you do?

You tell your husband you're leaving, explain to the kids that Mommy and Daddy have to live apart now—and of course all your friends and family think you're awful. Society in general does not look kindly on mothers who want to be happy, unless happiness is defined as cooking, baking, shopping, mending, cleaning, supplicating, repressing, denying, and a life spent cleaning vomit. Nothing else.

Mothers with careers are seen as cold. Mothers who travel with friends are negligent. Mothers who suspect they are *more* than just mothers, that they are humans with spirits that seek to be fed . . . they're just selfish or insane. They all break the age-old "mother contract" that says "If you prepare to bring a life into this world—prepare to end your own."

Eight months later you give birth to an eight-pound seven-ounce Asian baby boy. *Thank God.* Black hair, delicious creamy yellow skin. Like an opal in a blue blanket. Toru proposes to you and asks you to come to France with him. He's got a new job there, some real estate his family invested in, and he wants to build a life there with you. You consider it, chew on it, and then say *yes*. You all move to France—you, Rosie, Paulie, your new baby boy, and Toru. Luis is glad to give you custody because he says he can't wait for *the day you come crawling back, overwhelmed by your bad decisions*. You tell him not to wait up.

Paris is gorgeous. Intimidating, sexy, complicated . . . but gorgeous. You move into a little house on the edge of Paris, and the children are so quick to learn French they're translating things for you before you can even order a sandwich. Baby Billy is fluent by the time he's four. He goes on to study the violin, *a prodigy* you're told, and he receives a full scholarship to the Sorbonne.

Toru continues to work at his family's real estate company, and over time, because of the number of rich Asian people who want to own land in France, you become enormously wealthy. You all move into a grand chateau on the rue Marquis, in the old district where the big houses loom up against the French sun.

You have your own dressmaker, your own milliner, a stylist, a hairdresser, and a nail technician (who you fire after it's discovered she steals Manolo Blahniks from your shoe closet). The best part is you open your own fine French art gallery, which you name Le Mur Blanc, the White Wall. The perfect place to start a life or any other large work of art. A nice, clean blank wall.

Billy, who now goes by William, has his first solo concert at the age of fourteen. He begins to tour with his violin teacher, a slender man named Otto Van Parys who's twice his age. When, six years later, they announce they're getting *married*, when William is only twenty, it's more than a shock. Discussions are had, concessions are made, and they get married in a baroque church not far from the Arc de Triomphe. You're very proud of Toru, who ignores his traditional Japanese family's protests and gives his son away in the ceremony.

You don't die for many many years, and when you do it will be in the main gallery of Le Mur Blanc, as you are gazing into a deep scarlet slash across a beautiful canvas. Your heart stops right then. It was a beautiful life, and heaven, as it turns out, is the right to come back and do it all over again, starting on page one.

192

From section 119 . . .

It doesn't take long for them to come. The sirens become unbearably loud and then there are cops climbing all over you. They pin you, shove you, clamp handcuffs on you, push you around. At one point you're facedown on the bloody wet cement, at another you are spread-eagle against the cop car; they take your body and toss it around at random. Your arms and legs are no longer your own.

Jail. Courtroom. Sentence. Ten years for manslaughter. (The jury felt a little bad he raped you, still, women aren't supposed to shoot their rapists.) The women's maximum-security detention center is like a string of linked gymnasiums, no windows. High ceilings and nothing to look at but wall after wall of beige paint. You read books, you write letters, you try and stay away from the gangs and the dealers and the women who fight each other for money.

Prison is all about killing time. Slaughtering it with anything you can think of. Watching TV, playing cards, entering the monotony of prepared routine. People hate clocks. Can't stand to think about the time wasting, the minutes draining, *even now, even now, even now*. It's always there . . . the knowledge that you're wasting your time, your chances, your life.

Eventually, out of sheer boredom, and because the warden asks *if you want to*, you teach a small art class. Nothing much at first, just stupid popsicle stick crafts, but then you contact your old art school. You write them a long letter saying you wish you'd done things differently, but sometimes shit ends up on a stick and there's not much you can do. You ask them could they send art supplies? There's only so much you can do with a cardboard toilet paper tube and glue.

It turns out that the school thinks it's wonderful and politically correct to have a former student in prison, they think it's cool. They send paint and brushes and canvas and art history books. (But they can't send sharp objects. Prisoners cannot have anything that could be turned into a weapon.) They encourage you to *think free even if you can't be free*, which is horse shit, but who cares, they sent finger paint.

About a year later, the school wants to have a show that features the work from your class. A show called "Insider Art." The truth is the women's canvases aren't very good; they're all twiggy and rough and mostly primary colors (you couldn't get any of them to blend or feather, and one of the works is just a black canvas with white blocky letters that reads: I ALREADY GOT ONE ASSHOLE IN MY PANTS WHY DO I WANT TWO?), but it really doesn't matter—the school wants them.

The show goes well and then there's another. The local paper runs a story, which gets picked up by the AP wires. Then *Entertainment Tonight* comes to interview you (you're in hair and makeup for two hours before they think you look like a "sad but reformed, pretty but not too-pretty" artist in prison), and then Elton John calls the prison saying he wants to buy a painting.

Then all hell breaks loose. The shitty canvases created in your class sell to dealers and collectors and celebrities all over the world. There's apparently a high demand for paintings made by violent women—the more violent, the better. The most expensive pieces are made by one woman who can't even come to class. A beautiful husband-killer, named H. Thornswood, who's in confinement because of her aggression toward the guards. She makes these creepy little clay people (which someone says are haunted) that sell for a cool thirty thousand each.

Seven years later you get out on good behavior. CNN sends a camera crew in to cover you walking to a waiting limousine. You're now America's strangest and most unusual art dealer. You broker deals between prisoners and galleries. You sponsor retrospectives of inmate art, and you sell paintings for embarrassing amounts of money. You never get married, never have kids—freedom feels too good. Instead you build a community of women in recovery and you complete a body of your own work.

You die from a stroke when you're ninety-three. Your funeral is on CNN. At the memorial service your friends read from your journal (which then sells on eBay for two hundred thousand dollars). It seems everybody wants to know what goes on inside the mind of a bad woman. A woman who didn't have kids or a husband or a career—who picked up a gun and shot her rapist. A woman who went from a wet cinder-block car wash and ended up hanging in a gallery—like a rare sculpture made from flesh and bone and blood.

In heaven you are given a luminous opal tablet with the numbers. Your numbers. The number of people you helped in your lifetime, the people who you ignored the times your actually took time to guard something small . . . all in all you get a very low grade for your time on earth. You're definitely guaranteed a pretty shitty life the next time around. Probably in Afghanistan or Ohio.

193

From section 119 . . .

Run. *Out of breath*. Feet slapping down hard on the pavement like you're trying to pile-drive yourself into the ground. Your heart hammers in your chest—your breath tastes sour. You don't know how long you run, or how far, but by the time it occurs to you to slow down, your heart is shooting off like a machine gun and you think you might have a heart attack. You're miles away when you stop—and the pain comes flooding over you—your knees and legs, your chest and throat—everything is raw and cold.

At home you get busy. You've got to think clearly and act quick. You throw a couple of photographs of your family and some clothes into a suitcase, empty out the stash of cash your parents keep in a fake can of carburetor cleaner in the garage. Six hundred dollars. That's it—all the time you have to spare is gone. You've got to go—go *anywhere but here*. Where can you go to blend in? Where is it busy and frenetic and people are often overlooked or ignored? New York City. Perfect. Nobody cares about anybody there. Maybe you can even go to Europe. Hop on one of those freighters that crosses the Atlantic and start your life over in Paris. You buy a bus ticket to New York and sit in cramped, agonized panic for three days until you arrive.

Things get brighter as the city rushes around you. You've only just arrived and you're walking out of the station, just reaching the sunshine bursting down on the street, when somebody comes up behind you (somebody big like a refrigerator, and with hands strong as steel cables) and pushes you inside the propped-open door of a utility closet. *They/she/he/it* mugs you. (You are never sure *what* it was. It might have been a gorilla.) They take everything you have. Everything. Checks, wallet, money, suitcase, *shoes*. Everything. So there you are, not twenty minutes in the city, one minute everything ahead of you and the next you're picked clean as a newborn babe. A shoeless, cashless weakling freak. Fabulous.

You can't go to the police—they're the ones you're trying to avoid in the first place. You can't call home and you don't know anyone in New York. You walk down the street a ways. People look down, see you have no shoes, and avoid eye contact with you. They just walk faster. You get to a phone booth and look up the number of a shelter. The St. Francis Sheltering Arms. You walk thirty-two blocks to get there—but by the time you arrive at the weathered doors of the sad building, the woman standing on the steps handing out flyers says it's full up. *What now?*

You sit down on the curb to think. The sun is setting. You're hungry and cold. People pass you without so much as a glance. *You don't exist if you don't have shoes.* It's the perfect way to disappear. You got what you wanted—nobody gives a damn about you. It doesn't quite feel the way you'd planned on.

Then a little old lady, a little hermit crab of a woman, comes up to you. She's looking right at you with her filmy cataracts eyes. She's got a filthy trench coat on and plastic bags coming out of her pocket. There's a mangy dachshund tied to a rope that waddles behind her. "You in trouble? You need a place, little miss?" Normally, you wouldn't even respond to this kind of person. You'd assume she was crazy or deranged. Now *you* are this kind of person. "Sure," you say, and follow her.

She says her name is Minerva and her dog's name is Mr. Goldilocks. You follow them for thirteen blocks or so (you lose count, you're so drop-dead tired) and then they go down a steep embankment by the train tracks and over a slab of dirt and concrete populated by scrub bushes and crushed beer cans. It's an eerie place, the sort of place you imagine someone would dump a body. "In here." Minerva points to a dirty white shed door by the edge of the tracks. You open the door and see a large hole in the floor, like a manhole but bigger and with a torn rebar ladder jutting out of it. There's a pink Easter basket sitting next to it. "Down there," she says. *Down there?* Is she crazy? Isn't that the sewer or some metropolis for rats? She's insisting . . . and you have nowhere else to go. You're so tired at this point dying sounds refreshing, so reluctantly you step down the metal ladder that goes *down down down* into a dark tunnel underground.

She lowers Mr. Goldilocks down in the bright pink Easter basket and then climbs down herself. You can hear trains thundering past in an adjacent tunnel.

"Watch out for the rats," Minerva warns you. "They's big as dogs down here." *Like you weren't watching out for them already.* It's dark. Minerva fishes around in her deep pocket and produces a flashlight, which she shines ahead of you. The two of you slowly walk forward. *You must be crazy for doing this.* Who goes down into a dark tunnel in New York City with a complete stranger?

You follow Minerva down a twisting maze, the hall going down deeper and getting bigger and wider as you go until it looks like a cathedral. There is garbage strewn everywhere, paper bags and dead rats and old diapers. The smell is awful. You must be a mile underground now. There are shopping carts scattered around like silver fish lost in a black sea, and Minerva drops Mr. Goldilocks in one and begins to push it forward, clattering over the debris. She starts to sing "Happy Birthday."

Up ahead you see shacks, shanties made of particleboard and sheets of tin and cardboard boxes. Dozens of them. It looks like a refugee internment camp. *Something scampers over your foot.* There's a bonfire going in an oil drum and several old men standing around smoking cigarettes. "Don't mind them," Minerva tells you. "Crackheads has peckers like dried-up beef jerky."

You follow her through the underground shantytown to her "home," which is half a trailer connected to a larger room made of mismatched wood planks. She snaps on a light. "Got power down here," she says. "Running water too. All comes from the city but nobody pays. Nobody knows we here."

Sure enough Minerva has a working sink and a running refrigerator filled with Chinese take-out boxes. "Mr. Goldilocks likes egg drop soup the best, don't ya!" But Mr. Goldilocks is fast asleep in a little dog bed positioned right in front of a glowing space heater. Minerva hands you a pair of men's work boots. They're at least two sizes too big, but you cram newspaper up at the toes and they fit all right.

Once Minerva gets all her lamps turned on and reheats some Chinese food, you almost feel cozy. It's almost possible to forget you are miles beneath the street in some kind of apocalyptic underground third world country. *Almost.* At least you are safe and dry and warm. Without Minerva and Mr. Goldilocks . . . you wouldn't even have that. You sleep on an army cot that night, with a thick wool blanket covering you and Mr. Goldilocks snoring at your feet.

In the morning you get up and Minerva leads you back to the world. You still have no money—you're not sure what to do, and so you go with her to work, which is cleaning toilets at a Chinese take-out joint. They don't pay her money—they just give her egg rolls and old pot stickers when she's done. You get the same.

You go back to the tunnel that night. You'll just stick with her until you figure out what to do next. You explore a little and realize Minerva's house is only on the edge of the "city." It turns out over three hundred people are living underground—all with electricity and running water. There used to be more people, but they had a really bad fire and it scared a lot of them away. "Lotsa dead folks," one of the old men tells you. "We had to bury them deeper in the tunnel. No way we could get them out." Now he tells you the main trouble is making sure no officials from "up top" find them. There was some city workers that came close last year while working on the sewer.

You stay there for a week and then for another week. It's dark, it's hard to get to—but it's not that bad of a place to live. No mortgage, no property tax, no rent, no utility bills. You check the papers at the newsstands and you never see anything about your case, but you know they're looking for you. This makes the tunnel all the more appealing—no one in their right mind would go down there. No one would look for you there, because now no one knows it even exists.

Once you've been down there for over a year, you have that easily recognizable homeless sheen to you. Baggy mismatched clothes, stained shoes, matted hair. No matter how you scrub or clean, people can smell it on you. You've become completely invisible. It's actually quite comforting, knowing you can walk through the streets, and as long as you don't try to go into any restaurants or stores, no one is going to bother you.

You keep meaning to find a job, but being up top makes you more and more nervous. You think people might recognize you. They already look at you funny. You begin to only feel safe in the warm dark belly of the tunnel. Where you once dreaded going down, now you begin to dread going up. Then Minerva dies. In her sleep she shouts, "I said backgammon, fool!" and then seizes up. According to "tunnel rules" you automatically inherit her home and Mr. Goldilocks.

Time just sort of sleeps forward. You live down in the tunnel for twelve inadvertent years—every day assuming that tomorrow you'll probably move out. You paint a little, mostly on scraps of wood with paint stolen out of Dumpsters at hardware stores. You die in your sleep when the shanty next door goes up in flames. (Somebody's hot plate caught the mattress on fire.) You sleep through the whole thing.

They have a memorial service for you in the tunnel. They say a prayer and scatter your ashes on the train tracks right as a five o'clock commuter comes by. (They think they're your ashes; they're the ashes found in and around the frame of your bed.) The thundering wheels pick you up and roll you forward—bringing you all across the city.

When you go to heaven Minerva and Mr. Goldilocks are there, eating Chinese food by a fountain. "Not what I thought at all." She shakes her head. "No sex up here. I says to the guy I says, *What's the point of that? You got beef jerky peckers too?*"

194

From section 120 . . .

You testify in court while wearing a dark suit. No makeup, no nail polish. You have been briefed; you only answer the questions that are asked, you give neat clipped replies. You are supposed to cry, you have been *coached* to cry, and yet at the preappointed time you can't cry. The courtroom is hot. Your face burns, your temples pound. Sweat gathers under your armpits, in your clavicle. The room bends. *Why is it this hot?* The floor gives way as though the entire room were emptying down into an hourglass. Your forehead hits the wooden railing in front of you.

You smell roses. You keel over with a massive heart attack and die right there on the witness stand. The doctors will say your blood pressure combined with the amount of coffee and cigarettes you've recently consumed was dangerous. Add in the stress of the courtroom and it became deadly. These things are hard to predict.

You go to heaven through a silver stream of light and you enter a small sunny courtroom filled with case files. Tall walls lined with leather editions wait for you, and a round-the-clock butler routinely brings you coffee and cream in small porcelain teacups. You spend the rest of eternity looking up the reasons why some children are born with cancer, why humans hurt each other, where the Mayans went. It is all before you, in bound edition after bound edition. The answers.

195

From section 120 . . .

You're done. No trials, no testimonies, no front-page news or eternal Internet access to your face. You take the dark feelings of these events and you bury them. All the memories, the images, packed away in a little black box way down low inside you. Now you feel like the bottom of a lake bed—low and smooth and quiet. Covered with leaves and murk, water pressing heavy.

You tell everyone who asks that you're doing *much better*—because you *are* doing much better—and no one blames you for not testifying, *haven't you been through enough?* But that little black box where all the memories are stashed starts to rattle, mostly at night when you try to sleep.

A year later it's the anniversary *of the thing we do not mention* and you've gained fifty pounds. Nobody mentions it. *Hasn't she been through enough?* Let her eat if she wants to. Not polite to mention it. And the hunger—it's always there. Insatiable.

You have bad dreams. Dreams of killing people. Hunting them with rifles and saw blades. Hacking men to pieces, shooting every member of your family. *Horrible dreams!* It gets so you don't want to sleep—you can't bear to slaughter any more of your friends. Your counselor thinks you need a change; she encourages your parents to give you a leg up on a new endeavor—but what should you do? Something big. Something life-changing.

You go to work for a domestic violence center. You work with women from other countries who don't speak English and coordinate with translators and sometimes doctors to get them proper medical and psychological treatment. *Talk talk talk.* As long as we're talking we're not dying. *We're not giving up.* You get them to talk by talking yourself. You peel back the layers like opal onion peels, sweet, acrid piece by piece of you.

You become good friends with one doctor in particular, Dr. David Wilkins, a man from Chad who has a deep African accent and a broad smile. David is leaving soon; he's a member of Doctors Without Borders, where doctors donate their time and travel all over the world offering their services to the needy. David is donating twelve months of service in N'Djamena, which is the capital of Chad and the most undeveloped city in Africa. It's host to three climate zones, more than a hundred languages, and a rampant cholera epidemic. When David asks you to come with him, you pause, look deep into his warm eyes, and say *yes*.

The hospital is in the Paris Congo. It's a low stucco building with bars over the windows and garbage in the stairwell. Electricity is intermittent. The river of patients you treat have cholera, have malaria, have dysentery, have HIV, have chicken pox. They come like a damp river, with warm sweat and tough feet. You work by David's side; he stays strong when you are not, holds you at night when the fever or the exhaustion takes you.

Love thrives in hostile climates. You and David are married in October, in a civil ceremony at the local courthouse. After the ceremony little girls carrying baskets of flowers follow you down the street singing. You've never been so happy in your entire life. Three months after that you're walking past a popular café holding David's hand, when there's an explosion, sharp flying glass, like a tidal wave of transparent knives coming at you full force. You are both killed by the exploding pipe bomb.

Your last thought is this: How good the street smells. Like roasting coffee and oranges. How sweet the weight of your husband's hand.

In heaven you are given a luminous opal tablet with the numbers. Your numbers. The number of people you helped in your lifetime, the people who lived because of you, the children who were safe, the diseases that lost ground . . . all in all you get a very high grade for your time on earth. You're definitely guaranteed a wonderful life the next time around. Probably in Hawaii. There was only one thing you scored low on. You should have shot your rapist.

196

From section 48 . . .

You go to work at a shoe shop called Giovinetto, a small unmarked store in a back alley. There's no sign, just three stone steps down into a dark room lit by green bankers lamps. The front room is lined floor to ceiling with creaking wooden cubbyholes that hold all the repaired shoes. There's a yellow toe tag on each pair, some of which look very old, as if they might have been repaired a decade ago. The back room has two cluttered workbenches and a small kitchenette with a hot plate and a sink basin. There's a yellow cat that sleeps on top of the television.

You learn quickly that the owner, a little old man with long, tapered fingers named Signore Innocenti, takes shoes seriously. *Very seriously.* He adjusts his glasses and grumbles as he works. He specializes in repairing old shoes— *really, really* old shoes, like the pair of English cream silk wedding slippers from 1815. People bring him shoes from all over Europe, heirlooms or museum pieces—Signore Innocenti has a reputation for being one of the best vintage cobblers in the world.

His collection of tools is impressive. They hang around the room on perfectly precise pegs. You don't know what they're all used for—some look more like torture devices than tools. He shows you the awl, a needle thing used for stitching, which is so fine that if he pricks your hand with it (as he demonstrates), the wound neither hurts nor bleeds. He shows you the tools, but he wouldn't consider letting you touch *the shoes*. He makes that clear from the start. "These," he says with a thick accent, "these are mine. *Like children, si?* You don't touch, you don't bump into. You treat like small baby who is very sick. You be quiet, you walk soft, and you don't wake them up."

Your job is to stay behind the counter. You ring out customers and take orders over the phone. You're often sent to go *pick up* shoes around the city, as though it were an emergency and you were driving a shoe ambulance, running to rescue broken heels and torn seams. Signore Innocenti *hates* torn seams. He goes over them again and again with a magnifying glass before he starts to sew. "Always sixty-four stitches to the inch," Innocenti says. "Nobody put that many stitches in an inch today." You try to add comments here and there—whatever little you know about shoes, but anything you say is met with contempt. *"Manolo Blahniks are good, right?"* you ask, to which he nearly coughs up a blood clot. "I hate the Manolo!" he says. "He's a butcher putting out the shoes I hate! Don't wear the Manolo! Never the Manolo!" *Okay, okay. Yeesh.*

After that you pretty much don't say anything to him. You stick to your work and listen to Innocenti talk and talk and talk. He could talk the ear off a dead man. He fixes all different kinds of shoes. Bats, boots, clogs, ballet slippers, derbys, espadrilles, monks, oxfords, chopines. You watch him work on a pair of Italian silver Ferragamos from 1938—how he threads the looped needle and examines the worn heels—to think of the people who have stood in those shoes. The dances, the moonlit walks, the running and stopping. They are lives sewn together with thread and leather and glue. He is the one who carefully patches each life back together again.

You're getting a pretty good education in shoes just by watching and listening—you've watched him repair countless shoes and now you think you could probably make a shoe yourself. So you do. You go back to the shop late one night, unlock the door carefully so you don't ring the brass bell on the door. You go to the back room and turn on the lights and go to work. Your first try isn't very good. Your first shoe is a mangled man's loafer—a sloppy seamed chunk. At daybreak you clean up the workshop and sneak back out to catch a couple hours of sleep before you come into work again.

Your next attempt goes a little better—but not much. Your fingers can't seem to make the stitches right, and you do it over and over and over and over again before you can stitch a diamond loop without drawing blood. Your form is getting better too. You're attracted to the French Revolution heel—that is, *no heel at all*. Slippers. Everyone on the same level. Month after month you tinker and toy, blister and peel, cut and paste until you have five pairs of heelless, heavily embroidered Chinese slipper–influenced shoes. You call your first collection "Level."

After much worrying and nervousness, you show your efforts to Signore Innocenti. You line your shoes up on his worktable and wait for him to arrive. When he sees the shoes (after shuffling to the cash register, and grumbling about the price of cork) he stops dead in his tracks. He circles the table and then picks one of the shoes up. He studies it, turns it over and over in his hand. He runs his finger along the stitching, thumps the heel with his thumb. He clears his throat and goes to the hot plate, where he pours himself a cup of coffee. "Where they come from?" he says, peering over his glasses. "From me. I did them—I mean, I made them." He takes a sip of his coffee and then another. "Put them in the window," he says. "They're ugly, like frogs I see smashed on the highway, but maybe somebody with no taste will come in."

That's about as high a compliment as you're going to get. You hurry with them to the window, smiling all the way. Work is a joy that day, no customer too rude, no task too mundane. You love seeing your colorful shoes in the window, like puppies waiting for someone to love them.

But nobody seems to love them. You wait and wait and wait, but nobody buys the shoes. People are *nice enough* about them, you get compliments and words of encouragement, but you pretty much put the idea of making shoes out of your head until Kit comes in. Kit is a small, compact, impeccably dressed gay man. He talks with elaborate words and is always leaning forward, as if he might just be on the verge of taking flight. He comes in one day at the recommendation of his hotel concierge. One of his Berluti shoes has lost a sole and he rushes to Signore Innocenti's because "One must dine with the ambassador tonight, and one must make a bon vivant entrance." He always refers to himself in the third person.

As he drums his manicured nails on the countertop, waiting for you to fill out his claim slip, he gasps. "What are those?" he asks and in one bound is across the room holding one of your shoes in his hand. "Those are a local designer's," you say.

"Merde! Recherché and soigné!" he says. "They're fabulous!"

You step from around the counter. "They're actually my designs," you say, "and there's a lot more where that came from."

"You *bitch*," he says. "You beautiful, dishy *bitch*!" It turns out that Kit is a buyer for Barneys. Not just a buyer, the *head* buyer. He's in love with your shoes and your sketches and with you and with the very ground you walk on. "*They're so Barbarella meets Audrey Hepburn!*" he squeals. You have no idea what he's talking about, but within three days he's given you a contract to design shoes for Barneys. You don't have to make them—just *design* them. Barneys will have them made in Taiwan.

You leave Italy and move to New York, to a gorgeous airy brownstone at 96 Perry Street in the Village. You have an office on Madison Avenue and two solicitous assistants who cater to your every whim. Within a year your shoes are being sold at Barneys, and every Bergdorf Blond in the city is wearing them. You travel to San Francisco and Tokyo and Dubai on shopping sprees and "idea junkets" to think up your next creations.

You meet a man named Wesley, *a George Clooney look-alike*, who stops you in Delmonico's because you have a smear of cream cheese on your sleeve. When you look at him, you are thunderstruck frozen-in-your-place caught. He's a real estate developer, high-end buildings in the financial district, and he plays the banjo. He's this weird hybrid mix of sexy-salty-friendly-strange-high-powered-cute. The two of you are living together by the end of the year.

Your life in New York becomes a menagerie of dinners, parties, benefits, fashion shows, and trips to the doggie park. You work hard, you play hard, you love hard. You and Wes make a beautiful home at 96 Perry Street, and when you're not burrowed in at home, he takes you on trips with him all around the world. You're eating at a little delicatessen one evening, a place right across from his office downtown. You're smiling at him, reaching across the table to wipe a smear of cream cheese off his chin, and you're laughing, as you usually are when you're together, and he's saying, "*Leave it! Leave it!*" because he's always thought smears of cream cheese were good luck since he met you—when you look up and there's a flash of white light and an explosion so loud it goes to silence. Bits of glass are flying, you are flying, Wes is flying. It's all swirled up around and out—the white napkins like doves escaping out the window.

A man has blown himself to pieces outside the window. TERRORIST BOMBER IN MANHATTAN! the papers will say, but that's not the way it was at all. You remember that last moment perfectly, as if it were all poured into a snow globe you could hold in your hand. Nat King Cole on the radio, the big-bellied owner handing a pack of American Spirits to a young man across the counter, the fry cooks laughing at the grill. Two older women, maybe sisters, bowed over their bowls of soup, blowing to cool their spoons, an orange cat asleep on the windowsill. Wesley's face. His beautiful laughing face. There was nothing terrorist about it. You remember it perfectly. You were wearing your pink ballet slippers, the ones with the tassels. Now you're the one walking.

197

From section 123 . . .

You have the baby. You give birth to a six-pound boy . . . with Down syndrome. One in eight hundred babies is born with this genetic abnormality; it's caused by a single chromosome. They're not exactly sure how it happens—something random before conception. It's nature's glitch—not yours—that's what the doctors say, but that doesn't stop people from stopping you on the street and asking, *"What's wrong with him? How's that happen? Did you drink? Did your husband pee in you?"*

There's a theory that Down syndrome kids are savants—that they have an intelligence the rest of us can't understand. They move in a different space, tilt their heads and explode with laughter at the strangest things. They don't recognize religion or money. They don't understand race. It is as if they have been elevated from our ugly society and put on a white cliff out of reach. It is as if they have been touched by heaven.

Jóhann has completely turned around on his theories about genes. Gone are his ideas about superior bloodlines and the mathematical odds of perfection. He's gotten into several arguments with his supervisors at the lab—it seems he's changed his mind about almost everything he once believed. Now he protests against the government of Iceland, which passed the law for a national health database. He quits his work at the testing center and throws himself into researching Down syndrome.

He learns children with Down syndrome often have underdeveloped lungs and a very hard time breathing later in life. Getting their lungs to develop while they're young is essential, so when Ari's about seven, you begin a physical training routine for him that includes running along the ocean while wearing a small plastic mask that makes it harder for him to breathe, which in turn makes him breathe more deeply, which ultimately makes his little pink lungs expand and grow. It seems odd—to smother a child in order to get him to breathe, but these are the complexities of life. It is on one of these runs that Ari's seals come.

It happens like this. Ari is trotting along the rocky trail with his father one morning, huffing and puffing along like usual, when he stops in his tracks and just stares at the water. At first your husband thinks there is some problem with Ari's mask, and so takes it off him to inspect it—but as he does Ari points a tiny finger at the water and shouts, "Papa, they're here!" Jóhann looks up and is startled to see at least a dozen seals, not ten feet from the shore (much closer than they usually come), all with their sleek black heads out of the water, and their round unblinking eyes trained on Ari. "Papa!" Ari squeals and tries to run headlong into the water.

It was exciting enough at first, but then it starts happening every day. Every day the seals come right to the shore and swim alongside Ari as he runs. Every day he has to be nearly tackled so he won't run in after them. Word gets out about *Ari's seals* and people start showing up to see. Nobody has ever seen anything like it. Ari tells you fantabulous stories about the seals at night, how they are his family, and it really is rude not to go in the frigid arctic water after them.

You compromise and let him feed the seals sardines, which he hurls at them from the shore. Not only are you amazed by Ari's complete lack of fear and total familiarity with them, you swear the seals are *careful* around him. Swimming more slowly at the waterline and waddling up in the sand so he doesn't have to get his feet wet.

When Ari is fifteen he enters the Reykjavik Special Olympics as a short distance swimmer and takes fourteenth place (in the Special Olympics this is superstar status). He meets a girl named Ása, who also has Down syndrome. She becomes his girlfriend. *His true love.* He writes her poetry, calls her up and bellows rousing renditions of "You Are My Sunshine" into the phone. She paints him pictures on empty cereal boxes, which he sets up in a mini-fortress on the floor around his bed. They have a standing date every Saturday, and Jóhann jokes you should be so lucky to have such a love life.

When Ása's parents want to put her in a group home, where it will be much harder for your son to see her, you turn Jóhann's study into a flowery pink bedroom for her. (She is wonderful with color—loves pinks and lavenders and paints flowers all over the walls of her room.) Ari is so happy he composes an entire opera, a melody menagerie of "You Are My Sunshine," "L-O-V-E" by Nat King Cole, "Itsy Bitsy Spider," and other songs, which he performs for the family.

The four of you live together in a small house, and you start an arts program for handicapped children. Kids come from all over Iceland, Denmark, and Germany to study with you. The thing about working with "the handicapped" is that you realize you're the only one missing out on anything. These people don't care if you think they're stupid or slow or unable to compete. They're not even in the race. They left the race long ago—and the race really isn't any fun if the person you're trying to outrun has stopped miles back to admire an oversized monarch flexing its wings on a blade of grass. That race has already been won—and not by you.

Jóhann publishes several important books on genes, ethics, and spirituality. He wins awards and goes on book tours. If you had been told that living in Iceland with two Down syndrome children and running a school for the handicapped would bring you silly amounts of happiness, you would have thought the idea insane.

But it isn't insane, and it occurs to you that you found your happiness bit by bit, like you would find a honeycomb. First, find a buzzing little bee out in the wild and follow it until you lose sight of him. Wait right there for the next bee and then follow him, and then the next bee and the next bee and so on. They will, one by one, small thing by small thing, lead you to where you want to be. To the nectar. To the source.

You die in your sleep. It's a dream that gets really quiet and then opens up into deep blue water. Hellnar legend is right. We turn to seals when we die and heaven is not in the sky . . . it's deep in the ocean. Ari's seals show you the way down there. God and everybody lives in a crystal city at the bottom of the sea, in a fathom too dark and deep for any man to ever reach.

The very next day you swim back to the Hellnar coastline, and wait with the others to see Ari, who is a young man now but still runs every day along the coastline by himself. "Hi, Mom!" he shouts at you as you bob up and down in the water. He's beautiful.

198

From section 131 . . .

You buy a chunk of land in Brazil, where the climate is perfect to grow even the most unusual orchids: *Phalaenopsis hybrids, dendrobiums, miniatures*, they all thrive in the moist, breezy climate. Especially in the large vaulted solarium you build, which has automatically timed sprinklers and imported frosted windows, which protect the fragile sun-adverse petals.

The children run wild through the jungles that tangle around your property. They build forts and dig trenches—they collect insects and butterflies and keep them in open-air cages to watch them mate. The nearest school is over two hours away, so after they've had full days of sun and sweat you give them baths, and right as the sun is going down you pour yourself a big glass of wine and tutor them at the kitchen table. *Reading, writing, basic math*. When they get a little older you're going to have to hire a teacher to come. You're not taking on calculus.

You meet a man named Javier, a tall tan man with a bright smile and a way with working the earth. You originally hired him to be your groundskeeper and maintenance man, but after he showed you how to use a divining rod to find water in the forest and then saved you from a horrifically elegant-looking coral snake (he chopped off its head with a hatchet), you took him straight to your bed.

He loves orchids and he's kind to the children. There's a bit of a language barrier—but you've learned that can really work to a couple's advantage. You rarely fight because he rarely understands you and you never understand him. All you know is he has a great appetite, he protects you from snakes, and he's got a real king viper in his pants.

He also helps you in the nursery with the orchids. Every orchid you unwrap opens up a world of questions. Where is the orchid from? Is it found only in pristine rain forests or has it adapted to grow in a disturbed environment? How does the plant seat itself? Does it grow in the tops of trees or does it cling for its life against a sheer rock face? Are those particular forests protected . . . or do they no longer exist? Are there still native people there, practicing their traditions?

You love growing orchids, the science, the philosophy, the religion of it—but it isn't easy. There's blight. A black fungus that takes hold of one orchid, spotting its thick green leaves with black slimy sores, and then it takes to the next orchid and the next—and you lose over half your darlings in one horrible six-month stretch. There's constant disputes over property lines with the cattle rancher next door, trouble with the local hunters trespassing and poaching birds, and even a government raid on the property of your other neighbor, who was apparently growing coca leaves on his back forty and shipping them into Rio de Janeiro, where they were processed into high-grade cocaine. So much for living in the tranquil forest.

Then there's a hurricane, a monstrous storm with gale force winds and diamond-sharp hail, clicking down on the glass ceiling of your nursery. It's the sound of the tip-tapping wolf at the door, and you watch from cracked shutters in the house as the entire vaulted ceiling crashes down, letting the wind whip through your nursery, ripping your orchids in half, beheading them every one, flinging them through the rain like an oversized child having a tantrum.

You and Javier and the kids spend the next month carefully searching through all the debris for your flung orchids. Small clawed clusters of roots without stems or flowers and sometimes not even leaves. It's a grueling, heartbreaking task, but it becomes progressively easier over time, as many of the orchids (which are actually quite hearty in adverse conditions) are replanted and root and then eventually begin to rebloom. These actually become your favorite ones—the ones who survived a great hardship and then went on to flower anyway. You wonder if this is the way God feels with his creatures who manage to flower despite all possible odds. Like you.

The children grow up and move away. They both go back to America, where they have schools and cities and malls. You don't need those things. You haven't bought a new pair of shoes in a year. You wear your boots, jeans, and a tank top most days. For jewelry you'll stick the errant bloom behind your ear. For perfume you only have to rub up against the fragrant jasmine blooming over the back trellis, and for culture, you only have to spend a day in the greenhouse with Javier—and you're attending your own private opera, complete with color, drama, intrigue, and love. It is a beautiful, blissful life.

The cattle ranchers hire a man to kill you. They've long wanted your land for its fresh water access, and they must have gotten tired of negotiating. The man who comes to kill you doesn't care one way or another. To him you are a *stupid white gringa* with no business in Brazil. He breaks through the glass door of your greenhouse late one night when Javier is in town and you're alone trimming roots. The man slits your belly like a fish, while the orchids bend in the wind coming through the door.

In heaven you meet God. He thanks you for being a mother to the orchids, orchids in general being one of his favorite things. God isn't like you thought he'd be. He seems like a nice old man who's gotten behind on his paperwork. A man who is probably rethinking the whole "free will" thing. A man who has watched all the hallelujahs fade away and be replaced with city lights. A man with too many orchids and not enough mothers. A baffled king.

199

From section 131 . . .

You buy three and a half acres of woodsy, sea-blown land along the high bluffs above Long Island Sound, near the hamlet of Baiting Hollow. Perfect hummingbird habitat. You name your sanctuary the Baiting Hollow Hummingbird Sanctuary (BHHS). The land is wild, covered with wild cherry, oaks, pitch pines, beech, shade bush, and red maples. There are lots of dead branches for perching. (Hummers love to perch; they spend far more time waiting than eating. You know the feeling.)

You cultivate the craggy edges of the bluff with flower gardens, good nectar sources like hibiscus, mandevilla, and bougainvillea. The hummingbirds particularly like the six Million Bells and trumpet flower. Birders come from as far away as Japan to pay your (fairly steep) entrance fee and take photographs of these amazing birds as they zip from one bloom to the next. As they hover inches from your nose and then vanish, as they defy all laws of gravity and motion with their impossibly well-designed bodies.

The kids grow wild like the landscape and take to the sea like fish. To see them thundering down the shore, waving sticks, running headlong into the water brings your heart to a boil. They become tender landlords themselves, careful collectors of broken wings and torn nests. Junior veterinarians, nursing baby owls and bluebirds back to life—starting their own honey company with a collection of hijacked bees.

Time passes. Baiting Hollow is a paradise—a recognized environmental leader almost solely responsible for getting the hook-billed hermit hummingbird off the endangered list. Both the children graduate, go to college, and both become ornithologists. (Michael to Venezuela to investigate warbling-finch relationships, Molly to New Zealand to study the nearly extinct kokako bird.)

You meet, date, and fall in love with a local man named Henry. A towering watercolor artist who has gentle hands and cries at movies. He's an excellent chef—the things he can do with lobster are nothing short of astounding—and he cooks for you almost every night for the rest of your life.

You live a well-thought-out life until you're eighty-one. Then you die suddenly in a car crash on the main road by your house. You're on a rare trip out of the house when a drunk driver rear-ends you going eighty-two miles and hour. A local boy who had just lost his job on a fishing boat and who also had a blood alcohol level that could've killed a horse. Your last thought while you're spinning and spinning is not of Henry or the children or even your own life. You think of the hummingbirds. This spinning, their humming. Perpetual motion. *This must be what it feels like.* Then the picture goes black.

200

From section 137 . . .

You stay. It's a beautiful word, "stay." The Walker can wait. Well—no, it can't. They give your residency to a Brazilian filmmaker, a woman who sews together found footage, reels she finds in the trash cans of theaters and film schools, at garage sales and industrial business foreclosures. She splices them together and makes visual collages, moving storylines that make new meanings.

In Japan your life seems like a found-footage film, a disconnected series of events stitched together in a chaotic but beautiful way. You live with Toru in his polished cement studio for many years making art and exploring the details of Japan, which are too numerous to count. You become inspired by the vending machines of Japan, which dispense everything from aspirins and batteries to fried noodles and "used schoolgirl underwear." You begin to take photographs of these weird machines—their strange messages of economy and desire—and you blow them up wall-size.

Over time you make lots of friends and get to know all the shopkeepers near your apartment, the udon noodle guy, the smoothie man, the woman who somehow grows enormous lotus flowers in small aluminum buckets, but it's frustrating, you can only have second-grade conversations with them. All you can say in broken Japanese is: *"Hi. You. Mr. Tanaka! I need of the noodles which is big. Yes. Yes. I so sad when they gone. Okay. Thank you very much on the delicious fruit always. Okay. Bye. Bye."* They must think you're the village idiot.

Toru's mother dies suddenly and leaves him her country home. It's a small wooden house sunk into the foot of a broken mountain range on the bank of a slow cold stream with no name. It also has a small fragrance garden beyond the back door and an oval reflection pond, where two large idle koi live. They have names, Beginning and End. You renovate the old cottage into a studio and a gallery space. You have shows there and put together gatherings for young artists from Tokyo.

When snow comes to your bones, your hair white, Toru's face like a dried apple, you stay warm in the cozy house with your husband and the many friends who come to visit. They come with apple wine and purple plums, with chazuke and green tea. You sit and talk for hours and they look at your photographs and paintings, including your favorite one, your masterpiece, the subject of much talk, which hangs above the mantle.

It's the white painting you pursued in your youth. The one you chased, the one that lured you across the ocean to where the River Li and the mountains meet. You have finally caught that painting and there it hangs on a nail, like a prize stag above the fire. It's quite different from your other works, and perhaps that's why it's your favorite. Expensively framed in polished ebony is a perfectly blank, empty canvas. Raw, without paint, hopeful and ready as the day you began.

When you die, it's at the riverbed a half mile from your home. You're sitting perfectly still, looking up at the blue mountain when a blood clot rushes through your brain and stops your heart, which is full already.

201

From section 137 . . .

Leaving Toru feels wrong, and his soft, pleading voice makes a tight fist in your stomach. You're trying to be sure about your decision, trying to think it through. You're on a long walk when a total stranger gives you the sign you're looking for. It happens when you're walking through the blue smoke of Vendor Street, a narrow cobblestone alley where the wooden carts filled with prepacked bento boxes and shiny Nagano apples and salted pig are built so closely together that even cats can't slink between them.

There's an old woman who sells Japanese peaches on the corner. She has one brown eye and one blue—but she says the blue eye is the only one she can see out of. "Eat the peach!" she yells at you, holding a juicy one out. *"Eat it!"* she yells again and throws the peach at you, which hits you in the shoulder and soaks your shoulder with peach juice. It's stupid and maybe you're just looking for a green light anywhere, but something about that exchange hits just the right chord in you.

Eat the damn peach. Tell Toru you're leaving.

You go around to all the shopkeepers to say your good-byes. The Udon guy, the smoothie man, the woman who somehow grows enormous lotus flowers in small aluminum buckets, all the people you've come to know by walking past them or to them every day—but it's frustrating. You can't tell them how much you've appreciated their help while you've lived there, how even though you've only ever had second-grade-level conversations with them, you'll never forget them, and their sake and squid, their crème sodas and green tea have become your Japan. Your entire, whole Japan.

Instead, all you can say in broken Japanese is: *"Hi. You. Mr. Tanaka! Saturday I go home of my big country of the far away. Yes. Yes. I so sad. Okay. Thank you very much on the delicious fruit always. I so sad. Okay. Bye. Bye."* They must think you're the village idiot.

You return to America and after the polite personality of Asia, your home country seems like a big wet slap in the face. When did Japan leak so deeply into your blood? You compare everything. In Japan the streets are cleaner, the trains more efficient, the people more polite, the food fresher, the water better, the stars brighter. When you land in Minneapolis, it's March. (From the plane: large fields of scratchy brown and mustard yellow and dirty white, like a Rothko painting, like an Anselm Kieffer.) You immediately want to go back.

The Walker Art Center is a series of large brushed aluminum buildings next to a sculpture garden, which has a giant fiberglass spoon holding an enormous red, ripe cherry. It's common knowledge that people like to have sex on that spoon. The base of the handle is the perfect beginning of a backrest, and if couples are feeling really ambitious, they tiptoe across the bridge of the spoon, hike up the cherry, and have sex on the stem. You live across the street in the 510 Apartments, which has a delicious French restaurant called La Belle Vie in the lobby, as well as a clear view of the sculpture garden across the way.

You buy a secondhand telescope and set it up in your living room window, where you can zero in on the strips of white fleshy thighs under heavy winter coats. You see couples coupling like beached sea otters there regularly. Even in winter. You see the occasional slippery knob, the pinched faces and gloveless hands, steam rising off them at night. Having no other identifiable inspiration, you take telephoto pictures of these wintry chubby lovers, which you blow up green and grainy and tack on the wall.

Loneliness. All these slick unions make your isolation more acute. You place international telephone calls to Toru, but he won't answer. Neither will anyone else. You think about Japan constantly. You can't get a good peach to save your life here—they're mealy and dry—and what's worse is that you know this place has beauty, maybe not peaches or people but there's a poetry you know is there, you should be able to see, but you can't. You try to focus on your work and on the fact that you're an artist-in-residence at a prestigious museum—and that must mean something, although you don't know what.

Sometimes you walk through the city—down Hennepin Avenue to the train tracks that cross the Mississippi, a churning mud-brown river that reaches like a train trestle all the way down to the sea. Many people have tried to commit suicide by jumping off the bridge that crosses the river. The fall itself never kills them—they're killed downstream, after they're swept by the current over the dam and down into the rotating metal jaws of "the strainer," a hydraulic hatchet system designed to chop up trees and branches that come down the river.

At night sometimes you try to blow off steam by going out. To gay bars and coffeehouses and dance clubs. You like First Avenue, where you huff the occasional line of cocaine in the bathroom and dance all night. You're usually alone, unbothered by anyone, until one night when a tiny cinnamon-colored man approaches you. He seems like a shy, liquid-eyed doe backed by gorilla bodyguards. His jumpsuit is made from a creamy blue velour. It turns out to be motherfucking *Prince*. He's collecting women for a party back at his place. "Plenty of champagne and shamelessness, *Girl Chick*," he says. He's offering limo rides.

You think of Toru and the studio and the white painting. Why not get into the limo, what else is there to lose? You get in the limousine with about eight other girls. *Why not?* Live a little. You drive forty minutes out to Chanhassen, Minnesota, where the limo pulls into an underground parking lot. You're ushered up to a sophisticated sound studio, all aluminum and blond wood, which has been draped in silks and velvets, and has lit candles flickering everywhere.

There's alcohol, there's cocaine, there's meth, there's K. There's shit you haven't heard of. The girls are rolling around and the music is like a constant sonic boom. You have sex with one of the bodyguards because there's really nothing else to do. He's all shoulders and muscle. Grunts. The room is blurry as you're thrown around like a rag doll. Afterward you fall asleep on a purple, velvet-swagged couch and you don't wake up. There are dreams of underwater cities and peacocks that strut on the sandy ocean floor.

Whatever highball blend you took is racing around your capillaries, closing arteries and freezing your blood. You die at Paisley Park. In the morning the bodyguards bury you out back, behind the recycling bins, where there are lots of girls.

Your heaven is in Japan. It's a Zen center on the top of a nameless purple mountain. Well—it might have a name, but no one really seems to worry about names. You wake up clean, wearing a white kimono made of some rippling cream-colored silk. You live in a small stone house deep in the hill. Every day you get up, meditate, make tea, and go to work in a garden called *Roji-en*, or Garden of the Drops of Dew. It has cold stone lanterns, white sugary sand, jagged green rock, mustard-colored moss, blooming cherry blossoms, and thick-branched maple trees.

Your garden is connected to many others, which are all different. There's a rock garden that cultivates contemplation, the tea garden cultivates mystery, the water garden brings interconnectedness with nature. The entire space of heaven is intended to be a way to be in tune with a sense of space and rhythm, light and shade, texture and sound. Like earth, with its millions of little details, but better.

Whenever you're not cultivating your garden, you like to wander through the others and see what everyone else is creating. The Zen garden is our peace, and the garden bridge is a *yatsuhashi*, an eightfold Japanese bridge that zigzags over a small pond and forces a person to step carefully and take time to notice all the many small simple details around them that would otherwise go unnoticed. "It is good to have an end to the journey," they say, "but it's only the journey that matters in the end."

202

From section 126 . . .

Can you define your life by one moment? The cotter pin on which everything else swings? The moment you would take back—rewind, do over? You realize you made a mistake. A big, fat, hairy-eyeballed mistake. You run back into the building. *What were you thinking? You love Toru—you love him beyond his "deformity."* Your feet pound down the hall and you bang on number 1931—but Toru won't answer. You knock until your knuckles are red, until one splits and a small horseshoe of blood is stamped on the door. You are locked out. Panic floods you—you bang louder. Nothing.

You keep thinking of the white painting. *What you chase—isn't there, what you chase—isn't there.* You go outside. The sidewalk seems uneven. The solid crush of bodies as you cross the street carries you, like a tide, to Yoyogi station, deep, modern, well lit. Packed with commuters. What if he never talks to you again? What if you lose your connection to him—what if you lose him? What was his favorite food? *Was it yakisoba noodles? It might have been yakisoba noodles.* Will you forget it? What if you forget it—forget him? How much have you already forgotten? Did he smell like maple wood chips or pressed maple leaves? *What you chase—isn't there.*

You stay in Japan and go to work in a lithograph studio. It's two months later on a rain-soaked afternoon when you are sipping coffee in an *ko-hi-shoppu* (coffee shop) and read it in the papers. Ink fragments. *Celebrated Artist . . . Toru Nishigaki . . . Suicide . . . Window . . . Pavement.*

Toru Nishigaki. Suicide. Window. Pavement. You spill the coffee and burn the web of your hand. Sudden loss yawns in front of you. Toru. What did his fingertips feel like? Was it polished marble or polished wood? Where did you file him? Was it under forgotten? Under *sasoku* (left) or maybe *jin* (man)? Was it just *ji* (child)? You rush out onto the street, met by a world equally panicked. Blurred color, breathless speech, aching foreheads, and the birds with nowhere to go. The studio is three miles away and you begin to run. *What you chase—isn't there.*

After that, you can't seem to leave Japan. You join the large expat community of bedraggled artists, who live mostly around the slums. You try to paint, try to work, but nothing much comes of it. You think of Toru and his painting. He is easily located now by way of a marble headstone in a nearby graveyard. Memory has reserved him an easy place. You marry another artist, an Australian with a gold front tooth. The two of you paint in a run-down studio and work at an arts supply store. You're walking together by Yoyogi station one day when a passenger train—on time and full of commuters—derails and plows into the street. You go to heaven, which is a white painting. Nothing. All that fuss over a white void. What you chase—isn't there.

2o3

From section 126 . . .

You return home and after the polite personality of Asia, your country seems like a big wet shiny slap in the face. When did Japan leak so deeply into your blood? You compare everything. In Japan the streets are cleaner, the trains more efficient, the people more polite, the food fresher, the water better, the stars brighter. When you land in Minneapolis, it's March. (From the plane: large fields of scratchy brown and mustard yellow and dirty white, like a Rothko painting, like an Anselm Kieffer.) You immediately want to go back.

The Walker Art Center is a series of large brushed aluminum buildings next to a sculpture garden, which has a giant fiberglass spoon holding an enormous red, ripe cherry. It's common knowledge that people like to have sex on that spoon. The base of the handle is the perfect beginning of a backrest, and if couples are feeling really ambitious, they tiptoe across the bridge of the spoon, hike up the cherry, and have sex on the stem. You live across the street in the 510 Apartments, which has a delicious French restaurant called La Belle Vie in the lobby, as well as a clear view of the sculpture garden across the way.

You buy a secondhand telescope and set it up in your living room window, where you can zero in on the strips of white fleshy thighs under heavy winter coats. You see couples coupling like beached sea otters there regularly. Even in winter. You see the occasional slippery knob, the pinched faces and gloveless hands, steam rising off them at night. Having no other identifiable inspiration, you take telephoto pictures of these wintry chubby lovers, which you blow up green and grainy and tack on the wall.

Loneliness. All these slick unions make your isolation more acute. You place international telephone calls to Toru, but he won't answer. Neither will anyone else. You think about Japan constantly. You can't get a good peach to save your life here—they're mealy and dry—and what's worse is that you know this place has beauty, maybe not peaches or people but there's a poetry you know is there, you should be able to see, but you can't. You try to focus on your work and on the fact that you're an artist-in-residence at a prestigious museum—and that must mean something, although you don't know what.

Sometimes you walk through the city—down Hennepin Avenue to the train tracks that cross the Mississippi, a churning mud-brown river that reaches like a train trestle all the way down to the sea. Many people have tried to commit suicide by jumping off the bridge that crosses the river. The fall itself never kills them—they're killed downstream, after they're swept by the current over the dam and down into the rotating metal jaws of "the strainer," a hydraulic hatchet system designed to chop up trees and branches that come down the river.

At night sometimes you try to blow off steam by going out. To gay bars and coffeehouses and dance clubs. You like First Avenue, where you huff the occasional line of cocaine in the bathroom and dance all night. You're usually alone, unbothered by anyone, until one night when a tiny cinnamon-colored man approaches you. He seems like a shy, liquid-eyed doe backed by gorilla bodyguards. His jumpsuit is made from a creamy blue velour. It turns out to be motherfucking *Prince*. He's collecting women for a party back at his place. "Plenty of champagne and shamelessness, *Girl Chick*," he says. He's offering limo rides.

You think of Toru and the studio and the white painting. Why not get into the limo, what else is there to lose? You get in the limousine with about eight other girls. *Why not?* You drive forty minutes out to Chanhassen and the limo pulls into an underground parking lot. You're ushered up to a sound studio, which has been draped in silks and velvets, and has candles everywhere. *There's alcohol, there's cocaine, there's meth, there's K.* There's shit you haven't heard of.

You turn it all down. It suddenly seems sad. You came all this way to party but now the party seems boring. *Trite.* You leave the action and wander into the recording studio next door, where you noodle around on the piano. In the next room the girls are rolling around and the music is like a constant sonic boom. You sing a sad little made-up song. Then another. Keep yourself company while the party blares next door.

Then a figure emerges from the sound booth—you didn't know anyone was in there watching you. *It's Prince.* He's wearing an entirely different outfit—a key lime pants suit with a gold vest. He swings a green glass walking cane and sits down on the bench next to you. "Keep playing, *Girl Chick*," he says—and you do. Pretty soon the party people find you and drift in—and Prince makes them be quiet so he can hear your singing. He starts to harmonize, humming low and strumming a guitar that appears out of nowhere. You are in Chanhassen, Minnesota, jamming with *Prince* at Paisley Park.

The upshot is a very bizarre and big record deal. Prince has a new label called Sister Cream, an all-female label that features women's debut records, and you're the premiere artist. He brings his design team in to give you a complete new look. New hair, new makeup, new clothes. "He likes unknowns," his manager says. "He likes ingénues and women who nobody else has recognized. You're one lucky cherry."

Your record, *Too Pieces*, is soft and simple. You playing piano (barely) with a full orchestra backing you up. There are several feature solos from Prince on acoustic guitar—which makes the record go gold and then platinum.

You quit the museum—or rather, they quit you. With your touring and schedule there's no way you can maintain the program, plus they seem to think you've *sold out* or *bought in*, or something inappropriate for an upscale artist. Whatever.

You move to Santa Barbara and buy an enormous house overlooking the sea. The success of your album affords you a whole new lifestyle, one you're careful to protect. You invest your money wisely after you finish the tour. Then you step back out of the limelight. *Too Pieces* is the only album you ever make. Prince asks you to do another, but you gently decline and he finds another ingénue to focus on.

You live out the rest of your days in physical comfort but emotional disquiet. You never forget Toru—his crippled hand and soft heart. You try to contact him several times but your calls go unreturned and your letters unanswered. There are several affairs, and several more—with the most beautiful and handsome men—but you still can't shake Toru and his white painting—you go to your grave wondering where they both are.

Your afterlife is spent drifting through all the roads on earth you didn't take. It turns out that in the immense phone-book-sized rule book of heaven it says people who turn away from true love must spend a hundred years and then a hundred more looking for those they forgot to look for while they were alive. You keep walking.

204

From section 135 . . .

It's time to go. You say good-bye to Pierre. He pleads with you not to go, he begs. He produces a tiny diamond-chip ring he's been carrying around for weeks and asks you to marry him. *No*, you say. You *can't*. You already have your ticket—and once the winds come for you, there's nothing you can do but go. He dejectedly drives you and your luggage to the Le Havre port west of Paris where the boat is waiting.

It turns out the *O.H.* is a six-story ship with three hundred and fifty souls on board. There are no passengers, only crew. The crew members are mostly in the technology industry. Web site designers, software developers, IT managers, application managers, systems consultants, graphic designers. . . . They not only work on the boat, manning the bridge, cleaning the boiler room, and cooking in the galley, but as the *O.H.* sails all over the world, they collect new technology information. Every six months the *O.H.* pulls up anchor and heads for a new destination. California, South America, Paris, Rome, Tokyo, Iceland. Sometimes they do big jobs in the countries they visit, sometimes they're just visiting and collecting data.

You sail over the world. Europe, Tokyo, Bangkok, Venice, South America, South Africa, Bali, the Philippines, Easter Island, Bora-Bora, Texas. You miss Pierre, you miss him more than you thought you would. It isn't that you want to go back, just that you wish he was here with you. An uneasy worry shadows you—*did you let one of the loves of your life go?*

You work in the galley. You bake bread, chop vegetables, boil chickens, defrost beef stock. You work underneath a roly-poly Frenchman, a delightful guy named Darcy, who teaches you the difference between a beurre blanc and plain old butter. The job is tough—you're up at five a.m. every morning, which you never get used to. Your hands ache from all the kneading of dough and chopping of roots, and you still occasionally get seasick. There are beautiful moments too, like holding that first cup of steaming hot coffee each morning when all the pots are clean, and the sleepy kitchen portholes are lit yellow and blue and lavender, and Darcy's little bird, a yellow finch named Marmalade, trills madly at the light.

You make friends on the ship. There are late-night poker games, vicious Ping-Pong tournaments, impromptu water sports (chumming for sharks by hurling leftover pork chops and whole cakes into the ocean) and of course plenty of disastrous romantic episodes, making the *O.H.* at times a veritable *Days of our Lives*. You yourself have several affairs with men, but you never shake the memory of Pierre. You wonder what he's doing, who he's loving, what on earth drove you away from him. Of course you know it was the call of your own heartbeat you heard. Your need to search and see. You wanted to stay but you had to go, and there is the great schism of life.

Eventually a new man comes on board, a funny guy with animated eyes and strong hands. His name is Joel and he's a software programmer as well as a maintenance engineer, one of the wiry jack-of-all-trade creatures who can oil the engines, paint the bow, and rework the ship's elaborate navigation system. He kisses you within the first hour of meeting you. After some cursory introductions and him looking at you strangely, you start to heat up. It's like he's made of electrical coils or space heaters or something—being near him changes your core temperature. Then when you're alone he steals a quick kiss from you. You say, "Stop kissing me!" and he immediately kisses you again, which is when you know you love him.

You get married on the aft deck of the ship while drifting through the turquoise Caribbean. The captain presides over the ceremony and provides you with a vacation speedboat for your honeymoon, which is strewn with rose petals. Afterward the two of you live together on the *O.H.* The memory of Pierre shadows you from time to time but then eventually drifts away like a slow smoke, a gradual mist that darkens until you can hardly make out his shape in your mind's eye—and then in the constant kiss of time, he is gone.

Traveling by ship is so much more natural that sealing yourself up in a metal tube and flinging yourself blind, sightless across the ocean. On a ship there is no jet lag. No sudden illnesses or allergies to foreign germs. You acclimate as you go—nice and slowly. You see the landscapes change bit by bit, you have enough time to actually learn traditions and customs, you get used to the local food, as well as local bacteria. You buy twin pugs in Japan and name them Blitzkrieg and Snapple. They go with you everywhere, like fat, grumpy, little children.

Your family back home complains about your gypsy lifestyle, and every once in a while, under intense parental pressure, you and Joel try to get a "normal" life, but any apartment or house you live in seems thick and viscous, like a clod cave, like a monstrous prison you're paying to stay in. You miss the sea. Once you've got wandering shoes, they never come off.

You die years and years later in a restaurant in Bali, when you have an allergic reaction to local jumbo scallops soaked in coconut milk. (They were actually quite delicious.) After your third bite there's a tickle in your throat and you try to cough—but you can't. Your chest seizes. Blitzkrieg and Snapple start to bark. (One thing you love about Bali, you can bring your dogs *everywhere*.) You can't breathe—it's like something is squeezing your ribs together. Splitting them, cracking them. You try to call out for help as you go down on your knees, but there's only a rasping wheeze as your throat closes. Joel is beside you—clearing away the chairs and unbuttoning your shirt.

Waiters are flying around you like loosed doves, knocking over the water glasses, pulling Snapple off your leg and shoving Blitzkrieg away. Then it's like someone turned the sound off in the room. Spotlight on you. Big white light. You can feel the strength of Joel's hand and you smile. You went all around the world together. You saw bloodred bullfights and schools of bluegill and green parrots in love at a market in Marrakech. You were happy. The big white light blooms, and your spotlight escorts you offstage.

You reincarnate immediately. Others can wait up to a thousand years to come back—but you turn over in under twenty-four hours, like a kid ready to go on the roller coaster ride again. You're redelivered into the physical world as a sharp-eyed yellow-talon bald eagle with a wingspan over six feet. You're able to cruise up through the thermal heavens to a height where the currents carry you completely weightless, the giant planet beneath you, the edge of the atmosphere above. Sometimes you soar up and up and up to where the air turns to ice crystals and the jet engines roar, and then you drop, dead weight hurtling toward earth. You are caught in the spin and dazzle of the turning colors, the approaching details beneath you. You share the nest with the other soul you've been traveling with for many, many lives . . . its name changes, its shape—it's been called *Marie* and *Joaquin* and *Black Bear* and *Otter* and *Lucille* and *Joel* and now Bald Eagle. The name doesn't matter and neither does the shape. The soul is your mate and through every life you will find each other eventually. Sometimes you meet right away and sometimes it takes until almost the very end, but always and eventually you explore this beautiful broken world together, this comic tragedy, this careless velocity.

205

From section 135 . . .

You stay in Paris with Pierre and he proposes to you. You have an elegantly burlesque ceremony down on the waterfront with mimes for waiters and clowns as ushers. A friend takes you in his boat up and down the Seine while everyone on the banks of the grand river cheers and claps. Your parents come over for the wedding, and as a wedding gift they give you enough money to get the *Marionette Jolie* fixed up and running. (She looks so yar grumbling down the Seine late at night as the sun is setting and the café lights up on the boulevards are just twinkling on.) You and Pierre are able to take her down the Rhone River, to Lyon, Tournus, Chalon-sur-Saône, Macon, Tournon, Arles, Avignon, and Vienne. Every morning is a new gift to unwrap—a new world to see.

Pierre gets a job designing software for a German design firm and you move into a little cottage on the edge of the city. You have two children, Lisbon and Saône (two of your favorite places), and the girls love going for rides on the *Marionette Jolie* and hearing about the old days. (*You lived on the boat? You had to pump the bathroom out into buckets? You had cockroaches as big as chocolates?*)

Years pass, the children move away, Pierre gets promoted, old LeGrand dies of a heart attack, and you are made porter master. Life is very good. Then one day when you're fifty-eight and on the verge of retirement, a package gets checked in that never gets checked out. It's a simple white paper box. Heavy. No one pays attention or thinks of it when it explodes, sending passengers into the walls, sending the walls to the ground, sending the story of another terrorist bombing in Paris across the world. Just before the bomb went off you were trying to remember a poem and thinking you really need a manicure. Your nails look like hell.

206

From section 130 . . .

You go to Oahu with Albert. He shows you how to sharpen a bowie knife and eke out another ten minutes of oxygen from a scuba tank. He shows you how to freak out a barracuda with the bubbles from your hose and how to eat fire-pit-roasted lobster on the beach with your bare hands. He asks you all sorts of questions—like *What's your first memory? What's your favorite food? What makes you scared? What's one thing you want to do before you die?* He doesn't want to hear about your crappy marriage. "We all get into shit," he says. "The real story is how you got out."

The two of you spend your days surfing, your nights making love and then wandering on the beach looking for luminescent sand dollars. The best part is the cravings you used to have—the blood-boiling yearning for meth—dry up with all this sun and sand. It has no staying power anymore. You and Albert get married in Bali, on a lovely stretch of sugar-soft beach with a trail of little girls dressed in flowers around you. He gives you his bowie knife, and you give him yours. It's a fair trade—in the scheme of things. You live together for thirty blissful, sunny years before you're both drowned in an oceanic riptide while on vacation in Singapore. The waves were really huge that day. And beautiful.

Anyone who drowns near Hawaii becomes the eternal subject of Kanaloa, the Hawaiian god of the sea. Kanaloa is also the god of squid, which is what you and Albert become in the next life. Giant squids. Big and inky. Japanese scientists capture your image with a digital camera off the coast of New Zealand and wonder if Jules Verne might have been right about sea monsters. (He was. *They don't know the half of it.*) The photograph never makes dry land. You tip the scientists' boat with your gooey egg-colored tentacle and kill all three of them before you race on to catch up with Albert and the others.

207

From section 130 . . .

You say good-bye to Albert and he tells you to call him if you ever change your mind. You never know, you just might. For now, it's nice to have the number in your pocket, and nice to feel the erection in his pants when you hug good-bye. Meeting Albert has changed you. He didn't need money to be happy, he needed the beach.

You need something too. You need to feel free. You need movement and color, so you take your car and set out on a cross-country trip, stopping in every tiny town, at every strange roadside attraction you can find. *Rattlesnake farms, two-headed goats, mineral museums, and giant balls of twine.* You develop an affinity for truck-stop food (smothered pork chops, black coffee, lemon meringue pie) and a deep appreciation for just how many freaks live in this country. You also develop an ability to find a Narc-Anon meeting no matter where you go. You just head for any coffee shop on any main street and ask the most self-conscious-looking person in the room.

You're glad you're not doing drugs, because you can rule paranoia out as the reason you think someone might be following you. Has your husband tracked down his money? Maybe you shouldn't have wired money from Megan's account through Western Union. There's a dark blue Camry shadowing you with license plate number LIC 487. You thought you lost him in Texas . . . you laughed and thought you were imagining things, but in Gary, Indiana, the blue Camry reappears. Now you're worried. This taste of freedom has you set on never letting anyone else control you, or watch you, or hurt you again.

The Camry parks in the same hotel as you—on the far side of the pool. The guy has the nerve to get a hotel room *next to yours* and you see him hulking past the window quickly, like an old crooked wolf. Around two in the morning you break into his car with a crowbar, and inside the glove compartment you find a thick manila envelope with personal information about you. *Photographs, your social security number, a map detailing your trip so far.* A series of phone numbers. Your husband has hired this asshole to tail you. Maybe to kill you?

You lie down in the backseat of the car with your crowbar and you wait. You're not sure what you're waiting for. Around dawn the creep comes out and sees the broken window. Starts swearing. He gets in the car, never suspecting little miss embezzling wife is in the backseat. His head is down. Your hands are around the ice-cold crowbar. What are you waiting for? You sit up. You swing the iron like a baseball bat and catch him in the right temple. You probably didn't kill him, you just put him to sleep for a few hours. Time to get at least two states away.

You drive to Georgia, because you've always liked peaches, and you settle down in Savannah, with a history professor named Paul, who studies ancient Greek linguistics and grows prize roses. You never marry Paul, which causes something of a stir in the sleepy little town, especially when you have three daughters, Beth, Gillian, and Darcy. Still. No wedding for you. *Never again*. No paper is worth your freedom.

You may not subscribe to certain Southern customs, like the institution of marriage or drinking gin gimlets at noon, but you *do* subscribe to the institution of Southern food. *And how.* You learn to make red velvet cake, banana pie, fried chicken, fried grits, and Brunswick stew. You have oyster roasts and fish fries, chicken gumbo dinners and gallons of sweet tea. Your kitchen is always bubbling with good food, good gossip, and your good children, who grow up to become accomplished citizens of Savannah. An equestrian, an architect, and an artist. You must have done something right.

You die one hot summer day when you're sleeping on the porch swing and a wasp stings your tongue. The thing just drifts out from under some wisteria vines and right into your open mouth. You have an automatic reaction, your throat swells and closes, oxygen is cut off to the brain.

You lie in a vegetative state for three years before your children lobby to have your feeding tube removed. There are protests. You have to lie in this mucky, disgusting stew of a body until the blessed day the machines are turned off. Then you soar, silver clean and airy, up into a light yellow space, with fresh air and miles and miles of open fields. No doctors, no machines, just sunshine and birds.

It turns out you *did* kill that private investigator—but they say he had it coming, so instead of hell you'll get haunting. You're assigned to the Fitzpatrick house back in Savannah—a big blue house off Victory Drive. They have three children and a father with one eye. There you spend your days wisping and wafting, slamming doors, moving the children's school books, and hiding the father's glass eye. It's great fun.

208

From section 113 . . .

Nobody saw you take Ben's credit card receipt and sneak it into your pocket.
Nobody notices. You're just the high-paid girlfriend of a high-paying customer. There's just smiles and nods and *thank you*s on your way out. At home
you get online. You don't buy that much at first, just one or two things, a pink
cashmere sweater and some pearl earrings, because it makes you nervous. You
prepare yourself for Ben's phone call. *"Um . . . do you know about anything purchased online at Barneys?"* But that call never comes—he never says a word to
you. Not on the phone, not in person—nothing.

Does he know? Maybe he knows but doesn't care? Is this sanctioned spending? A whore's reward? *Why buy it yourself when the credit card is free?* You start
to spend in earnest. Leather jackets, art history books, eBay items of every
imaginable category. An antique brass monkey, an automatic Leica camera,
suede boots, rabbit-fur-lined gloves, a brass-handled umbrella, an antique gilt
mirror . . . you stop keeping track.

Ben moves you out of your ratty apartment into a posh third-floor walk-
up in SoHo. He likes to visit you in your well-appointed place, which is
filled with furniture he does or doesn't know he bought. You quit your job at
the school when it gets too tedious and now you casually send out résumés,
looking for something better. Ben doesn't mind taking care of things in the
meantime.

Sex changes. At first it was vibrators and anal plugs, then it went to sex
swings and latex masks, and finally one day you walk into the bedroom and
there's Ben, his red head bobbing up and down, and he's fucking some sort of
stuffed animal. A little stuffed baby whale. *"What are you doing?"* you shout,
and he withdraws his limp cock from a torn hole in the polyester fabric just
above the snout. It's Baby Shamu. Ben was fucking *Baby Shamu*.

After that things go downhill. The credit card suddenly stops working and now you're the one that doesn't know if you should say anything. How can you ask, *"Why the fuck isn't your credit card working anymore?"* or *"Can I have another credit card because I must have maxed out the other one."* Things deteriorate rapidly. The school has already replaced you and you can't get another job. You get evicted when you don't pay rent. Then *the police* show up at your door.

They take you into custody for *credit card fraud* and haul your ass to the downtown jail. Too embarrassed to call your family or friends, unable to reach Rocky or Ben (not that either would help), you sit there for seven days like a mossy gargoyle frozen on the bench before a judge will see you. He appoints you a bullshit county attorney who eats a tuna salad sandwich during the pre-trial, and after it's all said and done you end up motherfucking sentenced to a year in a minimum-security prison for credit card fraud. Your idiot lawyer says it's rat crap luck.

You still refuse to call your family. What are you supposed to say? "Hey, sorry I haven't called but I'm actually in jail"?

But what the hell are you going to do for a year? Play Ping-Pong? Write your shitty boring memoir? Who would read it? There's a prisoner–pen pal service sponsored by the Lutheran Church, a group who finds good Samaritans who are willing to write letters to locked-up losers like you. You request a pen pal (because anything beats Ping-Pong) and you get paired up with a man named Eddie, an ex-convict living in Reno. Instead of the pious stiff church lady you thought would write you, you get the good fortune of getting a beefy hunk who after several letters finally admits he fell in love with you the moment he saw your picture in the prisoner–pen pal Web link.

Eddie writes you letters and sends you presents (shampoo, floral-scented Tampax, clove cigarettes). He calls every Sunday and you convince him to tell your parents that you're living in Tibet among goatherds and you can't contact them right now, but you will in six to eight months.

When you get out of the joint (two months early for good behavior) you move in with Eddie. Where else can you go? You just have to get yourself cleaned up and then you can go home. Besides, Eddie needs you—his life is a mess. His rent is late, the electricity is turned off, his runny-nosed kid (you didn't even know he had a runny-nosed kid) is in need of a hygiene lesson and new school clothes.

You pitch in. You get a job at Wal-Mart folding clothes in the juniors section. That's all you do. Fold clothes. Day in, day out, you refold the mountain of glittery, rhinestone-studded, sequin-encrusted cheap clothes strewn across dressing rooms. Fucking teenagers. The place is like a Britney Spears–inspired death camp, the place where fashion goes to die.

Every penny you make goes to Eddie and his kid. Eddie needs a car for work; his kid needs medicine for asthma. The water heater bursts, squirrels chew a cantaloupe-sized hole in the roof, there's property taxes and his divorce papers and never enough beer. There's always something to buy, something missing, something needed, something broken. This goes on and on and you never go back to school, never move out; you just sit in his cinder-block house and wait for the next thing to break.

You gain weight. A lot of weight. What else is there to do when you watch television but spread out? You drink beer, develop Eddie's affinity for pork rinds and barbecue sauce. You still haven't contacted your parents—they can't see you like this. You'll get yourself together and then you'll call them. Right now your feet hurt all the time; it's hard to get to work. Your weight causes a whole host of medical problems; your heart, your blood pressure, your cholesterol all tank. Time passes, years roll by. You are now the lady everyone makes fun of. The kids in the neighborhood call you *Mrs. Fat Ass from Fart Town*.

You spend most of your time in an easy chair in the kitchen reheating pizzas and watching talk shows. Eddie is a disaster. He gets jobs and then loses them. He brings home the wrong things from the store. Why on earth he put a lava lamp on the stove, you don't know. But one day while you're sitting in your chair reheating a taco casserole while watching a talk show about *gold-digging whores and the men who love them*, the lava lamp explodes, shooting a shard of glass through your heart. There's white lava lamp goo all over the kitchen. You die just as the gold diggers are coming out onstage, just when one leggy blond is yelling at the audience, "I get what I want when I want it, see?" She doesn't care that they're booing. She shakes her head defiantly. "I get it all," she says. "I do what I want."

You go to hell. People who die watching the *Jerry Springer Show* have to go to a permanent Jerry Springer show in hell (because they shouldn't have been watching him in the first place). It's nonstop back-to-back shows with themes such as *You ate my baby! My husband is screwing the dog! People who confused fireworks with Tampax! I have sex with sofa cushions! I married my mother! Why can't you stop ramming butter up your ass?* And so on.

When you ask if you can go back to earth and try over again they tell you "sure, right after Jerry Springer is out of awful things to talk about." You take your seat.

209

From section 113 . . .

Enough is enough. You're considering credit card fraud now? You take the receipt out of your pocket and put it back on the table. Ben never knows you almost swiped his card and ran amuck with it—although sometimes he's such a tightwad you wish you had.

Then Ben's wife dies of a mysterious blood disease (you suspect Ben killed her, but you never know for sure), and he asks you to marry him. You say *yes*, even though he wants a prenup. Ben is okay for the short time you're married to him, but the best part is that he has the good manners to have a fatal heart attack only about a year later, leaving you with his entire fortune. Twenty-two million dollars.

With all your new free time and money you decide to paint in Paris and write your first book, *Diary of a Park Avenue Princess*, which gets fabulous reviews in everything from *Harper's* to *Vogue*. The media loves *your Harry Winston ways, your haute couture cufflinks, your million-dollar manicures.* Of course it's all utter crap—you don't like any of those things. You like jeans and tank tops. You eat hamburgers. Still, they eat it up like hard candy.

You depart this mortal coil a little early yourself—you're only forty when you have a sharp pain in your chest. All that money and still you didn't make time for a mammogram. Ah, well—not to worry. Heaven is *better* than Park Avenue. They have better stores and bigger limits on their credit cards. You can get a hamburger any time of the day or night. Honestly, you had no idea God was RuPaul Bunyan: part fashion model, part lumberjack. *Killer legs, pouty lips, flannel shirt, rippling muscles.* Beauty fused with brawn, but not too heavy on the brains—which actually, if you think about the way the world is, seems about right.

210

From section 89 . . .

You decide not to drink the wine. A strobe of images fires in your brain—like flashcards of everything that ever went wrong with your life. You head back for the courthouse, where you're forty-five minutes late for your scheduled hearing, but they (of course) are an *hour* and forty-five minutes behind so no one knows of your almost fuck-up. You sit down on the hard wooden pews of the courtroom and wait. By the time they call your name, they never even knew you were gone.

When the judge asks you why you were kicked out of Mercy House, you tell her *it was because sometimes the wrong things shine too brightly. You're just weak. You're a weak jerk and you tell her you deserve whatever she's got to throw at you. Throw fines, throw rehab, throw workhouse, throw jail time. Throw the book.*

The courtroom is quiet and the judge sits like a stone. In the end, she ignores the recommendations of your parole officer and instead orders you to finish treatment at St. Mary's rehabilitation center, known especially for their progressive program with women. You have been given a reprieve. You have been given another chance.

You go back to rehab, finish it, and with two of the women you meet in treatment you start a women's shelter/sober coffeehouse called the Daily Grind. You become known as "Mama," mother to all who are motherless. You're not crazy about the nickname, but you know it means all these people who stream past you like a quick river look at you as a mother to the motherless. That's worth something.

You get to see so many stories as the years go by—women struggling to save their children, to save themselves. Sometimes you're not sure what it all adds up to. Why there has to be so much trouble in the world.

Even still, you wonder what the world would be like if all these women had the power and the light they were meant to have from the get-go. If they'd all had tender hands raise them. *The sheer power they would have*. The things they would accomplish. You think of those elephants in the circus—the ones who are strong enough to break their chains but who choose to only remember what it was like when they were little, and so never try again.

That's what you see come through your shelter doors. Elephants. Noble creatures of strength and character, who just don't remember how to break the chains. All told you probably help over ten thousand women find better lives for themselves. Help them quit drinking, find jobs, leave their husbands, fight off their boyfriends, take care of their children. It's something. When you're older there are answers to questions you don't ask anymore. You die crossing Michigan Street one day when the 51A bus hits you. It was on time.

211

From section 149 . . .

"Your leg?" you ask, "they did this?"

He nods. "They broke it the night they found me." He looks over his shoulder. "They told me *Donna Maria* sent them and that she adopted you." Adopted you? The German hobbles off, and as you hurry down the street to Maria's house, it all falls into place. *The late-night meetings in the dining room, the easy way they moved through the city, the subservience and fear shown by everyone. Cosa Nostra.* You pack quickly, quietly. It's only your passport you can't find. You keep it in a drawer on your dresser in your room, but now it's gone.

At dinner that night, after the heaping plates of pasta are empty and the green salads gone, you mention it. Try to keep any fear or accusation out of your voice, just tell them your passport is missing. *They shrug.* Baldo belches, Marco rolls his eyes. No one says anything else. You carefully continue eating your salad, commenting on how *good and strong* the vinegar is. They're watching you. No question.

Time passes, it becomes like a noose around your neck—claustrophobic and suffocating. You try to contact your family but all mail goes through Donna Maria, all phone calls are monitored. You panic. Out of options, you run one morning down to the ferry, where the big boats run, and you lose yourself in a sea of strangers. Tourists from England, Ireland, Australia, Japan. You find an American couple and you beg them to help you. Perhaps it is your hysteria, or your nationality, or your tears, but the man (pale and doughy) seems to believe you. "Just get me to Rome," you say. "A train ticket to Rome. That's all I need." The wife pulls him to the side, confers, obviously complains, but they come back and grimly escort you onto the ferry.

It's a cat-and-mouse game once you're on the ship. You hide from the stewards, the captain, anyone who might know the Adonis family. At the port of call you scan the crowds nervously, thinking anyone might be the one looking for you. The couple buys you an express ticket to Rome. The man gives you a hundred euros and his name and address in case by some small stroke of luck you actually intend to pay him back.

You take the train to Rome and head directly for the American embassy to tell them about the Adonis family, the stolen passport, the intent to keep you in Sicily against your will. They don't believe any of your stories. "First of all," the bored man in the embassy says, "there is no *Adonis family* in Cosa Nostra. Second of all, they would want to keep an American in Sicily like they would want to keep a crocodile in their bathtub."

Once home, you never leave the United States again. Research as you might, you cannot find any evidence of an Adonis family connected with organized crime, but what do they know? What, is the mob going to post their official family connections on the Web? You wait for the day when Maria or one of her sons shows up on your door and blows your head off for deserting the family. You wait a long time.

Before you die by choking on a peach pit, which in the end will be the most significant detail of your life, you marry some guy who gets an erection about as often as he gets an interesting idea, which is to say hardly ever. You have two kids with him who you don't particularly like. They smell. You wait for the Adonis brothers. You watch. No one ever comes.

212

From section 149 . . .

You don't believe him—you give the German a good hard shove and knock him off his crutches. He falls hard on his elbow, crying out in pain. The commotion startles everyone on the street and a crowd gathers quickly. They automatically assume it's the German harassing the girl, not the other way around. They start to shout at him. *"Fucking Nazi!"* one of the shopkeepers says. *"Always making trouble!"* Someone gives the German a hard kick in the ribs, and the crowd goes down on him. Things get out of control. You stand back, away from the crowd, when Marco appears on his silver Moto Guzzi. The two of you take off down the bumpy cobblestone street while the crowd behind you moves in.

You drive out of the city, up to the foothills. Clear wind through your hair. Your face and legs baking in the sun. Marco's cologne smells like lemon, you bury your face in his thick hair. You spend the day together, looking at old relics and eating at a small roadside café. It's hard to say exactly when the precise moment was that you looked at him *differently*, but at some point you were holding his hand, leaning into him, pressing your lips against his.

The German dies. It's on the news and in the papers; he had clear ties to Cosa Nostra, although he was only a bit player, a thug used for petty crime. You find your passport, which you thought had been stolen, under the bed, knocked into the far reaches of the dark by a foot or a broom. When you realize your visa only lasts for six months, and when it's time to go soon, Marco gets down on one knee, right in the middle of the square, and asks you to marry him.

Maria throws the wedding—an extravaganza unlike any you've ever seen. Your parents fly all the way from home. Your mother is nervous and your father is curious, but by the end of the experience, so much wine, laughter, and dancing has passed through the wedding party that all rivers are bridged. They even talk about moving to Sicily if you ever have a grandchild, and it's only a year later you give birth to an adorable chubby baby boy, Vincenzo. (He has asthma and a bad heart—but he's your apple, your angel, your North Star, your Mount Vesuvius, your entire Italy.)

You open a shoe store in central Sicily, a popular boutique, which sells shoes not only from the cobbler up in the mountain but also from Milan, Paris, New York, and Tokyo. Rich women shop at your store, as do brides and wives who have saved up their money. Vincenzo grows up in the store, playing and sleeping around all these ebullient and demonstrative women, and so many people think it's *your fault* when he turns out to be gay. You couldn't care less if he's gay, straight, polka-dotted or cross-hatched. He's perfect.

Criticism dies down of course after he starts his own shoe line in Rome and then moves to Los Angeles, where he's the principal costume designer for big Hollywood movies. He sends big paychecks, and when you're too old to run the store anymore, he moves back to Sicily with his lover, Robert, and the two of them buy a villa in the hills and take over the boutique.

You live to be very old, older than anyone you know. Maybe it's the fish oil or the olives, but you live to be one hundred and eight. Maybe it's that your husband actually was in the mob and your whole family was protected at every turn. Who knows? You die while you are sleeping, with three cats curled up by your side.

213

From section 150 . . .

You follow Jed to New Zealand, where you study White Island, a horseshoe-shaped volcano rumored by the Maori to be haunted by twin brothers who eat white men. There was once a sulfur station on the shore, but the dig was abandoned when a landslide killed all of the workers, and a yellow cat was the only survivor. Despite the silent stone and unmovable boulders, the volcano is still active. It doesn't erupt lava, but it steams and vents and hisses, keeping your adrenaline up and your feet ready to run.

You and Jed live together in his house on the mainland and you travel back and forth to his jobs together, Taormina in the summer, White Island in the winter. You do this for over two decades, collecting data, taking pictures, completing fieldwork. Jed is a man of few words but has good intentions, and even though there are many nights you're lonely and you wish he would talk more—you love him. You never marry, Jed isn't the marrying kind, but you form a kinship, a bond with each other that's understood.

You have sex occasionally with the local boys, the ones who don't go off to college. You usually meet them while you're on your way into town running errands. You stop over at their small, cramped apartments and get sweaty on narrow single beds. Jed either never knows or never wants to talk about it. Maybe he understands that just like a race car or a piece of technological equipment, everything occasionally needs servicing.

Then one clear winter morning at the base of White Island, there is a sound like applause. A tremor. Jed looks up just in time to be crushed by a large, white sparrow-shaped rock that falls from high above. You refuse to bury his body and instead hire several Maori boys from the mainland to carry his broken body up the face of the volcano and toss him into a warm lava crater. You never go on another volcano again. Instead, you stay in the little house on the mainland, with its view of the sea, until you are old and brittle like hollow, burnt-out lava rock.

You die when you're seventy-four from the avian flu. Heat, thickness, fog. People praying. Your fever rises in the night, the cold air blowing outside, and you float over, float up, from where you can see everything.

214

From section 150 . . .

You tell Jed you've been away from home for too long. He's disappointed, but kisses you on the forehead and says good-bye. He gives you a map of Italy and a watch just like his, which tells the time in three cities. "Always keep one dial set to Italian time," he says, "and I will too."

You don't call your parents to let them know you're coming home—you want to surprise them. When you show up at the door it turns out they've replaced you with a wealthy, backstabbing, Hello Kitty–loving pixie of a Japanese foreign exchange student, who's staying in your bedroom, and she doesn't move out even when you're home again.

"We didn't know if you were ever coming back!" you father says, "and Nana is the best thing that's ever happened to us! You understand." It turns out this small, adorable Japanese exchange student has utterly seduced your parents. It's *Nana this* and *Nana that*. Why did you even bother coming home? You set your watch to Italian time. You miss Jed. At your "welcome home" dinner they make Nana tell you all about wacky Japanese customs and no one asks about your trip. This is hell. You hate it here—hate America *and Nana*, who is taking your parents to Japan to meet her parents.

Fine. Let her. You throw all your camping gear into the car and set out to get as far away from your family and the memory of Jed as you can. A place no volcanologist would go. *Alaska!* You drive the long black winding roads through Canada all the way to America's northernmost state. It's so beautiful up here you're sure enlightenment and closure will come. You can't torture yourself like this—you have to release the memory of Jed, you have to let go of him so you can move on.

You feel better as you drive. The scenery is so intense, the blues so blue, the trees so tall, the water so vast that you really can't think too much about your piddly little boy problems. You arrive in Anchorage and stop overnight at one of the pristine state-run campgrounds. It's off-season, only a few other people are there under the commanding, breathtaking landscape. You set up camp and get your little stove going. One burner, one kettle, one cup of hot tea. *Ah.* This is what it's all about. Maybe tonight you'll go into town and fuck a logger. No—you came here *to get rid of a man*, not acquire a new one.

You brought a little memorial candle for Jed, one you light ceremoniously as the sun sets. When it burns out, Jed will be released from your heart. Just wait and see. You weren't meant to be a volcanologist. See? You're in Alaska now. You pour yourself another tin cup of tea and stare into the deep, vast, endless night sky.

You must have fallen asleep because the next thing you hear is the sound of heavy crunching, like wood on wood and someone shouting at you. Heavy smoke and you're coughing . . . *what?* You can't see anything, you drop low to the ground and crawl. Firemen are everywhere, unloading yellow hoses and yelling. The red and blue lights from the fire trucks illuminate the thick smoke, and as you make it to the main road, everything around you looks like apocalypse.

Apparently your candle ignited a fire that eventually spreads across fifteen thousand acres of forest, burning down at least six homes and forcing hundreds of people to evacuate a thirteen-mile stretch of highway. *That's what.* Three dogs die in the fire and one moose as well, although she was seen the previous day lying down in the back pasture behind Ivory Jack's. Not a good sign as a rule. And if there was any doubt it was you who set the fire, "ground zero" starts at your stove, where dark charred grass spreads quickly away from your tent like a bridal gown of ash all the way to the valley below. If the wind had been blowing the other direction you'd be a smoking skeleton, and not much of one at that.

Not one but *three* photographs were taken from a nearby fire watchtower that show the fire started right at your camp. The only other people who were camping that night was a group of off-duty volunteer firefighters from Katchemak Bay. *Fuck.* Volcanologist indeed.

You are on the nightly news, the national news, the international news. You become Alaska's *enemy number one*, your mug shot posted on anarchist/survivalist chat rooms all across the state. The police have you in protective custody—they're afraid someone will kill you. It doesn't help that you're alone, and *what are you doing out here alone?* It seems *funny*. Then it comes out you've just returned from Europe and well—that's the last straw. No one knows *why* it's the last straw—it just is. You're a spy or a terrorist or just a fucking idiot.

The last morning of your life the stoic sheriff hands you a cup of coffee and stands perfectly still as you retch and claw at your throat. You look down and the last thing you see is the time in Italy on Jed's watch. *Two forty-five*. The sheriff looks out the window. "Get it over with already," he says. Alaskans don't fuck around. No one will ever indict him—they'll say you drank the antifreeze on your own. Who knew you were suicidal?

215

From section 158 . . .

You marry Christian in Galway, in a small ceremony that none of your family attends. Not *one* family member. None of her family comes either—they all produce really good reasons why they can't afford tickets, or are too busy, or too ill to attend. The truth is none of them wants to see either of you marry a girl. Their loss.

You get married in a commitment ceremony on the eastern shore along the cliffs of Moher, steep vertical cliffs that plunge down into the ocean and foamy surf below. You honeymoon in one of the crumbling castles that dot the verdant valleys. You ride speckled silver horses, eat vegetable stew, drink champagne, and stay in bed as long as you can. The two of you move into the old farmhouse.

You love the old haunted place, with its crooked doorways and tilted floors—so steep a marble tossed down will shoot to the eastern corner. Christian creates jewelry and you write, along with becoming a part-time shepherd for a nearby dairy farm that makes sheep's cheese. The two of you never have children, you never need to. You have two pet sheep, a dog, three cats, and passports that need pages sewn into them every year, because the two of you travel so much.

You live on the farm together until you're old women. You publish two books and she gets her jewelry advertised in *Vogue* and *Vanity Fair*. You're known as eccentrics, literates, and strange witches. You die as you lived— together. You're in a car crash along the cliffs of Moher. A sheep darted out into the road and Christian swerved to miss it. Your car went headlong off the cliffs and into the water below. Just before that you were laughing.

PRETTY LITTLE MISTAKES | | 507

ACKNOWLEDGMENTS

This book could not have happened without the elegance of Elizabeth Sheinkman, the velocity of Alison Callahan, and the childhood library of Carrie Kania. Special thanks to Salman Rushdie for telling me to push on the open door and to Joyce Carol Oates for her ongoing support and encouragement.

My gratitude to the London offices of Curtis Brown and the Elaine Markson Agency. Also to the entire HarperCollins staff, especially Jeanette Perez for her endless help, Kolt Beringer for his heroic production editing, Heather Drucker for her clever ways, and Bill Harris for truly Olympic copyediting.

Pretty Little Mistakes exists because of insomnia-fueled walks around Lake Calhoun with Bart Regehr, nonstop coffees with Tim Peterson, a kick the pants from Erin Fairie and Jim Zervanos, good advice from RD Zimmerman, strange glue from Kevin McIlvoy, farm fun with Jodi Read, good wigs and stolen mochi with Chris Strouth, the meticulous bartending of

Dr. David Wilkins, and nonstop propping-up from my best girl, Heather Thornswood.

The sex monkeys would not have made the book without Thompat Beene's enthusiasm for them, my computer would have caught fire without John Hegna, I couldn't have survived any of this without Minnesota Public Radio, and I would have slept in the streets of New York without Tony Bol and Katherine Lanpher.

Deepest thanks to my family, who endured much. To Colin, for his endless wisdom and encouragement, to JT for his smile and steadfastness, to my father for all the ham and cheese sandwiches, and of course to my dear darling mother, who taught me how to tell stories.

THE ADVENTURE

ISN'T OVER YET . . .

There's one more choice to make, and you can't go wrong with this one. Choose to take a sneak peak at *Million Little Mistakes*, Heather McElhatton's next book forthcoming in Spring 2008. Sign up to be notified when it's available at www.AuthorTracker.com.

MILLION LITTLE MISTAKES

You win twenty-two million dollars in the BIG MONEY SUCKA! lottery. For real. It does happen—and why not you? *Twenty-two million dollars.* You've been playing the same damn number for years, always cursing your luck, always wondering why nothing good ever happens to you, wondering when exactly the universe is going to cut you some fucking slack and then *pow!* You get what you want, like bare knuckles to the jaw.

There's a phone call at seven in the morning, thumping on the door, neighbors showing up, news cameras, strangers streaming in, weird gold Mylar balloons that are maybe supposed to be coins with BIG SUCKA! printed on them, the phone ringing nonstop, your mother wringing her hands, reporters knocking over a lamp, an official lottery man with smiley white bedrock teeth who hands you your large oversize Styrofoam check and squeezes your hand so hard it makes you make a weird face for your photograph, flashes pop, you're temporarily blind, you don't eat until midnight (dry cereal out of the box while standing up at the counter), and everyone, everyone, everyone asking what you're going to do with twenty-two million dollars.

You finally fall into a dreamless sleep at five in the morning. When you wake, it comes to slow focus, like a money gorilla out of the mist. *You are a multi-millionaire.* Yesterday you weren't—and today you are. Big Money and you're hungry. Been hungry. Not for food, nor a roof. Got that. Got all kinds of stuff. Something else. Something you meant to do, meant to get, always imagined you could—if only things had been a little different. More money, more time. Fewer detours. Fewer accidents. There was something else you wanted, something ice bright and burning in the greasy little waiting room of your heart. The one with all the torn magazines. The thing waiting. The thing you would have done if you knew you wouldn't fail. The adventure. The chance. The dream deferred. You know the one.

Now nothing can stop you from getting what you want. You have all the money and time in the world. Only you have to decide one important thing. One really crucial thing. You can either take one payment in a lump sum—which they would take taxes out of—or you can get a monthly check over the next twenty years. Either way—now you've got money to pay off bills, get yourself out of debt, help your friends and family out of their various disasters. Money is a lullaby for big people. Small green soothing notes in your head, a chorus repeating: *You're safe. You're safe. You're safe.*

If you take the lump sum, go to section # 2.
If you receive monthly payments, go to section # 3.